OUTSTANDING PRAISE FOR THE ROMANCES OF KAT MARTIN

Midnight Rider

"One fabulous read from a dynamite writer!"

—*Romantic Times*

"Another winner . . . Kat Martin keeps on getting better and better." —*Affaire de Coeur*

"What an outlaw! Dark, daring, dangerous, and delicious! A rich panorama of old California. I couldn't put it down."

—Georgina Gentry, author of *Timeless Warrior*

Devil's Prize

"Tempting, alluring, sensual, and irresistible."

—*Romantic Times*

"Enhances Kat Martin's first-class reputation."

—*Affaire de Coeur*

Bold Angel

"Sizzling with sensual tension and ripe with rich emotion, this medieval romance is a real pleasure."

—*Publishers Weekly*

Sweet Vengeance

"Kat Martin gives readers enormous pleasure with this deftly plotted, stunning romance." —*Romantic Times*

Gypsy Lord

"Kat Martin dishes up sizzling passions and true love, then she serves it with savoir faire." —*Los Angeles Daily News*

Innocence Undone

Kat Martin

St. Martin's Paperbacks

This is a work of fiction. All of the characters, organizations, and events portrayed in this novel are either products of the author's imagination or are used fictitiously.

INNOCENCE UNDONE

Copyright © 1997 by Kat Martin.

For information address St. Martin's Press, 175 Fifth Avenue, New York, NY 10010.

ISBN: 978-1-250-04142-5

Printed in the United States of America

St. Martin's Paperbacks edition / January 1997

St. Martin's Paperbacks are published by St. Martin's Press, 175 Fifth Avenue, New York, NY 10010.

10 9 8 7 6 5 4

To some of my best friends in the writing business, Meryl Sawyer, Olga Bicos, and Brenda Joyce, for all their help and encouragement through the years, and for understanding how difficult it is to undertake the task of writing a book. Thanks, guys—you're the greatest!

*C*hapter *O*ne

*S*tay away from me, ye bloody prig!"

"You little hoyden—how many times have I warned you? Now you're going to get what you deserve!" Newly commissioned naval lieutenant, Matthew Seaton, clamped his jaw against the fury surging through him. He had only just stepped out the front doors of his country estate, Seaton Manor, dressed in his brand-new, spotlessly clean officer's uniform. Now there were mud stains on his snug white breeches. Half a rotten apple made a wet, gooey streak on the collar of his dark blue coat. And the little hellion had done it on purpose!

He stalked toward her. "I've had enough of you, Jessie Fox. For the past two years, you've plagued me at every turn. You've picked my pocket, called me filthy names—now you've ruined my clothes. It's time someone took you in hand and it looks as though I'm the one who's got to do it."

"Ye won't catch me, ye sodden toad." Jessie backed up two steps for every step Matt took in her direction. "I'm smarter and I'm faster." In her filthy ragged breeches and torn homespun shirt, her dirty blond hair stuffed up beneath a motheaten gray wool cap, she looked more like a boy than a twelve-year-old girl. Reaching down, she snagged another rotten apple that had fallen from the tree beside the house. Matthew ducked as it whizzed by his ear, a fresh jolt of anger shooting through him.

"You little vixen, you're the scourge of Buckler's Haven.

You're a pickpocket and a thief—the bane of every traveler passing through the village. One of these days, you'll wind up in Newgate prison."

"Go to bleedin' 'ell!" Jessie shrieked as he grabbed for her, whirled, and sprinted away. She darted left, feigned right, and scooted just out of his reach. Matthew swore an oath beneath his breath.

"A bloody prig is what ye are," Jessie taunted, staying just a few feet away. "All dressed up so clean and fancy. Just because yer a sodden lord don't mean yer nothin' special."

His dark blond brows drew together in a furious scowl. "I can't believe you're a girl. You talk worse than any foul-mouthed sailor." He made another unsuccessful lunge, but Jessie just laughed. Turning, she raced off toward the gnarled old apple tree. A white wrought-iron bench sat beneath it. Jessie shimmied up the trunk, her thin legs working, carrying her toward safety among the branches.

If he hadn't been so tall, she would have made it.

Matthew smiled with fierce satisfaction as his hand clamped around the girl's slender ankle. With a yank that forced her off balance, she lost her hold on the branch above, screamed, and toppled backward. Matthew caught her just before she hit the ground.

"Let me go, ye sodden bastard!"

Gripping her shoulders, he shook her—hard. "You had better learn to behave, you little hellion." Another hard shake knocked the cap from her head, but Jessie remained unrepentant. Before he realized her intent, she had grabbed a shiny gold button on the front of his coat and wrenched it loose. The sound of rending fabric betrayed the rip she had made in the bright blue fabric.

Fury tightened the muscles across his shoulders. Ignoring the horror that now marked Jessie's face, Matthew dragged her over to the wrought-iron bench in front of the tree. "You've deserved this for a very long time, Jessie Fox, and now you're going to get it." To her wild shrieks of protest, he hauled her across his lap. "I warned you," he said. "And dammit, I'm not going to feel one bit guilty."

Jessie shrieked as his hand came down hard on her bottom, her tattered gray breeches little protection against the sting of his palm.

"Bleedin' sod!" she cried out.

Two, three, four.

"Bloody pompous prig!"

Five, six, seven. Another child would have been pleading for him to stop. Not Jessie Fox.

Matt jerked her upright, and she stumbled to her feet. Huge blue eyes stared into his face. It surprised him to discover they were glazed with tears.

"You're a hoyden, Jessie. The next time you start trouble remember the price you paid this day. If you don't change your ways, you're going to be sorry. Sooner or later you'll suffer the consequences, and they'll be far greater than this."

"Yer the one who'll be sorry," she said, sniffling behind a dirty hand. She took a step away, her bottom lip trembling, fresh tears welling in her eyes. There was anguish there, he saw to his surprise, and burning humiliation. "I'm gonna be a lady—a right proper lady wi' fine silk dresses and rich, 'andsome men to squire me 'bout. I'll show ye. I'll find a way. I'll be a real lady. Then—bloody lord or no—ye'll be sorry ye treated me this way."

Matthew simply shook his head. With a last glance into the waifish features of Jessie Fox, he turned away, ignoring a pang of regret. Not for what he had done. God knew she needed a good sound thrashing and perhaps it would do her some good.

Unfortunately, odds were far greater Jessie would continue her thieving, troublemaking ways and wind up in some dank prison.

Or more likely still, flat on her back in a room above the Black Boar Inn, earning a living as a whore—just like her mother.

Chapter Two

*F*or pity's sake, luv, 'e ain't the bloody king of England."

Feeling the faint tug of a smile, Jessica Fox turned away from the froth of expensive ball gowns strewn across the foot of her silk-draped bed. "No, I don't suppose he is. Perhaps if he were simply the king, I wouldn't be so worried about what I should wear."

"Ye'll look beautiful, no matter what ye choose." Viola Quinn, the buxom gray-haired woman Jessie had known since childhood, cast her an affectionate glance. "Odds are, the capt'n will be so taken wi' ye, he won't even notice what yer wearin'."

Jessie leaned over and hugged the heavyset woman who was more a mother than her real flesh-and-blood mama ever had been. "Thank you, Vi. You always say just the right thing."

Once a cook at the Black Boar Inn, at fifty years old, Viola Quinn was hardly a proper lady's maid, but Jessie loved her. And the aging marquess who was now Jessie's guardian had finally given in and brought Viola Quinn to Belmore Hall.

The hefty woman lifted one of the magnificent gowns strewn across the bed. "'ow 'bout the gold un'?" A glittering creation with a bodice shimmering with rhinestones. "The color'll match ye 'air."

Jessie shook her head, moving the long golden curls to which Vi referred. "Too formal. Lord Strickland has been at sea for the past two years. I want him to feel comfortable this eve."

Vi lifted another elegant gown. "What 'bout the ivory satin—perfect wi' yer pale, peachy skin?"

Jessie caught her bottom lip between her teeth, studying the demure neckline and simple capped sleeves. "Too plain. I don't want him to think I'm a wallflower."

Viola sighed. "Then what about this un'?" She held up an exquisitely fashioned, high-waisted blue silk gown with a moderately low-cut bodice. "The blue is the same shade as yer eyes, and the silver threads in the overskirt gives it plenty a sparkle."

Jessie grinned as she snatched up the gown and hurried across the room to the ornate cheval-glass mirror beside the window. She then surveyed the gown from several different angles.

"You're right, Vi. This one's perfect." For a moment she just stood there, staring at her reflection, the tall slender woman with the high, firm breasts, fine features, and freshly washed long blond hair.

Even now, it was hard to believe the lovely young woman staring back was really Jessie Fox, once a dirty little urchin who ran wild in the streets of Buckler's Haven. Poor pitiful little Jessie, the townspeople said. Living in squalor, no one to care.

Nothing but the daughter of a whore.

She felt Vi's hand on her shoulder, turned to see a tender look on the older woman's face. "It'll be all right, luv, ye'll see. Ye ain't the same as ye used to be."

Jessie went into Vi's plump arms, leaning her head on the stout woman's shoulder, crushing the beautiful gown between them. "H-He knows who I am, Vi. He knows the real me. What if he—"

"'E don't know the real ye—not anymore. Ye ain't some poor lit'l ragamuffin, like ye was. Yer the ward o' the Marquess o' Belmore. Thanks to 'is lordship, ye've a fine education. Ye've been schooled like a proper lady, and that's what ye are." The older woman chucked her under the chin. "It ain't what yer were born wi' that matters, it's what ye've made o' yourself that counts." She wiped away the tear that trickled down Jessie's cheek. "Remember that, luv, and everythin'll be all right."

Jessie glanced away. "I know it's silly, Vi, but I'm frightened. I can't remember feeling like this since the night that awful man nearly beat Mama to death at the inn."

Vi stroked her hair. "That was a long time ago, luv. There's nothin' to be afraid of 'ere. Papa Reggie will see to the capt'n. 'E'll take care o' everythin', just like 'e's done since the first day ye come 'ere."

Thinking of the kindness of the aging man upstairs, Jessie drew in a calming breath. "You're right, Vi." She straightened away from her friend and carefully laid the gown back down on the bed. "It's just that I want everything to be exactly right. The marquess's son hasn't seen me in years, but he's bound to remember the day—"

She broke off then, trying not to recall the last confrontation they'd had, one of the most humiliating moments of her life. Just thinking about the undisciplined twelve-year-old she had been—and the consequences she'd paid for her outrageous behavior—made her face go hot with embarrassment.

She leaned over and smoothed the gown. "Perhaps I ought to have it pressed. It's been hanging in the closet for a while. It might need—"

"The dress looks fine."

"Perhaps I should ring for a bath." She glanced toward the bellpull, fidgeting nervously. "Papa Reggie warned me not to be late. He says the earl is due to arrive at six o'clock, and he's always precisely on time."

Vi laughed, moving several of her beefy chins. "Ye've hours yet, lamb. I'm sure 'is lordship will get 'ere whenever 'e's supposed to, bein' a navy man and all, but ye ain't due at supper till eight, and that's still hours away. Ye've been runnin' like a whirlwind all day. Why don't ye nap for a while? I'll 'ave cook prepare a tray and when ye wake up—"

A brisk knock sounded at the door, interrupting Vi's words. Muttering to herself, she padded across the thick Persian carpet, turned the silver knob, and opened the door to find the tall stately butler, Samuel Osgood, standing in the hallway.

"Terribly sorry, Mrs. Quinn, for the intrusion, but there is a woman downstairs to see Miss Jessica. I told her Mistress Fox was unavailable this afternoon, but the girl seemed inordinately disturbed. I thought perhaps Miss Jessica might be able to spare her a moment."

"Of course I'll speak to her, Ozzie," Jessie said. "Did the girl give you her name?"

"Mary Thornhill, miss. She appears to be quite distraught. I thought—"

Jessie brushed past before he'd finished speaking and hurried down the hall toward the stairs. Mary was a friend of Anne Bartlett's, one of the Belmore tenants. Anne was nineteen, Jessie's age, heavy with child, the babe due any day. In the months since Jessie's return from Mrs. Seymour's Private Academy for the Deportment of Young Ladies, they had formed a tentative friendship.

Jessie crossed the marble entry, making the massive crystal chandelier chime overhead. A pale-faced Mary waited in the Red Drawing room, her expressive eyes wide with fear. "Miss Jessie—thank God you're here."

"What is it, Mary? What's happened?" A knot of worry tightened in Jessie's stomach. "It is Anne? Is it time for the babe to come?"

"Yes, miss. Lor', Anne's been fightin' to birth the child for hours. Somethin' ain't right, miss. That's why I come."

The knot twisted tighter. "Can't the midwife do something to help her?"

"The midwife's over to Longly village, birthin' another babe. Anne's got no one to help her but me, and I ain't doin' much good."

"What about her husband? Surely James has sent for a surgeon."

"Lor', James ain't there, neither. He's gone upriver; had a load of produce to sell in Southampton. I went for the surgeon, but he wouldn't come without payment in advance. Lor', I didn't know what to do. That's when I thought of you, Miss Jessie. I hoped you could loan us payment for the surgeon."

"Of course I will." The bloody whoreson, Jessie thought, but didn't say it. She hadn't said a swear word—at least not aloud—since the day four years ago that she'd arrived at Belmore Hall.

"I've got some money upstairs. You wait here—I'll be back in just a minute." Lifting her peach muslin day dress, Jessie raced up the sweeping marble staircase and jerked open the door to her bedchamber.

"What is it, lamb?" Viola hurried toward her.

"It's Anne Bartlett, Vi. She's in labor, but apparently the babe won't come. Mary Thornhill is going for the doctor. I've got to go to Anne."

Viola started toward the door. "I'll go wi' ye."

Jessie caught Vi's arm. "I can get there faster alone. If I cut across the fields, I can be there in fifteen minutes." Hurrying to her dresser, she lifted the lid on her inlaid mother-of-pearl jewelry box and pulled out a small leather pouch of coins she had saved from her monthly allowance.

"Take this down to Mary." She handed the pouch to Vi. "The doctor won't come until he gets paid. I'll see you back here as soon as I'm certain that Anne is all right."

Vi nodded. After all these years she knew better than to argue once Jessie's mind was set. The girl knew nothing about birthing a babe, but she was no stranger to blood or to pain. And she knew everything about survival, about determination and strength. She would get the girl through if anyone could. Vi took the coins and headed for the stairs.

Across the room, Jessie jerked open the door of her rosewood armoire, rummaged around in the back, and dragged out a bundle of ragged old clothes. "At least they're clean," she mumbled, thinking of the last time she had worn the shirt and coarse brown breeches she had stolen from a stable boy when she was just fourteen. God only knew why she had kept them, except that living hand to mouth with little to eat and nothing but rags to wear had turned her into a hoarder. Even in the luxury of Belmore, old habits were hard to break.

She buttoned the breeches, which fit a whole lot snugger than they had back then, and the shirt barely stretched across her now filled-out bosom, but the fields were muddy after last night's rain, and she wasn't all that good a rider. She didn't dare use a sidesaddle, as the marquess would insist, but figured she could make it mounted astride. Besides, no one but the grooms would see her, and they were all her friends.

Grabbing a brown felt hat that was part of the bundle, she shoved her hair up under the floppy brim and rushed out the door, heading for the servants' stairs at the rear of the mansion.

In the barn she ordered Jimmy Hopkins, one of the stable boys, to saddle the chestnut mare she usually rode. He adjusted the stirrups on the flat leather saddle, then gave her a leg up, grinning as he hoisted her onto the mare.

"Good luck, Miss Jessie."

"Thanks, Jimmy." Touching her floppy-brimmed hat in farewell, she leaned over the horse's neck and nudged her heels into the animal's ribs, hoping she could keep her seat and praying she could somehow help Anne and the babe.

"Hello, Father." Captain Matthew Seaton, Earl of Strickland, Commander of His Majesty's gunship, the *Norwich,* softly closed the door to his father's palatial suite of rooms at Belmore Hall. Resting atop his massive canopied bed, the aging Marquess of Belmore leaned back against the satin pillows propped against the mahogany headboard.

At the sound of his son's deep voice, his eyes cracked open and a corner of his mouth tipped up. "Matthew! Son! I'd begun to wonder if these rheumy old eyes would ever see the likes of you again." He reached out weathered, veined hands and Matthew clasped both of them firmly. Then he leaned over and gave his father an awkward, unexpected hug.

"I've missed you, Father." For a moment he tightened his hold, a rare show of affection for a man who'd spent nearly half his thirty years learning to suppress his emotions.

Being a captain in His Majesty's Navy demanded iron control, but eventually he would be leaving the navy, taking over his duties as son and heir, his older brother, Richard, having died of a riding accident. And he was worried about his father.

"Stand back, my boy, let me have a look at you. God's teeth, but it's been more than two years."

Matt obligingly stepped away, wondering if his father would notice the tiny crinkles he'd acquired beside his deep blue eyes, the darker bronze hue of his skin after so much time in the sun. His hair was still a dark, wavy gold, but it was longer now, brushing his wide white stock at the back of his neck, and the ends were streaked even lighter.

"If I didn't know better," the old man said with a chuckle, "I'd swear you'd grown another two inches. But then you were always tall, even as a boy."

"I'm a bit past the growing stage, Father." Matt smiled, thinking he was perhaps a little more muscled in the shoulders, a bit more solid in the chest. There was always plenty of work aboard ship, even for a captain. "I apologize for the clothes. I meant to change before I came in, but once I arrived, I was eager to see you."

"You look fine, my boy—wonderful, in fact. A welcome sight for these tired old eyes."

Dressed in a dark brown tailcoat, fawn riding breeches, a white lawn shirt, and tall Hessian boots, Matt had handed a waiting footman the reins to the saddle horse he had hired in Portsmouth and come straight up to his father's room.

"I hope I didn't disturb you. I didn't realize you would be resting."

"Nonsense. I would rather spend time with you than to waste the day lying here asleep."

Matthew smiled. "I'm glad to see you, Father. It feels good to be back home."

They talked for a while, spoke of mundane things, of the recoppering of his ship that had brought him back to Portsmouth after two grueling years on the French blockade. They spoke of his journey to Belmore, that he had left Portsmouth straightaway. Well, nearly straightaway. Matt neglected to mention the pretty little redhead who'd entertained him nightly while he concluded his business in the bustling harbor city.

"You haven't asked after Jessica," the marquess said with a hint of disapproval. "You must know from my letters that she is here."

"Unfortunately it took more than three months for your letters to reach me, but yes, eventually I learned that the girl was out of boarding school and in residence here at Belmore."

The marquess sat up a little straighter on the bed. He knew the subject was a sore one with his son. They had argued about Jessica when Matthew had last been home.

"I know the way you feel about the girl. You've made it abundantly clear on more than one occasion. But you haven't see Jessica in years—not since she was a wayward child. Certainly not since she has been under my tutelage. She's a woman now, Matthew. A fine, well-educated, spirited young woman. I thank God every day that she came to me when she did, that she had the courage to go after her dreams and convince me to help her obtain them."

Matt clamped down on a surge of irritation. "To my recollection, Jessie Fox never lacked for courage. As a child she ran wild, scrambling headlong into one bout of trouble after another. At twelve years old, she was a sharper, a pickpocket, and a thief. At fifteen, she was an unkempt, conniving little baggage who used every trick she knew to gain your pity and convince you to take her in."

"The girl was fighting for survival."

"And she did a damned fine job of it. By the time she turned nineteen, Jessie Fox had the finest education money could buy. She had her own carriage and four, and dressed as regally as a queen. She lives like royalty here at Belmore, and she has anything her treacherous little heart might wish for. You wonder why I'm not concerned for Jessie Fox? Because Jessie Fox doesn't need my concern. Obviously she's extremely proficient at taking care of herself!"

The marquess said nothing, just stared at Matt for long silent moments. "You make it sound as though Jessica has manipulated me into doing these things for her, that she has somehow taken advantage. The truth is, I'm the one who has gained the advantage."

This time Matt said nothing. He hadn't come to Belmore to fight with his father or argue about Jessie Fox.

"When your brother died," the old man went on, "I was devastated. You were gone and I was alone. It was a terrible time for me. When I couldn't stand the pain a moment more, I locked my memories up here in Belmore Hall and took myself off to Seaton Manor, but it was no better there. I was a bitter, lonely old man waiting for the end to come."

A wave of guilt spilled through him. "I'm sorry," Matt said. "I should have been here. Unfortunately, I didn't even learn of Richard's death until six months after he was gone."

"It wasn't your fault, son. You were exactly where you should have been, fighting for your country. But that didn't make things any easier for me." The trace of a smile touched his lips. "Fortunately, on a day when I was feeling particularly glum, I took a walk down by the lake and there the poor little urchin was. My life took a turn for the better the moment Jessica appeared."

"She just happened to be there the same time you were," Matt said with sarcasm. "It was simply an accident that the two of you chanced to meet."

"I don't know why she was there that day and I don't care. All I know is that she came there every morning after that and I looked forward to each of our meetings. When

Jessica was near, she brought life and joy into my world. She rekindled the spark that was dying inside me, brought me out of the darkness, and made me want to live. When she asked me to help her—when she told me her dream was to become a lady—it was my greatest pleasure to grant her that wish."

Matthew thought of the dirty little urchin who had challenged him at every turn. He had run her off on several occasions, but she had always returned, determined it seemed to spark his temper—though he remembered with relish the day he had finally given the little hoyden her due.

At fifteen, she was a ragged little thief who had preyed on his father's grief and tricked her way into his affections. He would never forgive her for it, and once he was home for good, he would see that the girl never took advantage of the old man again.

His father's gruff chuckle interrupted his thoughts.

"You won't recognize her, I'll warrant. She's quite a lovely young woman these days."

Matthew forced a smile. "You mean she's stopped throwing mud and rotten fruit? She's no longer the little cutpurse who fleeces unwary travelers out of their hard-earned coin?"

His father frowned. "'Twas that no-account half brother of hers who was the real villain. Jessica is spirited, yes, but she is too softhearted by half to ever have been truly bad. In the past four years, she's grown into a beautiful, intelligent young woman. If you will give her the slightest chance to prove it, you will see exactly what I mean."

Matthew studied his father's face. Once a tall, robust man, in the years since Matt had been away, Reginald Seaton's strength had begun to wane. He still had a leonine mane of snowy hair and thick muttonchop sideburns, but against the white of the linens, his skin looked pale instead of ruddy; his cheeks, no longer round, were slightly sunken in.

Matthew silently reined in his temper. He would deal with Jessie Fox later. In the meantime, his father's health was all important. He would do what the old man wished.

"I know the girl has won your support, Father. I don't countenance what she has done, but if having her here makes you happy, that is enough for me."

The marquess looked relieved. "Then you will treat her with the proper amount of respect?"

He made a slight nod of his head. What *was* the proper amount of respect for the daughter of a whore? Not much, he imagined. "In the meantime, if you will excuse me, I need to see that my horse is properly cared for." He looked at the Lord of Belmore Hall, saw the old man's eyes had drifted closed, and Matthew's dark look softened.

"Get some rest, Father." He clasped the old man's hand and gave it a final squeeze. "I look forward to seeing you and . . . your ward at supper."

With that he took his leave.

Jessie looked up at the sun, a fiery orange ball suspended above the horizon. Dusk was nearly upon them and she was only just now returning home. She bent over the neck of the chestnut mare she rode, urging the horse to a faster gait, flinging rich black soil out behind the animal's hooves, some of it spattering her shirt and breeches, already muddy from her earlier ride through the fields.

She had hoped to leave sooner, but the babe had been stubborn and the doctor's arrival late. Now she hoped her madcap, galloping pace would make up some of the precious time she had lost.

She glanced once more at the slowly sinking ball of flame. *Dear Lord, don't let him get home before I do.*

But the odds weren't good and she knew it. In her wrinkled, muddy clothes, her blond hair damp with perspiration and stuck to her forehead, she looked a fright. She prayed luck was with her, that Jimmy would care for the horse while she sneaked up the back stairs to her room.

Jessie smiled. At least Anne had finally been able to birth the babe, a little girl named Flora. When Jessie had arrived,

Anne had been sobbing with fear, certain she was going to lose the child, racked with pain and fearful for her own life as well.

Just when it seemed Anne would die of the pain, the doctor had come. The babe was breached, he said, but he had finally been able to right it and the child had come safely into the world. By the time Jessie left, both mother and babe were out of danger. A lump formed in her throat when she thought of the gift of life she had witnessed that day.

Jessie gasped as the horse stepped into a muddy trough, ending her musings and nearly unseating her. The animal slid for a moment and almost went down. Jessie's heart slammed with fear till the mare regained its footing and burst back into its ground-eating pace.

They were nearing the boxwood hedge behind the stable, almost home. Jimmy waved from the rear stable door. All she had to do was reach him, hand him the reins, hurry to the house and up the servants' stairs.

"Come on, Pagan," she whispered to the mare as the hedge loomed in front of them.

Leaning over the horse's neck, they cleared the hedge with ease—it was the landing that wasn't so fortunate, a huge mud puddle she hadn't remembered, slick on the bottom, impossible footing for the mare. A man stepped out of the shadows, distracting the horse at the worst possible moment. The mare shied sideways. The saddle went one way, Jessie the other, sliding off the horse and landing with a bruising jolt in the puddle of mud.

"Bloody hell!" She sat there sputtering, her hat long gone, her blond hair sodden with thick black ooze and stuck to her shoulders. Her neck and face were speckled with dirt, her shirt soaked through, as well as her breeches.

She glanced toward the man who had caused her horse to shy and her eyes came to rest on a pair of high black boots. Snug brown breeches covered long lean legs and trim hips, and rode low on a narrow waist. With dawning horror, she glanced up, past a wide chest and broad shoulders, to the tall man's hard, chiseled features.

Captain Matthew Seaton, Earl of Strickland. She should have known.

Except for Papa Reggie, luck had never been a friend to Jessie Fox.

"Well, if it isn't the infamous Mistress Fox." Sarcasm dripped from lips that were as well formed as she remembered. Eyes the darkest blue she had ever seen ran over her disheveled appearance without a hint of surprise, as if he saw exactly what he had expected.

Jessie felt sick to her stomach. She had wanted to impress him, to make the marquess proud. Instead she had made a fool of herself. She forced her chin up with a Herculean effort. "I-I'm afraid I must go in." She turned away from the earl, unable to find a response to the cold look on his face.

"I think that is a very good idea. Why don't we both go in? You can stop and say hello to my father on the way to your room, show him what a lady you've become."

Her mouth went dry. She kept her head up, though inside her stomach was churning. "Your father knows what I am better than anyone on this earth. Unlike you, however, seeing that I have obviously suffered a fall might cause him some concern. Since I do not wish him to worry, I shall change before I go in to see him. If you will excuse me . . ."

She turned away from him and started walking away. Her head had begun to pound and her ribs felt badly bruised. A faint pain throbbed in her ankle. She hadn't realized she had fallen so hard.

She didn't notice him walking beside her until she stumbled and he caught her arm.

"You were right. It was callous of me not to ask if you were injured."

She yanked her arm away. "I'm perfectly fine, thank you."

"What about your leg? You were favoring it just then."

"My *limb*," she corrected with pointed ladylike propriety,

"is also fine." She stepped down firmly, careful to hide the painful wince it caused. His brows narrowed but he made no reply. As she walked inside the house, Lord Strickland walked behind her, his midnight blue eyes burning into her back. She wondered what he was thinking, but muddy and bedraggled as she was, it wasn't too difficult to guess.

Viola was waiting in her room when she opened her bed-chamber door.

"We 'ave to 'urry," Vi said. "The capt'in 'as already arrived and—" She broke off when she turned to see Jessie and her eyes went wide. "Saints above! Poor lit'l lamb, what on earth 'ave ye done?"

Jessie's shoulders slumped. "What have I done? Imagine the worst, Vi. Imagine that I fell off my horse and landed in the mud at Captain Seaton's feet. Imagine that he saw me dressed in these filthy, ragged clothes."

"Dear Lord in 'eaven."

Misery washed over her. "I wanted to impress him, Vi, to show him I had changed." She felt the sting of tears, but blinked them away. "Instead I proved just the opposite. How will I ever be able to face him?"

The older woman set her hands on her ample hips. "Ye can face 'im, luv, because ye *'ave* changed. Ye'll go down to supper dressed in that beautiful blue silk dress, and ye'll play the part o' lady till 'is bleedin' lordship starts to wonder if that urchin 'e saw in the mud weren't some other gel."

Jessie turned toward the exquisite blue and silver gown hanging on the armoire. Until Papa Reggie had taken her in, she had only seen gowns like that through the windows at Seaton Manor, when she hid beneath the rosebushes and pressed her face against the panes. She had ached just to touch the shimmering fabric, to feel the smoothness of the silk against her skin. All she got were thorny pricks in her fingers and fresh rips in her tattered clothes.

She looked over at the copper tub sitting a few feet away beside a half-dozen pails of steaming water, ready and waiting to be poured in. Ugly thoughts of the past began to fade and excitement started pumping through her veins.

"You're right, Vi. This isn't the first time the captain has seen me at my worst. Tonight he'll see me at my best." She whirled toward the tub, stripping off her filthy breeches and muddy homespun shirt, kicking off her mud-caked riding boots.

In minutes she sat chin-deep in hot sudsy water, the scent of roses drifting across her skin. She washed her hair and rinsed it, then leaned back against the tub. Her ankle felt better and her headache was gone. Her courage had returned, along with a shot of determination.

The steamy water began to soothe away her tension. Her eyes were closed when Vi walked up with a clean linen towel.

"I take it the babe and its mama weathered the storm, and everythin' come to rights in the end."

Careful not to slosh water on the beautiful inlaid floors, she let Viola wrap the towel around her, then wrap a smaller one around her long blond hair.

"Everything came out fine. Anne had a little girl she named Flora. It was the most wondrous thing I've ever seen."

"Ye didn't stay there for the birthin', did ye?"

"Of course I did. I wanted to see how a babe came into the world. Now I know."

Viola sighed. "Ye know too much, luv, for a lass yer age. 'Tis a shame ye 'aven't been a bit more sheltered."

"It could have been worse, Vi. If it hadn't been for you, I can only imagine what would have happened to me after Mama died." A shudder rippled through her to think of the drunken man who'd accosted her in the taproom. When she'd refused the coin he had shoved into her hand, he had slapped her then started dragging her toward the stairs. Vi had saved her. Vi and the whores who had been her mother's friends. Women who wanted, just once, to see one of their kind escape.

She thought again of the babe, and a smile lit her face.

"At least, I was able to help. Perhaps if my life had been different, I would have been afraid to try."

"Ye've a good 'eart, lamb." Vi wondered if the tall, handsome earl could see clear of Jessie's past enough to notice.

*C*hapter *T*hree

Dear Lord, I'm going to be late. Jessie heard the ornate grandfather clock in the Tapestry Room strike a quarter past the hour just as she reached the imposing mahogany doors leading in.

Samuel Osgood, the butler, stood in front of them. "Good evening, Miss Jessica."

She stopped her hurried pace and took a moment to compose herself. "Good evening, Ozzie." Her hands shook a little. She smoothed them against the blue silk folds of her gown, hoping her courage wouldn't desert her.

"If I may say so, miss, you look quite fetching in that dress."

Dear, sweet Ozzie. She cast him a grateful smile. "Thank you, Ozzie." Squaring her shoulders, she took a calming breath, then motioned for the thin, stately butler to open the drawing room doors.

They slid silently apart and the beauty of the room settled over her, the flickering candelabra, the richly carpeted floors. With its painted ceilings and inlaid ebony furniture, the lovely room always had a calming effect on her. She was grateful for that feeling now.

She forced herself to smile as she walked in, moving toward the sienna marble hearth at the far end of the room where a small fire blazed and she knew the marquess would be waiting.

She spotted the captain, Lord Strickland, but didn't dare to glance in his direction. Instead she headed straight for his father, who smiled at her warmly, took her hands, bent forward, and kissed her on the cheek.

"Good evening, my dear."

"Good evening, Papa Reggie. I'm sorry I'm late."

The captain's dark blond brow arched up at the way she'd addressed his father. Obviously he didn't approve.

"Matthew, I should like to present my ward, Jessica Fox. Jessica, my son, Matthew."

His gaze felt hot as he assessed her, surveying her face then moving down her body, studying her as he had since the moment of her arrival.

"Mistress Fox." His mouth held a slightly mocking curve. Taking her gloved hand, he bowed over it with excessive formality as she rose from a graceful curtsy. He was wearing his navy blue uniform, gold buttons glittering down the front, the epaulettes on his shoulders making them look even wider than they were. Snug white breeches clung to long, hard-muscled thighs. In the light of the gilded sconces, his hair gleamed as golden as the candle flames.

His eyes came back to her face. "You're looking fit this evening. I'm glad you suffered no . . . ill effects . . . from your unfortunate mishap earlier."

She refused to rise to the bait. Only a flicker of embarrassment, the tiniest hint of pink, rose in her cheeks. "I'm quite recovered, thank you." She eased her hand away, determined not to let him upset her. "I'm afraid I'm only a passable rider. I should have been more careful, but I had promised Papa Reggie I wouldn't be late."

The marquess frowned. "What mishap has occurred, my dear?" His glance moved toward his son. "I didn't realize the two of you had already chanced to meet."

"It was nothing, Papa Reggie. A bit of a riding accident. Fortunately his lordship was there to offer his assistance."

She fixed a pleading look on the earl. The marquess would be mortified to discover the manner in which she had greeted his son. "I'm perfectly fine, as you can see. Neither of you need trouble yourself on my account any further." She knew the captain certainly wouldn't. He would probably rejoice if she were to break her neck.

She waited for the words that would accuse her, betray her as the same ill-mannered hoyden he had known before. Instead he lifted his crystal wineglass and held it up in a mock salute. "To your health, Mistress Fox." His lips curved faintly, then he took a sip of claret.

Jessie tensed as she waited for his next brutal sally, but he said nothing more. They spoke of mundane subjects, the break in the weather, the captain's journey from Portsmouth. Though he continued to watch her, his attention focused on his father. Perhaps he wouldn't bait her all evening as she had imagined. Perhaps the sight of her, gowned in silk and conducting herself as a lady, had given him pause. Whatever the reason, she was grateful for the respite, the chance to fortify herself.

He wasn't finished testing her, she was sure, yet his words hadn't been as biting as she had expected. He still believed she cared nothing for his father, that she was simply using him for her own selfish gains. She knew because he had said so in his letters. She shouldn't have read them; the marquess would have been furious, but her curiosity overrode her sense of caution.

Oddly, in the beginning the captain's presumptions were correct. She had plotted for weeks to gain the old man's attention. After her mother had died, except for Viola and the occasional unwanted presence of her half brother, Danny, she'd been left to fend for herself. After the drunken assault in the taproom, she was finally forced to leave the inn and set off on her own.

She had sought the marquess's help for he had always been kind to her. Whenever he came to the village, there was always a coin or two for her, as if even then there were some sort of bond between them. Almost from the start, she'd been drawn to him, and now she loved him like the father she never had.

But the earl understood none of that. He saw nothing but her misadventures, the lying, thievery, and cheating. He believed the worst of her and he meant to prove himself correct.

Jessie was equally determined to prove him wrong.

He made a grand show of extending his arm, and a slightly unsettling glint appeared in his eyes when she took it. She could feel the rough wool of his jacket, the heat of his body, and an unexpected warmth spiraled through her.

As nervous as she was, she felt a hint of amusement. What would the tall, handsome navy captain say if he knew the reason she had challenged him at every turn was to gain his attention?

What would Lord Strickland say if he knew she had always carried a secret *tendre* for him?

Supper finally came to an end. Papa Reggie had ordered an array of exquisite dishes—pheasant with oyster stuffing, sweetbreads of veal, roasted swan, turbot in lobster sauce, various vegetables and assorted greens, and a huge sweet molded in the shape of an anchor for dessert.

Throughout the meal, they made polite conversation, speaking of the English blockade, meant to keep Napoleon's French fleet from amassing for a British invasion, one of the country's greatest fears.

The captain's vessel, the *Norwich,* had been stationed off Brest and the Bay of Biscayne, assigned to the command of Admiral Cornwallis.

"We weren't as far from home as Nelson and the ships that were stationed in the Mediterranean," he said. "We were able to resupply every three months without much problem. Still, after two years without shore leave, morale aboard ship was getting pretty low."

Jessie sat up straighter in her chair. "You mean you never let those poor men off the boat?"

The captain's gaze shifted in her direction, cool in its regard. "You disapprove, Mistress Fox?"

Her fingers tightened on the crystal goblet poised half-way to her lips. "*Disapprove* is too mild a word. Good Lord, that is practically indecent. What about those poor men's families? Most of them were pressed into service. They were forced aboard those ships—then they weren't even allowed to go ashore?"

"A little less than half the crew was there at the hands of a press gang. Most were enlisted, and some of them were quota men—sent to the ships as punishment for crimes they committed. Personally, I believe the men in my command were loyal enough to return when their shore leave was ended. They had resigned themselves to their situation and were willing to make the best of it. Unfortunately, Admiral Cornwallis had other ideas." He pinned her with those midnight eyes. "May I remind you, Miss Fox, that *I* also remained onboard for the past two years."

Jessie bit her lip, a thread of guilt winding through her. She didn't doubt for a moment that Matthew Seaton was a fair and competent captain. He was the Marquess of Belmore's son, a man with the same noble blood as his father.

"I'm sorry, my lord. I realize you were only doing your duty. Someone must look out for England, no matter the cost. Two years just seems so very long. It must have been terrible for you."

His eyes clung to hers, trying to read her sincerity. "In a way it was difficult. At times, the waiting seemed interminable. When supplies ran low, we ate weevily biscuits and maggoty meat and drank water the color of bark. But with five hundred men in my command, there was countless work to do—it was certainly never boring. And there is the sea itself, endless and challenging." A faint smile curved his lips. "Rather like a beautiful woman—as dangerous as she is alluring."

She ignored the veiled reference that might have been directed at her. "I should love to sail somewhere. To feel the rocking of the deck beneath my feet and the crisp cool wind in my face. When I was a child, I often wished I were a boy. I would have run away to sea. I could have stowed away or even been a cabin boy." She flicked him a glance. "Perhaps one day I might even have served under you, Captain."

The smile turned to one of amusement. "Life is highly unpredictable, Miss Fox. One never knows the way things might yet turn out."

Warm color washed her cheeks. Surely she had imagined the nuance in his words. She glanced at the marquess and discovered he was frowning.

"Yes, well, I for one am certainly glad that you were born a girl, my dear." Smiling, he reached over and patted her hand, then gave it a gentle squeeze. "Boys are so much more trouble, and not nearly so entertaining."

When she glanced at the earl, she saw that he was the one who was frowning.

Matthew stretched out in an overstuffed chair while his father poured him a brandy. He was thinking of Jessie Fox—or more accurately, the woman Jessie Fox had become. He hadn't been surprised by her tardiness, though his father seemed inordinately put out by it.

"I believe it's a woman's prerogative," Matt had said, knowing damned well why the girl was late. Then she'd walked in, gliding past him in a whisper of blue and silver silk, moving gracefully toward the place near the hearth where he and the marquess awaited. She didn't spare a glance in his direction, just headed straight for his father.

Amazingly, Matt was grateful.

From the moment the girl stepped through the door, he couldn't think of a single thing to say. He'd stared at her as she crossed the room, unable to look away from the woman with the golden hair and startlingly clear blue eyes, several shades lighter than his own. Earlier in the day, when she was dirty and covered in mud, he'd had no chance to really assess her. Tonight he noticed she had grown several inches

from the gangly female he remembered, the thin, awkward-
ness of youth replaced by an air of grace and beauty he had
seen in very few women.

A long slender neck arched above smooth, pale shoulders; her hair was a rich silky gold. Her breasts rose proudly
above the bodice of an elegant gown the exact china blue of
her eyes. He noticed the tension in the set of her slender
shoulders, yet none of it showed in the exquisite lines of her
face. He would have given his fifteen years in the navy to
have known what she was thinking. But Jessie Fox was
nearly as good at hiding her thoughts as he was at hiding his
own.

His father's approach drew his attention back to the present. The older man pressed a brandy glass into his hand,
then leaned back against the red-flocked wall and rested an
elbow on the mantel. He looked healthier this evening, more
color in his cheeks, more energy about him.

"Well, my boy, what did you think of her?"

Matt smiled slightly. "You speak of her as if she were a
finely bred horse. The girl is lovely, if that is what you are
asking."

"I'm asking what you thought of her. You liked her, I'll
wager. How could you not? The dear girl positively radiates
life and warmth. When she smiles, it's as though a ray of
sunshine has just spilled into the room."

Looking at the spark in his father's eye when he spoke of
Jessica Fox, Matthew frowned, the thought he'd earlier entertained once more creeping into his mind.

He swirled the brandy in his glass, then glanced up at his
father. "Some years back, when you first told me about the
girl, I thought you were grooming her to be your mistress.
You assured me that was not so. Has your involvement with
Jessica changed? Now that I've seen her, I can certainly understand—"

The marquess's hand slammed down on the top of the
mantel, the slap of his palm like a crack of thunder across
the room. "Jessica is like the daughter I never had. She is

kind and caring, sweet and virtuous, and my thoughts toward her have never been other than those of a father for his child."

Matthew made a slight bow of his head. "I'm sorry, Father. I meant no insult to you or the girl." Oddly a feeling of relief trickled through him, mingled with the unwelcome thought that the girl would make a lovely mistress, indeed.

"I'm an old man, Matthew. I haven't been feeling well lately. You and Jessica are all I have in this world. The two of you mean everything to me. You are the future of Belmore, my very reason for living."

Matthew came to his feet. "I realize you're counting on me, Father. I've already discussed my resignation with both Cornwallis and Admiral Nelson. Unfortunately, they believe as I do, that a crucial confrontation between France and England is about to take place at sea, and until that happens—until England is safe from invasion, my place is aboard the *Norwich*. I cannot in good conscience resign my commission."

"I understand your loyalties run deep, Matthew, and I'm proud of you for it. However, captaining a ship in the middle of a naval battle is an extremely dangerous proposition. You are my only remaining heir. I cannot afford to lose you—duty or no."

"You know my feelings on this, Father. We've argued the subject before."

The older man sighed. "Yes . . . well, be that as it may, at present, that is not the matter I wish to discuss. The topic I'm concerned with involves my ward. It is the reason I allowed her to plead a headache she did not have, why I permitted her to retire to her room when the evening was not yet ended."

The marquess waved a blunt-fingered hand, indicating Matt should return to his seat, then sat down in a comfortable chair across from him. Bending forward, he drew a cigar from the rosewood box on the table between them.

"Join me?" he asked, pointing to the box, but Matt shook his head, taking a sip of his brandy instead.

His father held the cigar beneath the straight patrician

nose so like Matthew's, inhaling the aroma of expensive to-
bacco. "As I said, I understand that you still have commit-
ments to fulfill before your permanent return to Belmore.
But the fact is, with Richard gone, besides your duty to England, you have other, equally important obligations that
you must consider." The marquess snipped the end off the
cigar with a pair of silver nippers. Matt held a taper into the
flames of the hearth, then lit the end.

"Seaton Manor is already yours," the marquess continued,
puffing a wreath of smoke into the air. "Belmore and all of its
properties very soon will be."

"Don't say that, Father. You'll be running things for years.
There's no need—"

"Listen to me, son. I'm an old man. I'm ailing and I'm tired.
I would hand you the reins to Belmore tomorrow, if you were
home and ready to take over my affairs. The responsibilities
are beginning to weigh heavily on these old shoulders—I'm
asking for your help, son."

"Of course, Father. I'll help in any way I can."

The old man leaned back in his chair, took a long draw on
his cigar. A branch of candles flickered on the table, high-
lighting his silver hair.

"As I said earlier you and Jessica are the future of Belmore. Simply put—I want the two of you to wed."

"What!" Matthew surged to his feet. "Father, that is absurd."

"It is hardly absurd. You saw the girl tonight. There is no
more lovely creature on the face of this earth. She is intelligent
and charming. And she loves Belmore Hall nearly as much as
you do."

Matt clamped hard on his jaw, working to control his temper. "Father, I can't possibly marry your ward. I'm very nearly
betrothed already. You're well aware that Lady Caroline and I
have an understanding. We've known each other since childhood. It's been assumed for some time that we would wed."

"Yes . . . ever since you became my heir. Had the title not
passed to you, she probably wouldn't have had you."

Matt said nothing. In this his father was probably correct.

"Why are you so set on Lady Caroline?" he asked.

"Any man would be. Caroline Winston has everything a man could want—family, money, breeding. She's been gently reared and she's extremely attractive. Our temperaments are well suited and her father plans to dower her with a fortune—including the estate next to Belmore. The whole thing's practically settled."

"But it *isn't* settled. You have not offered for the girl, and I'm asking you to marry Jessica instead."

Anger slid through him. "Why, for godsakes? Jessie Fox and I hardly know each other."

"I told you why. Because I am a very old man. I am responsible for Jessica's welfare. I'm concerned for her future just as I am yours, and I want to see her well taken care of. With you as her husband, I can be certain she will be."

Matthew shook his head, unable to believe what he was hearing, fighting to remain in control. "Lady Caroline will soon be traveling to Winston House. I'm planning to call on her the moment I learn of her arrival. As soon as my resignation is tendered and accepted, I intend to make an offer for her."

His father looked at him hard. "Perhaps if you were in love with the girl, I would understand your reluctance where Jessica is concerned. But clearly you are not. You rarely mention her name."

"Love is the last thing I wish to feel for a wife. You loved my mother and her death nearly killed you. You've been grieving for her for the last twenty years. As I said, Caroline and I are well suited. That is more than enough."

For a moment his father said nothing, just took a long slow draw on his cigar. "I believe you and Jessica will suit."

Matthew's temper flared. "That's insane! The girl is a hoyden! We've done nothing but clash from the day we laid eyes on each other." He smiled with dark relish. "The last time she pulled one of her reckless misadventures, your darling little Jessie wound up over my knee. I gave her the thrashing she deserved and if she's not careful, I just might do it again!"

His father merely chuckled. "I'll grant she can be a handful at times. Jessica has a mind of her own and a bit of a penchant for trouble. She needs a man who can handle her, one who will not be afraid to take her in hand. She'll respect a man like that and she'll make him a very good wife."

Fury swept over him, so strong he found it difficult to speak. "She put you up to this, didn't she? She's afraid once you're gone, I'll have her tossed out in the street. Well, let me tell you something, Father—the conniving little baggage may have hoodwinked you, but she isn't fooling me. She's been after your money all along. Now she wants the Belmore title to go with it. You want me to marry Jessie Fox? Bloody hell—she's the daughter of a whore!"

The old man's face went pale. Matt cursed himself and his unexpected loss of control. From the corner of his eye, he caught a flash of blue through a crack in the door as someone hurried away.

God's blood—the little vixen had been listening. Matt studied his father's taut features, the way his hands gripped the arms of the chair. Already Matt regretted his words.

"You're wrong about Jessica," his father said with quiet dignity, some of his composure returning. "She knows nothing of this. It was simply my belief that if the two of you should marry, both of you would reap the greatest of rewards."

Matthew raked a hand through his hair, tumbling a lock of it over his forehead. "I'm sorry, Father. I shouldn't have lost my temper." He rarely did. Almost never.

"Perhaps I should have waited, given the two of you a chance to know each other better. I didn't because there isn't much time. And because of your involvement with Lady Caroline."

"I understand," Matt replied, once more in control. He dropped back down in his chair. "As I said, you have my sincerest apologies." Still, he couldn't help believing Jessie had manipulated his father in this, just as she had everything else.

"I've rarely asked you for anything, Matthew. What I'm asking now is simply that you set aside your prejudice and try to see Jessica as I do. Spend a little time with her. If you will do that, when your leave is up, if you still do not wish to marry her, I will not force the issue."

Matthew hesitated only a moment, then inclined his head in a stiff nod of agreement. His father was sick and he did not wish to upset him. Surely he could tolerate the girl for the next few weeks.

"As you wish, Father." After what she had heard, he wondered if Jessie would be willing to tolerate him.

Dawn streaked the windows, a dull gray hue that matched Jessie's mood. Her limbs felt weary, stiff, and cumbersome after her night of restless slumber. A slight headache throbbed at her temples. She had slept for only a couple of hours, angry and hurt at the captain's words. And yet she had known what he was thinking.

She shouldn't have been listening. She should have gone upstairs, as she had pretended to do. But she'd known there was something of importance on Papa Reggie's mind and she had been determined to discover what it was.

Dear Lord—marriage to his son, the future Lord of Belmore! It was ridiculous, utterly absurd.

Yet the moment she had heard the words, her heart had begun beating faster. He was the handsomest man she had ever seen, the epitome of the dashing hero in his navy blue uniform. When the girls at Mrs. Seymour's Academy had talked about their beaux, she had fantasized about Matthew Seaton, even dreamed what it might be like if he kissed her.

She had known it was silly, the musings of a foolish young girl, and yet when she thought of him, a tender yearning rose inside her. When she discovered he was finally coming home, that he would actually see her as the lady she had become, she couldn't keep her hopes from soaring. At last, all the years that she had studied until dawn, practiced her penmanship till her fingers ached and blisters rose on her thumb, repeated her

French till her throat was raw and her voice was gone—
would finally be worth the grueling effort—not that it wasn't
already.

Still, thinking of how different she was from the wild,
filthy little termagant the captain had known, there was that
one brief, sweet moment when she'd allowed herself to believe in her childish dreams.

Now she knew the hard, bitter truth.

Last night she had cried, ached bone deep at the brutal
dose of reality she had been forced to swallow. Today she
was herself again, steeled against what she could not have
and grateful to God for the wonderful gifts she *had* been
given. Besides, in truth, she knew the captain was right in
what he had said. He was an aristocrat, a member of the
nobility. The daughter of a whore was hardly a candidate for
marriage to an earl.

Still, if she lived to be a hundred, she would never forget
the cruelty of his words.

Searching through her wardrobe, Jessie pulled out a
lemon yellow morning dress, hoping it would brighten her
mood, then rang for the upstairs maid to help her fasten the
buttons. She wouldn't wake Viola. The older woman needed
her sleep, and she didn't want Vi's shrewd old eyes to realize
how ravaged she really was.

The tearful scene last night had been bad enough.

Today she was determined not to let the past defeat her.
She was happy here with Papa Reggie, happier than she had
ever been before. True, there were times she felt lonely,
times she felt isolated, as if she'd been born full-grown into
a totally different world than the one she had lived in before.

But there were also people here who depended upon her
and she was proud of how far she had come. She had more
important things to do than moon over a prig like Strickland.

It was barely light outside, just the first rays of sunlight
creeping in. Picking up the *Morning Chronicle* from a table
in the entry, always a day late with the mail-coach ride from

London, Jessie walked into the steamy kitchen. A huge iron pot boiled on the eight-burner stove, and she could smell fresh scones in the oven. The delicious aroma never failed to remind her how lucky she was to have food in her belly, that she no longer woke up hungry to face another bitter day.

Jessie waved and called out a greeting to Mrs. Tucker, the cook, as well as Nan and Charlotte, Cook's helpers, who labored nearby preparing food for the day. Then she looked down at the paper, walking toward the table as she read the headlines: *French Squadron Arrives in West Indies.* In smaller print, *General Nugent claims Jamaica not in danger of invasion.*

She came to a halt when she reached one of the benches, her attention still focused on the pages of newsprint.

"Interested in world affairs, Mistress Fox?" The captain's deep voice rumbled toward her from the end of the rough-hewn table.

Jessie's head snapped up. "Wh-What are you doing here?" Her heart lurched, twisted inside her. The words he'd said last night seemed to pound in her ears. Her chin went up a little higher. "You're supposed to be sleeping."

He noticed the pallor of her cheeks, looked as if he might say something, but instead his gaze turned hard.

"Sorry to disappoint you. I rarely sleep past dawn. The question, I think, is what are you doing here? I doubt my father expects you to labor in the kitchen."

"Hardly." A guilty glance strayed toward the paper. It was unseemly for a woman to be reading anything but a ladies' fashion journal, which Jessie found exceedingly dull. Her chin hitched a little bit higher. "In truth, your father frowns on my association with the servants. I, however, see no point in making extra work for them simply because I wish to rise earlier than most."

"Very thoughtful, Miss Fox. I had the same notion myself. Since we are both of a similar mind, perhaps you would care to join me?"

The newsprint shook a little in her hands. She didn't want

to join him. After what he'd said last night, she never wanted
to see him again. On the other hand, he didn't know she had
heard him. Surely she could brazen it out, pretend things
hadn't changed, behave as if she were simply the marquess's
ward and he the marquess's son.

That the cruel words he had spoken hadn't torn out a
piece of her heart.

She stared into his handsome face, noticed the perfect
symmetry of his hard, clean-shaven jaw, the way the gold of
his hair reflected in the sunlight streaming in through the
window. He had always been handsome, but the years had
given him a solidness, a depth of character that made him
even more attractive. Just looking at him made her heart
twist oddly and an unwelcome heat spiral into her stomach.

Her reply came out sharper than she had intended. "I'm
afraid I have plans for the morning. I've time enough for one
of Cook's scones then I must be on my way."

"Off on another of your madcap rides, Miss Fox? If that
is the case, I hope you will at least stick to the roads. I don't
believe either you or the horse could survive another mishap
like the last one."

Warm color swept into her cheeks, replacing her earlier
pallor. "I assure you, my lord, that is not my usual mode of
travel." But he didn't look convinced, and she wasn't about to
tell him she had raced off to help a friend. Assisting the birth
of a babe was hardly suitable behavior for an unmarried girl.
He would simply chalk up another mark against her.

She flicked a glance in his direction, saw that he studied
her, his eyes bold and dark, a lazy perusal that started at the
top of her head and ended at the curve of her breast. It made
her stomach go liquid and the color in her cheeks burn hot
once more.

He was dressed for riding, she saw as her gaze slid away, in
snug black breeches and a white lawn shirt, the same black
Hessian boots he had worn when she had first seen him. His
face was darkly bronzed, his hair still damp and slightly curling, the color of pirates' gold.

"Thank you, Mrs. Tucker," he said when the woman brought them tea and scones, and a slab of cold beef for the captain's heartier appetite.

"It's good to be seein' ye, Cap'n . . . even if ye do look like ye could use a bit o' me cookin'." She was a sturdy Irish woman, shorter than most, hardworking and pleasant natured.

He smiled and made a grand show of biting into one of the piping hot scones. Chewing thoughtfully, he swallowed and carefully wiped his mouth on a napkin. "And you, Maizie Tucker, are still the best damned cook this side of Dublin."

The stout little woman cackled with glee, then winked as she walked away.

Jessie turned her attention to the hot buttery scones. Smearing on a thick slab of honey, she rolled another in a napkin and prepared to leave. Then she felt his dark assessing gaze and stared up into the carved, compelling features of his face.

"I thought I would do some riding today," he said. "Get reacquainted with Belmore. Perhaps you would like to come along."

Jessie's insides clenched. He was asking her to ride with him, treating her as an equal when she knew very well it wasn't what he thought of her at all. Anger surfaced, hot at the back of her neck. Biting back a stiff retort, she shook her head, moving the thick blond braid that hung to her waist. "As I said, I'm afraid I have a prior engagement."

His eyes went a little bit dark. He had only asked her to please his father, she was sure, yet instead of looking pleased he looked incensed.

She smoothed her features, then smiled with nonchalance. "Well, I'm afraid I must be off." Reluctantly handing him the paper she hadn't had time to finish, she popped the last bite of scone into her mouth in a less ladylike manner than she had intended.

Lord Strickland's brow arched up. Jessie stiffened as amusement curved his lips. Shoving back the bench a little harder than she meant to, she rose to leave and the captain stood as well, his tall frame angled some distance above her.

"Have a good ride, my lord," she said a bit tartly.

He made a slight inclination of his head, the smile on his lips slightly mocking. "Enjoy your day, Mistress Fox."

Eager to be away from him, she made her way to the rear of the kitchen and down the back stairs, heading off toward her destination.

Chapter Four

Matt tried to concentrate on the fine print on the front page of the *Morning Chronicle,* but his thoughts kept straying to Jessie Fox. He hadn't expected to find her in the kitchen. Being the little sharper she was and knowing the way his father doted on her, he had imagined her in the dining room surrounded by servants catering to her every whim.

Then again, thinking of the mud-spattered Jessie he had encountered upon his arrival, perhaps the kitchen was where she belonged.

A cynical smile followed the thought. A woman who looked like Jessie Fox belonged in a man's bed. She wanted an education? He'd be happy to take up where Mrs. Seymour's finishing school left off.

He glanced toward the back door, thinking how pretty she had looked in her simple yellow dress. He smiled to think of Jessie Fox reading the London paper, then the smile slid away as he thought of his father's involvement with the conniving little baggage.

Recalling her abrupt departure, he found himself wondering why she had gone out the back door instead of the front. Where was she off to so early? What "prior engagement" could she have at six-thirty in the morning?

An ugly thought crept in. Jessica Fox was a beautiful woman. On the surface she had all the grace of a lady. But the fact remained, the girl had been raised in a whorehouse. She'd been fifteen years old when his father had brought her to Belmore—more than old enough, by the standards of the Black Boar Inn, to have taken up her mother's trade.

Perhaps Jessie Fox was not so innocent as his father believed. Perhaps Jessie Fox had a lover.

Matt snatched his riding coat off a hook on the kitchen wall and headed out the back door, letting it slam closed behind him.

No sign of Jessie in the stables. None of the carriages were gone. He ordered a groom to saddle him a horse, then strode off to take a quick look around. He tried the gardens, then walked down to the pond. Still no sign of Jessie. Perhaps he had been wrong and she had already returned to the house. He glanced back toward the barn. The groom held a tall blood bay gelding, saddled and waiting, pawing the earth in its eagerness to be gone.

He sighed. His time at Belmore wasn't nearly long enough. He had better things to do than worry about Jessie Fox. He crossed to the barn, took the reins of the horse, and swung himself up in the saddle.

Inside the old wooden carriage house, abandoned when a newer one of stone had been built, Jessie completed the last of her preparations for the class she would teach today. The place was cozy and warm. One of the grooms had acquired the task of building a fire each morning in the old iron stove, and thanks to Papa Reggie, the room was clean and well furnished, with bleached muslin curtains at the windows, tables and benches fashioned small enough for the children, and a desk and chair up front for her.

Jessie checked to be certain each student's slate writing tablet sat in its proper place in front of the child's usual spot, then glanced up just in time to see little Georgie Petersham, the cooper's son, dragging open the door. He was followed by ten-year-old Harold Siddon, then seven-year-old Amanda Jane Harvey, and her eight-year-old sister, Penelope. A few minutes later, Simon Stewart arrived, a gangly boy of fourteen, and nine-year-old Fanny Wills. It was a small but valiant gathering, children who had never had any formal schooling, yet all of them were eager to learn, just as she had once been.

"Good morning, children," she said in the ritual greeting.

"Good morning, Miss Fox," they replied in unison. Since her arrival from boarding school when she had first convinced Papa Reggie to start classes for the Belmore servants' children, their progress had been amazing. They were darling children. They tried so hard and she had come to love each one.

She smiled at them warmly, feeling a soft tug at her heart. It felt so good to be needed, to give something back for the wondrous gifts she had been given.

"Well, you all look bright eyed and bushy tailed this morning. Why don't we begin?"

Matt rode hard till midafternoon, assessing the growth of a cornfield here and there, pleased with the healthy looking sheep in a far distant pasture, stopping occasionally to speak to a tenant he hadn't seen in years.

He'd never thought to be master of Belmore. The title to his beloved home was meant to go to Richard. He had tried not to form too strong an attachment—perhaps that was the reason he had chosen a life at sea.

Now just looking at the rolling green acres, the robust crops, and burgeoning herds made something sweet unfurl inside him. One day this land would be his. His father was eager to pass on control, and except for the obligation he felt to the men of the *Norwich,* he was ready to leave his grueling life at sea. He was more than ready to face a new challenge.

Satisfied with what he had seen, Matthew finally turned his horse and started back toward Belmore. Just one more stop and then he would go home.

The sun angled over a clear blue afternoon sky when he dismounted from the tall bay gelding and tied the reins to the branches of an alder near the door to the old carriage house. Purposeful strides carried him toward the entrance, the muscles in his long legs aching a little, unaccustomed now to such long hours in the saddle.

Through a gap in the trees earlier in the day, he had glimpsed the old abandoned building, a favorite since his boyhood. He and Richard had often played up in the loft, fighting mock battles with their carved wooden soldiers, or simply making up adventure stories. He had hidden some of his most valuable childhood possessions up there, his seashell collection, a poem he had written, a favorite book of stories his father used to read to him before he went to bed. He wondered if they were still there.

Smiling at the foxglove and buttercups blooming along the little-used trail out in front, Matt shoved open the heavy wooden door, expecting to hear the sound of creaking hinges, to peer through a haze of cobwebs into a dark, dust-filled room. Instead the sight that greeted him brought him to a halt in the doorway.

Jessica Fox leapt to her feet behind a battered wooden desk, her eyes wide and startled by his unexpected appearance.

"Lord Strickland!" she gasped.

He surveyed the six small faces, all peering in his direction. "Mistress Fox. Once again you have managed to amaze me." Again that strange sense of relief. Jessie Fox, it appeared, had not gone off with her lover.

She gave him the coolest of smiles. "Children," she said, "we were very nearly finished even as Lord Strickland arrived. Take your readers home with you, and I'll see you all on the morrow."

Surprisingly they grumbled as if they didn't want to leave. Picking up their meager possessions, tattered jackets, woolen hats and gloves, and the single reader each child had been provided, they passed him by and shuffled out the door.

Jessie Fox remained exactly where she stood, her chin held high, her shoulders squared as if she faced an enemy in battle. In her bright yellow dress, the sunlight shining on her golden hair, she was the loveliest woman he had ever seen.

Heat uncoiled in his belly, began to pulse into his groin. Two years at sea had taken its toll. His nights with the redhead in Portsmouth hadn't been nearly enough.

Or perhaps it was simply Jessie Fox.

As he moved in her direction, he tried to control the stirring in his blood, the way it began to thicken and settle lower down.

"I don't . . . I don't suppose you approve of this," she said, gesturing toward the miniature tables and chairs. "Most of your kind does not." Her breasts rose with her breathing, shaping themselves into soft hills above the top of her dress. He wanted to reach out and cup them.

"My kind?" he repeated. "You mean the aristocracy, Miss Fox?"

She nervously dampened her lips, and a fresh surge of heat slid into his loins. Whatever she was, whatever she had been, Jessica Fox was a beautiful, sensuous woman. Unwelcome as the notion was, Matthew admitted he wanted her in his bed.

"Not all of the nobility," she said. "Not men like your father. The rest of them believe lower-class children should be kept in their places. Poverty and illiteracy provide cheap labor for those in the classes above them. And there is always the notion that should the poor receive an education, eventually they are certain to revolt."

He rounded the edge of the desk. "Ah, yes. As they have done in France. Teach these six small children and a hundred others like them, and sooner or later heads will roll. Is that about it, Mistress Fox?"

"Yes."

"And you think that is what I believe as well."

She stood her ground, though as he closed the last few paces her eyes darted several times toward the door. "I-I don't know what you believe."

"What I believe, Mistress Fox, is that if you are willing to teach these children and they desire to learn, then they should have the chance. I'm glad my father has agreed." He stood so close to her now he could see her small black pupils, inhale the scent of her perfume, the subtle fragrance of jasmine.

"That isn't what you thought when the marquess helped me," she said, a look of accusation in the cornflower blue of her eyes.

"No . . . I don't suppose I did." His mouth curved faintly. "Perhaps I was too busy dodging rotten fruit, or trying to keep you from stealing the coin in my purse."

"Or perhaps you were too busy with the girls in the rooms abovestairs at the inn."

He arched a brow. "I was only there a couple of times. I'm surprised you knew about it. You were only a child back then." He watched the way her eyes ran over his face, slowly came to rest on his mouth. "On the other hand, perhaps you know a good deal more about that sort of thing than my father imagines." His hand came up to cradle her cheek. He ran his thumb along her jaw.

"Wh-What do you mean?"

"I'm simply curious, Miss Fox. I wonder . . . are you really the innocent my father believes?" Or the conniving little baggage Matt suspected, a woman well seasoned in the art of pleasuring a man? It suddenly seemed the most important question in the world.

"I-I have to be getting back," she whispered as he settled a hand on her waist and drew her several inches closer, until their bodies barely touched.

"Not yet. Not for a few more moments."

"But I—"

"Do you know how lovely you are?" She trembled as he tilted her face up for his kiss. "Who would have suspected . . ." His mouth came down over hers, claiming the softness, testing the full, warm curves. He teased the seam between her lips, coaxing her to open for him, and felt her bottom lip quiver. Her palms pressed against his chest, hesitant, uncertain, perhaps even a little bit fearful.

Ignoring her reluctance, he deepened the kiss, taking possession of her mouth, thrusting deeply with his tongue. Jessie swayed and gripped his shoulders, making a soft little mew in her throat. Her legs seemed to weaken and she clutched his neck to hold herself up.

Bloody hell—he couldn't deny the truth a moment more. The girl was no whore. She was an innocent—a babe in the woods who'd most likely never been kissed.

He muttered a curse as he set her away, his body hard and throbbing, pulsing with unspent desire for her.

"M-Matthew?" It had a light, breathy sound when she said it.

"Easy, love. Just give it a moment." He would need far longer himself—a cold swim perhaps—but at least he'd discovered the truth.

She lifted a shaky hand and brought it to her lips. "You-You kissed me."

He almost smiled. She was lucky that was all he had done. It had taken an iron control not to drag her down on the desk, tear off her clothes, and make love to her there in her makeshift schoolroom. "You have my humble apologies, Miss Fox. I should not have taken such liberties."

She straightened, the dazed look fading from her face. Perhaps she had heard the insincerity in his voice. He wasn't sorry at all.

"Why?" she asked, her eyes cool now and suddenly remote. "Why did you kiss me?"

A corner of his mouth tilted up. "Because I wanted to, Miss Fox. You of all people should understand that. As I recall, you usually do exactly what you want."

Jessie said nothing. Her face had closed up, her expression becoming inscrutable. Her hands fumbled as she worked to gather up the papers strewn on her desk, but when she straightened, her spine was stiff, her chin high, and her shoulders squared.

"I have to be going," she said, intending to brush past him.

Matt caught her arm. "It was only a kiss, Miss Fox."

She turned and looked straight through him. "Don't do it again." And then she was gone.

Matthew stared after her, his body still hard, pressing painfully against the front of his breeches. No, he wouldn't kiss her again. He wanted her—yes—and if it weren't for his father, he would do whatever it took to have her in his bed. But he wasn't about to marry her.

Caroline Winston would be his wife, not Eliza Fox's daughter, no matter how tempting the little vixen had become.

In the days that followed, Matt vowed to stay away from Jessie Fox, and most of the time, he managed the task fairly well. But he couldn't avoid her at supper, and several times he accidentally came upon her somewhere in the house. Most mornings and one full day each week, she spent at the schoolhouse, teaching the children to read and write, how to cipher, and a bit of what was happening in the world.

When she wasn't with them, he discovered, she was usually in the Belmore library, pouring over a volume in French, or studying her Latin. She read the morning paper front page to back, absorbing each bit of news into a mind as thirsty for knowledge as any he had ever seen.

Whatever his opinion of her, she was serious about educating herself. To what end, he couldn't be sure. She was intelligent and outspoken about subjects that mattered to her. She was also nothing but trouble.

Like the morning a week after his arrival when Jessie sneaked into the house with her dress torn up the side and her hair tumbled down.

"What the devil happened to you?" he'd asked.

Hot color rose into her cheeks. "The children's ball . . . it got stuck in the sycamore tree. I had to climb up and get it down."

He gave her a mocking half smile. "As I remember it, Miss Fox, you were always good at climbing trees."

She went bone stiff, stuck her straight little nose in the air, and marched up the stairs to her room, leaving him smiling behind her.

Another time he had caught her arguing with a peddler who had stopped to sell his wares. She claimed the man had cheated the cooper's wife on the price of his goods and demanded he return the woman's money. The shouting match that ensued might have continued if he hadn't stepped in and put a stop to it.

Twice she came in with her gown covered in mud; once there was even a smudge on her chin. God only knew what she had been doing.

Nor did it matter. As beautiful as she was, as much as he desired her, Jessie Fox was still Jessie Fox. Beneath her polished facade, the girl was willful and hell-bent on causing trouble. Matt's jaw clamped. Even if Jessie's past were not a problem—a matter his father had so far been able to conceal—she was the antithesis of everything he wanted in a woman.

He wanted a wife who was sweet and manageable, an even-tempered girl like Caroline, a woman who would bear him children of the same gentle nature.

Jessie Fox was definitely not the woman for him.

Reginald Seaton, Marquess of Belmore, sat at the head of the long, polished mahogany table, his son on the right, his ward on the left, the most precious two people in his world.

Each night since Matthew's arrival, the three of them had gathered for supper and the meal had passed with cool formality. At times, Jessica had seemed almost hostile. Matthew ignored her to the point of being rude.

Reginald inwardly grinned. It was a very good sign.

He fixed his attention on his son, who studied his plate as if it absorbed his foremost attention. "How is the venison, Matthew?" he asked.

"Very good, Father."

"And the partridge, Jessica?"

"Splendid, Papa Reggie. The meal is quite delicious."

"I'm glad it pleases you. Tomorrow we shall be dining far more simply."

"Why is that?" they both said precisely in unison. Matthew

looked disgruntled. Jessica's sleek blond brows narrowed into a frown.

They both turned toward him and together they said, "Are we going somewhere—" Jessica's cheeks went crimson. Matthew's gaze held a spark of amusement, a sight rarely seen these days.

"After you, Miss Fox," he said, his eyes still sparkling.

"After you, my lord. I'm certain whatever you have to say is of far more consequence than whatever I might wish to say." There was a haughty little tilt to her chin.

Matt's attention remained fixed on her a moment more, then swung away. "Are we traveling somewhere, Father?"

"Actually, my boy, we are. There is a fair going on in Eylesbury. I haven't been to one in years. I should like to go once more before I'm too old to enjoy myself, and I should like the two of you to come with me."

Matthew frowned. "I'd like to go, Father, but I'm afraid I've already made plans."

"Yes, I saw that Miss Winston's footman left her calling card. I assume she is now in residence at Winston House."

"Yes. Since I had already promised to visit, it would be ill mannered of me to cancel."

"'Twould also be ill-mannered of you to break our agreement. I believe we had an understanding. Was I wrong?"

A swath of crimson colored the dark, sun-bronzed skin across Matt's cheekbones. Pride and honor were the words inscribed on the Belmore crest. Matthew lived by them more than any man Reginald had ever met.

His son made a curt nod of his head. "I shall send word to Lady Caroline." He smiled thinly. "Tomorrow we leave for the fair."

Jessica tried to look unaffected, but a radiant smile broke over her face. "A fair! I've never been to a fair, but I have wanted to go ever so badly."

"Never?" Matt asked, incredulous. "Surely at one time or another—"

She shook her head. "It was always too far to travel, or

something else got in the way. Then Mother fell ill and I had to tend her. After she died there was no money for such things." A dark memory flickered in her eyes, then it was gone, replaced by a blinding white smile. "I never got to go, but I've heard tales of how wondrous they are. My brother had a friend named Dibble who never missed a fair. He said the place was near to bustin' wit' coxcombs and gentry coves ripe for the pickin's. 'E said 'e could foyst a cove's purse and disappear into a crowd afore the blighter ever knew what 'it 'im."

Reggie inwardly groaned. The girl hadn't made a single slip since her return. She had told him once that she wouldn't allow herself to even think in the language she grew up with.

It was the strain of Matthew's presence, he knew, his proper navy son who wouldn't be moved one bit by the horrified look on Jessica's pretty face. He wouldn't give a fig that her cheeks had gone from peach to ashen, that her lovely blue eyes now brimmed with tears. He would simply think how right he was about her, how poorly they were suited, and that she would hardly make a respectable Belmore marchioness.

"Excuse me," Jessie whispered, easing back her chair. "I'm afraid the partridge did not agree with me after all."

"Jessica—" Reggie began, his weary old heart breaking for her, but it was Matthew who captured her hand before she could flee.

"Don't go," he said softly. "You have nothing to be ashamed of. None of us here is perfect, no matter how hard we may wish to be." He smiled at her with gentle warmth. "You've learned more in four years than most people do in a lifetime. You should be proud of what you've done, even if you aren't always perfect."

A tear spilled down her cheek. She wiped it away with the back of a hand.

"Stay, my dear," Reginald added softly. "Matthew is right . . . and we have plans to make for the morrow."

Slowly she sank back down in her chair, perching on the edge as if she still might flee.

Matthew spoke about a huge fair he had been to on Angel Hill in Bury St. Edmunds, regaling her with tales of his misadventures until he had her smiling again. She was looking at him differently than she had before, the way she used to look whenever Reggie spoke of his son.

As if he were some sort of hero.

Matthew was hardly that—if the look of naked lust in his son's blue eyes were any indication of what he was really thinking.

Damn and blast! He wanted this match, but the risks were great and he didn't want to see Jessica hurt. In her nineteen years, she had been beaten and starved, lived in squalor, and forced to survive on the streets. She didn't deserve to suffer at his son's hands as well. Perhaps the fair was not such a good idea after all.

Reggie eyed his two beloved children. Jessica was smiling softly, and for once his son was smiling back. Matthew wanted Jessica, but not enough to marry her. There was danger here, to be sure.

Reginald sighed. He was taking a terrible risk.

Then again, his son was an honorable man, and a chance for great happiness was worth the gravest sort of risk.

He would continue down the path he had chosen.

Chapter Five

The fair at Eylesbury was not as large as some. It had started years ago as a market, Papa Reggie had told her, then become a trade fair, allowing shopkeepers to stock up for the rest of the year.

As time went on, the fair expanded. A variety of shows were added, roundabouts, stalls for entertainment, and myriad other facets that each year enhanced the fair's appeal.

"The market was eventually moved to the outskirts of town," the marquess said. "Out where the beast market was, the place they sold cattle, sheep, and horses."

The square was a noisy, bustling place teeming beneath a warm late-morning sun. It was separated from traffic by wooden railings, which kept out livestock, horses, and carts. At one end, permanent stalls were set up where butchers, fishmongers, potters, and wheelwrights hawked their wares.

Around them, shopkeepers strolled beside beggars. There were innkeepers and pig-sellers, orange women and schoolmasters, gentry folk and members of the aristocracy, all thrown together, drawn to the sights and smells, colors and sounds of the fair.

"Look, Papa Reggie! A puppet show!" She dragged him off in that direction while Matthew smiled indulgently and walked along behind. They watched from the back of the crowd, Jessie laughing like a child at the antics of the puppeteer, who pulled the strings that raised the puppet's busy eyebrows, lifted a hand, and waved to her in the crowd.

Afterward they wandered along the aisles, Papa Reggie stopping here and there to purchase an item that happened to catch Jessie's eye, a colorful woven bracelet, a pretty shell, a beautiful length of red brocaded silk she had stopped to admire at a cloth merchant's stall.

"You've already bought me too much," Jessie protested. "I've a closet full of beautiful clothes—I don't need this, too."

"You like it, don't you?"

"It's beautiful, but you don't have to—"

"Leave him alone," Matthew put in with a smile. "He's having a good time spoiling you."

Reggie smiled, too. "Listen to the boy, my dear. For once the lad is right."

Jessica laughed and squeezed the marquess's age-spotted hand. "Thank you," she said softly, and caught a subtle shift in Matthew's expression, the blue of his eyes going a little bit darker.

They paused to watch a troop of acrobats somersaulting off each other's shoulders, then went into a sideshow where Jessie saw a real African native. He wore a bone through his nose and shells in his ears, and shook a deadly looking spear at the crowd. Jessie had never seen anyone look more fearsome.

Inwardly she grinned. Except perhaps Matthew Seaton the day he had given her the licking.

They walked out of the tent and back into the sunshine.

"Oh, Papa Reggie, I'm having so much fun. Thank you for bringing me here."

"Nonsense," he said with gruff authority. "I am the one who wished to come. I'm only grateful that you came with me." But his face had begun to grow flushed beneath his snowy hair and taking in his taut features, she began to worry about him.

"Unfortunately," he said, confirming her fears, "I'm not as young as I once was. My gout is acting up. I believe if the two of you will excuse me, I shall return to the Sword and Angel." The marquess had sent word ahead, arranging rooms for them at a well-appointed inn near the outskirts of town where they had spent the past night.

Jessie nodded and took his arm. "I think that is a very good idea."

"Agreed," Matthew said.

The older man pulled away. "Where do you two think you are going?"

"With you, of course," Jessie said.

"Don't be silly. You are both young and healthy. The two of you should stay and enjoy the fair. Matthew can see you back to the inn when you are ready."

"Oh, no, we couldn't possibly—"

"Isn't that right, my boy?"

Lord Strickland caught her hand and bowed over it with gallantry. "My father is right, Miss Fox. The day is far from spent, and you have not seen the rest of the fair."

"What about Papa Reggie?"

"There are least half a dozen Belmore retainers waiting at the inn. The footmen will see him there safely and his valet can see him settled in his room."

He glanced up at the aging marquess. "Is that about what you had in mind, Father?"

"Exactly so, my boy, exactly so." He bent and kissed Jessie's cheek. "Have a good time, child. I shall see you both later on this evening."

Jessie nodded. Even the twinge of guilt she felt at letting him return to the inn alone couldn't dim the thrill of being at the fair.

"I'll see my father to the carriage," Matthew said. "Wait for me here, in front of the cobbler's stall. I'll only be a moment."

"All right." Her eyes skipped over to the stall next door where a group of boys were battling to see who could eat the most hasty pudding. Prizes would be awarded to the winner.

"And don't wander off," Matt said sternly, pausing to glare

at her from a few feet away. "In this crowd, I'll never be able to find you."

She simply nodded and watched him meld into the milling throng. The marquess's hand came up one last time, then the men disappeared from view. Jessie took a couple more steps, drifting closer to the group of boys hunkered over their bowls of steaming oatmeal thickened with milk, flavored with sugar and butter, their spoons dredging up huge portions they shoveled into their mouths.

She smiled as she watched them, knowing only too well how badly each of the boys wanted the prize he would gain if he managed to stuff in the most.

"Well, kiss mine arse—if it ain't me long-lost sister."

Jessie's stomach tightened. She whirled toward the sound of the familiar voice. "D-Danny." A cold shiver snaked through her, leaving her shaking inside. "What . . . What are you doing here?" Beside him she spotted tall, bone-thin Connie Dibble, and a short, stocky, sandy-haired man she didn't know.

"What ya think we're doin', luv? Me and Connie and Theo here, come for the fair, just like yerself." Four years older than Jessie, Danny Fox wasn't a bad-looking sort, average in height and build, with light brown hair and brown eyes. It was the look in those eyes, the hard, flinty coldness that betrayed the man he was inside.

"Danny's got the right o' it, Jess," Dibble said. "Ye can't find pickin's the likes o' these anywheres this side o' London."

Jessie took a quick glance around, her pulse increasing with every second. No sign of Matthew, thank God.

"Lookin' for yer 'andsome sea capt'n, are ya, luv?" Her half brother laughed—more a cackle that sent another chill up her spine. "I seen ya wi' 'im. Did ya think I would forget who 'e is? Not bloody likely." He touched the slight lump near a point between his eyes. "The bastard broke me bloody nose."

Jessie stiffened. "What did you expect him to do—you were trying to steal his purse."

He ignored the words as if she hadn't spoken, reached out

and fingered the sleeve of her rose faille walking gown. "Yer dressin' pretty fancy . . . for a 'ore."

Her stomach twisted; the blood drained from her head. Danny had always been cruel. When she was little, he beat her unmercifully whenever he got the urge. And he had always been vicious with words.

"I'm not a whore."

He laughed again, the sound cold and hoarse. "Call it what ya will, luv. Ya ain't no different than ya were afore. Just cause yer fancy culley's got more blunt in 'is bleedin' pockets, don't make no difference a'tall."

"He isn't my culley."

Danny grabbed her arm, clamping down brutally. "Don't go lyin' to me, gel. I seen the way 'e was lookin' at ya. Man wanted to take ya right 'ere in one o' these stalls." His hand stroked softly across her cheek, his fingers cool and slightly damp, not a working man's callous anywhere on them.

The stocky man behind him edged forward. " 'Ow much ye want for a go at 'er, Danny?" He glanced over his shoulder to a narrow alley behind a row of stalls. "Me coin's as good as 'is, and me cods is near to burstin' just to look at 'er."

Jessie tried to wrench free, but her brother's hold only tightened, sending a shaft of pain up her arm. "Let go of me, Danny."

"Think yer better'n the rest of us now, don't ya? All yer lah-de-dah words and fancy clothes. Yer still a 'ore, missy. Nothin's gonna change the life ya was born to."

"I'm not a whore. I never was. You weren't even there when Mama died. You were too busy dodging the three-legged mare, trying to stay out of Newgate."

Danny's face went red at her reference to the gallows. A tic worked below one eye. He reached up and pinched her cheek. "Ya want the mort, Theo?" he said to the short, stocky man.

"Oh, yeah, Danny, I want 'er real bad."

"Gimme that purse ya just lifted, she's yers. Good swivin' might do 'er some good."

One glance at Theo's leering face and Jessie began to fight in earnest. "I'll scream!" she threatened. "I'll scream till they bring a constable over here!"

"No, ya won't." Danny wrenched her arm up behind her back. "Then yer culley'd be sure to come and I'd be waitin'— wit' this." A knife flashed silver as he backed her down the narrow space between two stalls, then into the dim light behind them. "Besides, ya wouldn't want any a those rich coves ya been runnin' wit' to find out who ya really are . . . now would ya?"

She tried to kick him, but her skirt was in the way and he only wrenched her arm up higher, jolting her with so much pain the bile rose in her throat. The next thing she knew she was lying on the ground beneath the stocky man, his thick body pinning her, his blunt fingers covering her mouth so tightly she could barely breathe.

He grunted as he wrenched open the bodice of her gown, grabbed her breasts, and gave each one a painful squeeze. Tears stung her eyes and began to slide down her cheeks. Her chest burned with the effort to drag in lungfuls of air with his heavy weight atop her. Dear God, how had her mother endured this? Gagging at the smell of the man's rancid breath, Jessie knew without doubt she would rather be dead.

She kicked and bucked, trying to dislodge Theo's thick body, but it only seemed to excite him.

"That's it, gel. Put some fight into it. I'll give ye a ride ye won't soon forget."

Jessie bitterly cursed him, words she hadn't allowed herself even to think slid onto her tongue, but the hand over her mouth kept them locked in. As hard as she fought, as fiercely as she struggled, she couldn't break free of his hold. A strangled sound seeped out as his hand moved along her leg, bunching up her long narrow skirt, then he was fumbling at the buttons at the front of his breeches, grunting with his effort to free himself and bury himself inside her.

"Let her go." Coming from a few feet away, the command sounded all the more deadly for its quiet tone.

Jessie's eyes slid closed, sending a fresh wash of tears down her cheeks. Matthew had come. She wasn't sure which was worse, enduring the brutal invasion of her body, or the condemnation she was sure to see when she looked into his face.

"I said, let her go."

The meaty hand slid away from her mouth as Theo scrambled to his feet then searched the dimly lit passage for his two companions. Jessie tried to speak, to cry out a warning, but her mouth was so dry she had to wet her lips to form the words.

"B-Be careful, Matthew! One of them . . . one of them has a knife."

He hardly spared a glance in her direction, just faced his opponent with his long legs splayed, his hands balled into fists, every muscle in his body tensed for action.

"Your brother and his friend have already been disposed of," he said.

A shiver slid through her. Had he killed them, then? The captain's features were set. Hard, dark, relentless. He had never appeared more deadly.

The beefy man just grinned. "It ain't them two, mate, it's me ye gots to watch out for."

Lowering his head, Theo charged like a maddened bull, knocking Matthew into the dirt. He wasn't wearing his tailcoat, she saw, and his white lawn shirt was torn and bloody, no doubt from his encounter with her brother.

Clutching the front of her rose silk dress with trembling hands, Jessie staggered to her feet, then frantically started searching for a weapon. Her brother had chosen this spot well. With the noisy contest being waged next door and the applause for the nearby acrobats, no one could hear their violent struggles.

Matthew was on his feet and landing blow for blow. Theo grinned again and there was blood on his teeth.

"She's a rum blowen," he said, circling for a better position. "Prettiest set o' dugs I ever seen."

Matthew growled low in his throat. Advancing on Theo, he swung a blow that caught the beefy man on the chin, knocking him backward and sending him sprawling into the dirt. The man merely grunted, shook his head, and staggered to his feet. Two left jabs, then Theo threw a roundhouse punch that would have brought a lesser man to his knees. Matthew dodged the full force of the blow, but it clipped him on the shoulder, spinning him around.

He took a quick blow to the stomach, then turned and threw a savage right to Theo's jaw, then another hard punch that sent blood flying from his nose and mouth. All the while, Jessie edged around them, her legs shaking and her heart pounding madly, searching for any threat from her brother or Connie Dibble and trying to find some way to aid the earl.

Dear Lord, she couldn't go for help. Calling a constable would end the fight but then there would be questions. Questions that could lead to questions about her and embarrassment for Matthew and Papa Reggie. She couldn't see them hurt that way.

Instead she found a heavy length of wood left from construction of one of the stalls, rounded on the beefy man still swinging blows at Matthew, and brought the wood down hard on his sandy head.

For a moment he wavered, his eyes fixed on hers in a look of disbelief. With a groan, he sank to his knees. His eyeballs rolled back, and he pitched forward into the dirt. Jessie stood above him, trembling all over, gripping the board like a club, ignoring the splinters that had tunneled into her hands. A few feet away, Matthew stood with his fists still clenched, blood on his face and the knuckles of his hands, his broad chest expanding with his effort to draw air into his lungs.

"Matthew?"

His head came up. His eyes swung to hers. She didn't realize the bodice of her dress gaped open, exposing her bare breasts, until she saw the hot dark look on the Earl of Strickland's face.

"Cover yourself," he said roughly, fury seething from every pore, "unless you wish to finish what that whoreson started."

Jessie stared into those hard blue eyes, felt the censure, the bitter condemnation, and a sob escaped her throat. She dropped the length of wood and turned away, grabbing the ragged edges of her bodice and holding them together with shaking hands. Her hair had come loose from its wreath atop her head and now hung in tangles around her shoulders.

She heard the captain's heavy footfalls, closed her eyes, and clamped down on her trembling lips.

"I told you to wait for me." His hands bit into her shoulders. He roughly turned her around. "I told you not to move from where I left you."

She shook her head, fighting back tears, ignoring the pain in her arm. "I-I only took a couple of steps, then Danny came. H-He must have been watching us. He thought I was your— your—" She broke off then, looked up at him through the tears she could not seem to stop. His mouth looked thin and grim. Tension bristled in every muscle of his long lean body.

Jessie forced herself to meet his unforgiving gaze. "Where . . . where is my brother? Did you kill him?"

A cold smile touched his lips. "I should have. That's what he was trying to do to me."

She nodded bleakly, feeling wretched at what had occurred. When she swayed against him, Matthew tightened his hold on her arms, forcing her to look at him.

"The next time I tell you to do something, you do it. Do you understand me? You don't do it halfway, you don't just pretend to do it, you do it."

When she didn't answer soon enough, he shook her— hard. "Do you understand?"

"Yes," she whispered, more miserable than she had been

since her days of near starvation after she had left the Black Boar Inn.

Matthew stared at her a moment more, then dragged her against him, wrapping her up in his arms. To her stunned disbelief, she felt him trembling.

"Do you have any idea the way I felt when I saw that bastard on top of you? I wanted to kill him. When he touched you, I could have torn him limb from limb with my two bare hands."

His palm cupped the back of her head, cradling her cheek against his chest, stroking gently through her hair. She could feel the rapid beating of his heart.

"I'm sorry," she said.

"You're sorry?" He tipped her face up. "That whoreson nearly raped you and you're the one who is sorry?"

She made a little sound in her throat and her knees went weak. Matthew swore foully as he caught her up in his arms. He said nothing as he strode back out of the shadows and into the crowd, nothing as his long strides ate up the distance to the carriage. Jessie closed her eyes and turned her face away from the curious glances of the people around them.

"I can't believe you hit him over the head," he said as he shouldered his way through the milling throng.

She moistened her lips. "I'm—"

"I know—you're sorry."

She smiled a little at that. "No . . . I'm not sorry I hit him at all."

A rude sound rumbled from his chest. "Little hoyden," he said beneath his breath, but the anger was seeping away. For the first time she realized it had stemmed not from what she had done, but from worry. Matthew had been worried about *her,* Jessie Fox.

A secret thrill shimmered through her, making her a little light headed. Careful to keep her bodice from gaping open, she slid her arm around his neck and nestled her head against his shoulder.

"I should have been more careful," she said as he rounded the corner toward where the carriage awaited.

"I'm the one who should have been careful," he said. "I should have guessed that something would happen." But Matthew was hardly the one to blame. Her brother was at fault, and if the captain had let him escape, he might just appear somewhere again.

Jessie shivered at the notion. Matthew must have felt it for he tightened his hold around her. She had never been held by a man before, not even Papa Reggie. In the taproom, men had patted her bottom and tried to fondle her breasts. Her brother had whipped her black and blue, and once he had blackened her eye.

But never had any man held her.

Jessie burrowed closer against him, inhaling the maleness of him, feeling the expansion of muscle over bone as he moved. She felt safe, protected, sheltered from the world around her. Her breasts brushed against his arm and a flutter dipped into her stomach. Something very like it had happened when he had kissed her, only then she'd felt hot and flushed and even a little bit frightened. Today she felt no fear, only a powerful urge to stay right where she was.

They finally reached the carriage and Matthew settled her safely inside. Tucking a lap robe securely around her, he leaned back against the squabs, his blue gaze dark and remote once more, his stern manner returning.

"You'll say nothing of this to my father. I don't want him unduly upset."

"No," she said. "Papa Reggie mustn't find out." But the same thing could happen again and both of them knew it. She was Jessie Fox, not the daughter of Simon Fox, the marquess's distant, deceased cousin and longtime friend, the tale Papa Reggie had concocted before he had sent her to school.

Her brother knew the truth and so did others. All it took was one slip, one incident like this one, and the Belmore name would be ruined. Four hundred years of pride and honor would be sullied—by her.

Jessie's heart twisted inside her. Dear Lord, she had not known until today how determined she was not to let that happen.

Chapter Six

*L*ady Caroline Winston stepped down from her carriage in front of Belmore Hall, her little maid, Emma, trailing along in her wake. Almost a week had passed since Matthew had sent his regrets, canceling his call at Winston House. She had heard nothing from him since.

In the meanwhile, word had reached her that the marquess's ward was in residence at Belmore Hall, a young woman several years younger than Caroline. Some of the Winston tenants had spoken of her, repeating tales of her kindness to the tenants of Belmore, and of course there was the gossip that always passed between the servants of two great houses.

They said that she was beautiful, with long golden hair and clear, bright, sparkling blue eyes. She had come from somewhere to the south, a country girl, they said, the daughter of the marquess's distant cousin.

Caroline was curious about the girl, and good manners required a social call.

Besides, she was worried why Matthew had not come to visit as he had promised in his letters and calling on Miss Fox would give her an excuse to discover the cause.

She was only slightly surprised when he greeted her in the entry, his expression warm as he clasped both her hands and bussed her lightly on each cheek.

"Caroline, my love, it's good to see you." He made no

excuses, said nothing about why he had not come, but his eyes were warm where they touched her, and she felt a sense of relief that his feelings for her appeared not to have changed.

"I'm glad you're here," he said with a wide, disarming smile. "I had planned to call on you before week's end, but now you are here and that is so much better. I've been eager to see you, Caroline."

A little thrill went through her. Matthew Seaton was tall, blond, and handsome. He was wealthy and titled, and the Belmore heir. "Oh, Matthew, I've missed you terribly." She went into his arms for a brief, warm hug, appropriate for a man who had been two years at sea and was nearly her betrothed. "It's wonderful to see you."

He started to say something when the marquess stepped into the marble-floored entry. "Lady Caroline. How good of you to come. Jessica has been so looking forward to meeting you."

Not if the tone of the old man's voice was any indication. Then again, perhaps the marquess was simply feeling poorly, as gossip said he had been of late.

She smiled, but suddenly she felt wary. "I'm quite looking forward to meeting her, as well." Matthew took her arm and the marquess led the way into a large formal drawing room near the front of the mansion. Across the way, a blond woman in a modish, pale blue muslin gown rose from a brocade settee beneath the mullioned windows. Jessica Fox was about her same height, but her figure was more rounded, more womanly, her skin more creamy than pale. Hair the color of finely spun gold glistened in the sunlight streaming in through the window. Caroline felt a sudden wash of fear at the beauty of the woman's face.

"Lady Caroline," the marquess said, "may I present my ward, Miss Jessica Fox." The old man said no more, nor did he make his excuses and leave, as she had imagined he would. Matthew stayed, as she had hoped, though she had the distinct impression he was there in some fashion to lend his support to the girl.

The marquess's ward moved forward. "It's a pleasure to meet you, my lady." The words came out with the grace and style of a duchess, and beside her the old man beamed.

"Jessica has been at Belmore only for the past six months," the marquess began. "Prior to that, she was a student at Mrs. Seymour's Private Academy."

Caroline turned to the beautiful Miss Fox and pasted on a smile. "I've a cousin who attended that same school," she said in her most dulcet tone. "Perhaps you know her. Frances Featherstone? Sir Albert Featherstone's daughter?"

"Why, yes," Jessie said. "I do believe I know her." She didn't add that Frances Featherstone was a malicious little gossip who hadn't a good word to say about anyone, least of all her. She wondered if Lady Caroline could perhaps be that same sort of person, then cast the notion away. Surely Matthew would see through a woman like that. Besides, it was unfair to judge a woman she barely knew simply because she was jealous.

She surveyed Caroline Winston with a close regard. She was as tall as Jessie, with a slender figure, light brown hair, and deep-set large brown eyes. She wore a modest but elegant pink silk gown trimmed with embroidered roses. Combined with her fashionable rose-flowered bonnet, it gave her a look of innocence, a demure sort of purity that set her apart from other women.

Jessie's insides churned and her mouth felt dry. She hadn't forgotten Matthew's words to his father. Caroline Winston was the woman he wished to marry. She was the picture of elegant gentility, the kind of woman every man wanted for a wife. Jessie felt sick to her stomach.

They all sat down in the drawing room, Matthew next to Lady Caroline, the marquess next to Jessie. Papa Reggie ordered the butler to serve them tea and cakes, and they came on a silver tray set with Sevres china. Reginald Seaton looked tired today, and now that Caroline Winston was here, a line of tension had formed around his mouth.

In contrast, Matthew appeared oddly relaxed. When he

looked at Caroline Winston, he wore a warm, friendly, open expression unlike any he had ever bestowed on her. He was comfortable with this woman, at ease in a way he never was with her. Jessie's nerves mounted and the teacup rattled as she replaced it in its saucer.

"I understand you're from somewhere to the south," Lady Caroline said.

"Devon," answered Papa Reggie.

"My family traveled to Exmouth last year."

Matthew smiled. "I hear the place is becoming quite a fashionable resort."

Caroline nodded. "Father has a brother there. Perhaps Uncle Henry knew your father," she said to Jessie.

"'Fraid that's not likely," Papa Reggie put in. "Simon Fox was quite a recluse. Lived near Bodmin, he did, he and Jessica. Stock-raising, country folk, not much for traveling. Isn't that right, my dear?"

"No . . . we didn't go out all that much. Mother had passed on, you see. Father was ailing and needed a good deal of care. I've traveled very little, I'm afraid." Her eyes touched the marquess's in silent communion, then her gaze swung to Caroline's and she forced herself to smile.

"I suppose you travel quite often," Jessie said.

"Yes. My family owns several estates besides Winston House, quite a large one farther north near Bedford, where we reside when we are not living here or in the city."

"I should love to hear about London. Lord Belmore says your family spends the Season there every year. It must be terribly exciting."

Caroline laughed, a soft, sweetly feminine sound, then as Jessie had hoped, she launched into a lengthy discussion of the balls, soirees, and ridottos she attended in the city each year. Even Matthew quirked a brow in silent salute for having turned the conversation so neatly away from herself.

As soon as they were finished taking tea, Jessie and the marquess made their excuses, which unfortunately left Lady Caroline with Matthew. He asked her to join him for a walk in the garden, and they left the drawing room smiling, their heads bent close together as they made their way out of doors.

From her bedchamber upstairs, Jessie watched them stroll the oyster shell paths of the formal gardens, pausing to examine a budding rose here, a row of tulips there. Matthew laughed at something Caroline said, his head falling back, his smile bright and easy. Jessie watched their lazy, tranquil progress, and her insides felt leaden. She thought of how he had seen her that first day, her tattered men's clothes covered in mud, her hair a sodden mass around her throat. She thought of the fair, the way she had been fighting like a wildcat, sprawled half-naked on the ground.

Dear God, for as long as she could remember she had wanted to be a lady. She would have done anything—anything to escape her life of poverty and crime. On the surface she had escaped. She dressed like a lady. She spoke like a lady. She read the classics and could even play a piece or two on the pianoforte.

She glanced back down at the couple in the garden, saw Matthew pluck a lovely red rose and hand it to Lady Caroline. All the hours of study, the walking for days with a yardstick strapped to her back, the volumes of poetry she had learned, the perfect intonations of French she had mastered—none of those things made her a lady in truth.

Lady Caroline slipped a gloved hand into the crook of Matthew's arm and they wandered off toward the greenhouse. Jessie had never seen him look so happy, so utterly content.

She thought of the way he had saved her at the fair, how safe she had felt in his arms. She remembered the way he had kissed her that day in the carriage house. If he wished to wed Lady Caroline, why had he been kissing her?

Jessie sank down on the bed. She knew enough about men to know the answer to that—God's breath, she had grown up in a brothel. A man's desire for a woman had nothing to do with marriage—at least not when it involved a woman like

Jessie Fox. Matthew might want her, but he would marry Caroline Winston.

It was a hard, brutal fact, one that brought a thick lump to her throat. But the bitter truth remained—Matthew Seaton would never be hers.

Unless Papa Reggie somehow forced the marriage.

For one brief, utterly selfish instant, she actually hoped he would. It was possible, she knew. Papa Reggie was a man used to getting his way, and it was obvious he wanted his son to agree to the marriage. The marquess was ailing. Matthew cared greatly about him. Papa Reggie would know exactly the way to manipulate his son into doing what he wanted. Perhaps she could have him after all.

The thought made her already churning stomach roll with nausea.

The truth was, even if Matthew acquiesced to his father's wishes and married her, he would resent her for it, perhaps even grow to hate her for destroying the life he had planned. Besides, she might not be a real lady like Caroline Winston, but even Jessie Fox had her pride. She cared for Matthew, in truth, more than cared. She had dreamed of Matthew Seaton for as long as she could remember.

But she didn't want a man who didn't want her. And she certainly didn't want him enough to ruin both of their lives.

Matthew and Caroline emerged from the garden and Matthew helped her into her waiting carriage, kissing her cheek as she climbed in. A simple, chaste, gentlemanly kiss, nothing like the fiery, passionate, all-consuming kiss he had shared with Jessie Fox. He would never take liberties with Caroline Winston, but Eliza Fox's daughter was another matter indeed.

It made her heart hurt to think of it, made her angry at Matthew when it wasn't really his fault. It was just the way of the world, and there was nothing anyone could do about it.

Besides, she didn't need Matthew Seaton. She didn't need anyone except Papa Reggie. She'd been happy at Belmore before Matthew came, and once he was gone, she would be happy again. She would speak to the marquess, she suddenly decided, convince him to let his son marry whomever he wished. It was a painful decision, one that made her chest feel heavy and tears sting the backs of her eyes. But it was the right thing to do.

Taking a deep resigned breath, she got up from the bed. Now that she had finally faced the truth, she just wanted the whole thing over and done with. Matthew was lost to her, but the fact was, she had never had a chance with him in the first place. It hurt to accept the truth, but she had been hurt before. In time, she would get over it.

Afraid she would lose her courage—or that Vi would come in, realize something was wrong, and try to dissuade her—Jessie paced the floor of her bedchamber, awaiting the hour the marquess usually awakened from his afternoon nap. As soon as the mantel clock struck, she headed for his suite of rooms at the end of the west wing, her stomach more jittery than ever.

His aging valet, Lemuel Green, answered her soft knock at the door. "Yes, miss?"

"I should like to see his lordship. Has he awakened yet from his nap?"

"Why yes, miss, he has. I shall tell him you are here."

She paced the sitting room, then turned at Lemuel's approach. "I'm afraid he's not feeling quite the thing, Miss Fox. But he allows that he will see you in his chamber, if that is your wish."

A tremor of fear slipped through her. Until these past few weeks, Papa Reggie had always been so healthy, so vital. But lately his health had been failing, and the doctor couldn't seem to discover what was wrong.

"Thank you, Lemuel. I shall go to him straightaway."

The valet nodded and allowed her to pass into the adjoining chamber.

"Hello, Papa Reggie."

"Come in, my dear, come in. Sit down right here beside me."

She seated herself on a rosewood chair at the side of the marquess's huge tester bed, reached over, and took hold of his hand. "How are you feeling?"

"A bit under the weather. Nothing to fret yourself about." He assessed her pale face and his once-handsome features clouded with concern. "What is it, my dear? You aren't still troubled over the Winston chit, are you? If you are, you shouldn't be. I thought you handled yourself very well."

"No, Papa Reggie, it isn't Lady Caroline." At least not directly. "There is a matter I wish to discuss, but if you aren't feeling up to it, perhaps tomorrow would be better."

"Poppycock. I'm only a bit tired, is all. Now, tell me what it is that has you looking so down in the mouth."

She had prayed the hurt wouldn't show. She took a calming breath and slowly released it. "It's about your son."

"Matthew? What about him?" He frowned. "That young buck hasn't been taking liberties with you, has he?"

Her face flushed a little as she remembered his fiery kiss. "No, no, of course not. It's nothing like that."

"Then what is it?"

"It's just that I have a feeling he may be interested in . . . paying me court." Dear God, if ever there was a bald-faced lie. "Because I'm your ward," she continued, careful to keep her fingers crossed and hoping she didn't burn in hell. "I'm afraid he may feel he has some sort of responsibility for my future. Perhaps he believes marrying me is the honorable thing to do, even if he has other inclinations."

"Such as Lady Caroline," he grumbled.

"Well, yes. Matthew can be quite chivalrous, you know." She thought of his gallant rescue. At least there was some truth to that.

"Yes—and he can also be a bit of a starchy prig."

Another time, Jessie might have smiled. "The point is, a marriage between us would surely be a mistake."

"Why, for heaven's sake?"

"Because the two of us are just too poorly suited. We have nothing in common, no friends, no similar interests.

The marriage would never work out and in a very short time, both of us would be miserable."

She squeezed his hand. "If things were different"—*if he wanted me for his wife*—"marriage to your son would be the greatest honor I could have." She glanced away, no longer able to meet his shrewd old eyes. "But the fact is, we are not in the least compatible. I would be unhappy and so would he. I have no interest in marrying Matthew and I don't believe he wishes to marry me. Since that is the case, I want you to discourage his suit."

"But this is preposterous."

She blinked at him, then stared as if she didn't understand, as if she hadn't heard the bitter argument he'd had that night with his son. "Why is that?"

Papa Reggie struggled to sit up straighter against the headboard. "Because . . . because you and Matthew would suit perfectly well. You have only to see the two of you together to know that. Any fool can see that you are very well suited, indeed."

Jessie forced a smile. "I've no wish to be married, at least not yet. I'm happy here with you, Papa Reggie. I'm not interested in Matthew and I never will be. And I am quite certain that he is not interested in me."

A slight noise drew their attention to the doorway leading in from the sitting room. Matthew stood rigidly in the opening, a black scowl lining his handsome face. "That certain, are you, Mistress Fox?"

Her heart started pounding. "How . . . how long have you been standing there?"

"Long enough to learn how poorly we are suited. Thank you for bringing the matter to my attention."

Papa Reggie glanced from Jessica to Matthew, who still wore a thunderous expression. The marquess said nothing for the longest time, then he gave up a weary, long-suffering sigh.

"Yes, well, I suppose Jessica is right. The two of you would never suit a'tall. I was a foolish old man to believe that you might."

Matthew arched a brow at his father's acquiescence, but said nothing more.

"Unfortunately, that does not solve our dilemma."

"What dilemma?" Jessie asked.

"My dear, I realize you are happy here at Belmore and of course I am more than happy to have you here with me. Unfortunately, I won't be around forever. My time is getting shorter and—"

"Don't say that." Her hold grew tighter on his hand. She loved Papa Reggie. She couldn't stand to think that he might abandon her, too. "I won't let you talk that way."

He patted the fingers that gripped his so fiercely. "My dear, I'm a sick old man. You, on the other hand, are a vibrant, healthy young woman. What you need is a husband and family of your own."

Jessie said nothing to that. It was a dream so sweet it made a lump rise in her throat. She loved children. Nothing would bring her more happiness than to have a child of her own.

"Therefore," the marquess continued, "since Matthew will not suit as a husband, we must find a man who will."

"What!" Jessie came to her feet.

"It shan't be all that hard, I assure you. A woman with your beauty . . . in no time a'tall, half the young bloods in London will be groveling at your feet."

"London!" Matthew said, stepping farther into the room. "You can't be serious, Father."

"Of course, I'm serious. I shall provide Jessica with a more than ample dowry. Once she has been introduced into Society, she'll be able to pick and choose."

"I-I can't possibly go to London, Papa Reggie."

"Oh? And why is that?"

"Th-The children, of course. Who would help them with their studies? They need me. I have to—"

"The children will not be a problem. We shall simply hire a tutor to work with them in your absence."

"B-But I cannot possibly go to London." She bit down on her lip, her hands suddenly shaking.

"Jessica, that is absurd."

Her chin came up. She battled a feeling of panic. "It is hardly absurd. What if someone discovered the truth? What if they found out who I really am?" She blinked back the tears that suddenly burned her eyes. "I won't let you do it. If anyone found out about me, the Belmore name would be ruined. I won't let you take that chance."

The marquess looked at her hard. "I'm afraid, my dear, you have very little say in the matter. I am your legal guardian. Until you come of age, it is my decision what you will and will not do. In this matter, you will do exactly as I tell you."

Jessie's eyes widened. He had taken that tone with her on very few occasions. Whenever he had done so, she had not doubted where Matthew had acquired his forbidding manner.

"Yes, Papa Reggie," she said meekly, sinking back down in her chair.

"For once the girl is right," Matthew said, surprising her. "You cannot possibly attempt to pass her off as a member of the nobility."

The marquess lifted his head, his face a thundercloud beneath his leonine mane of snowy hair. "Take a look at her, Matthew! A good, hard look. Can you really be that blind?"

Matthew's jaw tightened.

"Why, the girl is an Incomparable. You are the only one who cannot seem to see it. I assure you the rest of the ton will not have nearly so difficult a time." The old man held his son's dark gaze a moment more, then collapsed back down on the bed.

"Father!" Matthew rushed forward.

"Papa Reggie!" Jessie jumped up once more from her chair. "Are you all right?"

The marquess released a shaky breath. His face looked flushed and his heart beat too fast. "A bit too much excitement, I'm afraid. If the two of you don't mind, I should like a moment of rest."

"Of course," Matt said with a look of worry. Jessie nodded, feeling wretched for oversetting him in the first place.

"In the meantime," the marquess said, "you may begin to ready your things. Matthew, I shall expect you to accompany us. You have several more weeks before your leave is up. Jessica and I will need your support."

Matthew simply nodded.

"I shall send word ahead to have the town house opened and readied. We leave for London day after the morrow."

Matthew leaned back against the plush velvet squabs of the Belmore traveling coach. Jessie and his father sat across from him, chatting pleasantly, Jessie's bright blue eyes lighting at every new bend in the road. Another carriage followed, carrying Lemuel Green, the marquess's aging valet; the butler, Samuel Osgood, who often accompanied the family; and Jessie's tiring woman, Viola Finn.

Matt remembered the heavyset woman vaguely from her days in the kitchen of the Black Boar Inn. He still couldn't believe Jessie had convinced his father to employ a woman at Belmore with that sort of background. Then again, he couldn't believe his father now called Samuel Osgood "Ozzie," the way Jessie did. His father had changed in the years since Jessie Fox's arrival. Matt wasn't yet sure if those changes were good.

He glanced across at her and found her watching him from beneath the brim of her flowered straw bonnet. He gave her a lazy smile that said he had caught her at it, and flags of color rose into her cheeks.

She glanced back out the window, and his smile slid away. He couldn't help thinking of the way he had felt when he had heard her pleading with his father not to pursue a marriage between them. His chest had gone tight and he couldn't seem to breathe. He knew why she had done it. She had overheard him that night in the withdrawing room, furious with his father for even suggesting such a match, calling her the daughter of a whore.

Then she had met Caroline Winston, the woman he intended to marry. Caroline had wealth and position, something Jessie did not have. Caroline traveled in the same social circles he did, shared a similar view of life. They were better suited, she believed, just as he had said.

He wanted to marry Caroline and it appeared she wouldn't stand in his way.

"We've at least two more hours traveling time before we stop for the night," his father said, breaking into the silence. "What would you two say to a game of cards?"

Jessie looked longingly out the window, as if she feared she might miss something if her attention were to stray. "All right," she reluctantly agreed.

"Matthew?"

"Why not?" He might as well. He was getting damned uncomfortable sitting there watching the seductive movements of Jessica Fox's breasts, even confined as they were beneath the silk of her traveling dress. He could still remember the way she had looked that day at the fair, her blue eyes wild, her hair unbound, her lovely breasts bare. He could recall their exact shape and size, how the bottoms were fuller than the tops, tilting them slightly upward, the rose-colored nipples at the crests.

He tried not to think of the mind-numbing rage he had felt when he had seen another man touch them, wondered instead if they could possibly be as soft and ripe as they looked, but he knew enough of women to be certain that they were.

His breeches felt uncomfortably snug and he shifted on the seat, grateful for the lapboard his father had placed over their knees as they prepared to indulge in a rotating game of piquet. Damn, the girl might not be what he wanted in a wife, but as a mistress, she'd be all any man could ask.

It was a futile thought, the way his father felt about her, but one that stayed with him that night at the inn where they stayed, and even the next day as they rolled past the outskirts of London and on into the city.

The thought loomed again as he sat on the seat across from her and saw her smiling with delight at the sights around them.

"I vow, Papa Reggie—London is even better than the fair." Jessie gripped the sill of the open carriage window, her head poking out as the vehicle rumbled along. Dipping and swaying, it jolted over traffic-clogged cobblestone streets on its way to the Belmore town house on Grosvenor Square. "Could we go to the theater, do you think? I have so yearned to see a play."

"We shall go wherever you wish, my dear. Perhaps you would enjoy a night at the opera."

Her eyes lit up in that special way. "Oh, yes! I should love that above all things."

"Perhaps a day or two of shopping," his father said. "There is a jeweler I'm quite fond of in Ludgate Hill. I should like to buy you—"

"There is nothing I need, Papa Reggie. You spoil me terribly as it is."

His father smiled indulgently. "A woman can never have enough expensive baubles, my dear. 'Tis an impossibility, I assure you."

No new gowns? Matthew thought. No visiting the elegant stores from Charing Cross to White Chapel for the myriad items most women demanded, things they considered necessities in the fashionable world of the ton?

He wasn't sure he believed it. Then again, perhaps there was more to Jessica Fox than he had first imagined. The affection she felt for his father appeared to be real. Now it seemed she wasn't scheming after the Belmore title, as he had been so sure she was.

Then again, at twelve years old, Jessie Fox had been as skillful a pickpocket as he had ever seen. She cried buckets of tears at will, and even the most iron-hearted traveler wound up handing her a coin or two "to buy a scrap o' food for me poor, dyin' mother," who in truth was simply down with a case of bottle fever brought on by too much gin.

And there was Eliza Fox herself, a pretty but conscience-less little whore who would tumble a man for sixpence, then wind up with the contents of the poor man's purse while he lay unconscious in the alley. She was a good bit older than Matt, too hard around the eyes for his youthful taste, even though her breasts and hips were ripe, and being home from weeks at sea he had needed a woman badly.

Perhaps the real truth was that none of the things Jessie said or did were any more real now than they were then. Perhaps this warm, caring young woman his father treasured was simply an illusion.

It was possible. All too possible.

Matt settled back in the seat of the carriage, studying his cards and the girl on the seat across from him. Sooner or later, he vowed, he would discover the truth about Jessie Fox.

Chapter Seven

*I*n the end Papa Reggie won out. The marquess bought Jessie a lovely pearl necklace studded with tiny diamonds to add to the collection of beautiful Belmore heirlooms he had given her over the years. Then he insisted she go shopping with Viola for "whatever fripperies a young lady her age might need."

He had weighted her reticule with gold sovereigns for incidentals, told her to put anything she wanted on any of his numerous accounts, and forced Matthew to accompany them, armed with money as well. Apparently he was wise to the fact that nearly every penny of her monthly allowance went into her personal hoard.

What if something terrible happened? she would think, memories fresh in her mind of the awful nights after she had left the inn, nights she'd huddled in freezing haylofts, her stomach gnawing with hunger.

Fortunately, on Regents Street, Matthew had left them on their own.

"I'll be back in about two hours," he'd said. "I'll leave the carriage at your disposal and meet you in front of L. T. Piver's, the Perfume and Glovers', at exactly four o'clock." He gave her a stern look of warning. "One last thing, Mistress Fox. I would appreciate it if you would kindly stay out of trouble. Don't go anywhere except along this street."

She bristled then gave him a smart salute. "Aye, aye, Captain."

A touch of amusement curved his lips. "Behave yourself, Jessie. I'll see you in a couple of hours."

She had watched him walk away, unable to tear her gaze from the tall retreating figure with the stiff-spined military bearing, wide straight shoulders, indecently narrow hips, and long, lean, powerfully muscled legs.

"Well, luv, where shall we go next?" Viola's words finally dragged her attention away from him.

Jessie glanced from her heavyset friend to the fashionable carriages rolling past, the elegant shops with their tiny mullioned windows, the ladies and gentlemen of the ton who strolled by in their expensive clothes.

"Why don't we simply wander? Who knows what we might see." They started along the walkway, stepping into one shop after another, no longer self-conscious, now that Matthew had discreetly shown her how it was done. In Fugate's Umbrella Shop, she purchased a small, fringed, sky blue parasol she simply couldn't resist, though when the time came to part with the money, her hand shook a little as she handed it across the counter.

They walked past Mary the Fruitier's, Wedgwood's China Shop, a clockmaker's, and a haberdashery. Jessie paused in front of a tiny store nearly obscured by the two larger shops on either side. It was one of few that displayed items for sale in the window. The rest considered themselves far too exclusive for that.

Jessie leaned closer to the glass. "Look, Vi, have you ever seen anything so adorable?" It was a store specializing in items for children. A tiny pair of rain pattens sat in the window next to a baby's white christening gown, and a beautifully embroidered yellow satin quilt.

"Ye've always loved children, ye 'ave. Ever since I can remember." Viola eyed her shrewdly. "And I'll bet when ye' thought o' a babe, 'twas the 'andsome capt'n ye pretended was the lit'l un's papa."

Jessie felt the color seeping into her cheeks. "In truth, I might have dreamed about it, but I never really believed

I would ever have a family of my own. In my heart, I always believed I would wind up like my mother." She looked at Viola and smiled softly. "I would have, Vi, if it hadn't been for you."

The older woman flushed and waved a blunt-fingered hand, passing the matter off. "I 'elped ye get away, is all. Ye nearly starved to death doin' it. If it 'adn't been for 'is lordship, I don't know what woulda 'appened to ye."

"You were there when Mama died. You protected me from my brother. You're the best friend I've ever had, Vi." Impulsively, Jessie leaned over and hugged her. Then a thought struck and her eyes lit with excitement. "That's what we'll buy—we'll buy some things for you!"

Viola chuckled softly. "Don't be talkin' nonsense."

"It isn't nonsense, Vi. You'd like some new hats, wouldn't you? Maybe a new pair of shoes?"

Viola chuckled, then nodded her graying head. "If that's what ye want, 'twon't bother me to take a bit o' 'is lordship's blunt. 'Pears to me 'e's got more'n enough o' it."

Jessie smiled. "We'll go to the milliner's as soon as we finish here." She grabbed Vi's hand and started through the open shop door. "First I want to buy a few things for the children."

There was so much to choose from Jessie found it hard to decide what she wanted. She settled on a lovely little doll with a porcelain head for Amanda Jane, bought similar ones for Penelope and Fanny, then began to search for gifts for the others. She couldn't remember when spending money had ever been so much fun.

"Take a look at that, Connie, me bucko."

The scarecrow-thin man pressed closer, his gaze following the two women who had just left the milliner's store, their arms laden with packages as they walked on down the street. As soon as he saw them turn into a shop down the block, he flattened himself against the wall of the alley and turned to where Danny Fox stood grinning.

"She's even buyin' goods for the bleedin' old lady," Danny said, seeing the new straw hat Viola Quinn had been sporting when she came out of the store. "The lit'l tart's purse must be bustin' wit' the king's coin."

"Shall we nab it, Danny? Could be a bit tricky, what wit' all these nabobs 'bout, but at least the mort won't be expectin' us. She'd never think o' the likes o' us bein' 'ere in London Town."

Danny shook his head. He was dressed in his city clothes: dark gray breeches, a frilled white shirt, and a mustard-colored tailcoat, clothes he'd stolen from one of his doxy's coves. The breeches were a little bit shiny on the seat and the cuffs of the shirt were beginning to fray, but not enough so's anyone would notice.

"No need to rush thin's, Connie. We been followin' 'er this long, won't 'urt to wait a bit more. Besides, we got bigger fish to catch than the piddlin' coin she's carryin' in 'er purse. And we sure as 'ell don't want 'is bloody lordship showin' up again, ruinin' all our plans."

Connie nodded dumbly, his Adam's apple moving up and down. "Ye've the right o' it, Danny, yes sir. Better to wait, see 'ow thin's shake out, then make our move."

"I've the right o' it, Connie. Ya can count on Danny Fox to keep yer purse well 'eeled and yer 'orepipe good and tupped."

The two of them laughed and watched the women continue on down the street. There was no need to follow them now. Danny knew they were headed to his lordship's fancy town house. He knew where to find his sister when the time was right.

He laughed again, this time to himself. You could count on Danny Fox, all right—to take good care of himself.

Matthew propped a shoulder against the door leading into the drawing room, surveying the scene with a mixture of disgruntle and amusement. Jessie stood resignedly beside his father, dressed for the evening in an ice blue satin gown encrusted with rhinestones. Her golden hair had been woven into a crown, also laced with glittering stones. A beautiful diamond necklace encircled her slender throat, a gift from his father, and matching earbobs dangled from her small, shell-like ears.

He noticed her hands shook a little. Instead of a smile, she wore an expression better suited to a climb up the stairs to the gallows than a young woman making her social debut.

Perhaps it was the female Titan who stood in front of her, Cornelia Witherspoon, Lady Bainbridge. The dowager countess was a short, top-heavy bundle of energy his father had always held in a place of special regard, a woman it was said, who still carried a *tendre* for him.

"Yes, well, the gel will certainly do," said Lady Bainbridge, surveying Jessica from head to foot and several different angles in between. " 'Twas obvious from the moment I met her that your Jessica was gently reared. But you, Reggie, have created a masterpiece. I say, she is a testament to Mrs. Seymour's Academy . . . and, of course, to you, Reggie dear."

The marquess beamed while a soft flush rose in Jessie's cheeks. "She's quite something, isn't she, Corney?"

"Quite something, Reggie. The gel will set them all on their ears, I'll wager."

Matt glanced at his father, saw the soft, proud, protective expression the old man wore whenever he looked in Jessie's direction. She had won his affection completely. Reginald Seaton saw her not as the thieving little baggage she once was, but as the beautiful, intelligent young woman she had worked so hard to become.

Perhaps his father was right and he had been blinded by his memories of the Jessie he had known in the past. Perhaps until these last few days, when he had watched her proudly display the items she had purchased—gifts for the children in her tiny makeshift school, presents for Mrs. Finn and Papa Reggie, and only one small, inexpensive item for herself—he hadn't seen her as she really was.

Or perhaps she had honed her skills so well that she could

fool him and the rest of the ton as easily as she had duped his aging father.

Whatever the truth, it didn't matter. Matthew's course was set. Caroline Winston was the woman he wanted for his future marchioness. She was the perfect lady. She would make the perfect wife. He just prayed his father's grand plans for Jessie Fox didn't bring them all to social ruin before he could make that happen.

The old man cleared his throat. "I can't tell you how much we appreciate your support, Cornelia." He smiled at Lady Bainbridge, his eyes moving over the heavy breasts that rose with such gusto above the neckline of her black and silver gown. Her hair was the same gleaming silver, shot with what in her youth had once been a lustrous raven black. The marquess looked at her again, and though she didn't see it, there was a far different gleam in the old man's eyes than there had been before.

"I dare say, Corney, with you at Jessica's side, 'twill ensure her entry into Almack's and from there no door will be closed to her."

Lady Bainbridge smiled with satisfaction. "Never fear, Reggie. I shall see to it personally." She was a handsome woman, for all her years, and it appeared his father might finally have taken some notice. The old man had been married twice, but loved only once and only for a very short time, until Matthew's mother had died.

He watched the pair assessing Jessie Fox with a look of determination. Together they would find her a husband, but it wouldn't be Matt Seaton. Oddly enough, the notion made his chest go tight and a rawness gnaw at his stomach.

He glanced at Jessie, caught her looking at him as he had been looking at her, and the flush returned to her cheeks. He remembered the blood-pounding desire he had felt when he had kissed her, the way her mouth had softened under his, and heat pooled low in his belly.

In her nervous agitation, her breasts rose and fell above the neckline of her gown, and his body began to harden.

Damn, he needed a woman. And several mugs of grog—seaman's fare—wouldn't be half-bad, either. But he had promised his father he would lend his support to this campaign, and he meant to see it done.

He brought himself under control and came away from the door, stepping farther into the room. "The hour grows late, Father. I believe it's time for Miss Fox to make her appearance."

"Yes . . . yes, of course." The marquess turned to Jessie. "Are you ready, my dear?"

She moistened those soft coral lips. "Yes, Papa Reggie."

"Miss Fox," Matt said, tearing his eyes away from her mouth and extending his arm. She took it, resting a hand on the sleeve of his navy blue uniform coat, and he could feel her trembling.

"Cornelia, my dear." The marquess took the hand of the dowager countess and tucked it into the crook of his arm. They exchanged a look, then he turned and led the way through the marble-floored entry toward the massive carved front door.

At the bottom of the steep stone steps leading out of the Bainbridge town house, Jessie paused, halting Matt beside the statue of a great marble lion. In the soft yellow light of a street lamp, he could see how pale she was.

Her hold on his arm grew tighter. "I-I'm frightened, Matthew."

He was surprised she would admit it, especially to him. But the fact that she had softened something inside him.

"There's nothing to be afraid of, Jessie. My father was right—you look lovely tonight. Every young buck in the city will be throwing himself at your feet."

"Wh-What if I slip and say the wrong thing? What if I make a mistake?" Her eyes welled with tears. "They'll know I'm a fraud. They'll hate me for it and they'll hate your father, too. I can't go through with it. I can't take the risk. I can't—"

"Stop it, Jess." Matt caught hold of her shoulders, felt the tension rippling through her. "You aren't going to make a mistake. You've learned the proper social graces; you're probably better educated than any other woman there. You'll do the right thing because that is what you've worked so hard to do." He tipped her chin with his hand. "And I'll be right there with you. So will my father. We won't let you make a mistake."

Her eyes slid closed. Matt lifted a tear from her cheek with the end of his finger, and some of the tension eased from her body. When she looked at him again, there was something sweet and longing in her eyes. "Thank you, Matthew."

But he didn't want her thanks. His hunger had arisen with that brief, simple touch. What he wanted in that moment was to drag her into his arms, to press her luscious body against him, to plunder her mouth and fill his hands with her breasts. He wanted to feel the deep, suffusing pleasure that he had known before.

Instead, ignoring the pounding in his blood and the heaviness that pulsed lower down, he let her go. Taking her hand, he settled it once more on his arm and led her off toward the waiting carriage.

It was a crush of London's finest. Sleek black carriages, phaetons, barouches, and curricles lined the torchlit drive in front of the huge stone mansion at the edge of town, the London residence of the Earl of Pickering, Lady Bainbridge's second cousin.

Several hours had passed and Jessie's nerves were still strung taut, but the part she'd dreaded most was over. She had made it unerringly through the formal introductions and for the past three hours had been dancing in the gilt and mirrored ballroom. Crystal chandeliers hung from molded ceilings and bouquets of white roses scented the air from gilded vases. The entire house glittered like a diamond at sunset.

Jessie took in the beautiful sconces, the marble statues, and exquisite oriental rugs, and fought not to let the magnificence overwhelm her. Though she was used to the grandeur of Belmore, standing in such lavish surroundings, it was hard not to think of the past, of a smoky taproom, of half-naked women and lascivious men, of her dingy, airless hovel above the Black Boar Inn.

By sheer force of will, she pushed the ugly thoughts away, smiled and clung with quiet desperation to Matthew's hard-muscled arm. He was the first to partner her, leading her onto the inlaid parquet floor for a *countra* dance.

"Smile," he said gently. "You know how to do this. Nothing is going to go wrong."

She found reassurance in those deep blue eyes, and the smile came easier than she had imagined. The dance lasted nearly twenty minutes, yet with Matthew there to guide her, to lend her courage and strength, the minutes seemed to fly past.

After that, the evening became a blur. She danced with one young man after another, surprised to find four new faces waiting to take her previous partner's place. At first Matthew had remained close by, there in case she needed him, just as he had promised. Then Papa Reggie appeared with Lady Bainbridge, and Matthew slipped quietly away.

Three hours later she saw him again, dancing with an extravagant brunette, Madeleine, Countess Fielding, a widow, it was said.

A lonely one, it appeared to Jessie, if the way she draped herself over Matthew's arm and smiled with such exuberance was any indication. Jessie found herself hoping those ripe, milky breasts thrusting so determinedly upward would achieve their fondest wish and set themselves free.

She was a beautiful woman, older than Jessie, perhaps nearing thirty, with sea green eyes and a wide, luscious mouth. They danced past her during a rondele, and Jessie caught a whiff of heavy perfume. Matthew didn't seem to mind it's cloying scent—he was too busy enjoying the woman's blatant invitation. Only once did he glance in Jessie's direction. When he did, she gave the young Duke of Milton, her partner, the brightest, most beguiling smile she could muster.

She probably imagined the slight irritation she had glimpsed on the earl's handsome face. She blinked, and the next time she looked, he was smiling into the eyes of the luscious brunette.

They left the house party immediately following the lavish midnight supper, concerned that the marquess might be tiring and not wanting to tax Jessie on her first foray into Society. Or perhaps it was so that Matthew could keep his assignation with the countess.

Thinking about it left a film of tarnish on the evening's veneer of success.

"All those months on that stuffy old boat." Madeleine, Countess Fielding, reclined naked against the headboard of her huge red velvet-draped bed. Running an elegant finger around a tiny cherub carved into the polished wood, she trailed it lower, across Matt's bare shoulder, down his chest, and around his flat male nipple. "It's been too long, Matthew, darling."

He caught her wrist, lifted it and pressed it against his lips. "Too damned long, Countess. Not since before your most recent late husband. Which one was he, your second or third?"

A smoky laugh rumbled from a throat that was slim and pale, more so in contrast to the gleaming black hair draped over one bare shoulder. "Three, but who's counting? I've money enough, now that they're gone, I no longer need a man in my life." She smiled wickedly. "Except of course for pleasure." She bent over him, pinched the tiny flat nub of copper, and kissed him wetly on the lips.

Matthew kissed her back. Shoving a hand into her thick black hair, he dragged her down on the red silk counterpane, coming up over her and thrusting his tongue inside her mouth. He had taken her twice already and yet he was hard again, impatient for release but determined to prolong the moment.

"I shouldn't be here," he said as he sucked on the soft lobe of an ear. "We both know I won't be able to come here again."

She gave up a throaty purr and tilted her head back, exposing her throat like an offering. "Why, because of your Caroline? Perhaps if we are discreet . . ."

He shook his head. "You know I won't do that." He feathered her skin with small soft kisses. "I won't have her family embarrassed by rumors of my escapades with the beautiful countess, no matter how tempting she may be."

Madeleine sighed as she kissed his shoulders. "Time hasn't changed you, my darling. You're still too proper for your own good . . . but that, I suppose, is what makes you so attractive—being so stiff-necked and starchy in the drawing room and so terribly wicked in bed."

His mouth curved faintly. "And you, my love. I don't believe you've changed much, either. You're still as lusty as sin and twice as outrageous."

She started to laugh but he captured her mouth, and the sound seeped out as a moan instead. Her breasts felt heavy in his hands, soft and full and trembling, the ends pebbled hard with need. He pinched them gently, laved them with his tongue and bit the ends, then drew back to look at her.

"Wicked, is it? If that is what you're after, my lady, perhaps I can oblige." He knew her lusty appetites. They'd had a torrid affair between her first two ancient husbands. He teased her for several long moments, until he had her squirming on the bed, then pulled away, swinging his long legs to the floor.

Naked, hard, and pulsing, he fixed his eyes on her mouth as he stood up. "Come here," he said in the voice he used to command his men, and a glimmer of heat flashed in her sea green eyes.

Those ripe red lips curved seductively. She climbed out of bed but remained a few feet away.

"I said . . . come here."

She hesitated only a minute, then moved gracefully toward him, crossing the thick Persian carpet till she stood in front of him, her moist lips glistening in the flickering light of the candle, her eyes aglow with images of what he intended.

"Get down on your knees," he ordered, knowing she enjoyed a man with the will to command her, then watched as she slowly obeyed. "You'll get nothing more from me until you please me. I suggest, my love, you do it well or I shall wait until you have finished, then leave you in the state you are currently in. I doubt fending for yourself is what you've in mind for the balance of the evening."

She nodded weakly, trembling with excitement, eager to obey. Looking down at the hardened shaft jutting forward in silent demand, Madeleine set upon him with a vengeance, and Matt closed his eyes, allowing the hot sensations to wash over him. His body pulsed with heat and need, but his mind strayed away from the image of the woman at his feet.

It fixed on another, more fair than she, with silver-gilt, golden blond hair and breasts that tilted upward, exactly the shape to fill his hands. He imagined her tiny waist, long shapely legs, and slender ankles.

He groaned at the image, at the white-hot fire surging through him, at the feel of moist lips and a slick, urgent tongue. Heat washed through him, visions of pale skin and golden hair making his thick shaft pulse and burn. Clamping down hard on his need for release, he hauled Madeleine to her feet. Gripping her bottom, he lifted her up, wrapped her legs around his waist, and plunged her down hard on his erection, eliciting a deep, throaty whimper of hot pleasure-pain. Her head fell back as he squeezed her bottom. He lifted her up and impaled her fiercely again.

Long black hair brushed his thighs but it was golden hair he saw in the eye of his mind. Sweeter, faintly trembling lips clung to his, and the eyes he imagined were a bright china blue instead of a pale sea green.

He plunged faster, deeper, harder, felt the woman in his arms go rigid and call out his name. Several more deep thrusts and he came with a thundering rush that made him grind his teeth and bite back the word on his lips.

For the name he would have spoken wasn't that of his current paramour, nor Caroline Winston's, the woman he would marry.

Jessie Fox filled his thoughts and his senses until it seemed as if it were she who sheathed him, she who returned his passionate kisses, she who welcomed him into her bed.

Considering the hours he had shared with the countess, Matthew was astonished to discover how badly he wanted that to happen.

"Well, my boy, didn't I tell you? Didn't I say the girl was an Incomparable? Why, in little more than a week, she's set the whole damned town on fire." In the ballroom at Lord Montague's town house, Reginald Seaton watched his lovely young ward on the dance floor, her hair like spun gold beneath the chandeliers, her movements so graceful it made him ache inside.

He was so bloody proud of her. Not a single person of his acquaintance had ever made so much of themselves, ever risen so far above the place where they were born. Certainly he had helped her. If it weren't for him, the pitiful creature who had approached him that day at Seaton Pond likely would have wound up starving—or spending her life in Newgate prison.

But it was Jessie who had done the work, Jessie who'd spent endless hours studying, Jessie who'd exhausted herself practicing the speech and skills of a highborn woman. It was Jessie who had worked to make her dream come true.

Reggie smiled. She was a lady if ever there was one, the *crème de la crème* of all the young women her age. It made his old heart swell just to look at her, made his eyes grow misty, and love for her expand inside his chest.

It spawned a thread of irritation at his pigheaded son and urged him to goad the lad further.

"Will you look at that, Matthew? Why, they're standing in line for her. She's had three men offer for her just this past week, two viscounts and the Earl of Pickering. The viscounts haven't the blunt to afford her, but perhaps we ought to give some credence to the earl."

Matthew's hard gaze swung to his. "Pickering?" He made a rude sound in his throat. "The man's old enough to be her father. He's a slimy little toad with nothing to recommend him but the coin in his purse and the fact he's related to Lady Bainbridge. If he's lucky, he's got a bit of the old girl's blood running through his veins."

Reggie chuckled softly. "He isn't all that old, only eight years senior to you. Pickering's a gentle sort, I'll grant you, a bookish man, not the type to turn a young girl's head. But he would also demand very little, and he would lavish her with gifts. The earl is generous by nature. The man would give Jessica the moon."

"What he wouldn't give her is exactly what she needs—a husband who can handle her. A man who can control her reckless nature and keep her satisfied in bed."

Reggie smiled inwardly, enjoying the sting he could hear in his son's words. "Yes . . . well, that may be true. Jessica is extremely spirited. Perhaps someone else would better suit . . . someone, say, more like your old college chum, St. Cere."

"St. Cere!"

"Why not? The man's a handsome devil, certainly wealthy enough, and if rumor is half-correct, one needn't worry about his prowess in bed. Jessica loves children, and I should enjoy living long enough to see at least one grandchild. St. Cere would likely give her a house full."

Matthew's face looked carved in stone. "I can't believe you would seriously consider Adam Harcourt. The man is the worst sort of rogue. Aside from the scandal still connected to his name, he spends half his time with his mistresses and the other half gaming. And you may be certain the viscount plays deep."

"And wins mostly, the way I hear it. Besides a man can change. Before I met your mother, I was considered quite a rogue myself."

"Yes, well, St. Cere is different. He's as jaded as they come and ruthless when it comes to women. Besides, he's a dedicated bachelor. His marriage ended in disaster and he swears he won't be shackle-legged again."

Reggie cocked his head toward the dance floor. "Perhaps he has changed his mind."

Beside him Matthew went tense. The tall, dark Viscount St. Cere was enjoying a rondele with Jessie, who was smiling into his wickedly handsome face. Reggie was hardly pleased, though he made every effort not to show it. The man had a terrible reputation, and Reggie wouldn't for a moment consider him a candidate for marriage to his lovely ward, but the look of fury on Matthew's face was worth every moment of the ruse.

He glanced at his son, then smiled with glee at the winsome pair. "You see, my boy, with a girl like Jessica, the possibilities are endless."

Matthew's scowl went blacker. "If you don't want her ruined, I'd suggest you end her association with St. Cere before it gets started."

Reggie forced his brows into a frown. "Perhaps you are right. Maybe he isn't the sort we should encourage, though now that they've met, I'm not quite certain how to lay the matter to rest." He sighed dramatically. "If Jessica should take a liking to the man, it will be deuced hard to talk her out of it. She can be quite determined, once her mind is made up."

"There is scarcely a doubt of that," Matthew said darkly. He watched the dance end with what might have been relief, and the two of them parted. "Don't worry about St. Cere," he said. "At the earliest convenience, I'll speak to him myself. Once he understands the girl is under my protection, I'm certain he'll leave her alone." His look said the viscount had better or there would be bloody hell to pay.

Reggie felt another gleeful smile approaching. He wisely kept this one to himself.

*C*hapter *E*ight

*J*essie stood near the door of the terrace leading out to the small formal garden of Lord Montague's town house. A cooling breeze drifted in, scenting the night with the fragrance of damask roses. It was unseemly for her to disappear, even for a very short time, but oh, how she yearned for a moment alone.

Parties and balls, an evening at the opera, fireworks at Vauxhall Gardens, the theater in Drury Lane—it was magical, the days and nights in London, everything she had ever dreamed it would be. It was exhilarating, yet it was exhausting, too.

After the first few days, she'd begun to worry less about discovery. The Marquess of Belmore was a powerful man. The tale of his guardianship of a distant cousin's daughter was accepted without question, as it had been when she had gone away to school. And Lady Bainbridge's support put even the vaguest speculation to rest.

Her list of suitors grew daily. Surely, she told herself, one of them would serve well enough as a husband. They were attentive and rich, most of them were titled, surely she could come to care for one of them.

There was no question she would marry. It was Papa Reggie's fondest wish, and she would do anything to please him. He had taken her in when there was nowhere else to go, when she hadn't eaten in days, when she longed for a restful night of sleep out of the numbing cold. Everything she owned belonged to him, everything she knew, everything she had become.

Everything she was . . .

She loved him and she would do the only thing he had ever asked of her.

But oh, it was so much more difficult with Matthew near. She tried to ignore him, tried to control the flutter in her stomach whenever he walked into a room, or took her hand for the first dance of the evening, the one she always saved for him. She tried not to hurt when he lavished his attentions on other women and paid almost no attention to her.

She tried to focus instead on the gentlemen who paid her court, but none of them came close to Matthew's chiseled good looks and lean broad-shouldered build. With his imposing height, intriguing deep blue eyes, and dark blond, pirate's gold hair, he stood out among the others, making them pale in comparison. He seemed smarter, tougher, more in command of himself than the men who pursued her.

And in truth, he was.

Damn him, she thought. Damn him to bloody hell!

It seemed Matthew Seaton had been a thorn in her side since she was a little girl.

"Jessie! Jessie Fox! Jessie, is that really you?"

Her stomach clenched, rolled over on a wave of nausea. No one in London called her anything but Jessica. Dear God, had she been found out so soon? She willed herself to turn toward the sound of the voice. When she saw Gwendolyn Lockhart, her best friend at Mrs. Seymour's Academy, she went so weak with relief she nearly swooned.

"Jessie!" Gwen's arms flew around her and the women hugged, one tall, slender and blond, the other dark-haired and petite. Opposites in most things, yet alike in some way neither of them could quite understand.

"Dear heavens—Gwen, it's so good to see you."

The shorter girl grinned. "I can't believe you're actually here. I thought the marquess was ailing. I didn't think there was the slightest chance you'd be in London for the Season."

"He hasn't been all that well of late, but he insisted. Believe it or not, he's determined to find me a husband."

A dark winged brow shot up, the color of polished mahogany. "As often as you spoke of his son, I thought perhaps you and the earl—"

Jessie colored and glanced away. "Papa Reggie would have liked that, I think, but Matthew and I . . . we aren't really suited. Besides, he intends to offer for Lady Caroline Winston. They are nearly betrothed already."

Gwen looked at her long and hard. It was tough to hide anything from Gwen. "He's with you here in London?"

"He's helping Papa Reggie introduce me into Society."

Gwen waved her hands as if Matthew Seaton weren't the least bit important. "Well, you certainly don't need him—I imagine you've dozens of suitors already. Have you decided which one you want?"

Jessie laughed. "You make it sound so easy."

"It wouldn't be for me. But then I've never wanted a husband."

"It isn't easy for me, either, but something will have to happen soon. As I said, Papa Reggie's health isn't good. He'll worry until this is settled, and I don't want that." She forced a smile she suddenly didn't feel, then deftly changed the subject. "What about you, Gwen? How have things been going for you?"

The brightness dimmed in Gwen's big green eyes. With her perfect features, ruby lips, and full-bosomed figure, Gwen Lockhart was enough to turn any man's head. Except marriage was the last thing Gwen wanted.

"Things are about the same. My stepfather's as mean as ever. My mother tries to smooth things between us, but when it comes to Lord Waring, she's just not strong enough." The smile slowly crept back in. "It's better, now that we're here in the city. The earl is busy with his clubs and his mistresses. We rarely even see him—which is perfectly fine with me."

Jessie grinned. "Still the same old Gwen—thank God." Gwen Lockhart had always been outspoken. Perhaps that was one of the things that had drawn them together in the first place. Gwen said all the things Jessie used to say and now went to such lengths *not* to say. At Mrs. Seymour's Academy, Gwen was always in trouble. She couldn't seem to follow the rules, couldn't quite seem to obey. Jessie was the perfect student. She knew what she wanted—she dreamed of being a lady. She was determined to make Papa Reggie proud, and nothing was going to stop her.

In most ways the two of them were opposites. But Gwen had very few friends and Jessie was afraid to let anyone get close for fear she might somehow give herself away. Eventually a bond had grown between them that apparently time and distance had not weakened.

"Are you still writing your book?" Jessie asked.

Gwen nodded. "I work on it nearly every day." That was Gwen's grand dream. She wanted to be a writer, to pen novels and see them in print. "I realize when I'm finished, I shall have to send it off to a publisher under a man's name, but I shan't care one bit. *I* shall know that I was the one who wrote it." She grinned mischievously, flashing her small white teeth. "Which reminds me, guess where I'm going tomorrow night?"

Jessie's brows narrowed. She knew that gleam in Gwen's green eyes and it didn't bode well. "Lady Dartmouth's soiree?" she asked hopefully, knowing Lord Waring and his family would surely be invited.

Gwen glanced around to be certain no one was near. The music of the orchestra swelled as she leaned closer, disguising what she meant to say. "I'm going to a gaming hell in Jermyn Street."

"What!" The word came out louder than Jessie intended. She was grateful the music had risen so loud. "For godsakes, Gwen, you can't do that!"

"I have to, Jess. If I want to be a writer, I have to know what life is about. I have to see things, understand how things work. I have to experience life if I'm going to succeed."

Jessie understood dreams better than anyone. Still, there

were some things a lady just couldn't do. "You can't do it, Gwen, not this time. Can you imagine what would happen if someone found out? God's breath, you'd be ruined."

Gwen's lips pulled down in something close to a pout. "I thought you'd understand. At school you always seemed to. You knew how important my writing was—that it meant everything to me. You helped me the time I wanted to go to the cockfight and—"

"Yes, God help me, and I was terrified we'd be caught every minute we were there. We were both disgusted by all of that blood. It was hardly a pleasant evening."

"Yes, but the people! Such incredibly interesting *people*. I'd never seen the like of it before."

Jessie certainly had. Blacklegs and sharpers, mountebanks, and brothers of the gusset. She'd never been more grateful to get back to her simple room at school, back to clean linens and pleasant smells, away from all the ugliness she remembered only too well. Gwen had talked her into several other misadventures, but only because Jessie knew the ways of such things and was able to keep Gwen out of trouble.

"At any rate," her friend was saying, "I'm dressing up like a man and I'm going to one of the hells."

Jessie swallowed, imagining places even worse than the Black Boar Inn. "Where will you get men's clothes?"

"I'm borrowing them from my cousin. He's staying with us for the Season, but for the next few days he's visiting friends in the country. He's only just turned fifteen, a bit taller than I, but I'm certain they'll serve my purpose."

Jessie nervously wet her lips. Across the room, several gentlemen seemed to be watching, waiting perhaps, for the girls to return to the dancing. The music from the orchestra softened, so she lowered her voice to just above a whisper.

"Is there nothing I can say to stop you?" But even as her friend shook her head, she knew the answer to that. Jessie sighed. "I wish you hadn't told me."

"Why ever not?"

"Because now I shall have to go with you."

Gwen clapped her hands and grinned with a mixture of excitement and triumph, but Jessie merely frowned. Her friend knew nothing about places like the hells in Jermyn Street, but Jessie did. The men wore more expensive clothes but the object was the same—drinking, gaming, and whoring.

Not the sort of place for a lady, not even one as adventuresome as Gwen.

But Jessie loved Gwen Lockhart. Gwen was the sister she'd never had. Perhaps she could succeed one more time in keeping her out of trouble.

Leaning his tall frame back against the sofa in the study, Matthew blinked and blinked again, unable to believe his eyes. He stared harder out the window, but the image remained.

Surely his eyes were deceiving him. Surely Jessie Fox wasn't shimmying down a rope fashioned of bedsheets to the ground below her third-story window. Surely it was only an illusion.

Matthew watched the ease with which Jessie descended, amazed though he shouldn't have been. She'd been as nimble as an acrobat when she was a girl of fourteen. His jaw clenched as he watched her. He wouldn't have seen her if he hadn't snuffed out the lamp and remained in the study in darkness.

He'd been enjoying the silence, watching the glow of embers in the grate, thinking of the *Norwich,* wondering how his men were getting along without him, missing the smell of the sea and the damp salt air, missing the camaraderie between the officers and crew he served with aboard the ship.

He found himself wishing he were there instead of in London, that he were feeling the roll of the deck beneath his feet instead of being stifled by tedious evenings, pursued by a bevy of marriage-minded females—hungry for a woman he could not have.

Then he'd thought of Belmore and an odd sort of peace

settled over him. That's when he'd glanced out the window and seen Jessie climbing down—to his utter shock and dismay.

There was no mistaking the slender build, even dressed as she was in men's clothes. They weren't the same as the ones she'd worn before. Tonight she sported a pair of dark trousers, a white lawn shirt, and a wine-colored tailcoat, the clothes of a well-dressed young dandy. He wondered where she'd gotten them as he rose from his chair with a low, muttered curse.

Hell and damnation! The bloody little fool would bring them all to ruin yet.

Still, he did not stop her. He was determined to discover what exactly she was about. He followed her instead, to a hackney carriage waiting down at the corner. She glanced around, opened the door, and climbed in. Matt hailed another hack and bade the driver follow. He lost her once near Berkeley Square but sighted the carriage again in Picadilly and breathed a sigh of relief.

Until he saw the carriage change course, round the corner onto Jermyn Street and pull over, depositing two very small, very slight young "gentlemen" who walked without pause into a well-known place of debauchery called, quite appropriately, the Fallen Angel.

"Bloody hell." His pulse thrummed faster, whether from fear for the two young girls, anger that Jessie would risk herself that way, or a terrible suspicion of what Jessie Fox might be doing in a house of ill repute.

Why had they gone there? What the devil could they possibly want in a gaming hell like the Fallen Angel, a place that catered to the tastes of men who enjoyed administering pain? Perhaps they were meeting someone. Perhaps he had been wrong, perhaps Jessie wasn't the innocent he had come to believe, perhaps her taste ran to something far darker than simple passion in the arms of a lover.

He couldn't quite make himself believe it. More likely she was involved in some other sort of misadventure. Still, a tight knot clenched in his stomach. If it was true, it was past the time he found out. Matt set his jaw and climbed out of the carriage.

Jessie heard the front door close behind them, the sound like a death knell, and a shiver slid down her spine. It was dark in the entry, lit only by smoky oil lamps that lent an eerie glow to the huge, gilt-framed painting on the wall. It was the portrait of a voluptuous, pink-skinned woman who wore nothing but a scarf draped over her feminine parts, her melon-ripe, rose-tipped breasts poking upward from her nude, reclining body.

"Dammit, Gwen," Jessie muttered, "we shouldn't be here."

The little brunette glanced up. Jessie never swore. "We'll only stay a moment, just as I promised."

A tall, thick-shouldered blackamoor guarded the door to the main salon. He assessed them a moment but didn't try to stop them from walking farther into the room.

"Ohmygod—" Gwen's high-pitched whisper rose in astonishment. "Look at those women!" Rouged and painted, pale legs bare and breasts pushed up above their tightly laced corsets, the women of the Fallen Angel laughed at the men's coarse jokes and encouraged their lusty advances. Even the whores at the Black Boar Inn hadn't been so blatant. And they'd confined their activities to the privacy of the rooms upstairs.

"We ought to leave," Jessie said, but Gwen simply prodded her forward. They hugged the shadowy back wall and sat down at a table in a darkened corner.

A pretty little blonde walked up, her hips swaying seductively. "Evenin', milords. What can I get you?" She thrust her breasts very close to Jessie's face. "As you can see, I've more than enough to offer."

Jessie's cheeks burned with embarrassment. "A mug of ale for each of us, if you please." She strained to make her voice sound deep as she tried to guess what an aristocratic gentleman might drink in a place like this. "And don't dawdle, gel. We've another appointment. We won't be staying long." Which she hoped was an excuse for leaving their bowler hats on.

She was clothed from top to bottom, the back of her wrapped cravat rising an inch above her ears. Gwen wore a silly mustache fashioned from a chunk of her glossy dark hair. Jessie looked at her, glanced down at her own male clothes, and never felt more ridiculous in her life.

The girl still stood there. "Such a pretty pair. Are you sure there's nothin' I can do to please you?" She wriggled her breasts seductively. "We could all go upstairs. I could let you both 'ave a go. . . ."

"Not tonight," Jessie snapped, grateful the room was so dimly lit and that their table sat in a corner. "Just bring us the ale and be gone."

"Yes, milords." She bobbed a curtsy, making the silly little skirt on her skimpy version of a black-and-white maid's uniform flop up and down, showing her nearly bare bottom.

"My God," Gwen whispered. "Can you believe it?" She glanced from the saucy behind ambling away to the bevy of half-naked women draped over the well-dressed men at the gaming tables.

"I believe it," Jessie said.

A woman laughed as one of the men reached into the top of her corset and pinched a nipple. Coarse words and lewd remarks drifted across the room, along with the cloying scent of sweet perfume.

"God's breath," Gwen said, "the things men do for sport never ceases to amaze me."

"I hope you've seen enough." Jessie glanced around the smoky room, praying no one had taken notice when they walked in. "Every minute we're here the risk of discovery increases. We'll be ruined if anyone finds out who we are."

Gwen didn't answer, just studied the gaudy hall and its noisy inhabitants, mentally recording every ripple in the red flocked wallpaper, every wrinkle in the powder on the women's painted faces.

"Gwen, did you hear me? You've seen what you came for. It's time for us to leave."

A movement caught their attention. A man's big hands gripped the back of the chair across from them, and Jessie's head snapped up.

"That is extremely good advice," said Lord Strickland, his eyes as dark as onyx. "I'd advise you, Lady Gwendolyn, to do as your friend suggests."

Jessie just stared at him.

"Bloody hell," Gwen grumbled. Her gaze swung to Jessie. "You didn't tell him, did you?"

"Are you insane?" Inside her surprisingly well-fitting clothes, Jessie began to tremble.

"Lower your voices," Matthew warned, a hard edge to his words. "You managed to pick the most notorious spot on Jermyn Street—apparently to assuage your curiosity. Unfortunately, your intrusion for that purpose would not be appreciated. If they find out the two of you are women, I'll have to fight to get you out of here."

The saucy-bottomed maid reappeared, setting the mugs of ale down on the table. Matthew tossed a coin on the surface in payment.

"Evenin', 'andsome." The woman leaned forward, ran her fingers through Matthew's dark gold hair. "'Ow'd you like to come wit' me upstairs?"

He caught her wrist and dragged it away, smiled, but his mouth looked tense and hard. "Not tonight, thanks. Maybe some other time."

His dark gaze sent her running. He turned that savage look on Jessie and she cringed inside. "Get up very quietly. Don't look at anyone, just go back the way you came and out the door. Your hack is still outside. Get in and wait for me there."

"Y-Yes, my lord," Jessie said. Her heart was pounding so hard she could feel it clear to her fingertips.

Even Gwen looked daunted. They pulled their hat brims lower down and shoved back their chairs. Escaping past Matthew, they stayed close to the wall and made their way out to the street. Matthew appeared behind them before they had time to speak.

He jerked open the hackney door. "Get in the carriage." A muscle jumped in his cheek.

Jessie shivered as she settled herself against the seat, wishing she could pull the bowler hat clear to her shoulders. They rode in silence through the noisy cobbled streets, the rattle of iron wheels rumbling up from beneath the carriage. Dear Lord, of all people—why did it have to be him?

Still, as mad as he was, as much as she wished it weren't so, in truth she was glad he was there. It was the first time she had felt safe all evening.

Gwen pulled off her silly mustache and wadded it up in her hand. "This is my fault, Lord Strickland," she said into the tension in the carriage, which was as thick as a London fog. "It was I who wished to go. You mustn't blame Jessie."

Matthew's furious gaze swung to Gwen. "I would suggest, Lady Gwendolyn, you keep your lovely mouth shut and your thoughts—however entertaining they might prove to be—entirely to yourself."

She didn't of course. "But Jessica tried to dissuade me. She knew I would go whether she went along or not. She was only trying to help me find out what I needed to know."

Hard blue eyes locked on Jessie's. "If the way you help your friends, Mistress Fox, is by putting them in danger, you will never have very many of them."

Jessie said nothing. She had been trying to protect Gwen, not lead her into danger. But Matthew would never understand.

His expression turned even more fierce. "I ought to put you over my knee." His hard mouth twisted. "It wouldn't be the first time—as I'm certain you recall. If not, then perhaps another thrashing would serve well as a reminder."

Jessie flushed crimson. How could she forget the most humiliating day of her life?

"You were wearing breeches that day, too," he cruelly reminded her. "I gave you the licking you deserved, but apparently it didn't do much good. Perhaps the lesson would be better learned this eve."

Her face burned brighter, but her chin went up. "I'm not a child anymore, my lord. You can't tell me what to do, and don't you dare threaten me!"

His glance slid pointedly to her backside, outlined by the stylishly snug nankeen breeches she wore. "There isn't a whole lot, Miss Fox, that I wouldn't dare."

"Why you—" She started to argue, then caught the determined set of his jaw and fell silent. He would do it, she saw, if she challenged him a moment more. He was strong enough—and he was definitely mad enough. She eased back into the seat, wishing she could disappear into the worn brown leather.

Matthew's attention shifted. "And you, Lady Gwendolyn. You realize I shall have to tell Lord Waring."

Gwen's pretty face fell, her bravado escaping like the air in a leaky balloon. "Please, my lord, I beg you. I'll do anything. Just please don't tell my stepfather."

"I'm afraid you've given me no choice. I'll have to see you home and when I do, I'll have to tell him."

Gwen seemed to wither before Jessie's eyes. Knowing the cause, Jessie's heart went out to her. She frantically gripped Matt's arm. "Please, my lord. Gwen only wanted to know what it was like in a place like that. She's writing a book, you see. Her dream is to become a writer. She meant no harm, and nothing untoward really happened. Just this once couldn't you—"

"No, Jessie, I'm afraid I can't. Now that I'm involved, I'm responsible for Gwendolyn's welfare. It's my duty to—"

"Duty! That's all you ever think of—your duty and your bloody honor! You've never had a dream—you don't understand what it's like to want something with all your heart!"

"Jessie—Lord Waring has to be told. It's for Gwen's own good."

"But you don't understand—if you tell him he'll beat her. He'll cane her until she can't walk! She has scars across her back and all over her bottom. He enjoys it! How do you think she knew about the Fallen Angel? She heard him talking about what goes on in there. He's just like the men at the Black Boar Inn. They used to do those same things to Mama!" Jessie gasped at the tirade that had ended in betraying her most shameful secret, her terrified glance careening from Matthew's hard features across the carriage to Gwen.

Her friend just looked at her, mentally assembling the pieces of a heretofore unsolved puzzle. She reached over and squeezed Jessie's hand.

"You never talked about your parents," Gwen said. "And I never asked. I didn't care then and I don't care now. Thank you for trying to protect me. If a caning's all I get for this, I shall consider myself lucky. It is worth the price to know that I have a friend like you."

Matthew shifted, the muscles in his long legs rigid where they pressed against Jessie's in the confines of the carriage.

"There'll be no caning," he said softly from the shadows. "I won't tell Waring what happened tonight." He sat forward in the seat, his shoulders so broad they nearly touched both sides, a hard look fixed on Gwen. "But I want your word, Lady Gwendolyn, you won't try anything so foolish again."

She nodded meekly. "I promise." But Jessie saw the fingers she had crossed behind her back.

"Mistress Fox?" That same hard look drilled into her.

"The promise comes easily, my lord. A gaming hell is the last place I wish to be."

He eyed her a moment more. "Then we'll speak of this no further." His dark blue gaze didn't waiver. Leaning back against the seat, he studied her in silence as the hackney rolled along.

Jessie wondered what it was he was thinking.

"Why are you pacing, Matthew? If you've something to say, for pity's sake, go ahead and say it."

He was standing beside his father in the study of the town house. The hour was late. Jessie had already gone up to bed. "I'm worried is all. My leave will be up in less than two weeks and you'll be left here in London with Jessie—alone."

"I'm afraid I don't take your meaning."

"It's just that I'm worried is all. You still aren't feeling all that well, and even if you were, with no one to help you, it'll be harder to keep an eye on her, make certain that nothing goes wrong."

"Cornelia is helping, and as nearly as I can tell, things are progressing right on schedule. Whether you are here or not will hardly make a difference now."

Matt rested his hands on the back of a tufted leather chair in front of the desk, thinking about Jessie last night at the Fallen Angel and trying to chose just the right words. "I know how you feel about the girl. I'll even admit to a grudging admiration for her myself." Along with a growing lust, he silently added. "Considering her background, the girl has accomplished wonders."

His father beamed. "There is no question of that."

"Yes, well, be that as it may, the fact remains, Jessie Fox is still Jessie Fox."

"Meaning?"

"Meaning her past is still a problem. Even at home she has inadvertently slipped on occasion. Last night it happened again. She made a reference to her mother that couldn't have been more clear. Fortunately it happened in front of Gwen Lockhart, who, I'm happy to say, is apparently a very good friend."

"No one is perfect, Matthew."

"That isn't the point. The point is it could very well happen again. One slip—that's all it would take to expose her and ruin the Belmore name. It's an honorable name, one that's never known a single trace of scandal."

The marquess lifted the stopper off a crystal decanter of brandy and poured a generous portion into each of two cut-glass snifters. "A single trace of scandal that anyone's ever heard of," he corrected.

"What's that supposed to mean?"

"It means that nothing is ever as black and white, as cut and dried, as you would like to believe. There are always murky spots in the middle. I don't think our Belmore ancestors were as perfect as you have them pictured. They were fortunate to have kept whatever misdeeds they might have done blessedly silent. Even you, Matthew, with your rigid code of honor, surely you have done things you aren't proud of—or at the very least contemplated doing so."

That was beyond the truth. He wasn't perfect, far from it. And lately, the thing he contemplated most was what it would be like to take Jessie Fox to bed.

"I'm sorry, I didn't mean to sound condescending."

His father approached and handed him the snifter of brandy. "I won't deny Jessica's background is a drawback, but once she is married, the past can be laid to rest."

Matthew thought of Jessie dressed as a man and sitting in a Jermyn Street brothel. Though she hadn't gone there for an assignation, as he had thought she might have, she was as wild and reckless as ever. No matter what his father said, she was a threat to Reginald Seaton, to himself, and the Belmore name.

She was also the most tempting little baggage he had ever laid eyes on. He went hard just thinking of the way those breeches hugged her bottom, the way her white lawn shirt drew tight across her breasts.

An image of Caroline Winston rose up, all soft innocence and purity, a sweetly smiling face and gentle, ladylike ways. She was due to arrive in the city any day and he was looking forward to seeing her. Perhaps she could set temptation at bay. As soon as he was able, he would speak to her father, make their betrothal official. He had promised her that the last time he had seen her and he meant to keep his word.

He took a drink of his brandy. "All I'm saying is, the sooner she's married the better." Better for his father, for Belmore, and especially for him. "Find her a husband, get her settled and safely out of London. If you can keep things quiet that long, maybe this crazy scheme of yours will work. Until that happens, there is no way we can be sure."

The marquess sighed and sank down in an overstuffed chair. "Perhaps you are right. For me I don't care, but it would devastate Jessica if something of her past should arise. I shall endeavor to choose a husband wisely. It must be a man who will love her enough, should the subject ever surface, it will be of no concern. At any rate, as you have said, you will be gone by the time a betrothal occurs."

Matt ignored an odd squeezing in his chest. He wanted the girl for a mistress not a wife. He didn't really trust her and they would never suit. Still it bothered him more than it should have to think of Jessie with another man.

Chapter Nine

Jessie opened her hand-painted fan and used it to dry the slight sheen of exertion from her latest round of dancing. She was attending a soiree at the Duke of Milton's lavish residence in St. James's Square.

After the fiasco with Gwendolyn night before last, she was definitely on her best behavior. She had smiled till she felt sure her lips would crack, danced till her feet went numb, fluttered her fan, batted her lashes, and tried to entice any man who might be a candidate for marriage.

When she couldn't go on a moment more, she made her way to the card room, then stood quietly watching the deep play at the green baize tables. Huge stacks of money changed hands, tens of thousands of pounds. The betting was exciting to watch, perhaps even more so, since she would never take those same sort of risks herself.

"Shall we go in to supper, Miss Fox? I've a table waiting for us in the state dining room." Jeremy Codrington, Duke of Milton, stood at her side, impeccably dressed in a burgundy tailcoat, white pique waistcoat, and black breeches. A soft smile warmed his gentle features, slim straight nose, and well-formed lips. Sandy hair and brown eyes made him look younger than his twenty-four years.

She nodded, turning away from the play at the tables and trying to muster some excitement that the duke himself had asked her to join him for the midnight meal.

Jessie smiled. "I hope I didn't keep you waiting. I started watching the game and time slipped away." She took the arm he extended. "I could certainly use something to eat."

The duke glanced from her to the whist game she had been watching. "Do you enjoy gaming, Miss Fox?"

"No, I—" *get sick at the thought of losing all that money.* But she caught herself before she could say it. "I like to watch, but I . . . I'm not very good at cards, I'm afraid." That was a lie if ever there was one. She had learned to play as a child, could cheat even better than her worthless half brother. Perhaps that was the real reason she never played.

If she started to lose, she might be tempted.

"I could teach you sometime," the young duke offered. "I'm passably good, if I do say so myself."

That was just about right. Passably good. The poor man lost more often than he won. Then again, he could afford it.

She smiled and forced herself to nod. "I'd like that, your grace. I would be happy to learn anything you might teach me." He colored at the double entendre she had accidentally used, and she almost smiled. Of all the eligible young men she had met, the duke was among her favorites. He was soft-spoken and intelligent, and his conversations usually went beyond talk of the theater or the opera, or meaningless chatter about fashion.

They had actually spoken of the dread French invasion everyone so feared, of the opening of the new London docks and how it might affect foreign trade. They discussed news from Marseilles that the Toulon fleet had captured an English frigate off Cape Maria, talked of Admiral Nelson, the war, and Napoléon Bonaparte, the kind of topics she and Papa Reggie often discussed, subjects hardly appropriate to a young unmarried woman—any woman, in fact.

But the duke seemed intrigued when she had accidentally let slip that she read the morning papers. He enjoyed discussing important events and didn't seem to find it offensive that a woman should actually care what went on in the world.

Still, she was glad when the lavish ten-course meal had

been served and the duke returned to his guests. She had been so perfectly behaved these past two days, surely she deserved a moment by herself. Papa Reggie had already adjourned to the town house, but the countess remained to act as chaperone. She and Matthew were to see her safely home.

Inwardly she groaned at the thought. He had hardly spoken to her since the night he had dragged her from the Fallen Angel. When he did, she could hear the censure in his voice.

At least he hadn't told Lord Waring, as she had known he would not. Matthew would never break his word.

Unconsciously her eyes went in search of him. She spotted the Countess Fielding, but Matthew was nowhere near, which wasn't surprising since the beautiful woman had been fixing her attention of late on the roguish Baron Densmore.

Chiding herself for thinking of Strickland when she had promised herself she would not, Jessie reined in her searching gaze, eased through the crush of people, and made her way outside.

She stopped in the shadows at the edge of the terrace. Pulling off her gloves, she tilted her head back to watch the stars, the air cleared of soot by an earlier brief bout of rain. The earth still smelled damp, and droplets of water clung to the plants and the box hedge beneath the terrace railing, sparkling like crystal in the light of a distant torch.

"You shouldn't be out here, you know. At least not alone."

Jessie turned at the sound of the rough male voice, a shiver of unease drifting through her. Adam Harcourt, Viscount St. Cere. She had danced with the dark-haired man just once, spoken to him only briefly on a couple of other occasions.

"Good evening, my lord." Unconsciously, she took a step away. Something about him made her nervous, a harshness, a leashed sort of temperament that frightened her a little whenever she looked into the hard planes of his face. "I didn't intend to stay. I just . . . I needed a moment to myself." She glanced up once more at the stars, a blanket of jewels in a sky as black as the viscount's raven hair. "Sometimes the crush is a bit more than I . . ." She flushed a little at what she had almost said.

"A bit more than you can stomach?" he finished in his disturbingly cynical way. "I've had the same thought myself."

He moved a little closer, but this time she held her ground. "That isn't . . . that's not exactly what I meant."

"No?" A mouth that was sensuous yet somehow ruthless tipped upward at one corner. "I think that is exactly what you meant."

Her own lips tugged upward. It was exactly the truth. "Yes, I suppose it was."

He watched her from beneath a row of double-thick black lashes. "I stay in the city for a time, until all the hypocrisy begins to weigh me down. Then I return to Harcourt, which gives me ease for a while. Then I grow restless. I think of the pleasures I am missing and come back to London, where I resume my endless rounds of gaming and debauchery."

A jolt of surprise ran through her that he would speak so plain.

"Does that shock you, Miss Fox? Somehow I didn't think it would."

A thread of wariness spiraled through her. Did he know something of her past? Did he somehow suspect the truth? "Why . . . why would you think that?"

He shrugged a pair of shoulders almost as broad as Matthew's. He was just as tall and in a different, darker, more brooding way, nearly as handsome.

"Because there is a certain wisdom in your face. The kind that comes only from meeting life's challenges and somehow surviving them. It makes one wonder what could possibly have happened to make you look that way. It makes me ponder the secrets you must keep."

She caught a quick, jerky intake of air. "I-I have no secrets."

"No?"

"Of course not." She twisted the gloves she clutched in her hands, then steeled herself. She didn't like the discerning look on the viscount's hard-etched face. "If you'll excuse me, it's time I went back in." She started to brush past, but he caught her arm, stopping her just inches from his tall, powerful body. If he lowered his head, he could kiss her, she thought wildly, and for a moment she thought he would. A shiver of fear snaked through her, mingled with a fleeting urge to experience the unknown, to see if another man could make her feel the fire Matthew's kiss had sparked.

Lord Strickland's voice rang out as if she had conjured him. "So . . . Mistress Fox . . . I have found you at last." Matthew stood in the light of the torch just a few feet away, his body rigid with anger.

"I-I was just going in, my lord."

Adam Harcourt's expression did not change. His hand fell away from her arm. "Strickland. I heard you were in town for the Season." A corner of his hard mouth curved up. "I would say it's good to see you, but from the mood you appear to be in, I doubt that you would believe me."

Matthew did not answer.

St. Cere flicked a glance at Jessie. "I knew the lovely Miss Fox was your father's ward. I didn't know the girl meant anything to you."

Matthew's hand clenched into a fist. "Well, now you do."

The viscount assessed him a moment more, a long steady perusal that ended with a studied look into Matthew's icy blue eyes. Astoundingly, St. Cere broke into a smile. It softened his harsh features, making him look years younger. "Then I shall leave her in your care . . . and Matthew . . . it really is good to see you. I hope our paths cross again."

He was gone as silently as he had arrived, leaving her alone with the grim-faced man across from her.

"What the hell were you doing out here with St. Cere?"

"I wasn't *with* him. I came out here alone."

"And Adam just happened to stumble across your path? By Christ, the man is a rogue. Surely you could see his mind was on only one thing. Do you know what would happen if someone had seen the two of you out here alone?"

"We were only talking. There is hardly anything scandalous in that."

"Talking wasn't what St. Cere had in mind."

A shot of anger went through her, sending her chin up a notch. "How could you possibly know what the viscount had in mind?"

Matthew's gaze slid down to the curve of her breast, rising up above her gown with each breath. "Because I'm a man. Any man standing out here with you is hardly thinking of conversation."

Her chin went higher still. "It's hardly your affair. Adam Harcourt's intentions are none of your concern." She tried to walk past him, but his hand snaked out and grasped her waist, stopping her beside him.

"You're wrong, Jessie. You're masquerading as a relative. You're involving my father and the Belmore name—that makes it my concern."

"Go to bloody hell."

Anger darkened his eyes. A cynical slant twisted his lips. "Then again, perhaps you wanted the man to take liberties. If that is the case, perhaps I can manage in his stead."

The grip on her waist grew almost painful as Matthew hauled her against him, knocking the gloves from her hand. Bending her over his arm, he captured her lips in a hard, punishing kiss that told her just how angry he was. Jessie's palms pressed against his shoulders, trying to push him away, but his hold only tightened. She could feel his hard-muscled thighs through the front of her gown, taste the brandy he had been drinking. The smell of his musky cologne mingled with his own male scent. The rough wool of his jacket teased her fingers.

Heat swirled through her, tugged somewhere low in her belly. His mouth was no longer hard, the kiss no longer fierce, but soft and seeking, his tongue delving deeply, making the blood race like fire through her veins.

He shifted, bringing her closer, and she felt his hardened arousal. Slanting his mouth over hers, he deepened the kiss, probing, tasting, sliding his tongue across her trembling bottom lip. He teased the corners, then swept deeply inside. Her legs felt weak while her stomach tingled and her body pulsed in soft feathery waves.

Matthew!

Flames seemed to scorch right through her. Moisture gathered in the place between her legs, and her whole body tightened. Her fingers dug into the muscles across his shoulders and she heard Matthew groan.

Voices drifted toward them. A few feet away, on the opposite end of the terrace, laughter and shuffling feet jerked his dark golden head up. He was breathing heavily, slightly disoriented, as if he had forgotten where they were.

"God's blood," he whispered, pulling himself under control. When Jessie swayed against him, he swore softly, then carefully set her a few feet away. "I must be mad." Muttering something she couldn't hear, he raked a hand through his golden blond hair. Dimly Jessie realized he was shaking.

"Matthew . . ." It was all she could think of to say. She pressed a hand to her trembling lips and tried to control the fiery shivers still coursing through her.

He bent down and picked up her gloves. Straightening to his full imposing height, his bearing as erect as any admiral he might have served, he handed them to her.

"I apologize, Miss Fox. The fault in this is mine, not yours. Please accept my regrets . . . and my sincere promise that it will not happen again."

"Matthew . . ." It came out as a plea. She didn't want him to be sorry. She didn't want him to feel regret. She wanted him to kiss her again.

"Stop it, Jessie. Dammit—can't you see how wrong this is?"

She only shook her head. "I can't see anything anymore." Tears stung her eyes. Dear God, she didn't want him to see. "I wanted you to kiss me—that's all I know. If that is wrong, then I am the one who should be sorry." Turning away from him, she raced off toward the house, blinking to hold back the wetness.

Behind her, Matthew cursed softly, fluently, but he made no move to follow.

Jessie said a silent prayer of thanks, for the first person she saw as she entered the drawing room was Lady Caroline Winston.

Good sweet Lord. Humiliated, torn between guilt and an aching need for Matthew, she hurried in the opposite direction, making her way to the ladies' retiring room upstairs.

She wondered if Matthew would have regretted the kiss if he had shared it with Lady Caroline.

Henry Winston, Earl of Landsdowne, warmly clapped Matt on the shoulder. "I had hoped to see you long before this, my boy, but considering how many months you've been at sea, I realize how busy you must be, trying to put things in order."

The earl was a short, stocky, barrel-chested man with a fringe of gray hair around his balding head. It was obvious Lady Caroline had acquired her slender build from her mother's side of the family.

"I'm sorry I missed you at Winston House," Matt said. "I didn't realize my father planned to spend time in the city." They were standing in the drawing room of Landsdowne's town house in Berkeley Square. He had been with the earl, Caroline, and her mother for the past several hours, discussing the time he had left at sea, making polite conversation with Caroline and Lady Landsdowne. The latter had departed to call on friends. Now the earl was about to take his leave, giving him and Caroline a few moments alone.

Or at least as alone as one could be with the drawing room doors wide open and the house buzzing with servants.

"Caroline, my dear?" The earl turned an affectionate look on his daughter.

"Yes, Father?"

"I shall leave it to you to see that our guest receives proper treatment."

Caroline smiled sweetly. "Yes, Father." He bussed her

cheek, shook Matt's hand, then strode out through the drawing room doors.

Matt sat down next to Caroline on the horsehair settee. "I suppose this is as much privacy as we'll get until we are betrothed." And not much more until they were wed. He smiled. "Do you realize I have never even kissed you."

Sweetly feminine laughter bubbled up. "That's not true, my lord. You kissed me once when we were children—out behind the hedge in the formal gardens." She had seemed uneasy when he'd first arrived, on edge in some way he couldn't quite discern. Now that his attention was fixed on her, she resumed her easygoing nature.

Recalling the day she spoke of, Matt laughed, too. "I kissed you? Did I really?"

"Yes, you did. You said you had seen your stepmother kissing your father. You wanted to know how a kiss might feel."

"And you let me? I'm surprised at you, Lady Caroline."

Another sweet ripple of laughter. "It was hardly a matter of my letting you. You stole that kiss, my lord. Do you ever recall, Matthew Seaton, a time you didn't get something that you were determined to have?"

Yes, he thought, Jessie's pretty face rising up in the eye of his mind. He wanted Jessica Fox. He wanted to make love to her with a hunger that bordered on obsession.

It was the one thing he knew he could not have.

He forced himself to smile. "Time alone with you, my lovely lady, is something I want very much but plainly cannot have."

"It will happen soon enough, once the matter of our betrothal is settled." Her brows drew together. "That won't be much longer—will it, Matthew?"

He cleared his throat. "It's hard to be certain, but I'm hoping to see it done fairly soon."

Her features relaxed once more. "Father will be far more lenient once the marriage is set. He trusts you, Matthew—implicitly. He just doesn't want any unwarranted gossip."

Jessie rose in his thoughts again, sitting in a Jermyn Street hell. She was hardly concerned about gossip. Then again, perhaps that was unfair. Perhaps, as Gwen Lockhart had said, Jessie had simply gone with her friend in order to protect her. He had witnessed that instinct in her before.

For the first time he admitted how oddly appealing she had looked sported out as a dandy. This time instead of anger at what she had done, he found himself inwardly smiling. God's breath the woman had bigger cods than the brassiest man on his crew.

"Matthew? Did you hear what I just said?"

His head snapped up, his attention returning to Caroline, where it should have remained all along. "I'm sorry, my love. My mind must have wandered."

"I said I realize your leave is almost over. I was wondering if you would be attending the party at Lord Pickering's country estate at week's end? My father spoke to Lord Belmore. The marquess said he and Miss Fox would definitely be attending."

He knew about the outing. He had tried to dissuade his father, but the old man was bent on going. Which meant, since he didn't trust Jessie to behave, he would have to go along.

"I'm planning to attend as well. I didn't realize you would be there, too." He smiled. "At least I'll be pleasantly diverted." He captured her gloved hand between his fingers. "Perhaps I shall try for that kiss."

A soft flush rose in her cheeks. She was lovely. In a different, less dramatic way, just as beautiful as Jessie. He cupped a hand to her cheek and the soft flush deepened, stirring a gentle affection. He hadn't spent much time with Caroline over the years, but he had always felt comfortable around her. Caroline Winston was everything he imagined in a woman. Sweet, well-bred, and gentle. He could easily envision her as his wife.

Yet looking at her now, he suddenly felt as if something would be missing. Until this moment, it had never occurred to him that the woman he wed should stir the kind of passion Jessie fired with a single warm glance. Now he found himself wishing he desired Caroline Winston in the same lusty manner he did Jessie.

He tried to imagine Caroline in his bed, splendidly naked and writhing beneath him, begging him to take her, but instead of brown hair spilling across his pillow, he saw light golden blond. Instead of Caroline's soft pink lips, he saw Jessie's lush coral mouth, bruised and moist with his kisses.

"Have you any idea how long you'll be at sea this time?" Caroline asked, once more snapping his thoughts back to her. He cursed himself for not being more attentive.

"Unfortunately, I'm not sure. We've been blockading Napoléon's ships for the last two years. Something's got to break, and it's going to happen soon. Once it does and the fighting is over, I'll be out of the navy for good." Assuming he lived through the conflagration. The possibility of his death was the reason he'd been loath to make more definite plans.

"Oh, Matthew, I do so look forward to the day you'll be home to stay." She leaned closer and he could smell her light perfume, the soft fragrance of lilies. "We shall make such a perfect couple. Everyone says so. We shall have perfectly beautiful children and live in a perfectly lovely house." She smiled brightly. "I have always loved Belmore. Once your father is gone, the house and all of its splendid furnishings will be ours. I'm already planning the changes I shall make. It will be even more magnificent than—"

"My father has years yet to live," he snapped. "Seaton Manor is where we'll reside. If that does not please you—" The mortified look on Caroline's face brought his tirade to an end. God's blood, what the devil was the matter with him?

"I-I'm sorry," she said contritely. "I meant nothing untoward. I was just—"

"I am the one who is sorry. I shouldn't have snapped at you. It's only that my father has been ill. I'm worried about him and soon I'll have to leave." He got up from his seat on the sofa. "As I already should have taken my leave from here." His mouth curved only slightly. "We wouldn't want any unwarranted gossip."

Caroline frowned, sensing his change of mood. Even he was loath to explain it. "Yes, well, I shall see you at Benhamwood then."

"Yes," Matt said, bowing over her hand. "I shall look forward to it, my lady." But in truth, he discovered, he wasn't looking forward to it at all.

Caroline walked him to the door and the butler handed over his hat and gloves.

"Thank you for coming," she said sweetly.

"The pleasure was mine, my lady." He kissed her hand and wondered why he had never even tried to kiss her lips. For the past five years, he had planned his life around Caroline Winston. Now that life had somehow dimmed.

Silently, Matthew cursed himself—and Jessie Fox for making him want her so badly.

A warm sun sifted through the leaves of the plane tree beside the path Jessie walked toward the garden at Benhamwood. A soft breeze luffed through the branches, rustling the leaves overhead. Clematis bloomed and lilac scented the air.

The Earl of Pickering's country estate was magnificent, huge and stately, with more than a hundred bedchambers, a dozen elegant drawing rooms, and a lavish state dining room that seated two hundred guests. But it was the grounds Jessie favored.

A lake surrounded by willows dominated the rolling landscape; deer and sheep roamed the sweeping grass slopes ringed by dark green woodlands. In the days since her arrival, the wide, airy spaces had become her haven, giving her solace from the constant crush of people, the gossip and machinations of the wealthy elite who had gathered at Lord Pickering's estate. She wished Gwen were there, but Lord Waring and his family rarely attended such affairs, and Gwen couldn't come without them.

Walking through the gardens of the estate, Jessie plucked a pink climbing rose from a trellis along the path and absently twirled it between her fingers. She had always wanted to be a lady, and on the surface she was. But deep down inside, where she hoped no one could see, she wondered if she could ever completely accept the rigid code of conduct imposed by the members of the ton.

All of the wealth, all of the jewels and elegant gowns, came at a terrible price, she'd discovered. Every move she made, every word she spoke was scrutinized for the least impropriety. Even the dancing she so loved had its own stuffy rules that couldn't be broken. She found herself yearning for the freedom of her youth, longing for the peaceful days at Belmore, missing the children who expected nothing more of her than a warm, caring smile and a word or two of praise for their determined efforts.

And there was Matthew, of course.

He was here with Lady Caroline, spent most of his time in her company. It was obvious to all, his intention was marriage. And yet there were times when Jessie could feel him watching her, studying her every move. During the day he scrupulously avoided her, but at night . . . at night when he thought she couldn't see, his gaze was so intense it was almost as if he touched her.

During the time she had been there, her number of suitors had grown. Jeremy Codrington, the Duke of Milton, had spoken to her uncle. Amazing as it seemed, it looked as though he intended to offer marriage.

Jessie Fox married to a duke. It was almost funny.

Papa Reggie didn't think so. He and Lady Bainbridge were beside themselves, glowing with satisfaction and excitement as the duke's intentions grew more clear.

Tonight a lavish costume ball was planned. Jessie would be dressed as the goddess Aphrodite. Her gown, designed by Madame Dumont, the most sought-after modiste in London, was fashioned of snowy white silk. It draped over her hips and breasts, split up the side to afford a glimpse of her ankles, and clung sensuously to her body. An elegant topaz and diamond brooch held the fabric together over one shoulder, leaving the other one bare. She would wear diamonds in her hair and small golden sandals on her feet.

It was a daring gown, one she was surprised Lady Bainbridge had commissioned. Still, the party was to be a masquerade. She would be wearing a golden domino that covered most of her face and everyone had gotten into the spirit of being a little outrageous.

With that thought in mind, Jessie took a last comforting look at the quiet serenity around her, then started up the path to the huge, palatial house, hoping to rest a bit before evening. She was rounding a corner of the terrace when Matthew and Lady Caroline stepped into view.

"Oh . . . I-I mean, good afternoon, Lady Caroline . . . Lord Strickland."

His sensuous lips curved up. She remembered exactly the way they had felt pressed to hers and a soft coil of heat unfurled in her stomach.

"Good afternoon, Miss Fox," he said.

"I-I was just enjoying the gardens."

"Yes . . ." Caroline said, taking in Jessie's simple pink muslin gown, the fact she had left her hair unbound and falling around her shoulders. "They are lovely this time of year."

Matthew glanced behind her, searching the path she had strolled as if he wondered if she were alone. St. Cere was at Benhamwood, but he had gone hunting with some of the men. And he had spoken to her with only the politest formality since the night Matthew had confronted him on the terrace.

Jessie looked up at Lord Strickland, noticed the way Caroline's gloved hand rested with such propriety on his arm, and the warmth in her stomach changed to a queasy knot that started to churn.

"I was just going in," she said, mustering a smile. "Papa Reggie will be wondering where I am. I hope you enjoy your walk."

"Thank you," Caroline said.

Matthew said nothing. There was something in his eyes, something dark and illusive she had noticed of late but couldn't begin to fathom. Perhaps he was angry that she had gone off on her own, as she had a tendency to do. Perhaps he'd expected her to be more formally dressed, or maybe he was still upset about the kiss they had shared on the terrace.

Whatever it was, it didn't matter. Matthew's choice had been made, his future well in hand. Jessie Fox had no place in it. She swallowed back the ache that rose in her throat and continued into the house.

*C*hapter *T*en

*Y*ou look ravishing, my dear." Papa Reggie winked at her and smiled. "Doesn't she, Corney?"

Lady Bainbridge wore a satisfied smile. Dressed as Madame de Pompadour, her salt-and-pepper hair covered by a towering silver wig arranged around a miniature sailing ship, she surveyed Jessie's costume with approval. "Quite right, Reggie dear."

She tilted her head to the side as she studied Jessie's Grecian gown. "Elegant and graceful. Daring but not monstrously so. They shall simply admire her for being an Original."

Jessie smiled, wishing she felt more like an Original. Then again, perhaps Lady Bainbridge was right—there was certainly no one at Benhamwood the least bit like her.

They made their way from their third-floor guest rooms, down the stairs to the second-story ballroom, the countess beside Papa Reggie, who was dressed as Henry V. Jessie inwardly grinned. Even having lost a bit of weight from his recent bout of illness, with his leonine mane of hair, and imposing stature, the Marquess of Belmore made a very impressive king.

There was no sign of Matthew. He was leaving day after the morrow, returning to Belmore for the rest of his things, then traveling on to Portsmouth and his ship. Her chest hurt to think of it, but perhaps in a way it was best. At least she could begin to forget him.

They continued down the stairs and arrived at the second floor, where a gray-wigged footman, liveried in blue and gold, pulled open the gilt-trimmed doors. The lavish mirrored ballroom, decorated in bold colors to resemble a fair, beckoned them forward, and they passed beside huge bouquets of red and yellow roses.

The ball was well underway. The Earl of Pickering, dressed as Julius Caesar, asked her to partner him for a dance and after that her legion of admirers seemed to swell. The Duke of Milton was lavish in his attentions, and even Adam Harcourt sought her out for a dance.

It turned out to be a waltz, which Pickering risked censure by admitting he adored. In theory, Jessie knew how the dance was performed, but as scandalous as many of the ton believed it was, she had never had occasion to actually try it. She should decline the invitation, she knew, especially partnered with a rake like St. Cere, but the thrill of dancing the notorious waltz just wouldn't let her.

In the crush of the ballroom, she couldn't see him, then she felt his hand grip hers, solid and sure and somehow familiar. When she turned, it wasn't St. Cere but Lord Strickland whose sun-bronzed features stared into her face.

"It's only a dance," she defended, certain he meant to stop her. "I should like to try it just once."

Matthew surprised her by smiling, crinkling tiny lines beside his deep blue eyes. "And so you shall, Miss Fox . . . if you don't mind dancing it with me."

Pleasure filtered through her. Jessie smiled as his arm slid around her waist and he swept her onto the pink marble dance floor. She felt the warmth of his hand, the pressure of his thigh grazing hers as the music strengthened and he stepped into the rhythm of the waltz.

His eyes touched her face, held her gaze and did not falter. Her heart pounded, pulsed insanely through her veins. He was wearing his blue and white uniform, dressed as the captain of His Majesty's Navy that he was, the gold bars on his shoulders glittering the same golden color as his hair.

"Aphrodite. Very apt, I would say. Are you enjoying the ball, Mistress Fox?"

A soft flush rose in her cheeks. "I am now," she said softly, knowing she should not have.

His eyes went dark. The hand at her waist drew her a little bit closer. His gaze shifted over her features, came to rest on her mouth, and soft heat slid into her stomach. It felt wonderful to be held like this, to be dancing the forbidden waltz with Matthew, held in his hard-muscled arms.

"You're a wonderful dancer, my lord. And now that I have tried it, I have to say that I don't believe the waltz is one bit scandalous. I wish we could dance this way forever."

His eyes grew darker still. "Do you?"

"Yes . . ."

The muscles across his shoulders went rigid beneath her fingers. "Do you know what you do to me?"

Jessie just stared, her heart pumping madly.

"You're a fire in my blood, Jessie Fox. If it weren't for my father, there is nothing I would not do to have you in my bed."

She stiffened a little in his arms. He wasn't speaking of marriage—that he reserved for another. "You mean if it weren't for Papa Reggie—and Lady Caroline," she corrected.

Crystal chandeliers swirled above them. Other dancers spun past yet it seemed as if no one else were there. Matthew stared at her for long moments more, then his hold on her subtly shifted, increasing the distance between them until it was perfectly correct.

"My father says the Duke of Milton intends to offer marriage. Should that happenstance occur, do you plan to accept?"

Until that moment, she'd refused to think overly about it. Secretly she'd been hoping that something would change, that Matthew would discover it was Jessie he wanted, not Caroline Winston.

Her smile felt brittle, tight around the edges. "What is your advice, my lord? Do you believe I should marry the duke?" Her breath suspended as she waited for his words, her heart thundering louder than the music. She prayed he would say no, that he didn't want her to marry any other man but him.

The dance continued and they made a graceful turn. At the side of the dance floor, Lady Caroline stood next to Papa Reggie. Tension bunched a muscle in Matthew's jaw and she knew he had seen her as well.

"Jeremy is an honorable man," he said in a voice gone rough. "He's wealthy and powerful. If he asks for your hand in marriage, then undoubtedly you should accept."

The smile nearly cracked on her lips. "Very well, my lord. If Jeremy asks me to wed, that is exactly what I shall do."

His jaw clamped even harder and the lines of his face looked grim. He said nothing more, but when the dance finally ended, he returned her not to Papa Reggie, where Caroline also stood, but to Lady Bainbridge, on the opposite side of the dance floor.

She didn't see him after that, and the night grew long and tedious. Supper began at midnight, a lavish meal she barely touched. Lord Pickering served as her escort. Shortly after that, Papa Reggie retired to his room, his gout paining him, along with a goodly bit of fatigue.

Alone for a moment, Jessie wandered down from the upstairs ballroom, determined not to think of Matthew's words. She watched the gaming in one of Benhamwood's numerous salons, then strolled into the library, walked over and began to thumb through a leather-bound book: Joseph Lancaster, *Improvements in Education as It Respects the Industrial Classes.*

She started to skim the text, wishing she had time to read it, but her head had begun to pound. The bottoms of her feet hurt. She was weary and anxious for the night to end. She longed for her bed but Lady Bainbridge wouldn't hear of it. For the balance of the evening, this slight respite was all she would get.

She had just sat down on a small settee beside a lovely Queen Anne table when she heard someone shouting. A chilling scream followed, then a growing crescendo of voices that built and built and sent shivers of dread down her spine. Leaping up from the sofa, Jessie raced across the room and pulled open the tall carved doors leading out into the hallway.

"Fire! Fire in the east wing!" someone shouted. The news was followed by a stampede of people racing down from upstairs, the crush in the ballroom flooding out into the hall like an overflowing river.

The east wing! My God, the guest wing—Papa Reggie was up there and so was Viola! Racing toward the sweeping marble staircase, she battled her way through the onslaught of people, but for every two steps forward, someone shoved her several steps back.

"Where are you going, you fool?" someone shouted. "The whole place is burning down!"

"The marquess is up there!" she shouted. "I have to go and get him." The flames were visible now, licking at the curtains, spawned by the wind blowing in through the tall open windows. A few yards down the hallway, the beautiful gold flocked wallpaper went up like a candlestick, adding to the heat of the blaze. Staring upward, Jessie wet her lips, fear rising inside her. She started to move forward when she spotted a stout female figure wearing wide panniers and a tall silver wig.

"Lady Bainbridge!"

"Jessica! We were so worried—we have to get out of here."

"Papa Reggie—" She sagged with relief when she saw him in his long white cotton night rail, a stocking cap draped across one thick shoulder.

"Come, my dear," he said. "It is well past time for us to leave."

"What about Vi? She was sleeping in my room waiting to help me undress after the ball."

"I spoke to her in the hallway. She was worried for you. I sent her downstairs and told her I would see to your safety myself." The marquess glanced around as they started toward the massive front doors. "Where is Matthew? I thought that he was with you."

The blood drained from her face. "Matthew? Wasn't he with you?"

"No."

"Dear, oh, dear," said Lady Bainbridge. "He said something about a card game going on upstairs, but that was earlier. Or he might have simply gone up to bed."

"Oh, dear God." Jessie bit her lip as they were swept up in the terrified throng. She stopped when they pushed through the entry and stepped out in the cold night air, thick with soot and smoke.

"We have to find Matthew," she said. "We can't just leave him."

"Surely he is safe," Papa Reggie said. "He is probably already out here." But his face looked pale and lined with worry and so did the face of the countess.

"Is everyone safely outside?" Lord Pickering raced through the crowd, which had gathered beneath the trees some distance from the house, the women huddled together to watch the spreading flames. A bucket brigade had been started. Servants and guests worked feverishly to make a dent in the rapidly building blaze.

"There are people still upstairs," someone said, and a woman started crying. "Some are trapped in the rooms on the second floor. There may be others still up in their bedchambers."

"Oh, dear Lord." Jessie turned to the crowd. "Matthew!" she shouted, her gaze frantically searching. "Matthew, where are you?" The countess chimed in and so did Papa Reggie. They hurried through the crowd, hoping someone had seen him, but Matthew wasn't there.

Jessie's gaze swung back to the mansion. "He's still inside the house. I know it." Lifting the white Grecian gown up to her knees, she started running back toward the mansion.

"Jessica!" the marquess called after her. "Jessica, you mustn't go in there!"

But it was already too late. Breathing hard, she didn't stop till she stood inside the entry, where she paused to stare up the curving staircase into the inferno that raced through the second-floor halls. Matthew's room was on the third floor across from hers, but the staircase was already ablaze.

Perhaps he was outside and they just hadn't seen him, she thought frantically, but her heart said it wasn't the truth. "Dear Lord—help me." Racing down the hall, she rushed toward the rear of the house, the smoke so thick she could barely breathe. Choking on the black soot filling her lungs, she stopped in the dining room and grabbed a linen napkin, splashed water out of a silver pitcher onto the cloth, then tied the wet fabric over her nose and mouth.

The servants' stairs smoldered, blazed in several places, but she climbed past the flames and continued upward. She stopped at the second floor, called out but no one answered. She was breathing hard by the time she reached the third-floor landing. Taking a moment to catch her breath and get her bearings, she hurried down the hall, trying to remember which bedchamber Matthew had been assigned on their arrival.

Halfway down the corridor, she began to open doors, all the while frantically calling his name. Her eyes burned with soot, and tears for Matthew began to slide down her cheeks. A wall of flame erupted at the far end of the hall. Still no sign of him.

"Matthew!" she shouted, backing toward the stairs at the rear she had just come up. "Matthew—where are you?"

She heard his voice then, somewhere on the level below. When she turned toward the sound, she saw the stairs had blossomed into flame.

"Matthew!"

"Jessie!" He was racing up the burning staircase, running like a madman, wrapped in a water-soaked sheet. Barreling through the orange and red flames, he appeared like a specter on the opposite side, the edge of the cloth ablaze. He tossed the sheet away and kept on coming.

"Jessie!"

Then she was in his arms, clinging to him, repeating his name, and crying with relief that he was all right. "We have to get out of here." But Matthew was already moving, heading toward one of the bedchambers that hadn't yet been swallowed by the blaze.

"I can't believe you came up here," he said.

Flames pressed in on them from both ends of the hall. "Both staircases are burning. Dear God, Matthew—how will we ever get down?"

"The roof." He jerked open the door. "It's the only way out."

Jessie's stomach knotted. "We can't possibly jump three stories."

But he only tugged her into an empty bedchamber and closed the door against the heat. He didn't pause till he reached the window. "Look. A lower section of the roof joins the building just below the room next door. We'll have to jump from there. We can make our way toward the rear of the house and find a way down once we're there."

Jessie didn't argue as he urged her back into the hallway and into another bedchamber. The east wing was an inferno, orange and yellow flames eating at the walls, the temperature so hot each breath seared her lungs. They raced to the window and Matthew threw it open. Jessie ducked her head outside and saw the second-story roof below.

"Can you make it?" he asked.

"I'll make it."

"I'll have to go first, try to land on the ridge or grab hold of it, then I can catch hold of you."

Jessie just nodded. Matt squeezed her hand, then swung

his legs over the sill and launched himself forward. She fought not to close her eyes as he landed on the ridge of the roof and scrambled to keep from falling off.

Relief poured through her when she saw that he was safe.

As soon as he was settled, he reached up for her. "Jump!" he shouted. "I'll catch you."

She didn't wait. There wasn't time for that—the room was filled with smoke and the roof could go at any moment. She said a quick prayer for their safety, took off her sandals, and jumped. A gust of cold air rushed past. She felt a jolt of pain as her feet hit the hard slate roof, then Matthew's solid arms were around her, dragging her to safety.

"I've got you," he whispered, his head tilting forward against hers. She could feel him trembling, knew that her own body shook just as hard.

His fingers brushed her cheek. He tipped her head up. "We can't stay here. We have to leave before the roof gives way. Are you ready?"

She managed a shaky nod.

Matt gripped her hand as they picked their way along the ridge of the roof, then down a steep valley to a portion of the roof that was closer to the ground. "Doing all right?" he asked.

Jessie swallowed and wet her dry lips. "So far."

"Good girl." He helped her along a narrow walkway that led to the rear, as low to the ground as they were going to get. "We're almost there, love. Just hold on a little bit longer."

As frightened as she was, something warm trickled through her. He had never spoken to her that way. They reached the rear of the house and she glanced at the ground below. "Will you go first and catch me?"

He grinned, his teeth a flash of white against the black streaks of soot on his face. "I promise."

He jumped and hit the ground rolling, came up on his feet, and held his hands out for her. "Come on, love. You're almost safe."

Jessie smiled at him and jumped, sailing through the air, landing in his arms and knocking them both to the ground. She lay there a moment, sprawled on top of him, the air compressed from her lungs. She could feel the strength and hardness of his frame as he held her tightly against him, but the heat of the fire reminded them they were still too close and they hurriedly climbed to their feet.

Matthew caught her hand and they started to run, but she stumbled as a shaft of pain shot into her ankle.

"Damn. You probably sprained it when you landed." Sliding an arm beneath her knees, he swept her up and started walking, carrying her away from the blaze to a place of safety beneath a distant tree. Exhausted, he leaned against the rough bark of the trunk and sank down in the shadows, cradling Jessie in his arms.

Her head rested on his shoulder. She could feel his labored breathing and the powerful beat of his heart. One of his hands sifted gently through her hair.

"You went up there for me," he said softly.

Jessie looked into his dear, handsome face. "I had to."

Matt's hand trembled as he cupped Jessie's cheek. "You risked your life . . ." He still couldn't believe it. It was reckless, insane for her to endanger herself that way. He tilted her head back, stroked along her jaw. There was something in her eyes, something turbulent, and so compelling it took his breath away. Brushing a lock of pale hair from her cheeks, he bent his head and slowly settled his mouth over her lips.

Just the slightest pressure, the softest caress. Her bottom lip quivered beneath the brush of his tongue. Only a moment's pause, then she opened to him and he tasted her more fully. He knew he shouldn't, that touching Jessie Fox was forbidden, but the specter of death had been so near and he had almost lost her.

He thought how brave she had been, how fearless in the face of overwhelming danger. He stroked her cheek and silky strands of hair wrapped around his fingers. She smelled of woodsmoke, and her skin was warm from the heat of the flames. Only a moment more, he told himself, kissing her more deeply, but he couldn't pull away and the need for her swelled inside him. She whispered his name and he ravished her mouth, his tongue sweeping deeply, taking what he knew he should not have.

His hands found her breasts, cupped them, caressed them through the cool, slippery silk of her dress. Her nipple crested, grew pebble-hard beneath his fingers. He worked the bud, making it distend, and heard her soft little whimper of pleasure.

He should stop, he knew, but memories of the fire rose inside him and hot desire licked through his veins. He was hard with need, aching to be inside her. She could have died up there, died trying to save him.

His insides twisted to think what he might have lost. He deepened the kiss and the need to touch her overwhelmed him. Instead of letting her go, he unbuttoned the jeweled clasp on her shoulder, lowered the gown, and filled his hands with her breasts.

Passion rose like a hot blaze inside him. His loins grew heavy, thick with need, his arousal pressing hard against his breeches. He stroked her breasts, cupped them gently, molded them in his palms. They were as lovely as he remembered, the fullness tinged pink in the light of the flames, tilting seductively upward.

"Jessie," he whispered, aching for her, wanting to feel her beneath him, to sheath himself in her softness. Lowering his head, he took a dusky tip into his mouth. Her fingers dug into the muscles across his shoulders. Her back arched up. He teased her nipple with his tongue, drew her breast deeply into his mouth and laved it gently, then circled the crest until she whimpered and cried out his name.

Desire throbbed in his loins, rode him like a restless master. The Grecian gown climbed to above her knees. He slid it even higher, exposing a portion of her pale creamy thighs.

His hand skimmed over her flesh and the touch of her skin enflamed him. He needed her. God, how he needed her.

Reason receded. What if she had died? He couldn't think, couldn't force his mind past the heat and the smoke, the towering flames that all mixed together with his white-hot, blazing desire for her.

He kissed her again, deeply, thoroughly, touching her all the while. He was determined to reach the core of her, to feel her damp heat, to stroke her there, and give her pleasure, but the sound of voices began to seep in, carried above the crackle of the flames. He felt Jessie stiffen.

"Matthew?" She lifted her head, dazed, as if she had been in a trace, her voice honey-rough and more appealing than he ever could have imagined. "Oh, dear God, what have we done?"

He shook with the power of his need. "Easy, love," he said softly, fighting to regain control. Inwardly he cursed himself, incredulous at what he'd let happen, how completely he had lost himself. He buttoned her dress with a shaky hand and adjusted her clothes, trying to understand what had occurred, why he had behaved so insanely. But his mind remained muddled, as dark and smoky as the hallways inside the house.

Something had happened between them. Something important, he knew. Nothing was the same, would ever be the same again, yet he still could not fathom what it was.

"They're coming, Matthew. Your father and Lady Bainbridge. The duke and Lord Pickering . . . Caroline Winston." This last she whispered, her face gone suddenly pale.

He knew he should reassure her, say that what happened wasn't her fault, that everything would be all right. But things were happening too quickly. He needed time to think, to reason things out. In only a few short minutes, his life had been turned upside down.

"Matthew!" His father's voice rang out. "Thank God, the two of you are safe."

He eased Jessie away from him, checked to be sure her

clothes were in place, and rose to his feet. "We nearly didn't make it. It was touch and go for a while. Thank God, the roof didn't fall until we were down."

His father looked pale. The marquess turned to Jessie, still sitting beneath the tree. "Jessica, my dearest girl," the old man eased down beside her, "are you certain that you are all right?" Jessie looked into his worried face and immediately burst into tears.

Guilt knifed through him. How could he have taken such advantage? She'd been numb with shock and fear—she had nearly died in the flames. He cleared his throat, worked to make his voice come out even.

"She's twisted an ankle and swallowed a roomful of smoke, but other than that, she should be fine once you get her back home."

Jessie blinked and focused her big blue eyes on him. "We couldn't find you. I thought you were still upstairs. I was afraid you had fallen asleep, that you wouldn't wake up until it was too late."

"I was in my room when the fire first broke out. When I started downstairs, I saw people trapped in one of the second-floor card rooms. I helped them down the servants' stairs to safety. Father was there when I came out. That's how I knew you were up there. He told me you had gone back in to get me."

It was an incredible thing to do. He still could hardly believe it.

The Duke of Milton moved closer, bent, and knelt beside Jessie. "You are the bravest woman I have ever known." He clasped her hand in his long slim fingers and gave it a gentle squeeze. "The absolute bravest."

"Yes . . . she most certainly is," said Caroline Winston, who stood just a few feet away. Dimly Matt noticed she hadn't a smudge anywhere on her perfectly groomed person. She had obviously been among the first to leave. He wondered if Caroline had been the least bit concerned for his welfare.

"At least we're all safe," said Lady Bainbridge, whose wig was long gone, her Madame Pompadour costume torn in several places, the hem hanging down below her wide panniered skirt.

His father looked equally disheveled, his hands and face black with soot. Even the duke's face was smudged, his coat and breeches soggy with water from the bucket brigade.

"I'm sorry to say the house is a total loss," said his father. "Unfortunately, there is nothing more we can do. Since the stables are intact, our carriage and horses safe, I suggest we gather our servants and set off for home."

The duke slid an arm around Jessie's shoulder and she swayed slightly against him. "I agree. A return to London is the only sane course." His admiring gaze still clung to Jessie. "Miss Fox has suffered more than enough for one evening."

"I was speaking of Belmore," the marquess corrected. "My son must return to his ship, and I believe Jessica and I have had enough excitement for a while."

She glanced at Matt and her pallid cheeks infused with a hint of color. "Yes . . . I should like very much to go home."

"Of course," the duke said gallantly, helping Jessie to her feet. His attention swung to the marquess. "With your permission, as soon as Jessica is recovered, I should like to pay a call at Belmore."

Matt ignored a ripple of displeasure. The duke's intentions were honorable. He wasn't yet sure about his own. He needed time to think, time to sift through the confusion of feelings that had ensnared him since the moment he'd discovered Jessie was in danger, that she was risking her life for him.

"Of course, your grace," his father said to the duke, "we should be delighted to see you." But his eyes stayed on Matt's, trying to read his thoughts. "For now, however, I should simply like to take our leave."

Matt silently agreed. The sooner he escaped from Benhamwood and his tangle of emotions, the sooner he'd be able to think. He wasn't a man who acted rashly. Especially not in something as important as this. He steeled himself not to look at Jessie and set off walking toward the stables.

*C*hapter *E*leven

*J*essie wandered through the Belmore gardens, making her way to the little-used greenhouse at the opposite end. Since their return from Benhamwood, once her ankle was healed, she had begun spending time there when she wasn't with the children. She was working to prepare the soil, determined to fill the place with exotic plants, anything to absorb the empty hours and keep her from thinking of Matthew.

He had been gone three weeks, had left for Portsmouth just hours after their arrival at Belmore. His father's arguments that he should stay just one more day could not dissuade him.

All the way to Belmore, he had seemed oddly remote. He'd said nothing more about the fire, or what had happened between them. There had been only a single moment before his departure when the mask he wore slid away.

Standing out in front, his valise packed and tied on the back of his horse, he had offered his hand to his father, then gripped the older man's shoulders in a show of affection that was rare for him.

"Take care of yourself, Father," he said.

"As I pray that you will, my son."

Matthew just nodded. When he turned to Jessie, he lifted her chin with his fingers and looked into her eyes.

"And you, my lovely little hoyden, if you ever risk yourself that way again—for me or anyone else—the gravest danger you shall face will come from me." The soft look faded. He turned with brusque efficiency, mounted the saddle horse he had rented for his journey from Portsmouth, and simply rode away.

He made no apology for his passions this time. Perhaps he didn't regret what had occurred. Or perhaps he believed the fault was hers, that she should have stopped him—as any true lady would have done.

As surely Caroline Winston would have done.

Jessie's heart twisted to think of the way she had behaved. Ending Matthew's fevered kisses had never even occurred to her. They had battled the fire together and almost died. Life had never seemed more precious. Her love for him had never been more fierce.

Love. She had never admitted the word, though in her heart she had known from the start that's what it was. She had loved Matt Seaton for as long as she could remember. And yet what they had done was surely wrong.

Matthew belonged to another. He desired her, yes. He had never denied it. But a lady would have curbed the lust that drove him. She would have swooned at the feel of his mouth on her breasts, his hands skimming hotly up her thighs.

A lady would have been shocked and horrified.

Jessie shivered against the breeze that swept through the garden, fluttering the petals of a nearby rose. Like mother, like daughter, she couldn't help thinking. Remembering the scalding heat she had felt when Matthew touched her, Jessie was afraid it was the truth.

And yet she would never regret that night. She had never seen him so wildly protective, so achingly tender, so demandingly fierce. At the time she'd been certain he had felt something for her. But if he had, surely he would have spoken, told her he had come to care for her at least a little.

Matthew said nothing. It was clear he still intended marriage to Lady Caroline.

She recalled his words during the waltz: *Jeremy is an honorable man. He's wealthy and powerful. If he asks for*

your hand in marriage, then undoubtedly you should ac-
cept. Her heart ached to know he wanted her to wed another
man.

Last week the duke had come to call, just as he had promised. He had asked Papa Reggie to accept his suit, then pro-
posed most gallantly out in the garden.

Jessie had stalled, begged him to give her more time, told
him that she was still not recovered from her terrible night at
Benhamwood. The duke was persistent, penning odes to her
beauty and courage, praising her intelligence and wit. He
wanted her for his duchess, he said. There was no one else
who would possibly do. He didn't mention love, but spoke of
his undying affection, that should she refuse him, his heart
would scarce recover.

In the beginning Papa Reggie had been oddly silent on
the matter, considering that in London he and the countess
had hoped for just such a match. The day after his grace's
departure he had taken to his bed with another bout of the
ague that constantly plagued him, and she had sat worriedly
beside him. This time he spoke at length of the duke and his
proposal, pointing out the benefits of marrying a man of his
wealth and position. Jessie had smiled and nodded and felt
sick to her stomach.

Now as she plucked a long-stemmed red rose from among
those growing along the garden path, she wondered how
much longer the marquess would wait before he pressed her
to accept the duke's proposal?

"Do ye see 'er?"

Crouched behind the garden wall, Danny Fox looked at
his sister and smiled. "I see the lit'l baggage."

"I told ye she'd be 'ere."

"So ya did, Connie, me boy. I thought she'd stay in London
a bit longer'n she did." She would have, he was sure, spending a goodly sum of the marquess's blunt—as he would have
done—if it hadn't been for the bleedin' fire. Stories of the
terrible night at Benhamwood, of the death of two of Pick-

ering's servants and the loss of his magnificent country house were the talk of the city—and so were tales of Jessie Fox's bravery.

In every inn and tavern, they spoke of Lord Pickering and the woman who had run into the burning house to save her distant cousin. There was even an article in the three-day-old *Morning Post* Connie had found on the street and asked one of his friends to read.

"The gardner's gone off," the taller man said, interrupting Danny's thoughts. "She's standin' there all by 'erself."

He grunted with satisfaction. "Let's go talk to the chit afore someone else comes round."

Jessie turned at the sound of footfalls, then tensed at the sight of her brother's hard-etched face. "Danny, what . . . what are you doing here?"

"Well now, is that any kind o' a greetin' for yer long-lost brother?"

Jessie lifted her chin, refusing to let him intimidate her as he was always so easily able to do. "What do you want? We're a long way from Eylesbury, and Belmore has no fair. Why have you come here? How did you know where to find me?"

"I've me ways. I should think ya'd remember."

"I asked what it is that you want."

Danny's thin lips pulled down at the corners. "I'm sorry to say, I've come to be in a bit o' a pickle."

"You're always in a pickle, Danny."

"Yeah, well, thin's 'ave changed in the years since I've seen ya. I'm a married man now. Ya didn't know that, did ya? I'm a father, too. Got a lit'l blond gel looks like ya when ya was a babe."

"I don't believe you."

"Why? Ya don't think a mort would 'ave me?"

"Not if she had any sense."

"I've a wife—God's truth. Ya know I've always 'ad a way wit' the ladies."

That was no lie. He promised them the moon, gave them

the back of his hand instead, and they still wound up whoring for him.

"Even if you do have a wife, what does that have to do with me?"

Danny stepped closer, ran a soft, slightly effeminate hand over her cheek. "I need money, lit'l sis." He grinned, a too-slick smile that made her stomach feel queasy. "Ya've got more'n enough o' it. A lit'l for yer brother won't hurt ya."

"Forget it." She started to walk away, but Danny's harsh tone slowed her paces.

"Yer gonna pay me, gel. If ya don't, yer gonna be sorry."

Jessie stopped walking, a shiver creeping up her spine. She slowly turned to face him. "Are you threatening me, Danny?"

He held out his hands palm up in a placating gesture. "I didn't say that, now did I? Ya could 'ardly blame *me* if news some'ow leaked out who ya really are? That'd 'ardly be old Danny's fault, now would it, gel?"

Oh God, she should have known something like this would happen. If only she hadn't gone that day to the fair. If only he hadn't found her. "The marquess is a powerful man, Danny. He won't let you hurt me."

"The old man's sick, the way I 'ear it. Scandal the likes of that—the truth all over London that 'is precious lit'l Jessie is the daughter o' a whore—might just put 'im in 'is grave."

Oh, dear Lord, it was the truth. She stared into her half brother's brown eyes, actually more an odd burnished yellow that was always a little bit eerie. Her stomach churned while her mind frantically searched for a way out of her dilemma.

"All right, I'll help you—but I don't have as much as you think. I can give you what I've saved. I can't ask the marquess for more or he'll get suspicious. You'll have to be satisfied with the amount I've got."

He scratched his chin, which carried the slight rash of a recent shave. "'Ow much is that?"

"Almost two hundred pounds. It's my savings for the past several years."

He shrugged his shoulders, rustling the tailcoat he wore, the sleeves of which were a little too short. "I suppose it'll 'ave to do." He smiled tightly. "After all, a man's gotta feed 'is family."

She wondered if he really was married and felt sorry for the poor girl if he was. "I'll give you the money on one condition—you have to swear on Mama's grave this will be the last time you come here—the last time you ever ask me for money."

Danny's thin face actually went a little pale. He'd always had a thing about their mother. His love for Eliza Fox was the only streak of decency she had ever witnessed in him. "Say it, Danny. Swear on Mama's grave you won't ask me for money again."

He threw up his hands and sighed in resignation. "All right, I swear."

"On Mama's grave. Say it, Danny."

"On our poor dead mother's grave—are ya 'appy now?"

"Wait for me behind the garden wall. I'll be back in just a minute. Then I want you out of here."

It didn't take long to get the coins. The pouch felt heavy in her hands on the way back down the stairs. She had saved for so long . . . her hand shook as she handed it over.

"Thank ya, sister dear. Ye've a kind 'eart—'asn't she, Connie?" His smug smile did nothing to soothe her nerves. She watched him walk away but didn't relax until she saw his lean figure disappear down the road leading away from Belmore.

Matt paced the quarterdeck of the *Norwich*. The wind had freshened, snapping the white canvas sails above his head. The cool air held a salty tang and in the dim light belowdecks, the notes of a mouth organ drifted up from a seaman's hammock.

They were anchored off the French coast, blockading the harbor at Brest. Plymouth now served as their home port, but it would be nearly two more months till they returned there for supplies.

"Are you ready to begin the drill, Captain Seaton?"

Matt stopped pacing. "Aye, Lieutenant Munsen. You may begin whenever you wish."

The red-haired lieutenant, his second in command, gave the signal to clear the decks to prepare the ship for action, and the five-hundred-man crew of the *Norwich* began the well-synchronized movements that would prepare the sixty-four gun, two-hundred-foot-long ship of war to meet the enemy in battle.

A ship of the line could be readied for action in under six minutes, the gun ports opened, powder brought up from the magazines, shot carried up from the lockers. Since a number of the crew slept on the gun deck, their possessions had to be neatly stored. If not they were lost in the organized chaos of hammocks being stowed and mess tables hoisted up into the beams. Once the decks were cleared from bow to stern, the guns were loaded, run out, and made ready to fire.

The *Norwich*'s record was five minutes and twenty-seven seconds.

Matt checked the gold watch that hung from a fine-linked chain in his pocket. "Five minutes, thirty-five seconds. Not a new record, but definitely very good time. It appears, Lieutenant, you and the men didn't miss me much while I was gone."

Lieutenant Munsen smiled. "Believe it or not, sir, we're all delighted to have you back."

The ship had been recoppered, then returned to sea before Matt's shore leave was ended. During the time he spent away, he usually grew restless, began to yearn for the sea and his ship.

This time, instead of the peace he usually knew when he returned, he felt listless, unsettled in some way he couldn't quite name. Jessie rode hard on his mind. He thought of her actions the night of the fire. Running into a burning building—it was foolish—insane to take such a risk. Exactly the reckless behavior he might expect from Jessie Fox.

That she had done it for him was what amazed him. It

changed things, somehow, forced him to look through her rashness to the woman she was inside, made him want to discover what might drive her to act in such a way.

It occurred to him that Jessie was protective by nature. He had seen it with Viola Quinn, seen it with his father, and again with Gwendolyn Lockhart. Jessie would do anything for the people she cared for. If risking her life was any indication, apparently she cared a great deal for him.

But how did he feel about her?

He had asked himself the question a dozen times since he had left her. He wanted her. He couldn't possibly deny that. He lusted for her every waking moment and even in his sleep. That's what he had felt the night of the fire—lust—at least that's what he'd told himself on the journey from Belmore to Portsmouth. But weeks had passed since then. Long days and nights when he'd had time to think.

"Ah, there you are, Captain. I thought you might be up here. The drill went well, I suspect." Dr. Graham Paxton, a slight man in his thirties, was the senior medical officer aboard the *Norwich* and one of Matt's best friends.

"Better than I expected. Lieutenant Munsen performed well in my absence."

"Are you going to recommend him to your position when you retire?"

"Yes. I believe he'll make a very good captain."

"That time could still be some ways away, if you intend to remain on duty until we fight the French."

"You know I have to do that."

"There's been no recent news of French fleet movements. With Ganteaume and his ships still trapped, Villeneuve isn't strong enough to mount an attack."

"No, they can't engage us yet, but they are more than eager to do so. Villeneuve grows restless raiding in the Indies. Sooner or later, Napoléon will order his return and he'll attempt to ally himself with Ganteaume. This time, I believe Nelson will let him. He wants this confrontation. He wants the threat of invasion ended, once and for all."

The doctor looked off toward the horizon. He was a family man, married to a woman he adored, had a three-year-old daughter and a four-year-old son. "There'll be a number of Spanish ships as well. Together their fleet will be as large as our own, perhaps even larger. The battle will be costly, in both equipment and lives."

The doctor shrugged his shoulders, rustling the fabric of his uniform coat. "Myself, I'm no more afraid to die than the next man, but it bothers me to think of my children growing up without their father."

Matt had thought of that, too. It was the reason he hadn't gone ahead with his betrothal to Caroline. Yet this time, knowing the risk, he had finally decided to act. He had made a decision just that morning, or perhaps it had occurred during the long sleepless hours last night. He had skipped the morning meal and sat at his desk instead, penning one note after another until he finally found the difficult words he searched for. He was sending a letter to his father, asking the marquess for Jessie's hand in marriage—if the little hoyden would have him.

He wasn't sure when he'd be able to post it. Sometimes months went by with no inbound mail and no way to send word home. But at the very first opportunity, he intended to see it done, at least discover where he stood with her.

Even if she agreed to the match, he would have to tread carefully, and it couldn't happen soon. He would have to speak to Caroline first, allow her to save face, to be the one to end their unofficial betrothal. It wasn't a conversation he looked forward to. He felt guilty for misleading her, for breaking the promises he had made to her and her father, but the fact was he no longer wished to marry her.

Perhaps he was making a mistake, he couldn't be sure. In truth, Jessie was nothing like the wife he had imagined, but now that sort of woman seemed a pale imitation of the spirited young woman who had risked her life to save him the night of the fire.

Matthew found himself smiling. She would lead him a

merry chase, to be sure, but in the days since he'd been gone, he discovered he missed her stubborn independence, even her unwanted opinions on subjects heretofore reserved to the bastions of men.

In time she would learn her place. He would personally see to that. Jessie needed a husband who could bring her in hand and he was just the man to do it. In truth, he looked forward to the challenge.

Leaning on the rail of the quarterdeck, Matt glanced down at the holystoned deck, at the men unfurling sail, manning the capstan and the massive anchor cables, at the English, Scots, Irish, Welsh, and American crew he commanded. He had captained a ship of five hundred sailors—surely he could handle one small, fiery-tempered woman.

The restlessness returned. The doctor eyed him shrewdly. He wondered if his friend could tell how eager he was to return to England and home.

Jessie sat hunched over her desk at the front of her makeshift schoolroom. The children had already left for home, giving her a chance to go over the papers they had written. She smiled as she studied each child's essay on what he had done while she had been in London, pleased at the progress they were making.

A knock at the open door drew her attention to the footman who stood in the opening.

"His lordship wishes to see you, miss. He asks that you come to his chambers at half-past two."

A tendril of worry slipped through her. "He's all right, isn't he? His condition hasn't worsened?"

"No, miss. He's simply with his solicitor at present. He said he would be finished by half-past two."

She breathed a sigh of relief but it was short lived. She was afraid she knew what he wanted. He had mentioned the duke several more times, and though the marquess was feeling better, he hadn't improved as rapidly as either of them had wished.

Jessie stared down at the papers, but the blue script ran together in a blur. She worked another half hour, but her heart was no longer in it, and she found it difficult to concentrate. Finally she gave up and made her way back to the house to freshen up before her meeting. When she finished, she checked the small clock ticking above her mantel. Nearly two-thirty.

With a stomach that had been churning ever since the footman's arrival, she headed down the hall to Papa Reggie's suite.

"Miss Fox is here, your lordship, as you requested." The marquess's valet, Lemuel Green, stood at his bedside. The man had been in his service for more than forty years. "Shall I send her in?"

Reggie sighed. He wished he were feeling well enough to sup with Jessica tonight, speak of this over a pleasant meal, but he hadn't been well since Benhamwood.

"Yes, Lemuel, ask her to please come in." He plumped the pillow a bit behind him, propping himself up a little straighter against the headboard, then picked a piece of lint off the front of his burgundy silk dressing gown. "And open the window. The place has the foul stench of medicine about it."

The gray-haired valet nodded, went about his tasks, then left the room. A few minutes later, Jessica walked in. She was dressed in powder blue today, the same shade as her eyes. He had always liked her in blue.

He patted the chair beside his bed, recently vacated by his London solicitor, Wendell Corey, there on matters of his will. Wendell had declined his invitation to stay for supper. Jessica would be taking her meal alone again tonight. "Sit down, my dear."

She bent and kissed his cheek, sat down and smoothed her simple blue muslin skirt. "How are you feeling, Papa Reggie?"

"Fine . . . well, better, at least. I am certain, in a day or two, I shall once again be shipshape and back on my feet." He hoped so, but the truth was, he couldn't be sure. And if something did happen to him, Jessica would be left to fend for herself.

"I asked you here," he said, "because this morning I received another posting from the duke."

She studied the hands she clasped tightly in her lap. "I was afraid that was the subject you wished to discuss."

"You told me yourself, on more than one occasion, you found his grace to be the most agreeable of your suitors."

"Yes . . . Jeremy is a very nice man."

"I shall be honest with you, my dear. I had hoped, these past few weeks, to receive some word from Matthew. It is difficult for him to correspond, of course, confined as he is aboard his ship. But in truth, where Matthew has a will, he has always found a way. Knowing that, I don't believe his plans for the future have changed."

She stared at a place above his head. "I told you before that Matthew and I would not suit."

"I didn't believe that then, I do not now. I believe you care a great deal for my son and that perhaps he holds some degree of affection for you. But Matthew is not the sort to act rashly. In truth, it is not his way to bend overly much, once his course is set."

Jessica said nothing.

"Therefore, since it is my fondest wish to see you settled, I am asking that you accept the young duke's offer of marriage. I believe he cares for you greatly and I think, in time, that he could make you happy."

She said nothing for a while, blinked rapidly several times, then brushed at a tear that spilled down her cheek. "I'm sorry." She tried to smile. "Women cry at the oddest times, don't they?"

He reached over and patted her hand. Her skin felt icy beneath his fingers. "I know that you are uncertain, that you would rather not marry quite yet. If things were different, there would be no need for such haste."

"If my background were different, you mean. If there wasn't the risk of discovery."

"I'm afraid so, my dear."

"I have to know, Papa Reggie, what would happen if the truth leaked out. If the duke were my husband—"

"But you see, my dear, that is exactly the point. The Duke of Milton may be young but his wealth and power are immeasurable. Even if your past came to light, he would be able to protect you. No one would dare to question his choice of wife, or say anything untoward against you."

Her throat moved but she didn't speak for the longest time. "If . . . if I accept the duke's proposal . . . if I agreed to be his wife . . . how long before we would wed?"

Reggie sighed. He wished he could give her more time, let her get used to the notion, but he just did not dare. "The sooner, I'm afraid, the better. If something should happen to me before you were properly settled, I could not rest in my grave."

"Nothing is going to happen—I won't let it!"

He gently squeezed her hand, which had tightened into a fist. "I'm certain you are right. But the chance remains. When his grace was last here, we discussed the need for urgency, should you accept his offer, and he is agreed."

Jessica bowed her head. He could feel slight tremors running through her. When she glanced up, tears shimmered in her eyes. "Jeremy is intelligent and kind," she said softly. "I think he would make a good husband." She forced her lips into a smile. "I shall be happy to accept his proposal. A woman would be a fool not to marry the Duke of Milton."

Some of his own tension eased. "Quite right, my dear. I am glad you understand the importance of this decision."

She released his hand and came to her feet. "Since I am new to this sort of thing, if you don't mind, I shall leave the details up to you. Perhaps Lady Bainbridge could be of assistance."

"Of course, she will. Corney will be ecstatic at the news."

The too-bright smile remained on her face. "Then I shall take my leave. I should like to tell Viola. I'm certain she will be equally pleased." She bent over and kissed his cheek.

"Get some rest, Papa Reggie. I shall check on you again before I retire for the eve."

He simply nodded. He had done what was best, what his
ailing health had forced him to do. It wasn't the way he had
hoped things would turn out—Matthew's stubbornness had
seen to that.

His thoughts strayed to his son and it occurred to him
that in the end, Matthew might wind up paying the highest
price of all.

A rough sea dragged the *Norwich* into another heavy trough.
A slate gray sky hid the sun and boded a storm; a light mist
moistened the decks and clung to the sailors' woolen clothes.
Inside the wheelhouse, Matt stood beside the huge teak
wheel. He glanced up when Graham Paxton walked in.

"I hear we've received a message. Apparently we're about
to have company."

Matt nodded. "A signal came in from the *Dreadnought*."
Another ship in the line of blockade, the one nearest the
Norwich. "One of our sloops is headed this way, the *Weazel*
out of Plymouth."

"Perhaps she is carrying news of the war." The smaller
boats serviced the larger vessels, transporting communica-
tions, mail, and supplies.

"Perhaps." He didn't tell Graham that when the ship returned to Plymouth, she would be carrying news from him.
The letter he had written to his father. It sat in an isolated
corner of his desk and every day since he had penned it, he
had tried to come up with a way to see it posted.

At last he would have the chance.

"Do you think the French are headed this way?"

"I don't know," Matt said. "It certainly wouldn't surprise
me." In a way he wished they were. One way or another, his
duty to the navy would be ended.

The frigate arrived around noon, bringing a few fresh supplies for the officers' table, fresh vegetables, eggs, and cheeses,

but the message she carried wasn't news of the war—it was a personal letter for him.

Matthew's chest felt tight as he carried the missive down the ladder to the deck below, stepped inside his quarters and closed the door. He stripped off his jacket and sat down to read it—a message sealed with the Belmore crest.

His hands shook as he opened it. The navy didn't send special couriers except in the gravest circumstance. Had something happened to his father? It had been nearly two months since he had left England. The marquess had seemed pale and a bit strained on the journey from Benhamwood to Belmore, but considering the fire, that was understandable. Matt had been certain, once the old man was home, his health would improve.

Parting the thin sheets of paper, he nervously started to read, then relief rolled through him at the sight of his father's masculine scroll. The marquess was obviously alive. Was it Jessie, then? Tension swept back in. Had something happened to her? God knew as daring as she was—

His mind shifted from one thought to the next as he continued to scan the words, went from worry, to disbelief, to wrenching disappointment, and finally to towering anger.

"Damn him! Damn him to bloody hell!" He damned them both, in fact, Jessie for acting on the greedy nature he had convinced himself she did not have, and his father for using his considerable influence to bend him to his will.

He stared hard at the letter.

Dear Matthew,
   It brings me great happiness to inform you that our beloved Jessica has accepted a proposal of marriage from his grace, the Duke of Milton. Due to concern for my health, the wedding will take place one month hence, in London at St. James's Cathedral. Your superior officers have agreed to a short leave of absence from your ship so that you may attend. For Jessica's sake, it is imperative you do so. We must show his

grace and the rest of Society that our Jessica has complete and total Belmore support.

I look forward as always to your arrival.

> *With greatest affection,*
> *Your father, the Marquess of Belmore*

Matthew wadded up the letter and tossed it into the waste bin beneath his small oak desk. Half the crew had seen his face when he had received the letter. They had been certain, as he was, that an incident of gravest consequence had occurred.

His jaw tightened until the muscles cramped with pain. Perhaps it had. Perhaps he had been saved from the greatest folly of his life!

He stood up from his chair so fast he nearly toppled it over. He caught it before it hit the floor, righted it, and set it back beneath his desk, then started pacing, long strides and quick turns in front of the oak-manteled hearth. The captain's quarters aboard a ship of the line were lavish, elegant, and roomy. In that moment they seemed tight and confining, so airless he could barely breathe.

He strode across the cabin and opened one of the portholes, but the breeze that drifted in did nothing to cool the heat of his temper. He returned to the desk, rummaged through the trash, picked up and smoothed out the letter. Checking the date inscribed in blue ink at the top, he saw the posting was nearly three weeks old.

The sloop still sat alongside the *Norwich*, awaiting his reply to the missive. He should send word to his father, tell him he and Jessie could both go hang—that she hardly needed him to marry someone else.

He wouldn't, he knew, because his father's request for his presence had actually been no request at all. Couched between the lines was a direct command from his superiors. He was being ordered to attend the Duke of Milton's wedding. Allied together, his father and the duke wielded considerable power. A captain of His Majesty's Navy was no match for them at all.

He jerked open the drawer of the little desk and drew out the letter he had intended to send to his father, the letter that asked for Jessie's hand. He tore it in half, halved it again, then once more before he tossed it into the waste bin.

He strode to his berth and dug beneath it for his valise. The commander of the sloop would be anxiously waiting. Matt was certain the captain's orders were to carry him to London. The man undoubtly knew Captain Seaton would be coming aboard.

Matt wasn't certain whether to curse his luck—or thank God he'd been saved from the likes of Jessie Fox.

*C*hapter *T*welve

*T*hey had been living in London for the past two weeks, immersed in a whirlwind of preparations.

"Jessica can't possibly wed in so short a time," Lady Bainbridge had said. "Reginald, what on earth are you thinking?" But seeing that his course was set and the duke apparently agreed—perhaps was even grateful—she had finally consented to help, as the marquess had been certain she would.

From that day forward, Jessie hadn't a moment to herself. When she wasn't scurrying along behind the dowager countess, selecting everything from feathered bonnets to rare perfumes, she was standing for hours having her trousseau fitted, an ensemble of gowns even richer than the ones she already owned. A duchess dressed in the height of extravagance; nothing less would do.

With every pinprick she suffered, every muscle that ached from standing on her feet for so long, she wondered if her dream of being a lady wasn't a nightmare instead.

During the journey from Belmore and the first few days after their arrival in London, she had been concerned for Papa Reggie's health—after all that was the reason for the hasty marriage—but his condition hadn't worsened. He had in fact recovered a little of his strength. They were staying at the Belmore town house, immersed once more in Society, attending balls, soirees, the theater, and the opera, mostly in company with Lady Bainbridge, and often accompanied by the duke.

He was a gentle young man, as she had believed, pleasant by nature, attentive, and always trying to please her. Unfortunately *young* was the word that best described him. Though Jeremy was five years her senior, he had lived such a sheltered life he was more a boy than a man.

Which only made comparisons between him and Matthew more depressing. She tried not to do it, to keep their images separate in her mind, to see Jeremy's slender youthful visage in a completely different light than she did the stern, masculine contours of Matthew's handsome profile. Occasionally it worked.

Occasionally.

But there were times like this one, three nights before the wedding, when she stood in front of the mirror next to Vi, preparing to dress for supper, that she couldn't help thinking of Matthew, wishing he were the man she would wed.

Or that she didn't have to marry at all.

"It won't be so bad, luv." Viola patted her shoulder. "Remember to count ye blessin's, instead o' the thin's ye can't 'ave."

Jessie smiled a bit sadly. "Was my thinking so obvious, Vi?"

"Only to me, luv. I've known ye too long not to see what's plain on ye face."

Jessie sighed. "I know you're right. I'm lucky to be marrying a man like the duke. He's kind and sweet, he's generous . . . I don't think there's anything I could ask that Jeremy would not do."

"That's right, luv. 'E's a 'andsome boy, too, wit' 'is big brown eyes and sandy 'air, and all them pretty white teeth."

"Unfortunately, that's the problem. Jeremy's a boy, not a man."

Vi just laughed. "They all grow up, sooner or later. That's part o' ye job as 'is wife, to 'elp 'im grow into a fine upstandin' man."

"Is it? Somehow that isn't the way I imagined it." A memory arose of Matthew's burning kisses, his big hands caressing her breasts. There was nothing boyish about Matt Seaton. The Earl of Strickland was definitely a man.

"Chin up, luv. It's certainly better'n livin' yer life on the streets."

Jessie smiled slightly. "There's a world of truth in that, Vi, and believe me I haven't forgotten. From now on I'll try to count my blessings, just like you said."

It turned out that wasn't so easy.

Not when she walked into the drawing room later that night, and saw Matt Seaton lounging in an overstuffed chair.

Jessie caught her breath as he came to his feet, tall, lean, and hard muscled, his manner lazy, almost insolent.

"Surprised to see me, Mistress Fox? And I thought having me here was partly your idea."

"Wh-What are you doing in London? I thought you were still at sea . . . off somewhere on your ship."

He started toward her, his strides long and purposeful, the look on his face slightly mocking. "I came for your wedding, of course. Marriage to a duke, no less. You ought to be proud of yourself."

Jessie's insides quivered. Dear God, Matthew was here! And looking more handsome than ever, his face newly bronzed, the tips of his dark golden hair lightened by the sun, his shoulders even wider than she remembered. Her stomach knotted with tension. Marrying the duke was going to be hard enough. Now instead of her new husband, every moment would be filled with thoughts of the marquess's son.

"H-How did you discover we planned to marry?"

He came closer still, didn't stop till he loomed above her, forcing her to look up into his face. She caught the faint scent of his cologne.

"My father sent a letter. Kind of him, wasn't it? He arranged everything, of course, spoke to Admiral Cornwallis himself. My father can do nearly anything, once he sets his mind to it."

Jessie swallowed hard. "But why . . . ? Why would he do such a thing?"

A voice spoke up from the doorway as the marquess strode in. "Because, Jessica, my dear, as your guardian, I believed you needed the family's support—the entire family, and that especially includes my son, the Belmore heir."

Jessie turned to Matthew. She nervously moistened her lips. "How long have you been in London?"

"I arrived this afternoon. Father and I have been chatting. I'm glad to see that his health has improved."

"Yes . . ." Jessie said. "I was afraid for him to travel. I thought perhaps we should wait, postpone the wedding for a while, but he insisted. Your father is even more determined than you when he puts his mind to something."

A corner of Matt's hard mouth tilted. "And no less than you, Mistress Fox . . . when you are bent on marrying a duke."

Jessie stiffened. For the first time she realized the emotion behind his controlled veneer was anger. But why? Matthew didn't want her. In fact he was the one who had advised her to marry the duke. "Jeremy will make a very good husband. Your father wishes me to marry and I will not disappoint him. If I remember correctly, my lord, it was your wish as well. You said that if Jeremy should ask, then I should accept his proposal. You should be happy to learn I have done so."

His smile looked more wolfish than warm. "Oh, I am, Mistress Fox. You have my heartiest blessing." He turned away from her and strode toward the door. "Now if the two of you will excuse me, I have plans for the evening. I shall see you on the morrow."

"I was hoping you would sup with us," his father put in. "It's been weeks since we've seen you."

"Not tonight."

"Tomorrow then? 'Tis the last chance we shall have to celebrate before the wedding. I've planned a small gathering in Jessica's honor. 'Tisn't the usual thing, only a handful of guests, but the duke has agreed to come, as well as his mother, the duchess. Cornelia will be there, of course, and Gwendolyn

Lockhart has agreed to attend. I was hoping for your presence, as well."

For a moment he did not answer and she thought he might refuse. Then he made a slight bow of his head. "As you wish, Father. Supper tomorrow night." With that he quit the room.

Jessie sagged down on the sofa. "I can't believe he is here."

"Of course he is here. He is the Belmore heir. It is only fitting that he attend your wedding."

Jessie looked up at him, her eyes cloudy with anguish. "How could you do this?" she whispered. "Don't you know how much harder this is going to be, now that Matthew is here?"

"Jessica—"

"I'm sorry," she said, rising once more to her feet. "I know you meant well. I just wish . . . I just wish you had told me." Following in Matthew's wake, Jessie fled out into the hallway and back up the stairs to her room.

The next day seemed interminable. Her wedding gown hung on the door to her armoire, brocaded white silk shot with silver, high-waisted, with small puffed sleeves. The bodice was trimmed in blue, and a long blue and silver train would be attached once the gown was in place. As beautiful as it was, it only made her feel worse.

Dear God, Matthew was here.

She had thought not to see him for months, perhaps even years. She would be settled by then, coming to terms with her new husband. Instead he was only down the hall, would be seated tonight at the dining table across from her. She would be forced to smile at him, make pleasant conversation, when she wanted to throw herself into his arms, to kiss him and tell him that she was in love with him.

She wouldn't do any such thing. Matthew didn't want her, except perhaps for a brief tumble in his bed. With the duke she would have children. She would be safe from her past, and in time they would be happy.

Jessie paced the floor, tried to read, tried to embroider—nothing worked. The hours dragged. Even Viola could not distract her. She sighed with relief when the gray of dusk settled in. After bathing and letting Vi upsweep her hair, she began to dress for the evening in a midnight blue silk gown trimmed with black tulle and shiny jet beads. It was an elegant dress with a slightly low bodice, a contrast to her modest white wedding gown, making her look womanly and seductive. Secretly, she hoped she could make Matthew burn.

"Ye best get on downstairs," Vi said, patting her shoulder. "Puttin' it off won't make it one bit easier."

The clock ticked loudly, reminding her she was late. Good, she thought with a surge of spirit, knowing how Matt abhorred tardiness, though she hadn't really done it on purpose. A last nervous glance in the mirror and she sailed out into the hallway and down the stairs. A footman slid open the doors to the drawing room, which was warmed by the soft yellow glow of burning lamps.

"Jessica, my dear, come in, come in. We have all of us been waiting."

"Good evening, Papa Reggie." She smiled as she received his kiss on the cheek, but inwardly she was shaking. "I didn't mean to be late."

"It's all right, my dear. Brides are supposed to be indulged." He smiled. "Your betrothed is here, along with his enchanting mother, her grace, the Duchess of Milton."

Jessie dropped into a curtsy. "Good evening, your graces."

"You look lovely," the duke said, bowing over her hand. "Doesn't she, Mother?"

The older woman smiled at her with warmth. "Jessica will make a very beautiful bride."

Jessie was still amazed at the duchess's ready acceptance of their betrothal. She had no title, after all, and even if the story the marquess had created of her parentage were true, it would make her merely his very distant cousin. It was Jeremy, she suspected, who had convinced his mother to allow the marriage. Jeremy wanted her for his wife, and the young duke always got anything he wanted.

Any other young man would have turned out selfish and spoiled.

Jessie smiled at him and tried not to let her eyes drift in search of Matthew. Even then she saw him, standing next to Gwen, smiling at something her petite, dark-haired friend had said. Just seeing that soft look aimed in Gwen's direction sent a sharp stab of jealousy sliding through her.

God in heaven, Gwen wasn't interested in Matthew, or any other man for that matter. Her dislike of the male sex ranked only slightly below the hatred she felt for her stepfather.

"Matthew," his father said to him, causing his dark golden head to come up. "Now that Jessica has arrived, why don't we all go in to supper?"

Deep blue eyes swung to hers, paused for several long moments. "Good idea," he said, forcing his gaze away, a brittle smile returning to his face. He offered an arm to Gwen, then made his way to Lady Bainbridge, while his father escorted Jeremy's mother, a stately, still dark-haired woman in her early fifties.

Jessie steeled herself as Matthew walked past. She turned and accepted the duke's offered arm.

"The gown is lovely," Jeremy said. "It brings out the blue of your eyes." His gaze lingered a moment on her breasts, then settled with warmth on her face. She wished she could return that warmth, but instead she felt cold inside and slightly sick to her stomach.

Supper seemed as interminable as the day had been, a lavish meal of creamed sole, partridge, and venison served on gold-rimmed Sevres china. Silver platters brimmed with succulent dishes: pheasant eggs in oyster sauce, sweetbreads of veal, an array of steaming vegetables, and a lovely molded sweet in the shape of a heart for dessert.

It all tasted like sawdust to Jessie.

In deference to the war, Portuguese wines instead of French

accompanied each course, and she drank a little more than she should have. She tried to keep her gaze fixed on Jeremy, who kept staring at her as if she were a Christmas present he would soon unwrap.

Matthew's face showed not the slightest emotion. He made all the polite responses, laughed at the proper moments, and kept his attention equally divided between Lady Bainbridge and Gwen.

Only once did he falter, a single moment when their blue eyes clashed and held. His looked angry, somewhat resentful, though she still couldn't figure out why.

Her own gaze held regret, and perhaps a bit of yearning. She wondered if Matthew would recognize it for what it was.

After supper the men retired for cigars and port, and the ladies made their way into the withdrawing room. Gwen must have noticed how tense she was, for several times during the hour she mentioned bridal nerves and Jessie's upcoming marriage, and stepped in to save her whenever there was a lapse in conversation.

With the wedding so near, supper ended early. The guests went home, and the three of them retired upstairs to their rooms. She heard Matthew's footfalls as he paced the floor next door. Eventually they fell silent. As tired as she was, Jessie glimpsed the purple flush of dawn before she fell asleep.

Matt spent the morning at his solicitor's. Wendell Corey worked for his father, and also handled affairs at his own estate, Seaton Manor. Matt wanted to be certain that in his absence, things had been running smoothly.

The meeting took longer than he intended. There were problems with some of the tenants, several unsolved thefts, and some rents that hadn't been paid. He'd be glad when he'd finally be home and able to handle the problems himself.

Once the meeting was ended, he hailed a hack out front on Threadneedle Street and made his way to St. James, stopping to depart the carriage midway down the block. A few moments later, he pushed through the door to Brooks, one of London's oldest and most respected gentlemen's clubs. With its black-and-white marble floors, painted ceilings, and Roman busts, the place had an air of distinction—as good a place as any to forget his troubles for a while.

He surveyed the crowd, saw several of his acquaintances seated at the gaming tables, but instead walked toward the bar. He had come for peace and quiet and perhaps a bit of distraction. Unfortunately, it didn't take him long to discover he wouldn't find solace there.

Not when half the men at the gaming tables were discussing the Duke of Milton and his upcoming nuptials, speculating whether or not the lovely Miss Fox would be giving the duke an heir in less than the proper nine months.

There was even a wager upon it. Five thousand pounds. St. Cere and Baron Densmore.

Matt smiled coldly as he stared at the betting book. His old friend Adam Harcourt had redeemed himself in Matt's eyes by betting a small fortune there would be no early babe.

"What do you think, Strickland?" Lord Montague sauntered up to where he stood sipping a glass of gin. He didn't drink much and never during the day, but today he needed a good stiff shot of blue ruin more than he could remember. "You know the chit better than anyone here. Will Densmore prevail, or will the winner be St. Cere?"

He had never liked Montague. The man was a blowhard and a braggart, an overbearing lout who enjoyed making other people squirm. "I remind you, Lord Montague, the lady in question is my father's ward. He would not take kindly to your vulgar insinuations, and neither do I."

The beefy man just laughed. "Quite a lovely gel, she is, too. It occurred to some of us that you might be interested in her yourself. Ah, but then there is Caroline Winston, of course."

A muscle jerked in Matt's cheek as he clamped down on his temper. He had come to Brooks hoping to forget about

Jessie, forget the way he had felt just being near her last night.
Every minute had been torture, every second an agony of
jealousy and lust. She had never looked more desirable, more
womanly, never appeared more tempting.

All evening long, he'd fought memories of the fire, of kissing her and filling his hands with her breasts. He couldn't help
thinking that if he had acted sooner—or if Jessie had waited—
she would have belonged to him, not the duke. The desire in
Jeremy's eyes whenever he looked at her was enough to make
Matt's stomach queasy. If supper hadn't ended, he might have
been physically sick.

He turned a hard look on Montague. "My father is concerned for Miss Fox's future. He has been unwell of late, and
he is determined to see her settled. St. Cere will win the bet."

He recalled the look on Jessie's face when she realized he
had come to London. For a moment he thought she might
faint. She hadn't been happy to see him—that was more than
clear.

And yet there was something in her eyes, something sweet
and yearning. Perhaps that was the reason she made a point
of reminding him it was he who had convinced her to accept
the duke's proposal. It had deflated his anger like a rip in a
billowing sail.

"Then again," the earl was saying, "perhaps Densmore
will win. It needn't be the duke's get, you know. It could belong to someone else." His thick lips curved. "I should think,
for instance, a woman would have to care a great deal for a
man to run after him inside a burning building."

Matt's hand snaked out. He caught Montague by the lapels
and lifted him clear off the floor. His other hand balled into a
fist, which he held several inches from the man's veined, bul-
bous nose.

"Unfortunately, there are times when Miss Fox has more
courage than sense. She would probably have gone back into
that building even for a loathsome creature like you, if she
thought that she could save you. Bearing that in mind, I would

advise you to keep your slanderous thoughts about the lady to yourself."

"Y-Yes, yes, of course. Beg pardon, Strickland. Didn't mean anything improper. Shouldn't have said a word."

Matt slowly set him back on his feet. "No, you should not have." Conscious of the silence that now filled the room, and the group of men staring in his direction, Matt tossed back his drink, set the glass down on a nearby table, and strode off toward the door.

Out on the street, he paused to take a long, deep, calming breath of air. He walked a full block to ease his temper before he signaled for a hack. Still, anger pumped through him all the way home.

Anger and a hollow ache in his chest that went hand in hand with a silent resolution he would not be attending Jessie's wedding.

There were things a man could stand and things he could not. Watching Jessie marry the duke, picturing her in Milton's bed, was an even worse fate than he had imagined. He would rather face the entire French fleet single-handed.

To that end, he sent the footman upstairs with a request to speak to his father. It was early yet, though a sliver of moon hung over the horizon and the purple of dusk had begun to fall. Jessie was supping in her room, the footman told him, but his father was still about. He returned with the news the marquess would enjoy a glass of brandy with Matt in the study.

Which suited Matt just fine. Though he wasn't drunk yet, as soon as he finished this discussion, he meant to get so foxed he couldn't see. He would buy himself the prettiest whore in the city—one with long blond hair and firm, milk-white breasts. He would use her hard and often, bury himself between her pale thighs until the damnable wedding was ended, then he'd go back to his ship and be grateful he had never officially tendered his resignation.

Standing next to the sideboard, he unstoppered the crystal brandy decanter just as his father walked in.

"Matthew, my boy. I thought you'd gone out for the evening."

"Not yet, but that is my intention. Brandy?"

"If you please, though I probably shouldn't drink all that much, with such a big day tomorrow." He accepted the crystal snifter Matt poured him. "Perhaps you should stay home as well, get a good night's sleep before the wedding."

Matt's hand tightened around the bowl of the snifter. "That, I'm afraid, is the subject I wish to discuss."

The marquess sipped his drink. "Go on."

"I've decided I'm not going to the wedding."

"Don't be ridiculous. Of course you will go."

"No, Father, I won't. Jessica is marrying Jeremy, not me. Whether I am there or not, she will become the Duchess of Milton. She hardly needs me to see her down the aisle and she certainly won't need me when he takes her to his bed." He took a long drink, felt the soothing fire of the liquid. "I just wanted you to know that I wasn't going to be there."

His father set his brandy snifter down so hard the crystal rang and a little of the brandy sloshed up to the rim. "I will say this only once. You are going to that lovely girl's wedding. You are the Belmore heir and she is my ward. She is marrying into one of the most powerful families in England. You are going to be there when it happens. It is not a subject that is open for discussion."

Something tightened inside him. In the eye of his mind, he could see the duke bending to kiss her, taking Jessie in his arms as he claimed her for his wife. "I'm asking you to make my excuses. I haven't asked you for much, Father. I'm asking you for this."

His father's dark eyes bored into him. "Why? Why is this so difficult for you?"

Matt said nothing, just took a sip of his drink, then forced another heavy breath into his lungs. "I'm sorry, Father," he said softly. "I hate to disappoint you, but I won't be there tomorrow. Give Jessica my best regards . . . and of course give the duke my congratulations." Setting the crystal snifter down on the sideboard, he crossed the room toward the door. His father's voice stayed him for a moment.

"Dammit, boy, this isn't the way I wanted things to work out."

Matt continued walking.

"Devil take it, son, if you care so much, have the gumption to do something about it!"

Matt kept on walking. It was too late for that. It had been too late from the moment he had left her at Belmore. Perhaps it had been too late from the start.

Accepting the hat and gloves the butler handed him, he strode out onto the porch, down the steps, and into the cold London evening.

Jessie stared at the untouched tray of food beside her bed. The gravy had congealed atop the leg of mutton, the crust sagged on the kidney pie, and even the plum pudding looked appalling. The thought of a single bite sliding into her stomach made the bile rise up in her throat.

Turning away from the nauseating sight, she walked over to the window. On the street below, a night watchman stood at the corner, his stout figure outlined in the yellow glow of a street lamp. An elegant carriage clattered past, rolling off toward a grand ball somewhere.

Unconsciously, she twisted her betrothal ring, a bloodstone that represented March, the duke's birth month. It was a big gaudy piece of jewelry, embodying all the pomp and ceremony being a duchess entailed. It bothered her to think of the rigidly structured life she would lead in the years ahead. It niggled her conscience that what she was doing might not be fair to the duke.

Then again, as Papa Reggie had said, most ton marriages were arranged. Jeremy had chosen her and she meant to be all that he wanted in a wife.

Jessie left the window and sat down on the bed. She wished she could sleep, but even the glass of sherry she had consumed hadn't settled her nerves. Her head was pounding, throbbing against her temples, and her hands shook so badly she had to clasp them in her lap.

Tomorrow she would be married. The wedding would commence at ten, followed by a huge wedding breakfast that would last well into the afternoon. Seven hundred guests were invited, the cream of the London ton. Amazingly everything was ready.

Jessie sniffed, then wiped a tear from her cheek. She should be happy—ecstatic—tomorrow her lifelong dream of being a lady, of having a husband and a home of her own, would at last be fulfilled. She would be married to a handsome, influential man who could give her anything she wanted. She would be the envy of every woman in the ton.

She should be walking on air, dancing on clouds, giddy with euphoria. Instead, her insides felt leaden. Her chest ached as if a knife had been buried in her heart.

Oh, Matthew, why couldn't you have loved me? It wasn't his fault, of course. Love was fickle. She couldn't make Matthew love her any more than she could make herself stop loving him.

Pulling her quilted wrapper more closely around her, Jessie curled up in the center of the bed, drawing her knees up under her chin. Tears clogged her throat, burned behind her eyelids.

She gritted her teeth, determined to make them go away. She had nothing to cry about.

Nothing.

She was marrying a fine young man, one who would treat her well and give her the family she never believed she would have. A man who deserved a good and loyal wife. She would be that, she vowed again. She would do everything in her power to make Jeremy Codrington happy.

She only hoped in doing so, she would forget Matthew Seaton and find a bit of happiness for herself.

The nightwatch called the hour as Matt shoved through the doors of the Cock and Hen, a well-known brothel in Sloane

Street he used to frequent in his younger years. He had been drinking for hours, most recently at the Crown and Garter in Chancery Lane, before that the Globe in Fleet Street, the White Dove, and a half-dozen other seedy taverns in Drury Lane.

He had come to the Cock and Hen because he knew Sophie Stephens, the owner, and as drunk as he was, he figured if he didn't find a bed somewhere soon, he'd wind up beaten and robbed and left for dead in an alley.

Besides, he was determined to buy himself a pretty little whore and spend the balance of the night—what limited portion remained—in her bed.

He stumbled past the oversized lackey who stood guard beside the heavy front door and into the smoky interior. Half-empty gaming tables sat at one end of the room, where men played whist, faro, quinze, or hazard. They wagered on the lottery, or simply sat there drinking. The rest of the establishment's patrons were engaged in flirtation with ladies of the evening or sprawled in the arms of a naked wench upstairs.

Just as Matt intended to do. Or so he kept telling himself. So far, all he had managed to do was drink.

He made his way toward the bar, bumping into a chair and knocking it aside on his way. He spotted Sophie's red hair and smiled lopsidedly as she walked toward him, her broad hips swaying in a sensuous, womanly rhythm as old as the business she was in.

"Well, will ya look at what we got here." She eyed him up and down, taking note of his disheveled attire: His coat hung open and slightly askew across his shoulders, his stock was undone and hanging loose around his neck. "I don't believe we've had the pleasure of your company, milord, in as long as I can remember. Welcome back."

"Thank you, Sophie."

"What ya drinkin', luv?"

He eyed the empty glass he must have carried from the alehouse he had last been in. "Gin. And keep it coming. I plan to get a whole lot drunker than this."

"Whatever ya say, luv. Just you leave it to Sophie."

He watched her walk away, sat down at a table and turned to survey the rest of the inhabitants of the room. A pall of cigar smoke hung just below the ceiling, mixing with the faint, musky odor of sex. As drunk as he was, it took him longer than it should have to realize one of the men across the room was walking toward him, a scantily clad brunette clinging to his arm.

It took another few moments to recognize the man as St. Cere, especially with the viscount's coat off, his hair mussed, and his shirt unbuttoned clear to his very narrow waist. He was just as foxed as Matt was, only he seemed to be happier about it.

Matt struggled to his feet, reached out and clasped his friend's hand. "Forgot this was one of your haunts. Good to see you, Adam."

That brought the lift of a bold black brow. "Good to see you, too. I was afraid my slight transgression the last time you were in town might have cost me a friend."

Matt smiled, the curve of his mouth a little sideways. "I haven't all that many. I value what few I have." He'd been gone from home for so long, his closest friends now were officers he served with in the navy, except for St. Cere and a handful of others, men he had known since Oxford.

"Shouldn't have happened," the viscount said, referring to their nearly ended friendship. "Never good to let a woman come between men." He grinned, his teeth very white against his swarthy skin. "But that one . . . your Miss Fox . . . I can see how it could happen."

Matt set down his empty glass, wishing Sophie would hurry with another round of drinks. "I saw your wager. Five thousand pounds in defense of Jessie's honor. I hope Densmore learns a lesson."

"Which is?"

Matt smiled faintly. "Not to wager with you . . . especially when the bet concerns a woman." Adam laughed softly. "I wondered, though, what could have made you so certain."

St. Cere's mouth twisted up. "You, I suppose. I saw the way you came to her defense. Never saw you act quite that way. I knew you wouldn't touch her—not your old man's ward—and with you around she wouldn't get the chance to misbehave."

Matt almost smiled.

"And there was the lady herself. There is something about her. . . . She's a woman who knows what she wants, not one to be taken advantage."

Just then a nearly naked blonde walked up, her red rouged nipples bulging above her tightly laced corset.

"Here's somethin' to quench your thirst, milords." She set a bottle of gin and several water-spotted glasses on the table, then leaned over and pressed her full breasts into Matt's chest. "My name is Hanna," she said. "What do you say we take the bottle and go upstairs? I promise we'll have us a time."

She was exactly what he'd wanted, a voluptuous whore he could spend himself in until this nightmare with Jessie was over. "Maybe later. Right now I'm busy getting drunk."

The viscount idly squeezed the breast of the girl draped over his arm. "As I recall, you weren't much of a drinker. Couldn't be Miss Fox's upcoming wedding, could it?"

Matt tossed back the drink he'd just poured, picked up the bottle, and refilled the glass. "Join me?"

"Why not?" the viscount said.

Matt sat down and so did St. Cere, dragging the brunette up onto his lap. She giggled as he absently fondled her bottom.

Matt leaned back in his chair, inspecting the glass and its contents. His head was fuzzy, the room out of focus. The laughter at the gaming tables seemed to come and go in waves.

"Helluv it is," he grumbled. "I was thinking of marrying her myself. Wrote her a letter, but it didn't get posted in time." Bitterness rolled through him. "She could'av waited, but, of course, she didn't. Why would she—when she could marry a duke?"

Adam shrugged. "You're an earl and the Belmore heir.

Not a bad catch for a country girl. The way I heard it, your father pressed her to marry. Milton was there; you were gone. Did you tell her you wanted her?"

Matt tossed back his drink and refilled the glass. "She knew I wanted her. She didn't know I was thinking of marriage."

"Helluva difference, my friend." He grinned at the dark-haired whore. "Janie here knows I want her. She knows that before we're finished, I'm going to take her every way I can think of, and a few I'll figure out in the morning. But I'm not about to marry her—or any other bloody-minded female, for that matter."

Matt propped his elbows on the table, ran his fingers through his hair. "Doesn't make a tinker's damn now. She belongs to Milton. Tomorrow night he'll be the man in her bed."

Adam refilled both their glasses. "How badly do you want her?"

Matt stared straight ahead, his mouth going hard, the skin growing taut over his cheekbones. "More than I've ever wanted anything in my life."

Adam's glass slammed down. "Bloody hell, Strickland."

"You can say that again."

"Christ, man, what are you gonna do?"

"Not a damn thing I can do. By noon tomorrow, Jessie'll be married to the duke, and there isn't a bloody thing gonna change that."

St. Cere shook his head, tumbling heavy black curls over his forehead. "There's never been a woman I wanted I couldn't have. If there were, I'm not exactly sure what I'd do."

The woman on his lap began to squirm. "You want me, don't you, lovey? Why don't we go upstairs and you can show me just how much?" She wriggled seductively, but instead of getting up, St. Cere slapped her hard on the bottom.

"Sit still," he commanded. "I'll tell you when I'm ready to leave." Her lips curved down in a pout, but her eyes flashed with excitement.

Matt poured himself another drink. "Wish I could turn back the clock, but the fact is I can't. In the meantime, I'm gonna get falling down drunk and then I'm takin' that big-bosomed blonde upstairs. I'm not coming down till Jessie Fox is married and out of my life for good."

"Here, here," said Adam, lifting his glass of gin in salute. "Who wants to be leg-shackled anyway? I tried it once, and I tell you, from that day forward, a man doesn't have a moment's peace." He shot back his drink, then began to twirl the empty glass in his hand, studying the last drop of liquid in the bottom. "On the other hand, Milton is still a pup . . . hasn't the foggiest notion what he really wants in life. A woman like your Jessie needs a man."

Matt said nothing. His tongue felt thick, his head muzzy, yet he was still too damnable sober. He thought of Jessie with Milton and his stomach clenched. Jessie was his—she belonged to him, not to Milton. He knew it and so did she.

But it was too late. Too late for both of them.

He set his jaw, filled his glass, and tossed back another drink.

*C*hapter *T*hirteen

*S*t. James's Cathedral, a tall baroque structure in Ludgate Hill, was designed by Christopher Wren. It sat on the Gothic site destroyed in the great London fire of 1666, its tall spire dominating the skyline.

On this gray, misty morning, the ton collected there in growing numbers to celebrate the marriage of a peer, the handsome Duke of Milton, to his incredibly beautiful blond bride, the Marquess of Belmore's ward, Jessica Fox.

It was the wedding of the century, people said, perhaps not the largest, but certainly one of the most discussed. Few could imagine how such an extravagant affair could have been managed in such a short time—or why. Privately they speculated on the need for haste, but the duke and the marquess were powerful men. As the crowd passed through the portals of the towering monolith, only murmurs of congratulations passed through aristocratic lips, best wishes for a long and happy marriage.

By the time Jessie arrived, the church was filled to overflowing, the doors closed in readiness for the much-discussed event, except for those few who made a last hasty entrance then quietly seated themselves in a pew at the rear, among the dozens of rows that looked down at the altar.

Still outside the church, Jessie sat across from Papa Reggie in the Belmore carriage, which was decorated with blue and silver garlands and pulled by four gray horses. Lady

Bainbridge had gone ahead to make final preparations. Viola had left, too, gone to take a seat among those reserved for the family's close personal servants.

Staring out the window, her nerves strung taut, Jessie was poised on the edge of the seat. Papa Reggie reached for her hand and gave it a gentle squeeze.

"You are the loveliest of brides. I am so very proud of you."

Jessie turned toward him and tears collected in her eyes. She could feel them burning and struggled to keep them from falling. She had sworn the ones she'd shed last night were the last she would allow.

"Thank you, Papa Reggie." She smiled at him softly. "I can't tell you how much I appreciate everything you've done for me. You've been the father I never had, and I want you to know that I love you very much."

The marquess cleared his throat and his own eyes grew misty. "You are the one, my dear. You brought joy into days that had grown empty, breathed fresh life into an old man's soul. I will never forget you for it, my dear, dear Jessica." He bent forward and kissed her cheek. She noticed his hands were trembling. "The Duke of Milton is the luckiest man in England."

She swallowed past the tight ache in her throat, thinking how her life had changed since she had met him. She thought of the happy times at Belmore, of birthdays and Christmases, of treasured heirlooms and lavish gowns . . . and how she had felt when she'd worn them for Matthew. In an instant, his golden features rose up, his stern, beloved face and incredible dark blue eyes.

"It's time we went in," the marquess said gently. "Are you ready?"

Jessie glanced out the isinglass window behind the rear seat, searching back down the hill, searching for Matthew. "He really isn't coming, is he?" Papa Reggie had told her just that morning that he would not be there.

"No, my dear. He isn't going to come. Perhaps this way is best."

Half of her agreed. The last person she needed to see on her wedding day was the Earl of Strickland. The other half felt crushed in misery that he would not be there to lend his support. Why? she kept asking. Was he angry? Disappointed? Regretful? Perhaps he felt something for her after all.

She dragged in a shaky breath of air. "Gwen and the others will be waiting. As you said, it is probably past time we joined them." Lady Bainbridge and her bridesmaids, Gwen Lockhart and two of Jeremy's cousins, girls her age she had only just recently met.

He nodded. "Shall we?"

She took his arm and let him help her down from the carriage, then he bent and straightened her long silver train, making sure each blue silk rose rested in its proper place on the length of sheer white tulle. A crown of white satin roses encircled her head and a tulle veil flowed down over the train, nearly touching the floor.

They crossed to the huge front doors of the church, passing a line of liveried footmen, their journey protected by a runner of plush red carpet.

Two tall blond footmen, so matched a set they looked like bookends, pulled open the doors to the antechamber, where Gwen and her other two bridesmaids, along with Lady Bainbridge, waited nervously for her to appear.

"Oh, Jess, you look smashing!" Gwen leaned forward and hugged her. "The duke will burn every moment till he gets you into his bed."

Jessie felt a warm flush rising in her cheeks and the slight pull of a smile. Leave it to Gwen. "You look lovely, too. I'm so glad you're here. I couldn't possibly make it without you."

The girls all wore blue silk high-waisted gowns trimmed with the same silver threads as her own. Jeremy's cousins offered compliments and best wishes, praising her dress and her hair until Lady Bainbridge shooshed them to silence.

"It is time we got started," the dowager countess said. "There is a nervous young man in there, eager for his bride. I believe he has waited long enough."

Things seemed to happen in an odd, unfocused sequence after that, progressing either so quickly she missed them altogether, or so slowly each instant seemed to take an eternity.

Another set of footmen dragged open the main doors into the cathedral. To the compelling tones of a powerful organ, the girls began their long stroll down the aisle. Above their heads, candlelit chandeliers hung from magnificent ceilings, and silver candelabras flickered against the walls.

The scent of flowers drifted up, lilies, Jessie thought vaguely as she positioned herself beside Papa Reggie at the threshold, then she spotted the long-stemmed flowers at the front of the church, soaring upward from massive silver vases. All along the aisles, the soft yellow glow of tapers cast shadows on the people crowding the long wooden pews.

From the corner of her eye, Jessie recognized several faces: Lord Pickering, the Duke of Chester and his wife, Lady Dartmoor seated next to Lord and Lady Waring, the Countess Fielding and Baron Densmore. There were others there she knew, but they passed in a blur, except for Caroline Winston, whose smile Jessie thought looked relieved.

The next thing she saw was the face of her sandy-haired groom.

She couldn't recall the moment he took her hand. One minute she was standing beside Papa Reggie, the next she stood in the shadow of the duke.

The service was long and tedious. She didn't remember what was said, only that she knelt several times and was helped to her feet by the slender young man beside her. The choir sang from the loft, beautiful songs in Latin.

Standing at the altar, the archbishop presided, a tall, gaunt, imposing man even more impressive for his shimmering golden robes. He was speaking to them now, invoking God's blessing.

"Marriage is an honorable and holy estate," he said, "instituted by God, sanctioned and honored by Christ's presence at the marriage in Cana of Galilee, and likened by St. Paul to the mystical union which exists between Christ and His church."

She tried to catch the rest but her concentration drifted. She felt faint and overly warm, and the smell of wax and the sweet scent of flowers made her stomach begin to churn. Inside her chest, her heart thudded dully. It was hard to concentrate, even hard to breathe.

"Into this holy union," the archbishop said, "these two persons now desire to enter. Therefore, if any man can show just cause why they may not be lawfully joined together, let him now declare it or forever hold his peace."

For one long, heartstopping moment, she held her breath, secretly praying for salvation, but no white knight appeared to save her. She blinked and the moment passed. A throbbing had started in her temple and a buzzing filled her ears.

The archbishop droned on and the marriage continued. "Let us pray," he said, and Jessie bowed her head.

Her pulse pounded harder, rising in an odd, offbeat cadence. Her fingers shook in the young duke's hand. When she glanced up at him, she saw the expression she had seen before, the look of a schoolboy about to receive a new toy. It made her mouth go dry, made her want to run from the church all the way back to Belmore.

"Most holy and merciful Father," the archbishop was saying, "look down on these children. Guide and bless them, grant them—"

The crash of a timbered door slamming open ended his words. With the pounding in her head and the tightness in her chest, it took a moment to comprehend that there was some disturbance. The archbishop stared over their heads, his mouth gaping open, his eyes wide in astonishment. Jessie turned then, and so did the duke, just in time to see the Earl of Strickland standing in the doorway. His mouth was set, his jaw hard, his features determined as she had never seen them.

Jessie's heart slammed painfully, then squeezed inside her chest. "Matthew . . ." she whispered.

He couldn't hear her, of course, not with the rising murmur of the crowd and heavy thud of his footsteps as he started down the aisle in her direction. His golden hair was mussed, she saw, his long-legged gait none too steady, hitting one side of the aisle then the other, before he righted himself and strode on.

"Dear God . . ." Jessie stared at his utter disarray, the gaping jacket, buttoned crooked and fastened only in a couple of places, his neckcloth untied and trailing down the front of his coat. His shoes were muddy, the cuffs of his shirt unfastened beneath the sleeves of his jacket. Even his white lawn shirt was partially undone.

"Devil take it," the duke said with no little annoyance, "what on earth does the poor chap think he's doing?"

Jessie said nothing, just gazed at Matthew with a mixture of horror and a forbidden ray of hope. The archbishop looked as though he might have apoplexy any moment, while whispers of shock and disbelief rolled through the crowd.

The earl continued doggedly up the aisle and didn't stop until he reached them.

"M-Matthew?" Jessie whispered again, staring into the darkest blue eyes she had ever seen.

He grinned drunkenly. "Mine," he said, swaying so much she feared he'd topple over. Instead, he bent forward, settled a wide shoulder at her waist, then straightened again, scooping her over his shoulder, filling his arms with Jessie, her white brocade wedding gown and miles of her blue and silver train.

The duke began to sputter. "For godsakes, man, have you gone completely insane? You can't—"

Matt punched him squarely in the jaw, and he went down like a sack of potatoes. Jessie gasped and so did the crowd, which surged in unison to its feet. Matthew simply ignored them. He was busy trying to untangle his legs from her cumbersome train, cursing vilely, and trying to keep them both from falling down. He finally managed to free himself.

Ignoring the indignant catcalls being shouted in his direction, he started his staggering journey back up the aisle.

All the while Jessie simply hung there, the horror of what was happening so unthinkable she couldn't begin to sort out what to do. Her heart was racing, hammering inside her chest, but her mind remained mercifully blank. Like a trussed-up Christmas goose, she rode suspended over his shoulder, one of his big hands clamped possessively on her rump, the other keeping a firm grip on her legs. Around them, people were shouting, beginning to move about, but no one tried to stop them.

Color burned her cheeks. From her vantage point upside down, she caught a glimpse of Caroline Winston's horrified expression, and a few pews away Lady Bainbridge looked as gray as paste. Beside her—to Jessie's utter amazement—Papa Reggie stood there grinning.

Something warm trickled through her, unfurled in her tightly clenched stomach. For the first time she realized her white knight had actually arrived—tarnished a bit though he was—and the feeling trailing through her was relief. Papa Reggie was smiling—he had wanted this all along. If she went with Matthew, she would not have failed him.

The feeling of relief grew stronger, mingled with a blossoming of hope. Now if he just didn't fall down before they could make good their escape—

Matthew staggered through the doors, his steps even more unsteady, and the heavy timbers slowly eased closed behind him. Unfortunately when they did, they caught her train and part of her veil. His next step tore the beautiful train in half, ripped the silvery veil from her head and left it dangling. Her hair came tumbling down, long golden curls that tangled around his legs and threatened to trip him again, but Matthew did not pause.

Not until he reached the street and stopped to glance around for the Belmore carriage. Then he started off in that direction. While the footman stood there gaping, Matt said something to the driver, jerked open the carriage door and shoved her in, stuffing her train in as well and all that was left of her veil.

His foot missed the step as he climbed in and he crashed to the floor of the carriage. With a groan and a Herculean effort, he hauled himself upright. He rapped on the roof, signaling the coachman to depart, and the vehicle lurched into motion. He could barely sit up, she saw, was even more foxed than she had imagined.

Still, as he dragged her up on his lap, a little thrill shot through her. When he cupped her face between his palms and gave her a slow, thorough kiss, she didn't mind the smell of alcohol that tinged his breath and clung to his clothes. Instead she slid her arms around his neck and kissed him back, just as long and thoroughly.

Happiness swelled inside her. Whatever happened, whatever disaster awaited, Matthew had come for her. Jessie knew in that moment there was no place on earth she would rather be.

Of course, she wasn't quite so sure a few hours later, when they arrived at a small country inn south of London on the road to Guildmore. Matthew had slept off and on—passed out from drink, in truth—but roused himself when they reached the inn that was apparently his destination.

"Wait here," he said thickly, "I'll be right back." He was still reeling drunk, his clothes a rumpled mess and his hair in need of combing.

She watched him stumble toward the door and a trickle of unease filtered through her, the first since they had left the church. Matthew wanted her. He had told her so more than once. Last night he had gotten drunk, and this morning he had barged into her wedding and taken what he wanted. Now what did he mean to do?

She nervously chewed her lip until he returned, then climbed down from the carriage and walked in front of him into the inn. People gawked at them all the way up to the room he had let, Matt in his wrinkled, unkempt clothes, she in her torn wedding gown, her hair undone and tangled around her shoulders.

At least inside the room they could be private. No more astonished eyes and gaping mouths. She waited till he closed the door, then turned to face him, her stomach crawling with nerves again.

"All right, Matthew. You have brought me here. Now what is it you mean to do?"

A wicked look crossed those masculine features. "What I've been wanting to do since the moment you landed in that mud puddle at my feet." Smelling of gin and cigar smoke, he stumbled closer, a determined glint in his eyes.

He had come for her, saved her from marrying the duke. If he'd been at least half sober, she might have let him make love to her. It was what she wanted, she admitted, what both of them had wanted for a very long time. Instead, as his arms clamped around her and he hauled her against his tall lean frame, she grasped the handle of an empty porcelain pitcher that sat on the dresser. When he dragged her mouth up to his and began a ravishing kiss, she lifted it above his head and held it with a hand that shook only a little.

She hesitated at the soft feel of his lips. They were so warm and compelling they sent little sparks shooting through her. The pitcher wavered. She didn't want to hurt him. Dear God, she was in love with him. He had come for her, whatever his reasons, and she loved him even more for that.

His hand settled at her waist; he turned her a little, eased his knee between her legs, then pushed backward, toppling her onto the bed and sprawling heavily on top of her. Even as the air whooshed from her lungs, Jessie clutched the pitcher. She could barely breathe, he was pinning her so, the muscles across his chest flattening her bosom, his face against her neck, where he pressed soft, warm little kisses. A big hand cupped her breast and her nipple tightened inside her dress.

"Damn you, Matthew Seaton." She shoved with all her might, but he didn't move. Not an inch. Not a muscle. "You're not going to do this—not while you're so drunk." She shoved again with no result, then discovered that as heavy as he was, some part of her liked the feeling, liked the warmth of his breath on her skin, the muscled length of thigh parting hers, the hard ridge of muscle that throbbed against her belly.

"Matthew . . ." she whispered, running her fingers through his hair, combing it gently back into place. Instead of a response, soft snores drifted up, and Jessie went rigid. God in heaven—the big oaf was asleep!

Clamping down on a surge of temper, she lay still for a moment, collecting her strength. Relief rolled through her, tempered, she admitted, with a bit of disappointment. She let go of the pitcher and it rolled across the mattress but didn't fall onto the floor.

"Bloody hell, Matthew, you must weigh fifteen stone." Gripping his shoulders, she shoved with all her might and was able to lift him a little. She eased partway out from under him, lifted again, eased, and lifted, until she was finally able to crawl from beneath him. He slept facedown on the mattress, dead to the world and blissfully unaware of the uproar he had started.

She almost felt sorry for him. Captain Matthew Seaton, the very proper Earl of Strickland, had created a very large, very improper scandal. She might even have felt a little bit guilty if it weren't for the fact there was a very good chance the arrogant earl had ruined her life.

What to do, Jessie thought as she stood over him. Matt had come for her, but he had said nothing of marriage. He had simply wanted to bed her. He had carted her off for just that purpose, and if he hadn't been so drunk, odds were he would have seen it done.

Still, Captain Matthew Seaton of His Majesty's Navy had never behaved so rashly. He drank only moderately and never got drunk, yet he had ravaged the Duke of Milton's wedding, abducted the bride, and thumbed his nose at polite society. The consequences of his actions would be grave ones.

The consequences for her were even worse. If Matthew didn't wed her, she would be ruined. No decent man would have her. She would never have the home she so desperately wanted, never have children.

Jessie chewed her lip as she paced the floor, her head pounding again and her pulse way too fast. There was only one solution—Matt had to marry her. Surely he would see that there was no other way.

She mulled that over as she reached the opposite side of the neat little room and turned to pace again. He had destroyed her wedding, yes, but that might not ensure a proposal of marriage. He hadn't ravished her as he had intended. She was still a virgin and the truth of that could be proven easily enough. Matt had plans for his life and until today they hadn't included Jessie Fox.

Lord Strickland was the heir to Belmore and a very powerful man. Perhaps he would simply return her, make some sort of restitution to the duke, assure him her precious virginity remained intact, and go on with the life he had planned.

She didn't doubt that sooner or later, Caroline Winston would forgive him.

Jessie's stomach knotted. Matthew cared about her. What happened this morning had proved it. He wasn't in love with Caroline, and Jessie loved him so much she was certain she could make him happier than any other woman in the world.

She studied the man sprawled on the bed. Matthew was an honorable man. If he believed he had ravished her, he would marry her. He would have to or he wouldn't be able to face his father. She watched his heavy breathing. Should she or shouldn't she?

Jessie bit her lip. She had made some hard choices in her life: running away from the Black Boar Inn with no money and nowhere to go, approaching the powerful, unapproachable Marquess of Belmore and pleading for his help, going away to school to become a lady, traveling to London to find a husand and make a place for herself in Society.

One thing she had learned—taking no risk meant gaining no reward.

And a man like Matthew Seaton was worth any sort of a risk.

Jessie eyed him thoughtfully, studying those powerful shoulders, noticing the way they veed down to his narrow waist and hips. His coat had flipped up. His buttocks were round and taut, and long muscles outlined his thighs. She watched them flex and tighten as he moved on the bed and a knot of heat uncurled in her belly. Her palms felt damp and she swallowed against a dryness in her throat.

Her plan might not work, but the odds were in her favor. It wouldn't be so hard—she had seen naked men at the inn, on several different occasions. She knew what went on between a man and a woman. Well, she mostly knew. She'd caught glimpses of couples in the act several times and heard the women talking about it, though they were usually cautious, even protective, when it came to Eliza Fox's daughter. Still, her future was at stake, just as it had been before.

Her decision was made—she would do what she had to.

Jessie leaned over the bed and began to strip off the Earl of Strickland's rumpled clothes.

Feeling the heat and brightness of the sun behind his eyes, Matt cautiously lifted one eyelid then another. He slammed them closed against the agony that sliced into his head with just that one small contact.

Inside his skull, a thousand hammers were pounding, slamming against his brain like waves against the hull in an angry sea. He tried to wet his lips but his mouth was so dry he couldn't swallow. He shifted a little, moving out of the direct morning sunlight, and once more opened his eyes, but his eyelids felt gritty, and the pain in his head seemed to swell. His tongue felt thick and furry, and his stomach roiled, threatening to erupt.

For several long moments he lay back on his pillow, willing the pounding to cease. Damn blue ruin. Now he understood how the beastly stuff had gotten its name. Emitting a tight, pain-filled hiss, he stared up at the ceiling and for the first time realized he didn't know where he was. Not onboard his ship, that was for certain, since the only rolling motion was in his stomach. Not at the Belmore town house, which had lovely molded ceilings in every room.

He shifted again, barely turning his head, and felt an answering movement beside him. When smooth warm skin touched his leg beneath the covers, he bolted upright, then groaned at the pain that shot into his head.

Turning toward the lump beneath the sheets, he focused on the long, golden hair spilling over the pillow next to his. He couldn't see her face, yet relief of a sort trickled through him. The little blond whore at the Cock and Hen. At least now he knew where he was.

The woman made a sweetly feminine sound and rolled over just then, dragging down the sheet and baring one of her breasts. It was pale and well-formed, jutting deliciously upward, the nipple a soft dusky rose. As bad as he felt, he grew hard beneath the covers and recalled the sailor's adage that a proven cure for a night of abuse was to take his ease on a woman, drain the poison from his system, seamen said. The tempting little whore would serve well enough for that, as he was certain she must have last night.

He eased her toward him, shoving the hair back out of her face and baring a second lovely breast, which he cupped and began to stroke—and froze.

Jesus, Mary, and Joseph! The luscious little blonde wasn't the whore at the Cock and Hen. The woman was none other than Jessie Fox!

She opened her eyes and blinked, saw him staring at her

with unabashed horror, saw that her breasts were exposed, gasped, and jerked the sheet up to her chin.

A rosy flush burned into her cheeks. "Well," she said, nervously wetting her lips. "At least you are finally awake. You've been sleeping since yesterday afternoon."

He couldn't think of a single thing to say. Good God, what the hell was *she* doing here? He raked an unsteady hand though his sleep-tousled hair and almost wished he had another drink.

"I know this is probably a very stupid question, but what in the bloody hell are you doing in my bed?"

Bright blue eyes slid over his bare torso, down to the sheet that rode low on his hips. "You mean you don't remember?"

"Remember? Hell, I don't remember what day it is."

"It's Sunday. Sunday morning."

"Sunday," he repeated dully, trying to piece together the hours that seemed to be missing. "Yesterday you got married."

Her slim fingers kneaded the sheet. "Not exactly. Yesterday I was supposed to get married. Your timely arrival put an end to that."

Matt sank back down on the bed. "Tell me this is a dream."

"If it is, it's a nightmare, or at least it will be once we return to London."

The throbbing felt like an anvil in his head. He was dying of thirst yet sweat beaded on his forehead. Fighting a wave of nausea, he swung his legs to the side of the bed, wrapped a blanket around his hips, and stood up.

"I need a minute. When I'm finished, maybe you can explain to me exactly what's going on." But already the images were beginning to flash through his mind. Drinking and gaming with St. Cere till well past dawn, leaving the Cock and Hen in Adam's phaeton and heading for Ludgate Hill.

As he made his way behind the screen to wash his face and relieve himself, he caught an image of Jessie in St. James's church, standing at the altar next to the Duke of Milton.

He groaned again, trying to recall what had happened after that. Behind him he could hear Jessie rummaging around the room, apparently putting on her clothes, but in his mind he saw her luscious body lying in bed beside him, stark raving naked.

"You might want these," she said, handing a pair of wrinkled trousers over the screen.

"Thanks." He pulled them on and buttoned up the fly, then rounded the screen and stopped at the sight of Jessie in only her chemise.

Pink rose into her cheeks as he surveyed her slender form, curved so nicely in all the right places. "I-I'm sorry. The wedding dress is the only thing I have to wear. It's terribly uncomfortable. I didn't think you'd be offended if I wore just this for a while . . . I mean after what happened between us."

He slumped down on the end of the bed, his stomach rolling ominously. "God, Jess, tell me I'm remembering wrong, that I didn't drag you out of your wedding."

"I'm afraid you did, my lord."

"And afterward? What happened after we got here?"

The flush in her cheeks crept down her neck and across the top of her bosom. "Y-You started kissing me. You told me you were going to do what you had wanted to do since I landed in that mud puddle at your feet. You started to undress me, and the next thing I knew we had somehow wound up in bed."

He shook his head, unable to deny a ring of truth. "Damn." Then an awful thought struck. "Christ, I didn't force you? I wouldn't do something like that . . . at least I don't think I would."

Jessie glanced away. "You didn't force me," she said softly.

"Still, it was your first time. God, I hope I didn't hurt you."

She only shook her head. He started to say something more, when another thought crept in. He turned to the bed and jerked back the sheet, but there wasn't the slightest trace of blood. "I presume we did make love—"

The color rushed back into her face. "I-I don't know exactly what we did. You were on top of me, touching me, kissing me—"

"There isn't any blood. Maybe we never actually—"

"Blood?" Her face went suddenly pale.

"Virgin's blood. If you were a virgin and we made love, there would have been blood on the sheets." Even through the pounding in his temple, a shot of anger filtered in. If he wasn't the first, how many men had she slept with? The thought of her in bed with another man gouged a jealous hole in his stomach.

Jessie's features went taut. "Are you implying that I am not—was not—a virgin?" Fire stole into the depths of her light blue eyes. "I have never had a lover—if that is what you are saying. I-I mean until last night." Her chin shot into the air. "I told you I don't know exactly what you did. Perhaps you didn't quite—"

"Never mind—I believe I understand what may or may not have happened." Inwardly he groaned. As drunk as he was, God only knew what he had done to her—or left undone, as the case may be. As to her innocence, for the present he would have to believe her. Besides, if she had wanted to fool him, she could have put the blood there herself.

"It doesn't really matter what we did or didn't do," he said. "The fact is, you'll be ruined if I take you back. My father would be devastated, and it certainly isn't your fault this happened. We'll be married by special license as soon as I can make the arrangements."

Jessie said nothing, just stared at him and slowly nodded.

"In the meantime, we'll return to Belmore. At least there you'll be away from the gossip." He would rather go to his own home, Seaton Manor, where apparently he had been headed, but he couldn't take Jessica there. Too much risk of discovery.

"Matthew?"

He paused in the act of pulling on his shirt, which was wrinkled and smelled like an alehouse. "Yes?"

"I know this isn't the way you had things planned, but I promise . . . whatever happens . . . I'll be a good wife to you."

He glanced at her and thought how beautiful she looked in her simple chemise, how soft and vulnerable. Was she really the woman she appeared, or a sweetly alluring little whore? Crossing the several paces between them, he tilted her chin up with his hand.

"I'm certain you will be." He ran a finger across her trembling lips. She'd be a good wife, all right. He would see to it personally, no matter what truth he discovered. "Right now, the most important thing is to get us out of here as quickly and discreetly as possible. I've a friend in Weybridge. We can freshen up and borrow clean clothes there."

She nodded and turned away, went in search of her garments, then carried them behind the screen to put them on, her expression nearly as stoic as his. When the gown was in place, she came to him and he turned her around so that he could do up the buttons. It was a curiously intimate gesture, considering he couldn't remember what exactly they had done, one that stirred his desire for her. He found himself wishing he was stripping the gown away again instead of buttoning it up.

Matthew took a steadying breath. It was still hard to believe he was actually marrying Jessie Fox, something at one time he had wanted to do very badly. He was resigned to his fate, though it bothered him the way things had occurred. He had embroiled the Belmore name in scandal and forced Jessie into a marriage she didn't want.

Then again, perhaps marriage to the Belmore heir was

exactly what she did want, what she had schemed for from the start. His father said that Jessie loved Belmore nearly as much as Matt did. As his wife, it would one day be hers.

In truth, he didn't know what to believe. At the moment, his head was pounding so hard he did not care.

*C*hapter *F*ourteen

*B*y the time Jessie arrived at Belmore, several days later, she was a married woman. Well, almost married. The vows had been spoken, but the marriage had not yet been consummated. She told herself there hadn't been time.

Jessie paced the floor of her new suite of rooms at Belmore Hall, a luxurious accommodation done in ivory and gold that adjoined the earl's elegant, very masculine quarters of paneled wood and gold brocade. Unfortunately, her husband was not home.

As he had promised, they had stopped their headlong journey in Weybridge, at the country home of a school friend from Oxford, Adrian Kingsland, Lord Wolvermont. Wolvermont wasn't in residence, but they were welcomed nonetheless. The housekeeper, a thin, scarecrow of a woman who remembered Matt from his previous visits, provided them with guest rooms, where they bathed and changed into borrowed clothes.

Matthew left after that, for a meeting with the vicar of the local parish church. Word was sent to the archbishop, who for fifty guineas—double the usual, already exorbitant sum—arranged for a special license.

Jessie barely remembered the wedding that took place the following morning in the chapel of the small, ivy-covered church, only that it was nothing like the extravagant affair in St. James's Cathedral. Just a quick, simple ceremony and a brief, nearly passionless kiss. Through it all,

Matthew was politely formal and perfectly solicitous, if unsettlingly reserved. As for Jessie, she felt mostly numb.

They left the church as soon as the wedding was ended and set off on the road again. All the way to Belmore, the earl remained broodingly silent, his broad shoulders propped against the plush velvet squabs as he stared out the window, and he never touched her unless he had to.

It didn't bode well.

She knew he was pondering the enormity of what he had done, wondering perhaps if she had told him the truth, and feeling wretched about the scandal he had created. In four hundred years, there had never been a hint of aspersion breathed upon the Belmore name. That Matthew had been the first to cause it hung like a pall over his head.

He blamed her for it, she knew, though she couldn't imagine how she could possibly be responsible for his actions that day at the church. Still he'd remained distant and impersonal since the morning they had left the inn, and now as she stood at the window of her elegant bedchamber, she worried that the pointedly reserved way they had started might be the way they would go on.

Jessie wished Papa Reggie would come home. Surely he would know what to do. Word had been sent to him, of course, but he had declined to return, opting to remain in London so the newlyweds might have time to themselves. Privately, Jessie thought he was probably also speaking to the duke, working in Matthew's behalf to make some sort of restitution. In that, no doubt, he had his work cut out for him.

As for Matthew himself, instead of making her his wife in truth, her husband was gone. In his absence, she paced the floor, watching the long road through the rolling fields leading into Belmore, waiting with a tight knot in her stomach for his return.

He would, she was certain, sooner or later. But as the hours ticked past, she grew less and less sure. She fiddled with the edge of Belgian lace on her ice blue satin dinner gown, hoping against hope she had chosen one that would please him.

She wished Viola had been there to help her instead of remaining in London.

Mostly she wished Matthew were there.

Instead of with Lady Caroline Winston.

Standing in front of a forest green brocade settee in the drawing room, Caroline Winston held herself rigidly in check as she studied the dark, tightly drawn features of the Earl of Strickland. She and her family had returned to Winston House straightaway, after the humiliating scene her soon-to-be-fiancé had created in St. James's Cathedral.

"I appreciate your indulgence, Lord Landsdowne," the earl said to her father, who stood stiffly a few feet away, his jaw clamped in fury at the handsome man who should have become his son-in-law. "I'm extremely grateful you've allowed me to speak to Lady Caroline in person. I realize how difficult all of this has been for her, to say nothing of you and the rest of your family. I make no excuses for my behavior. I can only tell you how much I regret the embarrassment I have caused."

Earlier in the day, Matthew had sent a messenger with a note requesting a meeting with her father. He had apologized for what had happened in London and the distress he had caused the entire Winston family. He had asked to speak to Caroline, but her father had refused. It wasn't until sometime later, after a lengthy discussion and a number of heated words directed at the Earl of Strickland that her father had relented and finally agreed.

Now, attired in his full-dress uniform, his navy blue coat with its gold epaulettes and his tight white breeches, Matthew turned in her direction, leveling the formidable power of those intense, dark blue eyes on her face.

"Lady Caroline . . . I have come to tender my personal apologies for what has occurred. There are not words to tell you how sorry I am. Never once did I intend to cause you any sort of embarrassment. I am still at odds to discover exactly how it happened. Perhaps I will never be able to sort the whole thing out."

Caroline lifted her head. Her heart was beating, throbbing against her breastbone. Fury burned like bitter gall in her stomach. She had planned on marrying Matthew for as long as she could remember. He was wealthy and titled, and so handsome she would have been the envy of every woman in the ton. Anger rode hard on her control, yet she managed to disguise it.

"Perhaps it is not so difficult to understand. Perhaps you were simply in love with her."

Matthew said nothing for the longest time, just stood there with his jaw set, his bearing perfectly erect. "I have come to care for her, yes," he finally admitted, and Caroline's whole body went tense. "At one point, I even considered marriage— but never at your expense, my lady. Certainly I would have allowed you to cry off, whether our betrothal was official or not. You have been a true and loyal friend for as long as I can remember. Causing you any sort of distress is the last thing I wished to do."

Angry tears rose in her throat but appeared as a soft mist in her eyes. "I appreciate your coming here, my lord. I realize that all of us are human. Each of us has frailties and flaws, just like everyone else." She forced a wistful smile when she wanted to shriek out her rage. "I admit, that I believed you less flawed than most men, perhaps as near a paragon as any man I had met."

"Caroline . . ."

She held up a slim white-gloved hand. "But the fact is you are married and I must come to accept that. In time, I'm certain that I shall. For the moment, I shall refrain from wishing you joy in your marriage. Perhaps in time, I shall be able to do so and actually mean it. Until then, I pray God and the duke will forgive you." She started to walk away, but Matthew caught her hand.

"And you, Caroline? Will you also try to forgive me?"

How could she? He had made her a laughingstock, destroyed her well-laid plans for the future. She had waited for him when she could have had any number of other suitors. She kept her expression neutral, though she thought her face might crack. Finally she nodded. "I shall try, my lord."

She turned away from him then, left him there with her father, and made her way upstairs. For days she had been aching with rage and pain and wallowing in fury. Matthew had humiliated her in front of the entire London ton. He had made a fool of himself, embarrassed the duke, and destroyed her future. But it wasn't completely his fault—Jessica Fox had driven him to it.

She was a treacherous bit of fluff, a conscienceless little vixen who had led him on, charmed her way into his heart, and brought disgrace to the noble Belmore name.

Who was this woman, this harlot who had stolen Matthew away? Caroline raged. Where had she come from? Why had no one ever heard of her? Perhaps Frances Featherstone had been correct. From the start her cousin had been suspicious of the way she kept to herself and never seemed to know anyone else of the marquess's acquaintance. Perhaps even Matthew did not know the whole truth about her.

In that moment, Caroline imagined an entire bevy of secrets she might unearth about the lovely but conscienceless Miss Fox. In her mind, she envisioned Matthew's horror when he found out, pictured him down on his knees begging Caroline's forgiveness, pictured Jessica Fox, disgraced in front of all of London. Matthew would admit the error he had made, perhaps even find the means to correct it.

Caroline smiled, the images dulling the sting her pride had suffered. If there were any sort of justice, Jessica Fox would be punished for the pain she had caused. And Caroline Winston was just the person to accomplish the task. Yes . . . she vowed, as she slowly climbed the stairs, sooner or later, one way or another, the Countess of Strickland would pay for what she had done.

* * *

It was dark by the time Matt arrived back at Belmore. As terrible as the scene at Winston House had been, as ashamed as he was for the hurt he'd caused Caroline and her family, in some strange way he felt relieved.

Since the moment he had awakened at the inn and realized he had abducted Jessie from her wedding, he had been drowning in a quagmire of guilt and regret. He had sent a message to the duke containing his personal apologies, offering to make financial reparations, to print a public apology, and more, then written his father for help with the endeavor and left the rest up to him. After all, the old man had gotten what he'd wanted all along, and he was far better at those sorts of machinations than Matt was.

The other step he had taken was somewhat unexpected, even to him. He had written to his direct superior, Admiral Cornwallis, tendering his previously discussed resignation— with the provision, of course, that his services would be available should word arrive that a naval encounter with the French loomed anywhere on the near horizon.

He was a married man now, with a new set of responsibilities. He hadn't planned it this way, but after what had happened, he would simply have to adjust.

He climbed the steps to Belmore with a different air than when he had left, walked into the marble-floored entry, and handed his bicorn hat and white cotton gloves to the butler, who stood stoically beside the door.

"Good evening, your lordship."

"Good evening, Osgood. I'm looking for Lady Strickland. Has she already retired upstairs?" Today he had made his peace with Caroline and her father. He had written to the duke and to Admiral Cornwallis. There was only one person with whom he had yet to set things straight.

"At present, my lord, her ladyship is dressing for supper. She has arranged for the meal to be served at eight . . . if that meets with your lordship's approval."

He studied the look on Samuel's face, catching the hint of

disquiet. Somehow the servants had discovered that he hadn't yet bedded his new wife and they were not happy about it.

Matt shook his head. "No, I'm afraid it won't suit at all. I'd like supper served in my suite—something special. And flowers and candles on the table." He turned and started up the stairs. "And send up a bottle of champagne. Your mistress may be nervous on what is to become her wedding night."

The tall, stately butler actually grinned. "Yes, milord. I shall see to it personally."

"Thank you"—Matt smiled—"Ozzie."

The older man's ears turned a little bit red, but he nodded and hurried away. Matt continued up the stairs and went into his room, to find his valet had already laid out his clothes on the huge gold-draped four-poster bed, and a nice hot bath had been prepared. He quickly shed his uniform, climbed into the tub, folding his long legs up as best he could, leaned back, and for the first time since his marriage, allowed himself to think of Jessie.

He had practically ignored her these past few days. His conscience had been riding him hard and Jessie was the cause. He knew it wasn't her fault, yet part of him blamed her for it. If she wasn't so damned beautiful . . . if he hadn't wanted her so damned badly . . .

Ah well, the truth was, he was married. Jessie was his wife, but he had barely acknowledged the fact. Tonight he intended to make up for the time he had lost. The doubts he still harbored about her innocence gave him pause, but the truth of that matter would soon be revealed one way or another. Until then, he would give her the benefit of the doubt.

He thought about the night they had spent at the inn and hoped, if she really was the untried maiden she claimed, his drunken, pawing attentions hadn't been so loathsome she would be inhibited with him this time. Even if she was, he believed, with patience, sooner or later, she would come to enjoy the physical acts of love.

Just thinking about it made him hard beneath the warm, sudsy water. He wanted Jessie Fox, more now that she was his wife than ever before. He could almost taste the smoothness of her pale creamy breasts, the berry flavor of her lips. He imagined the slickness of her passage as he eased himself inside her, the sweet sensation of her muscles tightening around him.

Matt cursed roundly. If he kept that up, he would take her too swiftly and he didn't want that. He wanted to woo her, make love to her slowly, show her the joys of passion and give her incredible pleasure.

He might be starchy in some things, but never in bed. He wanted her to feel that way, too.

Checking the clock on the wall, he climbed from the tub, toweled himself dry, and with the help of his valet, began to pull on his evening clothes, a pair of dark gray breeches, a silver waistcoat, and navy blue tailcoat. He pictured what Jessie might wear, but secretly wished he would find her exactly as he had that morning at the inn—dressed in nothing at all.

His mouth curved faintly as he finished dressing. Whatever had motivated him to abduct her, Jessie was his wife. He had wanted her since the day she'd come riding hell for leather into the stables and wound up in the mud at his feet. Marriage was a high price to pay for his lust, but pay it he had. Tonight he meant to claim the prize he had paid for so dearly.

His body stirred at the thought, his shaft rising up, making his breeches fit too snug. Visions of the evening ahead made his loins grow thick and heavy, conjured images of Jessie naked and writhing beneath him. He tried not to think how he would feel should he discover she had lied, that her innocence was a ruse and he was merely another in an endless string of lovers.

As he walked to the door, he forced his hand to relax from where it had balled into a fist.

Dressed in the ice blue satin gown she'd had altered, now that she was married—well, almost married—to fashionably display more of her breasts, Jessie stood in front of the ornate cheval-glass mirror, surveying her appearance and hoping she looked seductive. Minerva Towser, the thin young girl who was acting as her lady's maid until Viola's return, had just informed her that the intimate dinner she had planned for the evening, assuming Matthew returned, would be served in the drawing room of his lordship's suite.

Just hearing the news made Jessie's palms go damp. At the earl's request, her intimate supper was going to be even more intimate than she had planned.

An uneasy shiver ran through her. Did he mean to make love to her then, make her his wife in truth? Or perhaps it was simply there was something of a private nature he wished to discuss.

That set her heart to pounding. Dear God, what if he had discovered what she had done at the White Dove Inn? What if he'd found out that she had tricked him into marriage? Or worse yet, what if he'd discovered it was Caroline he wanted and decided to annul the marriage?

Jessie took a deep, calming breath and forced aside her fears. There was no reason to believe the worst. Better to face him with hope in her heart and a small prayer for strength. Better to expect no more than a partner for supper and perhaps a bit of conversation.

Bearing that in mind, she checked her appearance in the mirror one last time, took several deep breaths, and pulled open the door leading from her suite of rooms into his. It was bathed in candlelight, she saw, the heavy silk draperies, lovely molded ceilings, walnut paneling, even the beautiful linen-draped table that was set with china and crystal—all appeared washed in gold.

As did Matthew himself, from his sun-bronzed face and dark golden hair, to his corded neck and long-fingered, masculine hands. Dear God, and she was married to him!

Matt glanced up at the sound of the opening door, but for several long seconds did not move, just allowed himself the pleasure of watching Jessie walk into the room. When a soft, uncertain smile touched her lips, he smiled at her in return.

"Good evening, my lady." He started toward her then, striding across the room in her direction as if pulled by an invisible cord. She was wearing blue, he saw, the same shade as her eyes, the décolletage lower than she'd ever worn before. High full breasts rose above the plunging neckline, and a memory of them naked stole into his thoughts, mocking his resolve to go slow. He was hard before he even touched her, his loins heavy and full. His smile was soft but his eyes burned with purpose. Tonight she would be his.

"G-Good evening, my lord. I hope I haven't kept you waiting."

His mouth curved up. "If you had kept me waiting half the night, it would have been worth it." He lifted her hand, turned it, and placed a kiss in the center of her palm. "I am the one who is late. For the past few days, I've been remiss in my duties as husband. I apologize for that—something I seem to be doing a lot of lately." She smiled and desire rolled through him. "Tonight I mean to make amends."

A spot of color rose into her cheeks. Jessie glanced off over his shoulder. "I-I realize you've had a good deal on your mind. I hope you were able to resolve those matters to your satisfaction."

"In so far as it was possible." He let his gaze travel over her, taking in the gold of her hair, the curve of her cheek, the arch of her throat, where a tiny pulse fluttered at the base. "But the past is not what I wish to speak of tonight." He handed her a glass of champagne, tiny bubbles fizzing above the gold rim of the long-stemmed crystal. "As a matter of fact, it is my most fervent hope, as the evening progresses, there'll be very little need for conversation."

The crystal goblet trembled in Jessie's hand. She moistened her lips with the tip of her tongue, and heat tugged low in his belly. He reached for her, slid an arm around her waist and drew her against him, bent his head and captured her lips. They were as soft and sweet as he remembered, and trembled slightly as he urged them to part. His tongue swept in, tasting her more fully, making his shaft ache and throb.

God, he wanted her. He deepened the kiss, slanting his mouth to fit hers, crushing her soft full breasts against his chest. He could feel her fingers digging into his shoulders, feel her nipples growing hard beneath her dress. He wanted to rip the fragile silk away, to bare those lovely white mounds, to take them deeply into his mouth, to lick and suckle them until she moaned.

Instead, with an iron control, he tore himself away. When he spoke, his voice sounded deep and rusty. "I believe, Lady Strickland, Cook has fashioned us a treat. Since I have plans for you for the balance of the evening, perhaps we should get started."

Jessie nodded, the color even higher in her cheeks. "As you wish, my lord." She accepted the arm he offered and they crossed to the intimate table before the hearth. Her gown brushed his thighs and the blood pulsed in his groin. He pulled out her chair and seated her, then took a seat across from her. The footman began to serve the meal, but all Matt could think of was the softness of her lips, the tiny circle of her waist, the crush of her breasts.

No wonder he had braved the wrath of a duke to have her. Perhaps Jessie Fox would be worth it.

Supper proceeded right on schedule, each course presented with exquisite care, the meal perfectly cooked from start to finish. Neither of them ate very much, the tension hung too thickly between them. Conversation lapsed into the brush of hands and heated glances, blue eyes searching blue, and more wine consumed than food.

By the time the last course was served, Jessie thought her nerves might snap, and Matthew seemed even more restless than she. He ordered the sumptuous dessert of gingerbread and custard left on the table, pressed the last of the footmen into retreat, followed the man to the door, and worked the key.

"I must have been insane," he said, turning in her direction, fixing his gaze on her mouth. "I should have passed on supper altogether." With that he strode toward her, pulled her to her feet, and dragged her into his arms. The kiss he took was burning, a hot, hungry kiss that left no doubt of his intentions, a wet, thorough kiss that seared clear into her bones.

"I have vowed to go slow," he said gruffly, "but if you aren't out of those clothes in the next ten minutes, I believe I shall tear them off you piece by piece."

Jessie flushed crimson. "I-I'm sorry, my lord. I shall call Minerva straightaway." She turned but he caught her arm.

A corner of his mouth curved up. "You've no need of a maid. Tonight I will act as such." His eyes slid from her mouth to her breasts. "Turn around, Lady Strickland."

Jessie's stomach tightened then rolled. She did as he commanded, trying not to notice the little tugs of heat darting through her. With each pearl button that came undone, her heart skipped a little bit faster. By the time he slid the dress down her arms, past her hips, and onto the floor, her pulse fired like a trip-hammer, and goose bumps-skittered across her skin.

"Do you know how much I want you?" he whispered beside her ear, planting soft, moist kisses along her jaw. His arms wrapped around her waist, pressing her back against his chest. She could feel his arousal, thick and hard against her bottom. He nibbled the lobe of an ear, then turned her into his arms and kissed her, a hot, deep-tongued kiss that made her insides curl and damp heat slide into her belly.

"Matthew . . ." She barely noticed when he lifted her chemise off over her head, leaving her in only her white silk stockings and pink satin garters.

Not until he took a step away.

Jessie's cheeks burned with embarrassment, but she didn't try to cover herself, just lifted her eyes to his face. It was dark with heat and hunger, tightly leashed desire, and something else.

"You're lovely," he said in a voice gone rough. "I have thought of those beautiful breasts a hundred times." Deep blue eyes ran from her bosom to her waist, then traveled past her navel to the thatch of golden curls at the juncture of her legs. Heat coursed through her, made each place he studied begin to burn.

"There are a thousand ways I mean to love you," he said. "Still . . . I wonder if even that will be enough." Fire rippled through her with every word. His eyes scorched a path across her skin.

"Come here, Jess." Hunger glinted in his eyes, fierce and unmistakable.

Part of her wanted to run, to protect herself at all costs from this man who meant to claim her. The other part wanted this to happen, wanted more of the pleasure he promised with every heated glance, every kiss, every touch. She moved closer, till the wool of his coat brushed her nipples, making them go instantly hard.

Then he was kissing her again, plunging his tongue into her mouth, sweeping deeply, ravishing her will as he meant to ravish her body. A big hand cupped her breast, sending waves of heat shimmering through her. He gently upbraided the nipple, making it tighten until it puckered and began to burn.

"Dear God, Matthew . . ." For years she had loved him. Now she wanted him as she never would another man. She kissed him back with scorching passion and found that it wasn't enough. She wanted to feel the smoothness of his skin, to taste his salty heat, to touch him the way he was touching her. She remembered the night she had stripped off his clothes, how smooth and tan was his skin, how long and lean his muscles.

"Take . . . take off your clothes." Frantically she pushed at his coat, shoving it off his shoulders. "Please . . . I need to feel you . . . I have to, Matthew." She thought she heard him groan. Then he was stripping the coat away, jerking off his stock, unbuttoning and shedding his shirt. In the light of the candles, dark golden hair formed a broad swatch over his suntanned chest, and thick slabs of muscle rippled across his shoulders.

When he stood before her naked, he reached for her again, and pulled her into his arms. He kissed her long and deep, then he was picking her up, striding across the room and into his bedchamber, laying her in the center of his massive bed and following her down. His mouth took hers in a thorough, ravishing kiss, then he was kissing her neck, trailing kisses along her shoulder.

He drew a hard, aching nipple into his mouth and Jessie moaned. Her breasts felt swollen and the place between her legs throbbed and burned. He must have known it, for his hand traveled there, sifting through the downy golden curls, then easing her legs apart. When he slid a finger inside her, Jessie sucked in a breath at the pleasure that rippled through her. She was hot and slick and pulsing, on fire with heat and need. Every time his finger eased in and out, a wash of heat swirled into her belly. She knew what he intended, but even her fear of the huge male ridge he meant to bury inside her wasn't enough to stifle the desperate longing.

A second finger slid in, delving deeper, probing and stretching until she thought she might scream with the pleasure. She arched upward, unable to control herself, searching frantically for relief.

"Please, Matthew . . . I can't . . . I can't . . ."

"Easy, sweeting. Trust me a little bit longer." He kissed her again as he rose above her, his tongue thrusting deeply. "Open for me, Jess, let me love you."

She whimpered softly, straining upward, her legs parting as if they had a will of their own. Guiding himself inside her, he eased his way into her slick, damp heat, stretching and filling her in a way she couldn't have imagined. When he reached the wall of her maidenhead, he paused, his head dropping forward onto hers.

"Thank God." He looked at her again and he was smiling with such incredible warmth, tears stung the backs of her eyes. "Don't be afraid," he said. "It will hurt only just this once."

She cupped his dear, beloved face with her hand. "I'm not afraid, Matthew. Not when I'm with you."

"Jess . . ." His mouth took hers, savagely, almost pain-fully, distracting her and firing the heat that already roared through her veins. His tongue thrust deeply, harshly, just as his body thrust past the thin barrier of her maidenhead, tearing it in two. His hot kiss muffled her cry, but his body went tense, every muscle straining for control.

"I'm sorry," he said, but he didn't look sorry. In fact he had never appeared more pleased.

She took a few deep breaths, but already the pain was receding. When Matthew began to move, she felt only the friction of his lean hard-muscled body, the heavy thrust and drag that sent fiery shivers through her limbs. In minutes she was arching against him, meeting each of his powerful thrusts. Waves of heat washed over her; flames seemed to scorch through her veins.

"Matthew . . ." she whispered as a tight, spiraling sensa-tion began to curl in her stomach. Her mouth went dry and her nipples tightened while the rest of her drowned in liquid heat. Several more deep thrusts and she felt his muscles stiffen. He plunged deeply, dragged himself out and plunged in, and the tight spring inside her snapped free.

Jessie clung to his neck and cried out his name, saw bursts of white light behind her eyes and felt a sweep of pleasure so heady she started to weep. Joy washed over her, a feeling so profound it left her boneless, limp and sated and numb.

"Jessie . . . love . . . are you all right?"

She blinked and the tears rolled down her cheeks. She shook her head. "Yes . . . no . . . I'm not exactly sure. Mat-thew . . . it feels so wonderful."

Soft laughter rumbled in his chest. He kissed her gently, then eased off her and lay at her side, pulling her into his arms. "You're right, my love, it does feel wonderful." He ran a finger along the bridge of her nose. "Apparently I did a very poor job of ravishing you the first time."

Her stomach muscles tightened, a trickle of fear sliding through her. "Wh-What do you mean?"

"I mean, my lovely countess, that you were still a virgin."

For a long time she said nothing, her insides tight and uncertain. "I suppose I should have known. If I had—"

Matt frowned. "If you had, what, Jess?" He rolled onto his side to face her, his features suddenly dark. "If you had known you were still a virgin, you would have gone back to London and married the duke?" He sat up in the bed, naked and utterly splendid. "Listen to me, you little vixen. Milton is out of your life for good—I am the man who is your husband. Perhaps you would rather have had it the other way, but it's far too late for that."

"That isn't what I meant. I only meant—"

"I don't care what you meant. It's no longer important. You're my wife—mine. I intend to see you don't forget it." With that he pulled her beneath him and kissed her again. Not a soft, gentle, lover's kiss, but a hard, male, possessive kiss that warned her she was his. Jessie reveled in it. When he slid himself inside her, thrusting deep and hard, she rose up to meet each of his thrusts.

He thought she wanted the duke, and though she wasn't yet ready to tell him, the only man she had ever wanted was him. Jessie gave herself up to the pulsing rhythm of his hard driving passion and the knot of spiraling pleasure curling once more in her belly.

*C*hapter *F*ifteen

*M*atthew awoke before dawn. Beneath the canopy of his big tester bed, Jessie lay sleeping beside him. The rumpled bedsheet tangled around her, leaving a rosy nipple exposed, a slender foot bare, as well as a trim bit of ankle. Just looking at her half-naked among the tousled linens made his body begin to grow hard. He wanted her again and before he left the bed, he would have her. He had paid for the right to her body with his name and his wealth, yet this need he constantly felt for her bothered him.

It bothered him to realize the lengths he had gone to keep her from marrying Milton. It worried him that he cared too much, a thing he was determined not to do.

Loving a woman was not in the plans he had set for himself. He knew only too well the hurt that could come of it, had seen his father's grief, watched him pine for his beloved wife for more than twenty years. His stepmother had suffered as well. She had loved the marquess deeply, but he never loved her. He was never able to forget the woman of his heart. In the end, the second marchioness had died a lonely bitter woman, scornful of men and regretful of her marriage.

Matthew looked at Jessie, sleeping so peacefully in his bed. She was his wife. One day she would bear him a son, the next heir to Belmore. He would provide for her as his father had wished, keep her well satisfied in bed, indulge her feminine whims as much as he could, and try to be a good husband. Aside from that, he meant to keep his distance, bring his emotions back under control as he had always been careful to do. For a time, Jessie Fox had nearly been his undoing, but that time was past. He meant to make a new beginning.

Matthew reached toward her, looped a silky blond curl behind her ear, then bent to kiss the delicate rim. Jessie arched upward in her sleep, baring one of her breasts, and Matthew's arousal strengthened. She was his wife and he meant to enjoy her. The notion seemed even more appealing, now that he had fashioned his new resolve.

Smiling, Matthew bent his head and took a soft pink nipple into his mouth.

The first week of marriage drifted into the next. Though she had hoped they would spend time together, Jessie saw Matthew only briefly. Usually he was up and out in the fields before dawn and he didn't return until nearly dark. He had always worked hard. She shouldn't have expected him to change, she told herself, just because he had married, but she couldn't shake the notion that he distanced himself on purpose, that he didn't want to get too close.

She tried to tell herself his remoteness would fade. He was simply unsure of his feelings, or perhaps he was uncertain of hers. Whatever the case, the only time it seemed they were easy together was when they were in bed, a place he was extremely skillful and not the least bit prudish.

At times she wished they never had to leave the privacy of their rooms.

Apparently Matthew did not agree. Well before dawn, he rode off for a meeting with James Bartlett to discuss increasing their crop yields. Jessie had sent a basket of fresh-baked bread along to Anne and the baby, then once the sun was up, set off for her makeshift school.

It was late in the afternoon, the children already gone, when she heard her husband's footfalls. Jessie sat at her desk preparing the text for the following day's lesson as he walked in, his long-legged strides not stopping until he stood on the opposite side of the desk a few feet away.

"So this is where you've been hiding." His features looked a little bit tense and she wondered at his thoughts.

"Good afternoon, my lord."

"Yes . . . it's a very good afternoon." His gaze remained steady on her face. There was something in his eyes, the glint of some emotion she could not read.

"Your meeting went well with James Bartlett?" she asked, flicking nervously at a piece of lint on her clothes.

"Extremely well." His voice turned a little bit gruff. "He said to relay his heartiest thanks for helping Anne with the difficult birth of their babe."

Jessie flushed. Dear heavens, no wonder he seemed upset. A young unmarried woman helping to deliver a babe— she had hoped he wouldn't find out. "Yes . . . well, there is certainly no need for his thanks. I was glad I could be there to help her."

"As I am glad," he said softly, taking her by complete surprise.

"You are?"

"Yes." He rounded the desk and took her hands. "And I am also extremely sorry."

"Sorry? What for?"

"For the way I treated you that day, Jess. For the awful things I said." He kissed the back of her hand by way of apology. His guard seemed to be down as it hadn't been all week. He gazed into her face. "If my father had known, he would have taken a horse whip to me."

Jessie felt warm inside, and suddenly very hopeful. "I wanted you to see me as a lady. I planned the evening for weeks. In the end, I certainly made a muddle of it."

He lifted her hand and kissed it again. "Perhaps in the beginning, but with very good cause. I only wish you had told me."

She stared into those blue, blue eyes. "I was afraid you would be shocked."

He smiled, crinkling the lines at the corners of his eyes. "Perhaps I was . . . just a little. But that is most probably the thing that attracted me to you in the first place." Jessie laughed as Matt pulled her into his arms. He lowered his head and kissed her, a soft, warm, searching kiss that made her go weak in the knees.

"Once I imagined making love to you right here," he said in a husky voice. "On the top of your battered desk, scattering all of your papers."

Jessie glanced toward the door and saw he had closed and locked it. "You did?"

"Yes, I did."

She glanced back toward the door. "You don't intend . . . ?"

A dark golden brow arched up. "Don't I? I believe it is past time I made amends for causing your horse to rear and toss you into the mud."

She grinned and pressed her hands against his chest. "So—you finally admit it was your fault!"

"I do," he said, bending her back over his arm. "And as I said, I shall have to make proper amends." Dipping his head, he captured her lips, at the same time clamping his hands around her waist and lifting her up on the edge of the desk.

Jessie gasped as he unbuttoned her blouse and freed her breasts, then cupped them with his hands and began to massage them gently. Teasing her nipples into tight little buds, he lowered his head and began to suckle there, drawing them deeply into his mouth. Jessie whimpered at the hot little sparks dancing through her, the feel of his lips and tongue. She barely noticed that he stood between her legs, that he was hoisting up her skirts, bunching them around her waist.

Another heady kiss distracted her while he pulled up her shift and eased her toward the edge of the desk, all the while kneading her breasts. He tilted her head back and kissed her throat, dropped several hot kisses on her shoulders, then he knelt in front of the desk.

"Matthew . . . ?" Jessie whimpered as his big hands cupped her bottom and he pressed his mouth against the rapidly heating core of her. "Dear God . . ." She could feel his warm breath, then his tongue parted her sex and slid deeply inside. He laved her there, teased and suckled until her breath came in tiny panting gasps and she moaned and arched against him. Relentlessly, he continued, stroking with infinite care, making her writhe and squirm. A sweet tension mounted inside. Her body tightened to a fine, taut edge and she rushed headlong into climax.

Then he was pressing her down on the desk, unbuttoning his breeches and thrusting himself deeply inside her. He was thick and hard, filling her to the hilt, arousing her and making her cry out his name. She clung to him as he pounded into her, each stroke deep and determined, scorching her with heat. They reached their peak together, both of them trembling, clinging to each other, their clothes damp with perspiration, their bodies languid and numb. Then Matthew was easing away, helping her up from the desk and holding her tightly against him.

His hand stroked over her hair. "I mean what I said, Jess. I'm sorry for the way I acted that day. And I'm proud of you for having the courage to help Anne birth her babe."

Tears sprang into her eyes. Jessie brushed them away with the back of her hand. *I love you,* she wanted to say. *I always have.*

But it was too soon. She was afraid of what he might say, of what he might think. Afraid he might guess the lengths she had gone to in order to ensure they would marry. Instead she went up on her tiptoes and kissed him, thankful that she was his wife, grateful for the fierce way he desired her. For now it was enough.

Another week passed. Viola had arrived two days ago, and now Papa Reggie sent word that he would be returning as well. Three days later, he rolled up in the Belmore carriage.

"I see the two of you are none the worse for wear," he said that first night at supper. "Neither has shot the other. The chambermaid says she has little need to make up her ladyship's bed, since it is rarely slept in. Apparently the two of you suit fairly well, after all."

Hot color flooded Jessie's cheeks. When she dared to look at Matthew, she found his mouth curved wickedly.

"I very much doubt, Father, there was ever a question Jessica and I would suit in that regard. However, you will be pleased to know that we have also found other things in common."

Jessie's head came up. "You're speaking of the children? You'll tell them about life aboard the *Norwich*?" She had asked him, but he had not yet agreed.

"I'll speak to them, love, if that is your wish. But I was referring to your greenhouse."

"My greenhouse? What about it?"

"Did you know that when I was a boy, planting flowers was my favorite pastime? Not very masculine, I suppose, but I loved it just the same. Watching you, I've discovered I still do."

Papa Reggie cleared his throat. "'Tis hardly untoward for the son of a landed nobleman to love the soil. I was glad for your interest. I still am."

"How is Lady Bainbridge?" Matthew asked him, changing the subject, and it was the marquess's turn to look embarrassed.

"Delightful as always. The woman is a gem. Can't credit why it took me so long to notice."

Matthew smiled and so did Jessie. Their eyes touched and something sweet passed between them.

Perhaps the evening would have continued in this very pleasant vein, if Ozzie hadn't appeared just then at the dining room door.

"A visitor has arrived," he announced to the earl, his manner slightly disturbed. "In fact there are two of them. They both look a bit disreputable. I wouldn't have let them in except the gentleman claims to be her ladyship's brother."

Jessie sucked in a breath, her heart picking up its tempo. She and Matthew rose to their feet at exactly the same instant, followed closely by Papa Reggie.

"Father, you and Jessica stay here," Matt commanded. "I'll see to the matter of Danny Fox."

"I'm coming, too," Jessie said. "Danny is still my brother." Matthew started to argue, but she swept by him and out the door.

Her brother was lounging in the small drawing room he had been shown to, slumped with nonchalance on a spindle-legged tapestry sofa. He came to his feet when she walked in.

"Well . . . if it ain't the countess 'erself."

Jessie stiffened, unnerved by him as she always was. At first she didn't see his companion huddled at the end of the sofa, the small child bundled in dirty rags, tiny nose smudged with dirt, fingers poking through her holey mittens. When she did, her heart very neatly turned over. She forced her gaze to her brother. "Hello, Danny."

"I'm surprised to see you, Fox," Matt said as he moved farther into the room. "I thought I made myself clear—I warned you in no uncertain terms never to come near Jessica again."

For the first time, she noticed the thin scar running from beneath her brother's jaw along his throat into his open collar. A remnant of the knife fight they'd had at the fair. Definitely a warning.

Then Matt saw the child. Even bundled as the little girl was, dirty and shivering with cold, the blond hair and blue eyes were unmistakable, a smaller, nearly mirror image of Jessie.

"Who is she?" Matt asked, but Jessie already knew.

"Lit'l Saree 'ere is me daughter." Danny gestured toward the child. "Sweet lit'l tike she is, too. Been wit' me since 'er mama died, just three weeks past. Man like me's got no place to raise a child. Thought maybe me sister could 'elp, now that she's a countess and all . . . and seein' as 'ow she's always 'ad a way wit' the lit'l un's."

The little girl just sat there, staring straight ahead. Danny ran a hand over the top of her head, smoothing back her hair.

Jessie thought the child might have flinched, but the movement was so slight she couldn't be sure.

Afraid to look at Matthew, Jessie started walking toward the tiny blond girl. "How old is she, Danny?" Kneeling beside her, Jessie pulled the dirty woolen blanket more closely around her, but the child continued to shiver.

"'Bout four, I guess." He grinned. "Lit'l Saree's the reason I wound up shackle-legged in the first place. Mary's father come upon us in the 'ayloft. By then the gel was three months gone and I 'ad to pay the piper." His odd yellow eyes slid to Matthew. "Sort o' like what 'appened to the earl, 'ere."

Matt took a threatening step forward, but his father caught his arm.

"I gather you are proposing to leave the child with us," the marquess said, and Jessie swung hopeful eyes in his direction. She couldn't imagine leaving a child with Danny Fox. He hadn't the temperament for raising children, resorted to the back of his hand—or worse—most of the time. Jessie could personally attest to that.

"I was 'oping me sister could 'elp, bein' the girl's aunt and all. Lit'l Saree wouldn't be much trouble. She'll do whatever ya say, and she don't talk much. Not much a'tall."

Jessie could see that. Through the whole discussion, the child sat there mutely, staring at Jessie as if she were looking at a larger version of her own reflection.

"Mama?" she said, reaching out with a look of wonder to touch Jessie's golden hair. Jessie's throat closed up. She fought to blink back tears.

"Matthew?" she said, turning toward him. Her heart thudded painfully, tried to hammer its way out of her chest.

"We need to talk, Jess."

She nodded, both hopeful and fearful at the same time. She glanced at Papa Reggie as they walked out of the room, but his expression remained inscrutable. Since his return from London, he'd made one thing perfectly clear: From now on, Matthew was the head of the Belmore household. His decision was law—the marquess would not interfere.

It took a man of great wisdom to make such a choice. She respected him for it, but right now she wished it were he she faced not her husband. She couldn't begin to imagine what Matthew might say about raising someone else's child.

She felt his hand at her waist, strong and purposeful as he guided her into the study and solemnly closed the door. He said nothing for several long moments, just studied the painful emotions flickering across her face.

"For once Fox is telling the truth. The child is obviously your niece—the resemblance is uncanny."

"Yes . . ." Jessie wet her lips. "Viola knew my mother. She said as a child, we both looked the same."

"Having her here will compound the problem of your past. More lies will have to be created. More people will be involved in the deceit . . . to say nothing of the grave responsibility you will be undertaking as the little girl's substitute mother." He looked at her hard. "That is what you are thinking, is it not? You wish to raise the girl yourself?"

Her chin went up. Her stomach crawled with nerves. "My brother will treat her badly. I'm certain he already has. He used to beat me black and blue whenever he got the chance. Once he cracked a rib. Another time, he blackened both of my eyes. He used to—" She stopped at the look of horror on Matthew's face. It was replaced by one of fury.

"I should have used that knife for more than just a warning," he said blackly, his hand balled suddenly into a fist.

"It doesn't matter now. I only mentioned it because of little Sarah. I can't stand to think of a child being treated that way, especially if the child is my niece."

"No," Matt said, coming up beside her. He cupped her cheek with his hand. "The child can't stay with your brother. But there are other ways we could help her. The question remains, do you wish to keep her here?"

Jessie lifted her gaze to his, her heart there in her eyes. "The house is so big and she is so small. You won't even notice she is here. She can play with the children at the school, and Vi will help look after her. I'll make certain she doesn't get in your way. If you let her stay, Matthew, I promise you won't be sorry."

How could he possibly be sorry? Matt looked into those beseeching blue eyes and knew that if it made Jessie happy, it was exactly what he wanted to do.

The thought completely unnerved him. He didn't want that kind of involvement with a woman. He never had. He had vowed to keep his distance—had meant to keep that vow.

And there was something else, something that warned him to be wary. Thoughts of his father's determined wish that he and Jessie marry. Jessie's love for Belmore—almost as great as his own, his father had said. She had vowed to become a lady from the time she was a child. Now it had happened, just as she'd said.

Unconsciously, Matthew's jaw clamped. It was all so neat, so orderly. Jessie was his wife, just as his father—perhaps even Jessie—had planned. Never mind that his rashness had been the ultimate cause.

He cared for Jessie—too damned much to suit him. Now he was giving in to her wishes again, agreeing to raise the spawn of her no-good half brother. It was dangerous, he knew. People might wonder about the girl, begin to get suspicious, since no mention of the child had ever been made before.

Still, she was little more than a babe, and aside from Danny Fox, Jessie was all the family she had.

Matt cleared his throat. "The child may stay," he said gruffly, "but I want Fox gone." He strode toward the door and jerked it open with that single purpose in mind.

In the drawing room, the marquess knelt beside the girl and spoke in comforting tones. Fleetingly it occurred to Matt that his father might be pleased to have the child stay as well. He fixed an unrelenting glare on Danny Fox, but didn't speak for so long the thinner man started to fidget beneath his harsh regard.

"Your daughter may stay on one condition."

"Now wait just a minute—" Fox rolled to his feet, his demeanor suddenly aggressive. "I never said for certain I wanted to leave 'er. I just said I 'oped me sister would 'elp."

Matt said nothing, just let his hard look bore into the other man. He had known Fox wanted money. Danny knew his soft-hearted sister well, knew that once Jessie saw the child, she'd be determined to protect her. "How much?"

Danny's eyes glinted with triumph. "A thousand pounds."

"I'll give you five hundred. Not a farthing more. You will take it and you will never set foot on this property again."

"Well now, yer lordship. Ya drive a bleedin' 'ard bargain . . . askin' a man to give up 'is own flesh and blood."

"I'm not asking you, I'm telling you. Either you take the money, or you take the girl." He ignored the strangled sound that came from Jessie's throat. "Either way, you won't be allowed inside this house again. The choice is yours—what's it to be?"

A cold smile curved the slender man's lips. "Why, the blunt, yer lordship. No matter 'ow much it might pain me, a man's got to do what's best for 'is kin."

Matt smiled thinly. "That's what I thought." He started for the door. "Leave the child and come with me." Walking past Jessie, he headed for his study. In minutes he had written out a bank draft and pressed it into Fox's hand. A few minutes later Matt slammed the front door closed, leaving him standing on the porch.

Matt watched him through the window till he disappeared into the night and wondered why he didn't feel a stronger sense of relief.

Jessie sat at the front of the schoolroom. Across from her, six small heads bent over their desks, a seventh, this one tiny and blond, sat staring straight ahead. For hours Sarah hadn't moved.

Jessie watched with a heart in tatters. The child was so broken, so alone. While the others were working on their lesson, she crossed the room and took Sarah's hand, led her away from the building and out into the sunshine. A thin fog had left the morning crisp, but the day would be warm. Still, Sarah kept her small arms wrapped tightly around herself, hugging her newly sewn yellow muslin dress as if it were a treasure.

"It's pretty here, isn't it, Sarah?"

Sarah didn't answer. Since the night of her arrival, she'd said only that single word. *Mama?* As if it were a question, as if she couldn't understand why she and Jessie looked so much alike. Then she had sunk back into her shell, never speaking, pretending not to notice her surroundings.

But she did.

Every once in a while, Jessie saw the spark that came into her eyes when she discovered something new and wonderful, the way it had this morning when she had received her first new dress. Oddly enough, it was Matthew who had brought it, a present he had purchased in the village, one of a dozen new dresses he had ordered, but the only one that so far had been completed. Until today, Sarah had been wearing clothes borrowed from the servants' children, clean but slightly worn.

Even those had garnered several soft touches and winsome smiles—when she was sure no one was looking. The rest of the time, her thoughts remained safely locked away.

"How's she doin', Miss Jessie?" Simon Stewart, the oldest of her students, walked up. They still used the informal address, though she was certain Matthew wouldn't approve if he found out. "I finished my assignment. I saw you come outside with little Sarah."

"This is all very new to her. I imagine she misses her mother. I don't think she quite understands what's going on."

"Why don't you tell her? Children is—are—smarter than people think."

Jessie smiled. "I did tell her, Simon. But I'm not sure she believes me."

The gangly boy knelt beside the little girl. Already the

children were fond of her, touched in some way by the fears she kept locked inside. "Miss Jessie always tells the truth, Sarah. She likes children. There isn't a one of us wouldn't like havin' her for a mother. You don't know how lucky you are."

Jessie flushed. It was wonderful to know they cared. "Thank you, Simon." She watched him walk away, thinking how far he had come since he had started at the school. She glanced down at the child, whose eyes still followed the gangly youth. "He's a good boy, isn't he, Sarah?"

Sarah watched him disappear but made no effort to acknowledge Jessie's words.

"How about something to eat?" she said, and caught what might have been a flicker of interest in the little girl's powder blue eyes. "We'll go see Cook just as soon as the children are finished with their lessons."

No response. Jessie bent and scooped her up, propping her against one hip. The little girl's arms slid around her neck and Jessie's heart squeezed painfully. She cursed her brother for the hundredth time. She thought of the marks she had seen on the child's back and legs when she had put her to bed, and knew exactly the kind of things Danny had done to frighten her so badly.

A flicker of unease settled over her. She hugged Sarah against her, suddenly afraid of what would happen if her brother ever got hold of the child again. She wouldn't let him near her, she vowed, but she couldn't shake the feeling. It darkened what had started as a lovely day.

Chapter Sixteen

They couldn't hide from the scandal forever. At least that's what Papa Reggie said.

During his weeks in London, he had mollified the duke with the repayment of expenses the man had incurred in preparation for the wedding, a tidy sum to be sure. The marquess had returned the bloodstone betrothal ring and given him, in Matthew's name, an incredible ink-black, seventeen-hand Thoroughbred racehorse so obviously destined to become a champion the duke had finally, grudgingly, acquiesced to forgetting the duel he intended, and even agreed not to give the newlyweds the cut direct the first time he saw them in Society.

"Now the trick," the marquess said as they sat in the breakfast room that looked out over the garden, "is to ease back into the mainstream of things." He scratched his chin. "A wedding celebration here at Belmore might be a good place to start."

Jessie looked at Matthew, whose expression had turned dark, then back to the white-haired man across the table. "I-I don't think that's a good idea, Papa Reggie. Perhaps we should wait. Give things a bit more time to cool down."

"Poppycock. The longer we wait, the more difficult the task will become. We shall keep the whole thing very simple, an outdoor fest for the tenants, a dinner and ball for the landed gentry, the local squires, and any of the nobles we can convince to come. I shall call upon Lord Landsdowne myself. If he and Lady Caroline will agree to attend, the way back will be far easier."

Matt's face turned even harder, and Jessie's stomach did a nauseating swirl. "Surely the Winstons will refuse."

"They will come," the marquess said. "You may count on it." He smiled in that determined way that reminded her of Matthew. "I hold a second mortgage on Winston House. The earl is quite determined no one of his acquaintance should learn about it—Landsdowne won't dare to refuse."

"Matthew?" Jessie turned to him. The final say, she knew, would now be his.

He took a sip of his thick black coffee, set it down with a clatter in his saucer. "As difficult as it may be, my father is right. We have to think of the future. There is the Belmore name to consider. We'll do as he suggests."

Preparations for the festivities swung into motion the following day. Jessie wasn't surprised when Lady Bainbridge arrived to help them. In fact she was imminently relieved.

And the marquess seemed years younger when the countess was around. Seated in the drawing room, Lady Bainbridge affectionately patted the older man's arm.

"As usual, Reggie dear, you have hit on the very thing. It is customary for a member of the aristocracy to hold a celebration of his marriage for his neighbors and friends in the country. 'Tis the perfect avenue for the newlyweds to begin their journey back into the fold."

But Matthew was obviously unhappy about it. Jessie supposed he was embarrassed by the scandal. He was, after all, a very proper military man. But perhaps it was something else. Jessie worried that it was the encounter he faced with Lady Caroline. Perhaps he still carried a *tendre* for her, maybe even loved her.

Once he had said it wasn't so, but then he had expected they would marry. Since then he had lost her. Perhaps his unknown feelings for her had now become clear.

Jessie bit her lip, praying it wasn't the truth. But Matthew was a man who didn't show his emotions. She had no idea the way he really felt, except that he remained a bit of a prig.

In the matter of her gowns, for instance. He had let it be known, in no uncertain terms, that no other of her dresses should be lowered in the bosom.

"I don't give a bloody damn about the current vogue," he'd argued. "I won't have every man-jack in London staring at your breasts."

Jessie stiffened. "You're being totally unreasonable, Matthew. Every woman in the ton—"

"I don't give a tinker's damn what every woman does. It's you I'm concerned with. Since I am the master of this household, as well as *your* lord and master, you will bloody well do as I say." He had stormed from the room, leaving Jessie fuming behind him.

She didn't speak to him for the balance of the day, barely acknowledged his presence at supper, but when she retired to bed, she found him already upstairs, silently pacing the floor of her bedchamber.

"I realize you are still angry," he said, eyeing her rigid posture, "but our disagreement has nothing to do with what happens between us in here." Determined to make his point, he had dragged her into his arms and kissed her so thoroughly she forgot how angry she was. Jessie found herself kissing him back and the next thing she knew he was lifting her up and carrying her over to the bed.

After a passionate round of lovemaking, she curled against him, deciding it really didn't matter whether she was the height of fashion or not.

Another time they had argued about her jaunts around the country. It had been weeks since she'd visited the Belmore tenants. She missed seeing them and was determined to discover if friends like Anne and James Bartlett were still faring well.

"Where do you think you're going?" Matt approached her in the stables as she made ready to leave.

"I thought I told you. I wish to visit some friends."

"I presumed you'd be traveling with a groom." He glanced around. "I don't see one here."

"I am not a child, Matthew. I'm quite capable of riding by myself."

"You may not be a child, but you are behaving like one. You will take one of the grooms with you, or you will not go."

"Matthew—"

"I'm sorry, Jess. You don't know what kind of danger you might come upon out there. And a woman by herself is always fuel for gossip. I don't want you stirring up any more of that."

She didn't bother to remind him it was he who had stirred up most of the gossip of late. "Everyone needs a little time alone, Matthew. I've come to enjoy my rides around Belmore. I mean to continue as I have in the past." With that she climbed up on the mounting block and settled herself in the sidesaddle. Just as quickly, Matt reached up and hauled her down.

"You'll go with a groom, my lady, or not at all. Which is it to be?"

Fury coursed through her, making the riding crop tremble in her hand. "You are my husband, Matthew, not my jailer."

His expression remained stern. "Make your choice, Jessie."

"Damn you!"

A corner of his mouth kicked up. "I thought you gave up swearing."

"You would make a saint utter profanities."

Suddenly, he moved closer, till his body pressed full-length against hers. "Perhaps staying home would be best, after all. There is a pile of fresh straw in one of the tack rooms. I imagine if we closed the door, I could find a highly improper use for it."

"Matthew!"

He ground himself suggestively against her and she felt

his hardening arousal. "Then again," he said, "there is a saddle slung over one of the feed barrels. I can easily imagine bending you over, lifting your riding skirts, and—"

"Ohhh, you are a devil!"

He kissed the back of her neck. "Forget your ride, Jess. Stay here with me."

She knew what he was doing, and yet she trembled, half tempted to give in. If it weren't for seeing Anne and the baby . . . "All right, Matthew, you win. Jimmy can come along."

He grinned wickedly and brushed a kiss on her lips. "Are you sure that's what you want?"

Her heart was pumping, her cheeks tinged pink with heat. She glanced down, saw the way his riding breeches gloved the bulge of his sex, and wasn't sure at all. "I-I'm quite sure, my lord."

Matthew chuckled softly, apparently reading her thoughts. She let him help her back up into the sidesaddle, then watched as he left to fetch Jimmy Hopkins, the youngest of the Belmore grooms.

"Matthew?" she called after him.

"Yes, love?"

"You are a very wicked man."

He laughed triumphantly, pleased to have gotten his way in this as he did most everything else.

Yes, even with his faults, Matthew had been a good husband. She loved him more each day and she couldn't stand the thought that somehow she might lose him.

But he had never mentioned his feelings for her, and he always kept a certain distance between them. Now he'd be thrown together again with Caroline Winston. Caroline was everything Jessie was not and seeing the two of them would make that abundantly clear. The wedding celebration might be the entree into Society the Earl and Countess of Strickland needed, but Jessie dreaded it with all her heart.

As she nudged her gray horse forward, she felt an icy chill of apprehension.

* * *

The day of celebration finally arrived. Beginning with an afternoon of skittles and beer in one of the meadows nearest town, a fete attended by nearly five hundred of the country folk thereabouts, the festivities progressed on into the evening with the lavish dinner and ball. Sixty servants assisted. A dozen musicians were engaged to perform at the dance, which was held in the gilt and mirrored Belmore ballroom.

Most of the people who attended Jessie didn't know, but the Lord Pickering was there, Lady Bainbridge's cousin; as well as her son, the earl, a tall imposing, silver-haired man who had lately been out of the country. Adam Harcourt, Viscount St. Cere, was present, as well as the Countess Fielding, which meant Baron Densmore was also in attendance.

There was a small, selective group of military men: Admiral Dunhaven, a weathered, stern-faced man Matthew had served under a few years back; Captain Eustace Bradford, whose ship, the *Gibraltar*, was in Portsmouth for repairs, as well as a young lieutenant named Wescott, and several other naval officers who were Matthew's friends.

An imposing man Jessie knew of but hadn't yet met arrived midway through the evening—Adrian Kingsland, Baron Wolvermont, and for one of the few times that night, Matthew smiled with genuine warmth.

"Adrian!" Her husband strode forward, sincerely glad to see his friend, unlike some other of his guests. "I was pleased to learn you'd returned from the fighting on the continent. I hoped very much you would come." Born a second son as Matthew had been, Adrian Kingsland was a captain in the cavalry, decorated several times for valor. Late last year, on the unexpected death of his mother's uncle, he'd inherited the Wolvermont title and estates, but had not yet resigned his commission.

The handsome baron smiled. "I was surprised to hear you had married, but it looks as though it suits you."

Matthew smiled. "I might still be a bachelor if it hadn't been for you—at least indirectly. I can't tell you how much

I appreciate you and your staff's generosity. Thank you, Adrian."

"Anytime, Matthew. I only wish I had been there myself." He turned as Jessie stepped up beside her husband and a pair of penetrating emerald eyes assessed her from head to foot. The baron was tall and broad-shouldered, with thick, dark chestnut hair and an arrogant, sensual mouth. For the first time that evening, she was grateful her gown wasn't cut fashionably lower.

His words were for Matt, who hadn't yet realized her arrival, but his eyes remained on her. "If this lovely creature is your bride, my friend, I understand why you stole her from Milton." It was the first time anyone had dared to make a reference to the farce they'd played out at the church. Matthew looked at Wolvermont with a hint of disapproval.

"I imagined you would," he grumbled, sliding an arm possessively around Jessie's waist.

Wolvermont just laughed, a deep, male, slightly rough-textured sound. "Lady Strickland, it is indeed a pleasure." He bowed extravagantly over her hand, and in his perfectly tailored scarlet and gold cavalry uniform, he was a devastatingly handsome man.

Matthew must have read her thoughts for the baron's continued flattery made his jaw go taut. After a moment more of conversation, he whisked her away to entertain other of their guests.

One of them, she already knew. A wealthy young squire named Sir Thomas Perry. Though not quite as tall, in a different, more genteel, less commanding way, he was nearly as handsome as Wolvermont. With light brown hair and hazel eyes, he was an intelligent, hardworking man in his twenties, a man Jessie didn't know well, but liked and respected.

"Good evening, my lord," he said to Matthew. "Lady Strickland, it's good to see you again."

"I'm glad you could come, Sir Thomas."

Matt frowned even as he shook the young squire's hand. "I didn't realize you and Lady Strickland were acquainted."

"We met one day while we were both out riding," Sir Thomas said. "Lady Strickland was visiting some of the Belmore tenants." He smiled at her with warmth. "Her ladyship is quite a stunning woman."

Jessie smiled. "Sir Richard has paid calls at Belmore several times since."

Matt's eyes locked with the squire's. "But not lately," he said matter-of-factly—far too matter-of-factly. "Not since I have been in residence."

Jessie flushed as she recognized Matthew's growing animosity.

Sir Thomas smiled thinly, sensing it as well, his own ire rising at the subtle insinuation. "I apologize, my lord—you are quite correct. I was remiss in not calling sooner. I shall endeavor to remedy that in the future." He gave Jessie a warm, too-intimate glance. "A pleasure, Lady Strickland." Turning, he walked away.

Jessie looked at Matthew, saw he worked a muscle in his jaw. "You never mentioned Perry. How long have you known him?"

"I-I met him when I first came home from boarding school."

"And he called on you at Belmore?"

"He simply paid his respects . . . to Papa Reggie and me."

Matt stared after him, watching the handsome squire disappear into the crowd. "I wonder if he will continue in that vein . . . now that you have a husband."

Jessie bristled at the anger she saw in his face. "Sir Thomas was never anything but a gentleman. He doesn't deserve your abuse and neither do I." She started to say something more, but now was not the time for an argument. "Excuse me," she said instead, "I believe I see Lady Bainbridge coming this way. She appears to be looking for me."

Matthew smiled, but it held no warmth. "Why don't we both go speak to Lady Bainbridge?"

Standing inside the door to the ballroom, Caroline Winston watched Matthew standing beside Jessie Fox. One hand rode possessively at her waist, while his jaw flexed anytime a man happened to glance in her direction.

Caroline's stomach knotted. She had known that Matthew was enamored of the woman—the terrible scene at the church had proven just how much. Still, it hurt to know his feelings for the woman hadn't lessened, had perhaps grown even stronger.

Damn you, Jessica Fox. Damn you to the fires of Hades. How had she seduced Matthew away so completely? Used her luscious body, no doubt. Tempted him with her high full breasts and incredibly long slender legs. Perhaps she had gone to him, given herself to him without benefit of marriage. Perhaps she had even enjoyed the things Matt had done to her . . . or at least pretended she did.

Caroline knew the kind of woman who responded to the lusts of a man. Carnal women, tarts and slatterns, lightskirts and disgusting creatures like Madeleine Fielding.

Though she had begged and pleaded with her father not to come this evening to Belmore, he had been firm in his resolve that his daughter and wife attend. Caroline had greeted Matthew and his . . . *bride* with sugary sweetness, though every word tasted like bitter gall in her mouth.

Now the evening was almost ended and somehow she had survived it. Day after tomorrow, her family would return to London to complete the last few weeks of the Season. Caroline would be humiliated once again, but eventually it would pass. Matthew was the one at fault, not Caroline. Matthew and his *wife* would bear the brunt of the scandal.

So far Caroline had taken no action against the woman who had caused her so much grief, but now, seeing Matthew so entwined in the Fox woman's web, she vowed again to do so.

Once she was back in London, she would hire a Bow Street runner, a man who would, for a price, dig until he discovered the truth about Jessica Fox. She wanted to know every detail, every possible secret that might be used against her. There had to be something. Few people were as pure as they seemed.

Caroline watched the beautiful blonde being guarded so
jealously by the man who should have been *her* husband,
and a cold stone settled in her stomach. It wasn't fair—it just
wasn't! Somehow, someway, Caroline intended to ruin Jessica Fox.

The evening progressed from bad to worse, as far as Jessie
was concerned. She was angry at Matthew for being so possessive, yet at the same time, she couldn't help a tiny glow of
warmth. Perhaps he cared for her more than she believed.
Perhaps he was beginning to feel something besides merely
lust and husbandly duty.

Earlier in the evening, he'd been excessively polite to
Lady Caroline, but nothing more than that. No warm look
passed between them; they both behaved with the strictest
propriety.

Then again, that is exactly what Matthew and Caroline
would do.

It was well past midnight when the last guest entered the
ballroom, a petite, dark-haired woman whose eyes searched
for Jessie even as she walked through the ornate gilded
doors. Gwen Lockhart looked radiant in a peach moiré silk
gown, her glossy chestnut curls forming ringlets around her
face, her breasts displayed a bit more prominently than her
age and unmarried status allowed.

"Jessie! God, I thought I'd never get here." She glanced a
bit nervously at Matthew, who stood beside her as he had for
most of the evening. "Good evening, Lord Strickland."

"Good evening, Lady Gwendolyn." Matthew glanced
around. "I didn't see your mother . . . or Lord Waring. Have
you come with someone else?"

"Not . . . not exactly." She looked beseechingly at Jessie.
"I'm sorry, my lord, would you mind very much if I spoke to
Jessica alone? There is something important we need to dis-
cuss."

Matthew glanced around the ballroom and Jessie followed his gaze. No sign of Lord or Lady Waring . . . or anyone else Jessie could think of who might have brought Gwen.

"Who have you come with, Lady Gwendolyn?" Deep blue eyes fixed on her face and Gwen wet her lips.

"Jessica?" she pleaded.

"Matthew, if you don't mind, Gwen and I—"

"I'm afraid I do mind." He glanced toward the terrace, his jaw set once more. He gripped Gwen's arm, then took Jessie's none too gently. "I believe the three of us need to speak." Propelling them out onto the terrace, he didn't stop until they had reached a private corner where no one could hear them.

"Now then, my lady," he said to Gwen. "I would like very much to know with whom you have traveled here from London."

Her shoulders went rigid, her small pointed chin coming up. "I told you, I wish to speak to your wife—alone."

"Not until you answer my question."

"Matthew," Jessie put in, resting a hand on his arm, "perhaps it would be better if—"

"No." He glared at Gwen. "Lady Gwendolyn, I have asked you a question. I would appreciate an answer."

"You . . . you are a tyrant, Lord Strickland. I cannot imagine how Jessica puts up with your high-handedness. I vow I shall never marry—especially not a man like you."

Matthew's mouth curved up. "Tyrant I may be. Now, answer my question."

"All right—if you must know—I came here by myself. I hired a carriage in London, spent the night at an inn, and if a wheel had not broken, I should have arrived here hours ago and not missed most of the evening. Are you satisfied?"

Matthew frowned. "Why? Why did you come on your own?"

"Because I knew this was important to Jessica. I wanted to lend my support, as she has always lent her support to me.

My stepfather would not come, nor allow my mother and I to come, so I came on my own."

Jessie sucked in a breath. "Dear Lord, Gwen, you know how angry Lord Waring will be—you should not have risked yourself that way."

"I don't care. I am sick unto death of Lord Waring. I'm a grown woman. I wish to live my life on my own."

"Lady Gwendolyn," Matthew said, more gently than Jessie would have expected. "It is noble of you to think of your friends, but it is also highly unseemly for a young, unmarried woman to be running around the countryside unchaperoned."

"I told you I don't care."

"Fortunately, I do. Tomorrow, I shall send word to your family that you are here, that you are well, and that you'll be staying a few more days. Lady Bainbridge will be leaving by then and you may return to London with her as chaperone. If you are lucky, perhaps the dowager countess will intercede on your behalf with Lord Waring."

Gwen nodded stiffly. "As you wish, my lord." Jessie reached over and squeezed her hand.

Surprisingly Matthew smiled. "In the meantime, you might as well enjoy yourself. There are a number of handsome young men in attendance. I'm certain they saw you come in. Allow me a dance, then I shall leave you to them."

The dance was his way of giving Gwen his protection, and Jessie's heart swelled with gratitude. Gwen actually smiled.

"Thank you, my lord. Perhaps you are not such a tyrant after all."

But of course he was. When he began a country dance with Gwen, and Adrian Kingsland asked Jessie to dance, Matthew's warm look faded and his features turned grim.

"I believe my friend Strickland is having a bit of trouble adjusting to the role of husband," Jessie's partner, Lord Wolvermont, said.

"What do you mean?"

"I mean I have never seen Matthew jealous. I didn't know he had it in him."

Jessie glanced at her husband's stony expression as she and the baron danced past. "I realize he is overly possessive, but jealous? That is something altogether different. Do you really think it's possible?"

Wolvermont smiled, a devastating flash of white that undoubtedly sent half the women in London to their knees. "Why is that so hard to believe?"

Because he wants me but he doesn't love me, Jessie thought, but hadn't time for any sort of answer before the dance came to an end. Matt left Gwen in Lady Bainbridge's care, then tugged Jessie toward the doors leading out to the foyer and away from the ballroom.

"Matthew, what on earth are you doing? We can't possibly leave with so many guests still here."

But her husband's steps didn't slow. He led her up the stairs and down the hall to his suite, hauled her in and closed the door. "Every man in there has been wanting to drag you off somewhere since the moment you entered the ballroom. Since that right belongs to me, I am the one who shall exercise the privilege."

"Matthew!" His hard kiss silenced her protest, started out fierce, almost punishing, then turned gentle, coaxing, and achingly tender. In minutes he was stripping away her clothes, filling his hands with her breasts. Thoughts of the ball began to fade. Papa Reggie was there, after all, as well as Lady Bainbridge. And somehow what was proper seemed to fade into unimportance. Vaguely it occurred to her that her stiff and starchy husband was becoming less so all the time.

A golden, late-morning sun washed over the rolling green Belmore fields. In the distance, tracts of barley corn had been harvested, the yellow straw left to fodder for the cattle later on.

Standing on the terrace, Adam Harcourt studied the distant fields then returned his gaze to the gardens below the terrace wall. At least a dozen guests remained at Belmore, people who had traveled any sort of distance, friends from London, or other parts of the country, Matt's military friends in the navy.

A late breakfast of ham, eggs, pheasant, Cheshire cheese, cold tongue, chocolate, tea, coffee, and scones was being served out of doors beneath a big green-striped canopy, but it was the girl in the peppermint-striped day dress who had captured Adam's attention.

"Ah, so there you are." Matt Seaton strode toward him, turning his attention away from the girl. "I wondered where you'd gone off to."

Adam smiled faintly. "I was enjoying the view." Matt followed his gaze to the petite dark-haired beauty. "I saw her come in late last night. You were remiss in not giving me an introduction."

Matt frowned. "Her name is Gwendolyn Lockhart. She's the Earl of Waring's stepdaughter. She's an innocent, Adam, hardly someone you'd be interested in."

Adam continued to watch the girl, enjoying the way she moved, not delicately like most women, but with energy, life, and zest. "Those eyes of hers are magnificent . . . as green as new leaves. I've seen her before . . . I'm sure of it, but I can't think where it might have been."

"Leave her alone, Adam. The girl is a friend of Jessica's. She's here by herself, which means she's under my protection."

"By herself? You don't mean she came on her own?"

Matt sighed. "The girl is even more of a handful than Jessie. She has a penchant for trouble and a family who doesn't care a fiddler's damn about her. She has far too much audacity and far too little common sense. Aside from that, she is too naive to handle a worldly man like you."

But Adam simply smiled. "Now I know where I've seen her. She was the girl in the Fallen Angel . . . the one who came in with your wife."

Matthew froze. "Bloody hell." His scowl went even blacker. "I was hoping no one saw them."

"I don't think anyone else knew who they were. I wouldn't have suspected if you hadn't come sweeping in like Sir Lancelot and herded them out of there."

Matt's eyes swung to his, studied him for a long, silent moment. "I'm surprised you would frequent a place like that. I didn't realize your tastes ran to that sort of thing."

Adam simply shrugged. There wasn't much in the last eight years since his abominable marriage had ended that he hadn't tried at least once. "Almost anything can be pleasurable . . . at times. Pain isn't usually my preference, however. Lord Chasen's son, Philip, wished to go. Since I had nothing better to do, I agreed to go along."

Matt said nothing.

"I don't suppose you'd tell me why your wife and her friend were there."

Strickland's gaze swung to the girl in the garden, who now stood talking to Jessie. "Lady Gwendolyn fashions herself a writer. She wishes to pen a book, and in order to do so, she needs to experience life—or at least that is what she believes. Jessie went along hoping in some way to protect her."

Adam grinned, etching dimples into his cheeks. "And you arrived to protect the pair of them. I imagine, once you got them out of there, you were their greatest threat that eve."

Matthew laughed, relaxing a little. "I suppose I was. I wanted to thrash them both." The smile slid away. "Apparently Waring does more than enough of that. It's the reason Jessica is so protective." He looked hard at Adam. "I've said more than I should have, but I wanted you to know and I trust your discretion. Leave the girl alone, Adam. She has more than enough trouble already."

Adam didn't answer. His gaze had shifted back to the lovely dark-haired girl. Her laughter rang out at something Jessica said, a clear, sweet, crystalline sound. An image of her appeared, dressed in men's clothing, her glossy dark curls poking out from beneath her oversized bowler.

What kind of woman would risk her reputation just to

know what went on in a place like that? An interesting one to be sure. He was more curious about her than ever. And determined to obtain an introduction. He made his way through the guests down the steps to where the lady in pink stood next to the Countess of Strickland.

Chapter Seventeen

*J*essie watched the tall, darkly handsome Viscount St. Cere walking toward them in the garden. Gray-eyed and leanly built, elegant and perfectly groomed, St. Cere had an aloofness about him, a dangerous, unreadable temperament that Jessie had always found unnerving.

"Lady Strickland." He bowed gracefully over her hand.

"Lord St. Cere . . . Matthew and I were pleased you could join us."

"If you are pleased I am here, then I must have done the right thing in driving him that morning to St. James's church."

Jessie's eyes widened. "So you were the one who encouraged him." She smiled at him softly. "I shall be forever grateful, my lord." The viscount smiled, and Jessie thought perhaps there was a side of him that was softer, more approachable than she had first thought. She turned to Gwen, who fidgeted a little beside her.

"I don't believe the two of you have met," Jessie said, making the formal introductions.

"A pleasure, my lady." The viscount smiled as he bowed over Gwen's hand.

Gwen smiled back, her eyes skimming over the fine cut of his clothes, the thick black, softly curling hair. Approval shone in those big green eyes, and an interest that made Jessie suddenly nervous.

"Our hosts have provided what promises to be quite a sumptuous repast," St. Cere said to Gwen. "If you are hungry, my lady, perhaps you would care to join me."

Her thick dark lashes swept down, but they couldn't hide the color in her cheeks. "I should like that very much, my lord."

But Jessie didn't.

Dear Lord—St. Cere was the biggest rake in London, a conscienceless rogue who had seduced half the women in the ton. Gwen was young, and where men were concerned, still extremely naive. True she was intelligent and not easily fooled. She was also bound and determined to experience life, and Jessie wasn't sure to what lengths she might go in order to do so.

In truth they made a handsome pair, both of them dark-haired, she petite and the viscount so tall, but they were hardly suited. St. Cere was a cynic, jaded even by aristocratic standards, while Gwen was a confirmed optimist whose every waking moment was consumed with the need to discover the joys of life. The only thing they truly had in common was the obvious attraction each of them held for the other and the fact that neither of them had the slightest interest in marriage.

It was a dangerous combination, one that set Jessie's nerves on edge. She watched St. Cere eyeing Gwen as if she were a juicy piece of meat and rushed headlong toward the house in search of her husband.

Matthew sat in a tufted brown leather chair in the study, the door firmly closed, Admiral Dunhaven and Captain Bradford seated across from him. Each of them sipped mugs of strong black coffee.

"So Villeneuve has sailed at last from Ferrol." The French admiral had broken away from Admiral Nelson at Toulon some time back and sailed for the West Indies. Eventually, he had put into port in Spain, after an inconclusive battle with a squadron commanded by Sir Robert Calder.

"We believe he picked up at least fifteen Spanish ships

while he was there," Admiral Dunhaven said, "though the report has not been confirmed."

Matt leaned forward, the news he had awaited infusing him with tension. "And you believe he is headed for Cádiz?" A port on the tip of Spain near Gibraltar.

"In Admiral Nelson's estimation, as well as my own—yes, we believe he is. In fact he could reach there at any time."

Matt studied the admiral's weathered features: the hawk-like nose, thin lips, and busy gray brows. "Once Villeneuve arrives, will Nelson confront him?"

He nodded, his mouth set grimly. "Absolutely. As soon as the Frenchman's destination is clear, Nelson intends to begin amassing his ships."

"And the *Norwich*?"

"Will undoubtedly be among them."

Matt straightened in his chair, a hundred thoughts running through his mind. "When do I leave?"

"Not quite yet, but I'm certain you'll be called. Admiral Nelson intends to win this battle. He wants to enter the fray with the best men in His Majesty's Navy. With your experience, Captain Seaton, and your spotless record, clearly that means he will want you."

Matt nodded. Part of him hummed with the old thrill of excitement, the heady need to stand in command of his ship and lead his men to victory. The other half thought of Jessie, of little Sarah, of Belmore and his father, and all of his new responsibilities. The pull was equally strong to stay there. Unfortunately, he owed this final duty to England.

"I'm at your service, Admiral. I made that clear before I tendered my resignation. As soon as word arrives, I'll be on my way for Portsmouth."

The general came to his feet and so did Matt and Captain Bradford. "You've a little more time, I should think," the admiral said. "Break the news to your family. Prepare them for your departure."

"Aye, sir."

They exchanged a few last minute concerns, then the

men retired to retrieve their things for the journey back to Portsmouth. Part of him wished he could go with them. He had waited for this battle, readied his men and equipment, for more than two long years.

The other part wished the war was over. That he could stay at Belmore and never spend a moment more thinking about the hardships and suffering he was certain to encounter when he returned to sea.

By supper that night, the number of guests at Belmore had dwindled to less than a dozen. Gwen Lockhart sat at the far opposite end of the table from Adam Harcourt, beside the Earl of Pickering. Lord Strickland had arranged it that way, Gwen was sure, or perhaps it had even been Jessie. They wanted to protect her from St. Cere, and in truth, she supposed they were right in their concerns.

Adam Harcourt was a rogue of the very worst sort. His very name was shrouded in scandal, dark tales of his long dead wife and her lover, Harold Cavendish—the man who had shot her. Gwen wasn't supposed to know, of course, but since that morning, she had dragged bits and pieces of information from a dozen different sources, and at last the picture had been clear.

Poor Lord Harry, the impoverished second son of the Marquess of Havendale, never had a chance against a vamp like Elizabeth Harcourt, Lady St. Cere. She convinced Lord Harry that she was in love with him, that St. Cere was a black-hearted beast her parents had forced her to marry, a man who took her against her will, a man she loathed the very sight of.

She did loathe him on occasion, when he shunned her bed for one of his mistresses, a habit he'd begun after discovering her in the throes of passion with one of his grooms. Still, St. Cere had wanted an heir so he had continued to bed her. He was a skillful lover, and Elizabeth insatiable in her appetites.

It was poor Lord Harry who was tortured in the end, discovering the woman he had pictured as the long-suffering, nearly virginal wife of the sadistic viscount, *en flagrant dilecto* with her husband—and obviously loving every moment of it.

He had shot the viscountess, plunged a knife into St. Cere's back, then thrust the same blade into his broken heart.

Since then, it was said, the viscount had no use for women, except of course in bed, and that he still carried the scar of Lord Harry's blade. He was a well-known rake who immersed himself in deep play and drank too much, spent his time in houses of ill repute, and was even rumored to have deflowered several young ladies barely out of the schoolroom.

Gwen believed every word of it. It was there in each hot look, every wicked glance. He was a woman's worst nightmare—but oh, dear Lord, he was sinfully handsome. He made her insides flutter just to look at him, made her yearn to know the secrets she had only begun to imagine since that night at the Fallen Angel.

Even sitting as he was at the far end of the table, she could feel his eyes on her, feel those cool gray orbs slowly deducing the size and shape of her breasts.

Gwen shifted uncomfortably in her chair, her thighs rubbing together, a trickle of perspiration beading, then running down the line of her cleavage. He was every forbidden fantasy she had ever had, and she wondered insanely what it would be like to kiss him.

Surely she wouldn't consider such a thing. Surely she wouldn't dare. But as the evening progressed and she felt his silver gaze again and again, she found herself making excuses to leave, to wander alone out into the garden, hoping insanely that the viscount would follow.

Now as she strolled the crushed gravel path, Gwen fluttered her hand-painted fan, cooling the heat in her cheeks and ignoring the odd, inexplicable tension that had enveloped her all evening. When she reached the gazebo, a shadowy quiet spot at the rear of the garden, she climbed the stairs into the dark interior, then fidgeted as she watched the lights of the house through the tall mullioned windows in the distance.

It wasn't long after that footfalls crunched on the gravel path. Gwen's head snapped up as the tall handsome viscount climbed the stairs to the gazebo. He paused for a moment, then continued walking till he stood directly in front of her. Moonlight slanted in beneath the eaves. She could see the slightly arrogant tilt of his lips, the cool gray color of his eyes.

The corners of his mouth curved up. "You're a bold little vixen, aren't you?"

Gwen's mouth dropped open. "What!"

He chuckled softly, his gaze running over her, taking in the heightened rise and fall of her breasts, the stubborn tilt of her chin. "Half the women in London are afraid to walk in my shadow, but not you, Lady Gwen. I don't think you are the least bit afraid."

She was afraid, just a little, but she wasn't about to admit it. Instead she shrugged her shoulders. "What is there to be afraid of? You are simply a man, are you not? No matter what the gossipmongers say."

His sleek black brows drew together and his sensuous mouth went thin. "So you know about that."

"Yes."

"I should have guessed. Did they fill in all the gruesome details?"

"I believe so, yes."

"I'm flattered you had that much interest."

Gwen arched a brow. "I'm a writer, my lord. I enjoy studying people. I find you an interesting man."

The smile returned, softer now. "A writer . . . yes. That is what Strickland said."

"Did he?"

He nodded, the moon tracking blue-black waves through his hair. "He made a point of it when I mentioned I had seen you that night—at the Fallen Angel."

Gwen hissed in a breath, her legs suddenly unsteady. For

the second time in the last several minutes, she felt out of control. "Y-You were there that night . . . at . . . at the Fallen Angel?"

"I was there. You don't make much of a man, you know, even dressed as one. I've far greater hopes for you as a woman."

Gwen let that pass. She couldn't get over the fact he had been in a den of debauchery like the Fallen Angel. "You don't look like the kind of man who would enjoy a place like that."

"You mean a brothel? I assure you, my sweet, most men enjoy the pleasures of the flesh, purchased or otherwise."

She shook her head. "I meant a place that caters to men who enjoy . . . inflicting pain. Somehow I wouldn't have guessed . . . I didn't imagine you would like hurting women." She turned away from him then, her stomach leaden with disappointment, and feeling oddly close to tears. "Excuse me, I have to go in." She started past him, but the viscount caught her arm. She hoped he wouldn't notice she was trembling.

"I've discovered a number of forbidden pleasures in the last eight years. Pain can be an enjoyable diversion, I suppose. If the woman wishes it, I am willing to oblige. It doesn't matter to me, one way or another."

"I-I really have to go."

But he didn't release her arm. Instead, he lifted her chin and looked deeply into her eyes. "I can see that you have been mistreated. I would never hurt you, Gwen."

Her bottom lip trembled. Her eyes burned with tears. This wasn't going at all the way she had planned. "I shouldn't have come out here." She blinked and a drop of wetness slid down her cheek. He lifted it away with a long dark finger.

"No, you should not have. But I am glad you did." His eyes remained on hers, silver eyes, unreadable eyes. Then he bent his head and very gently kissed her. It was a feather-soft touch, barely a brush of his lips.

"Good night, Lady Gwen."

She could still taste him on her lips, feel the heat of his

mouth, and the touch of his hand on her skin. "Good night, my lord." She turned away from him and didn't look back, just streaked down the steps and out of the garden, into the house through the open terrace doors, and up the stairs to her room.

She had almost made it to safety when Jessica appeared, hurrying toward her down the hall with a worried expression.

"Gwen! Where on earth have you been?"

She glanced away from Jessie's close regard, her mind still clouded with thoughts of the man in the garden.

Jessie's eyes ran over her face. "Good heavens, what is wrong? You look pale, yet you are flushed at the same time."

Gwen sighed with resignation. Jessica would not give up till she knew the truth, and besides, she was Gwen's best friend. "It's him," she said, gripping Jessie's hand, dragging her inside the bedchamber and closing the door. "Feel my heart." She clamped Jessie's hand against her chest. "Dear God, 'tis still beating like thunder."

"You don't mean St. Cere? Tell me you are not speaking of that *him*?"

"Of course, I am. Who else could it be? Surely there is no one else like him."

"That is for certain. No one else could possibly be as dangerous to you as St. Cere."

Gwen sighed again and leaned back against the door. "I know. The man is a danger to any woman of an age to realize what one is, but Lord he is handsome." She looked up, her eyes still lit with an inner glow. "I do not believe he is as bad as they say. I simply do not believe it."

"He doesn't believe in marriage, Gwen. He is absolutely dead set against it."

"Good—so am I."

"It's different for a man, Gwen. You know that as well as I do."

"Perhaps it is. I do not care." She rolled her eyes. "Besides, all he did was kiss me."

"He kissed you?"

She nodded. "It was the softest, sweetest kiss you could possibly imagine."

Jessie's brows came together as she assessed that bit of news. "That doesn't seem a'tall like St. Cere." Her back went straighter. "It doesn't matter how sweetly he kissed you. You mustn't go near him again. Promise me you won't, Gwen."

"Why ever would I do that, Jess, when you know very well I will do so if I wish."

Jessie frowned. "You deserve a man who will make you happy. St. Cere can't possibly do that. Be careful, Gwen. At least promise me that."

"I'll be careful," she said. But even as she spoke the words, it occurred to her with stunning force that she didn't want to be careful—not when it came to St. Cere. She wanted to be bold and daring, to discover things about him—and herself. She wondered whether he would return to the city, and half of her prayed he would.

The other half prayed he would not.

The last of the guests departed Belmore the following day. Jessie had been careful to keep Sarah away from the visitors, except for Gwen and Lady Bainbridge, who both fell in love with the golden-haired child.

"She never speaks?" Gwen asked. "Never says a single word?"

"No."

"But she very definitely understands," Gwen said, watching the little girl rocking in her tiny chair.

"Oh, yes. We communicate surprisingly well, considering. Matthew has trouble, of course. He has no experience with children. I don't think he's quite sure what to do with Sarah."

"She likes him. Her eyes follow him whenever he comes into the room."

"He brings her presents. He takes her out to the stables to look at the horses. He just doesn't say very much. I suppose in that they are alike."

"Perhaps they are communicating better than you think."

They were standing in the doorway to the nursery, watching Sarah play with the clever little rag doll Viola had made for her. Jessie smiled softly. "Perhaps they are." She found herself wishing she and Matthew could communicate even half that well.

"She's a darling little girl," Gwen said. "Her hair is even lighter than yours. It's amazing, really. With the blond hair and blue eyes all three of you share, the child could be yours and Matthew's. In time she'll feel like a member of the family."

"In time . . ." Jessie agreed. "For now she is still uncertain. That's the reason I thought it best to keep her away from the guests. I didn't want her frightened any more than she already is."

Gwen's eyes skipped to the child. "I had a lovely childhood . . . before my mother remarried. I never knew my real father, since he died when I was so young, but I've always imagined him as a great white knight in shining armor. It made living with Waring that much worse." She glanced up at Jessie. "I know what it's like to be treated as brutally as Sarah. She is lucky to have found you and Lord Strickland. Now she will be safe."

Jessie reached for Gwen's hand. "What about you, Gwen? What will Lord Waring do to you for coming here without his permission?"

She shrugged, but tension settled in her shoulders. "I don't know. He has been busy with his whores of late. Perhaps, as your husband said, Lady Bainbridge will be able to intercede on my behalf."

"You say you do not wish to marry, but surely taking a husband would be better than living like this."

Gwen shook her head. "I would simply be changing one master for another. I wish to be in control of my own fate, Jess. Sooner or later, I shall find a way to accomplish the task."

Jessie hoped her friend was right, but she wasn't so sure.

Now as she watched Gwen waving through the window of Lady Bainbridge's sleek black carriage on its way back to London, she wished there was some way she could help her friend. In truth, there wasn't much she could do. She thought of little Sarah, waiting for her upstairs. At least she'd been able to help her niece. With their guests finally gone, she'd be able to spend more time with the child.

And perhaps with her husband.

Unfortunately, in the days that followed, she and Matthew grew even farther apart. He seemed tense and worried, on edge most of the time, though he tried not to show it.

Jessie's own worry grew. What was happening to them? He was pulling away from her as he had done before. Was it Caroline Winston, or something else? Perhaps it had something to do with the war. He had seemed ill at ease when he had left his meeting with Admiral Dunhaven. Surely he would tell her if he was preparing to leave.

She wanted to ask him, but she was afraid of what he might say. They had never discussed their feelings, never spoken of the future. Matthew had thus far been a dutiful husband, and wildly passionate in bed, but that didn't mean he loved her. Or needed her. Or had even come to accept her as his wife. In truth, she wasn't his social equal and never would be, no matter how extensive her ladylike facade.

With each day that passed, Jessie grew more and more uncertain. She had no idea where her life was headed, knew only that she was married to a man who wanted her in his bed, but had never intended marriage. She had tricked him into that and although he had brought it on himself, deep down she felt guilty.

Then another problem appeared, one she had thought resolved, and her worries grew ten times worse.

"Excuse me, milady." The butler stood in the doorway of the tiny schoolroom, where Jessie worked at the blackboard, drawing a makeshift map of England for the history lesson that day.

"Yes, Ozzie?"

"One of the boys just arrived from the village. He said to give you this. Said I wasn't to deliver it to anyone but you."

She glanced at the children. Six pairs of eyes had swiveled toward the door. Jessie walked in that direction. "Thank you, Ozzie." Nodding, he turned and headed back to the house. "Children—when you have finished your assignments, you may be excused. That will be all for the day."

They shifted around in their seats, shuffled their papers, then bent their heads to the task. Meanwhile, Jessie walked out on the porch, wondering at the message she had received. She broke the wax seal and tore open the missive, but didn't recognize the handwriting. Her heart skipped a beat as the words began to register—she knew exactly where the note had come from.

Danny!

Simply put, he wanted more money. He couldn't write the note himself, but whoever had penned it, clearly knew of the meeting Matthew had left yesterday morning to attend, a gathering of local landowners and their tenants in nearby Beaconsfield. He wouldn't be returning until tomorrow.

In the meantime, Danny wanted another five hundred pounds, and if she didn't give it to him, he was prepared to tell all. He would leave for London first thing in the morning and go straight to the London papers. Gossip was news, and after her fiasco with the duke, any more would be disastrous, especially such a sordid secret as this.

Jessie's stomach knotted. The Belmore name had suffered enough already. With a scandal of this magnitude, the family would be ruined, banned from Society forever. Dear God, what should she do?

Jessie reread the note, the foolscap shaking in her hand. She couldn't let Danny continue to blackmail them, yet she couldn't risk exposure. She had to think of a way to stop him, and it had to be tonight.

Straightening her spine, she stepped off the porch and headed back toward the house. She was supposed to meet her brother behind the Wayfarer Tavern at the edge of the village. *Lord, if Matthew were only here.*

Well, he wasn't, and by the time he got home it would be too late.

Besides, since the wedding celebration, Matthew had resumed his former demeanor, becoming aloof and withdrawn. She wasn't sure what was wrong. She didn't know if she had done something to displease him, or if perhaps he was upset at being saddled with her brother's child. News like this would only make things worse. It would be better if she told him after the problem was resolved.

Jessie chewed her lip, trying to work things through. She thought of Papa Reggie. He was always there to help her, but his health was just too frail. She couldn't take the chance of oversetting him again.

And there was Danny, himself. He was her brother—which made him her problem, not Matthew's or anyone else's. She would have to deal with Danny herself—and this time she'd make certain he didn't trouble them again.

A soft wind whispered through the leaves of an overhanging tree. High among the branches, an owl hooted into the night and Jessie shivered. It was a dark night, with only a sliver of moon. Now that she had reached the tavern, she was glad for the covering of blackness that disguised her movements. She didn't want anyone to see her with Danny Fox.

"Evenin', lit'l sister." Her brother pulled the watch fob from the pocket of his saffron brocade waistcoat, flipped open the lid, and checked the time. "I figured ya'd come. I do believe yer even a few minutes early."

Jessie drew the hood of her cloak up a little higher, hiding her face in shadow. Early for their rendezvous she might be, but it was already late and it would be nearly midnight before she got back to Belmore.

"I've done as you asked. I didn't have that much money. I brought what I've saved from my allowance, along with some of my jewelry. It's worth more than five hundred pounds, even if you don't get market value when you sell it. That is the best I can do on such short notice."

Danny just smiled. "Any port in a storm, I always say." He reached for the reticule she held in her hand, but Jessie stepped away, shaking her head.

"It isn't going to be that easy, Danny. Not this time." In the other hand, she held the small derringer pistol she had stolen from a drunken sailor the night she'd left the inn. She lifted it from the folds of her cloak and pointed it at Danny's heart.

"I'll give you the money, just like you asked. But understand this—you've badgered me and my family for the very last time. My husband warned you not to come back, but you didn't listen. Now I'm warning you. If you come near me again, if you threaten me or any of my family or try to come near Sarah, I'll kill you. I won't hesitate. I won't feel sorry about it. I will simply stick this gun in your face and pull the trigger."

She stepped closer, pressed the muzzle against his cheek, and watched his face go pale. "Do you believe me?"

He tried to smile, but it came out shaky and forced. "Surely ya wouldn't 'urt yer only kin."

"You aren't my kin—not anymore." Jessie lowered the pistol, pressed it into the fleshy part of his arm. "I said I would kill you." She was amazed at how steady her hand was. "Do you believe me, or do you need some proof?"

"Ye Gods—ya don't need to shoot me! I believe ya, gel." He eyed her from top to bottom, saw the resolve in her face. "Ya've turned out even 'arder'n yer ma." If she hadn't known better, she would have sworn she heard approval, the first she'd ever received from Danny Fox.

She handed over the reticule, heavy with money and jewelry. "I want you gone from here, Danny. I want you out of my life for good. I meant every word I said. If you ever utter a word against me or mine, you are dead."

The pistol didn't waiver, but inside she was shaking. She

meant what she told him—every word. She would protect her family no matter the cost. She hoped she had convinced him.

"Good-bye, Danny." He didn't say a word, just stood there staring as she walked away. In minutes, she had mounted the horse she had left in the stable at the rear of the tavern and started back down the road to Belmore. She prayed this time they'd be safe from Danny Fox.

Matthew watched in silence as his wife rode past, but where his fingers clutched the reins, they tightened into a fist. It was purely a matter of timing that he had seen her riding away from Belmore. He had almost stayed with Squire Montrose, returned home in the morning as he had planned, but thoughts of sleeping in his own bed, of making love to his wife and having her curled beside him, drove him to leave the warmth of the squire's friendly hearth.

He had almost reached Belmore when he noticed a lone rider leading a horse from the stable. He couldn't make him out very clearly, just saw him guide the animal to a shadowy tree stump, and position himself in the saddle. It was a side-saddle, he realized, which meant the rider was a woman—and the first stirrings of worry speared through him.

He had watched the woman ride away, certain now that it was Jessie, furious at her for leaving the safety of Belmore, and determined to discover what in God's name his wife was up to this time. He had followed her at a distance, hoping she wouldn't spot him, but she seemed oblivious to her surroundings, intent it appeared, on reaching her destination. It turned out to be the Wayfarer Tavern.

All the way there, Matt's stomach churned, his mind envisioning a dozen different scenarios. Knowing Jessie as he did, there could be a hundred different reasons she might go to the inn, but one suspicion continued to grow stronger.

Sir Thomas Perry wasn't among the gentry who had gathered for the important yearly agricultural meeting. His absence was remarked on, an unexpected illness it was said. Now Matthew wondered . . .

Perry had called on Jessie several times at Belmore before his arrival. He was young and handsome, and obviously found his wife attractive. Perhaps there had been something between them long before he'd come home, something that had grown, now that her position as the future marchioness of Belmore was secured.

He watched Jessie arrive at the inn, deposit her horse in the stable, round the tavern, and disappear into the darkness at the rear. He'd seen the man almost immediately, but he was too far away to hear what they were saying. He couldn't make out their faces, but the height and build was right for Perry. He saw Jessie hand him something, she paused and moved closer, perhaps into his arms.

Matt leaned back against the wall, his breath coming hard now, short white gasps in the chill night air. He closed his eyes and the weight of despair rolled over him. As soon as he brought himself in hand, he would go to them, confront them.

It was clear to him now, what he had feared all those months ago when he had first seen Jessie at Belmore—that sooner or later, the daughter of a whore behaved like one. Even a woman as educated and refined as Jessie Fox.

He dragged in several more calming breaths, but when he turned back to peer around the wall, Jessie and her lover were gone. He moved frantically then, determined to find them, to drag them out of their cozy bed upstairs, if that was where he found them. Instead, he caught sight of Jessie, mounted once more on her horse and headed back toward Belmore. There was no sign of the man she had met, but it didn't matter. Before the night was ended, he would know who that man was.

Moving silently toward his horse, his stomach churning, his muscles taut with fury, Matt swung up in the saddle of his weary horse and started back down the road to Belmore.

He was in no hurry. He knew where his wife was headed. Once he got there he would go to her, force her to tell him the truth.

Perhaps, by the time he reached home, he could turn his white-hot rage into an icy control.

*C*hapter *E*ighteen

*E*ven in the warmth of her bedchamber, Jessie still felt chilled. She had stripped off her riding skirt and now wore a comfortable white cotton night rail beneath her blue velvet wrapper. Matthew wouldn't be home till morning, and after her confrontation with Danny, she felt strangely cold.

Seated on a tapestry stool in front of the small oval mirror on her dresser, she absently pulled the last of the pins from her hair, then began to stroke her silver-backed bristle brush through it. She wished Matthew were home. She needed to feel his arms around her, to absorb some of his strength. For a moment she almost imagined she heard him, that he was climbing up the stairs. It was silly, but .. .

Jessie paused, certain now that indeed someone was coming, footsteps that sounded familiar. Matthew was home! Leaping up from the stool, she jerked open her bedchamber door to find him standing in the hall. He still wore his navy woolen greatcoat, she saw, the cape wet with dew from his late journey home. He hadn't paused long enough to leave it on the coat tree downstairs.

Perhaps he was as eager to see her as she was to see him.

"Matthew!" She threw her arms around his neck and dragged him into the room, dropping small soft kisses all over his face as he came forward. "I didn't think you were coming home."

"I'm sure you didn't." He set her away from him, turned

and shrugged out of his heavy coat, tossed it over a chair. "I decided to return tonight instead of tomorrow." An odd smile lifted his lips. "I couldn't wait to see you."

"Oh, Matthew—I'm so glad you're here."

"Are you?"

"Yes, I . . ." She started to tell him about her brother, about the money he had demanded, but something held her back. The tight look on Matthew's face, or perhaps it was the tension in his tall, hard-muscled body. "Matthew? Is something wrong?"

"Why should anything be wrong?"

"I-I don't know."

He stepped back from her then, let his eyes run over her from head to foot. She surveyed him as well, noticed his riding clothes, a dark brown tailcoat, soft doeskin breeches that molded his thighs, and knee-high black Hessian boots.

"If you are so glad to see me, perhaps you will show me how much. Take off your wrapper—I want to look at you."

She smiled a bit uncertainly as she untied the sash on her robe. "I didn't know you were coming." Removing her wrapper, she faced him in her simple cotton nightgown. "If I had, I would have worn something that would please you."

His mouth curved up, but it wasn't really a smile. "You will please me well enough," he said, "and soon." His eyes moved down her body, paused at the dark aureoles that outlined the tips of her breasts, then moved down to the shadow at the juncture of her legs, backlit through the garment by the yellow light of the fire.

"I-I missed you," Jessie said, fidgeting beneath his regard, unnerved a little by his matter-of-fact inspection. She wanted to tell him what had happened, how much she had needed him tonight, but his forbidding expression kept her silent.

"Did you?" He moved closer and unconsciously Jessie backed a step away.

"Yes . . . yes, I did. I wish you had gotten here earlier." That was an understatement.

"Well, I'm here now." Another thin smile. "And I intend to make up for lost time." His hand clamped around her waist, iron-hard as he dragged her against him. He stared at her a moment, his eyes dark in the shadows cast by the fire, and completely devoid of emotion. Then he lowered his head and took her mouth in a ravaging kiss. It wasn't the least bit tender, just fierce, brutal, punishing.

Jessie broke away, taking several steps backward and nearly tripping over the bench at the foot of the bed. "Matthew, what is wrong?"

His eyes came to rest on her mouth. "I apologize, my love." A cold smile twisted his lips. "Apparently my need of you is greater than I thought."

Jessie took another step away, trembling now as her back came up against the wall. "Tell me what is wrong."

"The only thing wrong is that I have not had you since yesterday morn. I mean to have you now. Come here, Jessica."

He had never spoken to her in that tone of voice. Never. She only shook her head.

"Then I shall come to you." He crossed the distance between them, didn't pause until he towered above her. He studied her hard for a moment. "Remove your night rail."

Jessie wet her lips. "I'm your wife, Matthew. I've no wish to refuse you, but—"

"I said to remove your clothes!" Gripping the delicate embroidery at her throat, he ripped the gown clear past her waist. Jessie gasped as the cool air rushed over her breasts, but the sound was muffled as his mouth crushed down over hers. He drew her hard against him, his hold so tight she could barely move. His hands engulfed her breasts, began to massage them, abraded the nipples until they grew stiff beneath his fingers.

Jessie shoved against his chest, determined to resist him. She tried to turn her mouth away, but he only caught her jaw and deepened the kiss. His heavy arousal thrust against her belly, thick and hot and hard. All the while his tongue

swept in, delving deeply, tasting her and demanding a response.

The kiss continued, no longer brutal but thorough and
arousing, expertly seductive, sapping her will to resist. The
hands on her breasts began to tease, to stroke with exquisite
skill, until each one ached and swelled, sent little tongues of
flame into her stomach.

Her resolve grew weaker as her body grew shivery and
warm. She found herself kissing him back, allowing him to
work his magic, looking forward to each stroke of his hand.
He was her husband, after all, and she wanted him.

Tangling her fingers in his thick dark golden hair, she
pressed herself more fully against him, started working the
buttons on his shirt. A soft whimper escaped as his lips left
hers to trail hot kisses along her throat and shoulders. He
bent his head and took a breast into his mouth, bit down on
the end, sending a shot of pleasure-pain rippling through her.

"Matthew . . ."

He kissed her again, delving deeply with his tongue,
stroking her into submission.

"Lift your nightgown, Jessica," he said softly.

Her hand trembled, hesitated only a moment, then began
to obey, catching the hem and lifting it to the top of her
thighs.

"Higher," he commanded. "I want to see you . . . touch
you."

She held the gown above her waist, baring herself to him,
mesmerized by the heat that burned in his dark blue eyes.

"So soft," he said, dragging a hand through the thick blond
curls above her cleft, then stroking downward, to separate the
plump folds and slide a finger inside. "You like this, don't you,
Jessica?"

She whimpered and arched against his hand. He stroked
her smoothly, expertly, and she was desperate to touch him
that same way. The final button popped off his shirt and she
tore it open, seeking out the muscles that rippled across his
chest. Unconsciously she lost her hold on the gown, but before

it could fall to the floor, Matthew had caught the fabric and pulled it off over her head, leaving her naked, her skin awash with the glow of the fire.

"Unbutton my breeches," he softly commanded, punctuating the order with a long, hot, deep-tongued kiss. "Touch me, Jessie. You know that's what you want."

She wet her lips. "Yes . . ." Her fingers fought with the fastenings until one by one they popped open. He was huge and pulsing, fighting to burst free of the confining garment, then jutting forward into her hands. She stroked him there, admiring the silky feel of him, the texture of satin over steel. Another tentative stroke and she heard him groan. His hands gripped her bottom, cupping the roundness, squeezing and testing the firmness.

"Spread your legs for me, Jessie." She did as he said, mindlessly parting for him, feeling his hands there, plunging deeply, then his hardened sex sliding back and forth. In a single long thrust, he filled her, driving her back against the wall, lifting her up off the floor.

She cried out at the savage force, yet her body welcomed him eagerly, drawing him deeply inside her. Heat washed over her, wave after burning wave, as Matthew plunged into her again and again. Her fingers dug into his shoulders; her mouth searched out his lips, claimed them in a fiery kiss that grew even more fierce as his tongue swept in to match each long stroke of his body. Her head fell back, her shoulders pressed against the wall, each of his driving thrusts raising her several inches. The fierce, incredible pleasure dulled her senses. She couldn't think, could barely remember to breathe.

Dear God, she had never seen him like this, so insatiable, almost feverish. It made her own heat soar, made her burn for him until all she could think of was Matthew, all she could feel was the pounding, pulsing rhythm and the thrusts of his tall, muscular body.

"That's right, Jessie. Take what you want. Do it now. Come with me."

With that harsh command, she broke over the edge. Heat

speared through her, pinpricks of fire that spread through her body and glittered behind her eyes. She felt Matthew stiffen, felt his last few hard-driving thrusts, and collapsed against him, grateful his powerful arms were there to hold her up.

She didn't remember him carrying her over to the bed, but the canopy and curtains loomed above her when she opened her eyes a few minutes later. She lay there naked and sated, her body tenderly battered from his powerful lovemaking—but Matthew was no longer there.

Jessie shivered, a tendril of fear snaking through her. He'd been so angry. She shouldn't have made love to him, should have made him tell her what was wrong. Instead, she'd given in to the powerful attraction she always felt for him. She had responded with abandon and now she was afraid.

She listened for his movements in the room next door, but the place remained eerily silent. Where had he gone, she wondered? Why had he left her alone? She had never seen him the way he was tonight, so strangely out of control. He had made her wild for him, and yet she had sensed his anger.

She tried to tell herself his fury was not aimed at her, that it was something else. Perhaps his meeting in Beaconsfield had gone badly. Perhaps that was all that was wrong. In the morning, he would feel better, be in control as he usually was. She would go to him then, speak to him and clear the air.

Jessie scoffed at herself. She had never been a coward, yet where Matthew was concerned, she was constantly unsure. She would talk to him on the morrow, tell him about her brother, about the threats Danny had made and the money she had given him.

She had to tell him—she was his wife, after all, and she owed him her loyalty. Still, she was worried about his reaction and concerned for little Sarah. The child made the threat to the Belmores even greater—Matthew had said so himself. Now with Danny's reappearance, would her husband be so worried he would send the child away? She didn't think he would, but she couldn't be sure.

Jessie closed her eyes, her heart thudding dully. Tomorrow she would know what to do. Tomorrow things would be clearer. Sliding beneath the satin sheets, she pulled them up beneath her chin, her body still tingling from her husband's violent lovemaking, her breasts still tender from his touch. Tomorrow she would tell him, discover what was wrong.

Jessie closed her eyes, but she couldn't fall asleep.

A leaf drifted down in the shadowy light of the lanterns, crunching beneath Gwendolyn Lockhart's slippered feet as she passed beneath the branches. Gowned in emerald moiré silk shot with gold, she strolled the gravel paths of Vauxhall Gardens, wondering how late the hour had grown.

It was amazing she was there, considering her parents fury on her return from Belmore. But earlier, during the carriage ride into the city, Lady Bainbridge had agreed to speak to the earl in her behalf, and Gwen had once more avoided a brutal caning, her guardian's favorite form of punishment. Instead she had simply been confined to her room for the next two weeks, except of course when her parents believed it necessary for her to make an appearance in Society.

Which had occurred this eve. Her mother's favorite charity, the Society for the Betterment of the Poor, was sponsoring a night at Vauxhall Gardens, a yearly money-raising event, and this year Lady Waring was in charge.

Her mother had been fretting for days, working late into the evenings on the final preparations. Last night she had spoken to her husband.

"Please, Edward, I beseech you—you must let Gwendolyn come. It would be highly unseemly if my only daughter did not attend the function I've been planning for nearly a year."

In the end, Lord Waring had relented, something he did only rarely, and agreed to let her go—not that Gwen really cared about attending another of her mother's boring charity functions. But this one was at the gardens, one of Gwen's favorite spots, and even these past few days cooped up inside the house had been too long.

She sighed as she strolled the main promenade of the gardens, a wide gravel path bordered by rows of towering elms, grateful to have finally escaped her parents' watchful eyes. Her mother was so busy she didn't notice when Gwen slipped away, and Lord Waring was engrossed with the lovely young widow, Lady Burton, he had been eyeing of late.

Gwen turned off the Grand Walk that led to a Gothic temple complete with fountain, onto a narrow, less traveled path where she could listen to the song of a nightingale and enjoy the pleasure of studying the huge silver moon.

For a moment she remembered another night, another midnight stroll in the gardens that had led to a feather-soft kiss. She hadn't seen St. Cere since her return to the city but she hadn't expected she would. Her stepfather would never allow him to call and the viscount knew it. And Gwen wasn't sure he would want to come if he could.

She smiled to think of him though, so wickedly handsome just his image made her insides flutter and her heart trip a little too fast. If it hadn't been for the sound of footsteps on the path, she might have continued her musings, conjuring the viscount's brief kiss one more time. Instead she turned—and went stock-still.

"Don't stop smiling, Lady Gwen." Amazingly the voice hadn't come from her thoughts, but from the tall dark man himself. "You've the loveliest of smiles," he said. "I've been looking forward to seeing it again."

Her knees quivered beneath her skirt. "Lord St. Cere . . ."

He bowed gracefully. "At your service, milady."

Her heartbeat thundered, pulsed like a drum inside her chest. "What—what are you doing here?"

"I came to see you." He smiled at her obvious disbelief. "I often donate to your mother's charity for the poor. I knew about tonight's event and that Lady Waring was in charge. I hoped that you might come."

Gwen said nothing. She couldn't take her eyes off his mouth. It curved only faintly, firm, full lips that spoke of seduction more eloquently than any words.

"I've been watching you all evening," he said. "There was no mistaking your boredom. I assumed, in light of your past misadventures, that sooner or later, you would find some means of escape."

She should have been piqued at his ungentlemanly reminder, but instead she found herself smiling. "You're quite right, my lord. I've been trying to get away for the past several hours. Thank God for my mother's near-vapors and my stepfather's unrelenting lust."

St. Cere's eyes slid down to the curve of her breasts and his bold black brows pulled into a frown. "Knowing Lord Waring as I do, I'm not sure that is a blessing."

Gwen glanced away, not liking the turn in conversation. "No . . . neither am I." She looked at him and forced an overbright smile. "They'll be angry if I'm gone too long. Since we are both of the same mind and well rid of them, we should make use of the time we have."

The viscount's beautiful mouth curved up, gouging winsome grooves in his cheeks. "My thoughts exactly." He extended his arm, and Gwen took it, the soft wool of his coat brushing lightly against her skin. They spoke of the beauty of the moon and of the weather, then of her writing and his favorite sports. Horse racing was his passion.

"I haven't missed Derby Day at Epsom Downs in more than twenty years, not since I was a boy."

"I love to ride. I should love to have a horse of my own, a fine, spirited Thoroughbred."

"Yes," he said. "A beautiful mare with a sleek chestnut coat and a spirit to match your own."

Gwen's stomach went liquid, all soft and buttery. She smiled at him and thought she had never met a man whose eyes could see into her soul. All the while, he led her deeper into the gardens, turning once more off the path onto an even more dimly lit trail. They paused beneath a giant elm and he pulled her into his arms.

"You're different from other women . . . fresher somehow,

determined to learn about the world, not just sit idly by and be indulged by it."

"I must learn about things if I'm to succeed as a writer."

He paused in the pathway, looked down into her face. "What of marriage, Gwen? And children? Every woman wants that. Surely you do, too."

She stared into his deep gray eyes and for the first time in her life, felt the sharp edge of yearning for the things he spoke of.

"I do not wish to marry," she said, repeating the words that came almost by rote. "Marriage is little better than slavery. The man keeps his mistresses, enjoys the world and all it holds, while the woman sits at home and does nothing but care for his children. She sees only the things he allows, experiences only what he permits."

"What about love?"

"I don't believe in love." She glanced away. "Though if there were such a thing, I imagine it could be very beautiful. If a man and woman were in love, they could share the joys of life, experience them together. If they loved each other, they could protect each other, care for each other, not hurt each other as most married people do."

The viscount said nothing for the longest time. "If you do not marry, there is much you will miss. How will you learn the joy of being with a man?"

She looked up at him, certain this was where he had been leading. "I will find someone to teach me."

His eyes fixed on hers and a hand came up to her cheek. "I could teach you, Gwen. I could show you all about life and loving. Together we could share endless hours of pleasure."

Gwen moistened her lips, her mind bombarded by the images his seductive words created: Adam Harcourt peeling off her clothes, his long dark fingers caressing her breasts, his beautiful mouth taking hers again and again. As if he had read her thoughts, he bent his head and kissed her, molding his lips to hers in a way that was infinitely tender yet infused with sensuous heat.

Cupping her face between his hands, he deepened the kiss, slanting his mouth over hers, fitting them perfectly together. The heat expanded, began to slide through her limbs. His tongue coaxed open her mouth, then swept in to taste her more fully. Inside her chemise, her breasts swelled, brushing against the fabric, making the tips grow hard.

The viscount pulled her closer and Gwen slid her arms around his neck. Pressed full length against him, she stood on tiptoes to reach him, her breasts crushed into his chest. Somehow his thigh had slipped between her legs and now pressed against her woman's flesh, making it moisten and pout. He shifted a little, lifting her up, and heat swept through her.

"Adam . . ." she whispered, her fingers sliding into his hair. At the sound of his name, he stirred, raising his head. He seemed to be fighting a battle as he gently eased himself away, his breathing fast and even more ragged than her own, his eyes a dark silver gray.

"I want you," he said. "So much I ache with it. I've thought about you every night since I left Belmore."

"Oh, Adam, I've thought about you, too."

He might have said more, but they both heard someone coming along the trail. He pulled her into a more shadowy spot that would hide the flush in her cheeks, then stepped a discreet distance away and waited for the person to appear.

"So . . . this is where you've gone off to." The Earl of Waring's strides were long and formidable. "I might have known you wouldn't be alone."

The viscount eased a bit in front of her, blocking Lord Waring's approach. "The lady and I met by chance along the path. We were merely enjoying a moment of conversation in the moonlight."

Her stepfather turned his hard gaze on Gwen, but she didn't glance away.

"I was just starting back," she lied, wishing she could stay with Adam all evening.

"As was I," the viscount said. "I would be happy to see your stepdaughter safely returned."

"She would be more safely returned with a pack of wolves, St. Cere. I shall see Lady Gwendolyn back after I've had a word with her in private."

Adam paused a moment more, as if he were loath to leave her, then made a slight inclination of his head. "As you wish, my lord." Turning away, he walked off down the path, his steps long and graceful. In moments he was gone, vanished as silently as he had appeared.

"Do you realize what a man like that could do to your reputation?" Hard, dark eyes bored into her.

"We only spoke for a moment."

"A moment with St. Cere is too much. The man is a bounder. Your virtue is hardly safe with a man like that."

But Gwen was more worried about her virtue at the hands of Lord Waring, who had taken several steps closer, forcing her back against the trunk of a tree.

"We-We ought to be returning," she said. "Mother will be worried."

"Your mother is otherwise occupied." He lowered his head, set his mouth on her shoulder, then began to trail wet kisses along her neck.

Revulsion washed over her. Gwen pressed her hands on his chest and tried to shove him away, but he was a big man and he only pulled her closer. "I'm going to kiss you, Gwen."

"No!"

He tried to cover her mouth with his wet lips, but she turned her head away.

"I'll scream," she said. "I swear it!"

"You do and I'll whip you. I swear *that* to you!"

Tears welled up, began to burn her eyes. Waring looked triumphant. He started to lower his head, but a deep voice interrupted.

"Excuse me—" St. Cere stood in the path just a few feet away. His mouth was curved in a smile but it didn't reach his eyes, which glittered with barely leashed fury. "I'm sorry to interrupt, but Lady Gwen must have lost this on the path. I thought I had better return it."

It was a lacy white handkerchief. Not one of her own. The viscount was using it as an excuse to come back and protect her from Waring. How had he known?

"Th-Thank you, my lord." Gwen stepped around Waring to accept the handkerchief. "I didn't realize I had dropped it." She forced herself to smile. "We were just starting back." She clamped onto St. Cere's arm, gripping it so tightly she felt his muscles bunch. "I'm certain Lord Waring won't mind if you escort me."

She gave him no time to object and neither did St. Cere. "A pleasure, my lady." Together they started down the gravel path, her stepfather's footfalls a few feet behind them, his murderous expression boring into their backs. Adam's hand covered her fingers where they rested on his arm and he gave them a reassuring squeeze.

"Thank you for returning," Gwen whispered.

"I never intended to leave you alone with him."

She gave him a tremulous smile. "And the handkerchief? Must you now return it to its proper owner?"

His mouth tilted briefly. "I imagine Lady Bainbridge will want it returned. Perhaps you might see it done."

A thread of warmth slid through her. "Yes, I would be pleased to take care of it." But mostly she was pleased that the handkerchief didn't belong to one of his legion of women.

It appeared, at least for a time, the viscount's attentions were firmly fixed on her.

*C*hapter *N*ineteen

*T*he gray of dawn slanted into the study. Matt sat up on the brown leather sofa where he had finally fallen asleep, his neck stiff, a day's growth of beard on his face. His head was pounding from the brandy he had consumed, his clothing wrinkled and muddy from the ride he had made last night.

He ran a hand over his face, his thoughts still sleep-muddled, yet nothing could disguise them completely. The events of last eve loomed like a heavy iron weight above his shoulders. He had followed Jessie back to Belmore, then returned upstairs to confront her, make her admit her treachery and discover the name of her lover.

Instead he had released his anger in another, more primitive fashion, allowing the savage lust he felt for her to run its rampant course. He had taken her brutally, almost viciously.

Still, as angry as he was, he had been careful not to hurt her.

Matt raked a hand through his disheveled hair, thinking of where he'd gone wrong. He had thought that once his fury was spent, his precious control would return, but he had been mistaken. Even after their savage round of love-making, his anger simmered beneath the surface. Far too hot to risk a confrontation. This morning, he had vowed, when his icy calm returned, he would force his wife to admit her affair.

Now, as he climbed the stairs, entered his suite of rooms, and rang for his valet, he still could not summon the will to face Jessie. In the weeks since their marriage, an odd sort of change had begun to occur. His desire for her had grown, not lessened as he had expected, and though he had tried to fight them, there were other feelings she stirred—feelings of protectiveness he had not realized he possessed, concern for little Sarah and a yearning for children of his own, a gladness in his heart whenever his wife walked into the room.

He had vowed not to let his guard down, to keep his emotions in check, but he had failed. He'd allowed himself to *feel* as he hadn't done since the death of his mother. Not since his brother had been killed.

Now he was paying the price.

Matthew bathed and changed into fresh riding breeches and a white lawn shirt, his eyes more than once straying to the door between their rooms. His head still pounded, but it was the leaden feeling in his stomach that bothered him the most, the hollow ache that seemed to swell every time he thought of Jessie. Even his anger at her betrayal couldn't make the feeling go away.

"I'll be out until nightfall, Rollie," he said to his valet. "In the meantime, you may begin to pack my things."

"My lord?"

"I'll be leaving for Portsmouth on the morrow. I've been waiting for word from Admiral Nelson, the order to return to my ship. I've decided to wait there rather than here."

"Very good, sir." The young man watched him walk away, wondering no doubt at his sudden haste to leave. Jessie could deal with the servants' gossip. He wouldn't be there to hear it.

Tucking his riding gloves into the waistband of his breeches, Matt headed out the door, along the hallway, and down the stairs. He had almost made it to the bottom when he spotted a small figure standing in the shadows beneath the mahogany banister watching his descent. He slowed a little as he approached, not wanting to frighten the child away.

"Sarah?" He paused in front of her, went down on one knee at her side. With her small pointed chin and straight little nose, she looked so much like Jessie it made an ache throb in his chest. "What are you doing out of bed, sweeting? It's too early for you to be up, and it's far too cold."

She just stared at him, her blue eyes searching his, her hair as pale as moonlight. He straightened away from her, glancing around for the butler, hoping Ozzie would take the little girl back to her room, but the man was nowhere near.

When he knelt back down beside Sarah, she lifted her arms to him, silently asking him to pick her up. He did so without thinking, noticing how cold her small feet were against his arm, wondering why she didn't have on her slippers. "Where are your shoes?" he said. "You'll catch a chill if you don't wear them."

Her tiny arms slid around his neck, and she rested her cheek against his shoulder. Wisps of baby-fine hair brushed his cheek and the tightness in his chest grew more fierce. They reached the nursery and walked past where Viola lay sleeping, to the smaller room that was Sarah's. At the foot of the bed, he set her down, but when he started to pull away, her small arms clung to his neck.

Big blue eyes fixed on his face, then slowly filled with tears. "Papa . . ." she said, pressing a soft kiss on his cheek then resting her small head against his shoulder. Matt's chest went so tight he couldn't breathe.

He cuddled her back in his arms, sat down on the bed and just held her. He wasn't sure which of them felt more lost, more alone, little Sarah—or himself.

He wasn't certain how long he sat there, simply holding the little girl in his lap. He didn't move until she had drifted off to sleep, and then he sat there a few moments more.

Finally he placed her carefully back in her small feather bed and backed away, wondering what it might have been like to have children with Jessie. What their marriage might have been if his wife had not betrayed him.

He wondered now if he would ever have a child of his own, and it crossed his mind that last night when they'd made love, Jessie might have conceived. He scoffed as he walked down the hall, thinking that after what he had seen at the tavern, he wouldn't even know if the child was really his.

The ache continued to throb but with each bitter heartbeat, he clamped down harder on his emotions and soon the hurt began to fade. Eventually he would feel nothing, just the same emptiness he had known before he'd married Jessie, an emptiness that he had foolishly allowed her to fill.

With a last harsh glance at her door, Matt descended the stairs and walked off toward the stables.

All night long, Jessie thrashed beneath the covers and worried and didn't fall asleep until nearly dawn, then she slept far later than she'd meant to. Minnie came in just minutes after she stirred, babbling gaily as she usually did, but Jessie barely heard her. She felt drained and exhausted and yet she was tightly on edge. She was worried about Matthew, about the anger she had sensed in him last night, and what he would say when she told him about her brother.

She climbed out of bed, still a little sore from their fierce round of passion, dressed hurriedly in a plum silk day dress, then let Minnie pull the bristle brush through her hair. The girl was her lady's maid now, since Vi spent all her time now with little Sarah.

"Don't fuss with it, Minnie. I don't have time."

"Yes, mum." Still it took agonizing moments just to draw it into ringlets atop her head and leave the rest curling loosely down her back. She wanted to look pretty for Matthew, but she was already late and with each passing moment, her nervousness mounted.

She kept thinking of the way they'd made love, so fiercely, almost violently. At first she had been frightened, but the notion of danger only heated the fires of her lust. In the light of day she was a little ashamed of her unbridled passions and worried that they might have been the reason that Matt hadn't stayed.

She checked her image in the mirror and took a deep breath, prepared to beard the lion in his den. She couldn't put it off any longer. She had to know what her husband was thinking, no matter how painful it was. With a brief prayer for courage, Jessie pulled open the bedchamber door and headed for the stairs.

"Good morning, Ozzie," she said to the butler who stood in the entry. "Have you seen Lord Strickland?"

"I'm sorry, milady. His lordship has already gone."

Jessie's shoulders sagged. "I was afraid of that." She nervously chewed her lip. "Do you know where he went?"

"No, milady. But Rollie said he wouldn't be returning until nightfall."

Jessie inwardly groaned. Another day spent on pins and needles. "Thank you, Ozzie." The words came out softly. Where had he gone? Why was he avoiding her? After last night, she didn't know what to think.

The day was hellish, long hours that no amount of diversion could dispel. She avoided Papa Reggie, afraid he would notice the fear in her eyes, afraid he would press her to explain. Instead she worked in the greenhouse, then returned upstairs to her room to change for supper. It came and went, and she managed to hide her worry from Papa Reggie, who grumbled that Matthew should have sent word if he wouldn't be home. The marquess retired early, but there was still no sign of her husband.

It wasn't till late in the evening that she heard him enter the room next door. Panic gripped her chest. Her heart began to pump in an odd, erratic rhythm. Taking a deep breath for courage, Jessie smoothed the folds of the ivory silk gown she had worn down to supper and started across the floor to her husband's suite of rooms.

Untying his wrapped cravat as he walked toward the fire, Matt shed his dark green riding coat and unbuttoned the throat of his full-sleeved white lawn shirt. He was tired from his long day of riding, of trying to exhaust his mind and heart of thoughts of Jessie.

Sooner or later, he would have to face her, yet something

continued to hold him back. He was surprised to discover how badly he dreaded the moment, dreaded speaking the words that would end the days of promise he had known since they had been together. He wished he could hate her, but mostly he just felt empty.

And lonelier than he had ever felt before.

Perhaps it was his fault, since he was the one who had forced the marriage. Still, she was his wife now, and he didn't deserve her betrayal.

His head came up at the knock at his door. His stomach twisted as he realized the sound came from Jessie's room and that she meant to come in. It was time, he supposed, and his jaw clamped at what lay ahead. A memory rose up of her standing in the shadows behind the tavern whispering to her lover, but he forced it down, bottled it up with the rest of his emotions.

Crossing the thick Persian carpet in his sitting room, he jerked open the door, then stepped back as Jessie walked in.

She was dressed in ivory satin, her hair done in an elegant crown, her breasts displayed with a subtlety that only made them more alluring. Her head came up as she turned to face him.

"Good evening, my lord."

A grim smile settled on his lips. "Good evening . . . my lady." Jessie caught his tight expression and her face went a little bit pale.

"I-I'm glad you are finally home."

"Are you?"

"Yes . . . I . . . there are several matters of importance I wish to discuss."

He arched a brow at that. "Are there, indeed? Strangely enough there are matters I wish to discuss as well."

She walked toward the hearth and he tried to ignore the way the firelight shimmered in her hair, the way the ivory silk mimicked the smoothness of her skin. He tried to ignore the knot that balled hard in his stomach.

"Shall you begin, or shall I?" she asked.

"Why you . . . my love . . . of course."

Jessie cleared her throat. Though she appeared in perfect control, there was an edginess about her and a weariness in her expression. A pang of feeling broke over him. He ruthlessly tamped it down.

"I wish to speak to you about last night," she said.

Tension rippled across his shoulders. "Last night?"

"Yes."

"If you're referring to our lovemaking, I'm sorry if I hurt you. That was never my intention."

Twin spots of color rose into the whiteness of her cheeks. "You did not hurt me."

"Then tell me what it is you wish to discuss."

Jessie wet her lips. She opened her mouth to speak, but her eyes strayed to the pair of leather valises packed and lying open on his big tester bed.

"Y-You are leaving? Where . . . where are you going?"

His smile was wolfish and cruel. "Portsmouth. I am returning to my ship. I had meant to await my orders here, but last night I . . . made a change of plans."

"You're going off to war?" Her voice rose a notch, sounded high pitched and strained.

"You knew I would go if they asked."

"Yes, but I-I didn't know they had. I thought you would tell me, give me a chance to prepare."

"Prepare for what, Jessica? Surely you don't mean to say you care that I am leaving?"

"Of course, I care! I'm your wife. You'll be putting your life in danger. How could you think that I would not care?"

Matthew looked at her, saw that she was trembling. Each word rang with sincerity, yet he knew it was a lie and his careful control began to crumble. "So you care for me, do you?"

"Yes, I—"

"If you care so much, why did you go to the Wayfarer Tavern? Why have you taken a lover?"

"What!"

"Early last night, I returned from Beaconsfield. I saw you leaving, Jessica, and I followed you. I saw you with your lover behind the tavern. I'm not certain who he is, but before this night is ended there is no doubt that you will tell me." His eyes bored into her, flashing his contempt and the rage that threatened to explode.

Jessie just stood there, her face so pale it appeared translucent. She said nothing for the longest time. Then her lips went taut with anger.

"Yes, your lordship, you may be certain I will tell you who the man is. As a matter of fact, that is the matter I wished to discuss."

Something sharp jolted through him, leaving him disconcerted and suddenly uneasy. He couldn't seem to make sense of what was going on.

A few feet away, Jessie locked her fingers together, clutching them against her stomach so hard they turned pale. "Yesterday a boy arrived from the village. He carried a letter addressed to me. It was obvious from the content that the sender knew that you had gone off to Beaconsfield. Since I didn't wish to overset your father, I was left with no choice but to deal with the matter myself."

With a hand that shook, she reached into the pocket of her gown and drew out a wrinkled scrap of paper. Her eyes grew bright with angry tears. "This is the note I received, the reason I went to the tavern. The man you saw there was my brother—not my lover." She stuffed the note into his hand, blinked, and the tears rolled down her cheeks. "I have no lover, Matthew. I do not want one. The only man I have ever loved is you."

Pain squeezed hard in his chest, wrapped around his heart and squeezed again. He stared at Jessie, then down at the letter. By the time he had finished reading the note, his hand was shaking so badly he could no longer make out the letters. His eyes found Jessie and he saw her beautiful face streaked with tears. The anger was gone now, replaced by a look of hurt and terrible aching pain.

He searched for something to say, clawed desperately to find the right words, but his mind was a void, a dark fathomless pit without a single shred of light to help him find the way.

She gazed at him a moment more, then lifted her chin, turned and swept out of the room, closing the door behind her.

Even as the hollow sound faded, Matthew scanned the letter, each word condemning him to a hell of his own making. He had wronged her. Again. Condemned her unjustly. Again.

His jealousy had done it. And his prejudice. His secret, insane belief that because her mother was a fallen woman, Jessie was somehow doomed to that fate, too. Her blood wasn't as pure as a truly aristocratic woman, a lady like Caroline Winston.

Perhaps it wasn't.

But her heart was just as pure, perhaps even more so. He knew that now with a certainty that had eluded him until today. How could he not have seen?

Matthew blinked, amazed to discover tears had gathered in his own eyes. He hadn't cried since he was six years old. The day his mother had died. She had told him that day that she loved him. No one had ever said it since, not even his father. Not until tonight.

His chest felt leaden as he walked to the door between their rooms. He lifted the latch and pulled it open, stepped inside, then stood staring at the woman he had so bitterly wronged. She faced away from him toward the hearth, standing there in silence, her head held high, but her slender shoulders shook with the force of her despair. How many times would she prove him wrong before he learned that he could trust her? How long would she try in vain to win that trust?

He crossed the room, his bootsteps silent on the thick oriental carpet, came up behind her, and gently rested his hands on her shoulders. Slowly he turned her to face him.

"Jessie . . . love . . . I'm sorry."

She said nothing, just lowered her eyes and stared at the front of his shirt.

"I shouldn't have jumped to conclusions. I should have come to you, asked you to explain. I can't tell you why I didn't. I can only say that I've never been jealous of a woman. I didn't know what it could do to a man."

She lifted her gaze to his face. "You've never trusted me, have you? Not even after we married. You think because of my mother—"

"Don't say it, Jess." He drew her closer, into the circle of his arms, then tightened them around her, his heart aching to think how his cruelty had hurt her. And guilty because she had stumbled upon the truth. "You aren't like your mother. You're nothing at all like that."

She pulled away from him before he could stop her, stumbled back several paces. "But I am, Matthew. In some ways I'm exactly like her."

Matt shook his head, aching to hold her, to wipe away the wetness sliding down her cheeks.

"Last night when you came into my room," she said, "I knew that you were angry. You frightened me at first, but then . . . then you started kissing me, and I-I wanted you. Dear God, how I wanted you. I liked the things you did to me, Matthew. I didn't care that you did them in anger. You made me burn for you, ache to have you inside me. No wonder you don't trust me—I behaved no better than the women upstairs at the Black Boar Inn!"

Matt gripped her shoulders. "Stop it, Jess!" He pulled her into his arms, crushed her against his chest. "You're a beautiful, sensual woman. I thank God every day for giving me a wife who returns my passions." When she started to argue, he shook her, forcing her to listen. "There is nothing wrong with what we do. Nothing! I told you that the night I took your innocence. I am the one at fault here, not you. I was a fool, Jess. A crazy, jealous fool." He tipped her chin up. "I'm sorry, Jess. Can you ever forgive me?"

Her fingers curled into the front of his shirt. She tipped

her head forward and the tears on her cheeks soaked through the fabric onto his chest. "I love you, Matthew. I would forgive you almost anything." But when she looked up, there was a sadness in her eyes he had never seen there before.

He stroked her hair, hating himself for the breech he had forged between them, knowing that any day he would be called away to war.

"I shouldn't have doubted you, Jess."

She pressed her face into his shoulder and he could feel the fine tremors racing through her. "Are you still going away?"

He kissed the top of her head. "Not until I have to. I've been meaning to tell you I'd be leaving, but I didn't know how. I didn't want Father to worry and it just never seemed the right time."

She drew a little away. "Is that what has been the matter? Before last night, I mean. You were worried about going to war?"

"I was worried about leaving. At least now that we're married, you'll be safe. If anything should happen to me—"

She pressed her fingers over his lips to still the words, and he noticed that they trembled. "Don't say that, don't even think it. You're coming back to Belmore. Once you do, you won't ever have to leave again."

He searched her eyes, a faint thread of hope returning. He had hurt her, yes, but maybe it wasn't too late. "No . . . once I come back, I won't ever leave."

Teary blue eyes clung to his face. I love you, they said, and Matthew allowed himself to believe it. He had never wanted a woman's love, yet the words curled warmly around his heart. The weight on his shoulders began to lift and the hope he felt began to strengthen. He would come back, he vowed. He would come back to Belmore and Jessie.

Then he thought of the blood and the fighting, of men maimed and dying, of widows who cried for the husbands who would not return.

And he prayed that his vow would hold true.

* * *

Adam Harcourt lounged at the end of a sofa in the Cock and
Hen on Sloane Street. It was gaudy, smelled of smoke and
cheap perfume, but it was clean and reputable. Sophie Ste-
vens, the owner, saw to that. Besides, the pretty little dark-
haired whore who sat on his knee reminded him faintly of
Gwen.

Adam absently fondled her bottom. He had gone there
purposely to see her, meant to bed her until his fever for
Gwen Lockhart had cooled to at least a slow boil. He had
thought of nothing but making love to the outrageous little
hoyden since he had kissed her that night in the Belmore
gardens.

The fever had grown at Vauxhall. He remembered each
of her luscious curves, her sweet lilac scent, the exact softness of her lips. Not since before he married Elizabeth had
he wanted a woman so badly—a sweet young girl named
Mary. But Mary had been betrothed to another and Elizabeth Radmore meant for him.

After the way things had turned out, he was grateful he
never felt the least flicker of love for the woman he had
married.

But he was worried about his feelings for Gwen. There
was something about her, a combination of innocence and
bravado, that drew him as no other woman ever had. She was
like a dangerous fire that burned out of control, as wild and
passionate as Elizabeth.

And yet they were nothing alike.

His wife had been coldly calculating, selfish and indulgent.
Gwen was tantalizingly sweet, innocence left unguarded. He
had to keep reminding himself that he was a dedicated rake,
that he meant to bed her but keep his heart safely locked away.

He bent and kissed the whore's pretty throat. Sweet Rachael was a start. She would soothe the ardor he carried for
Gwen and allow him to temper his unruly emotions. He
would separate his feelings for Gwen and allow himself to

feel only lust. He would bed her sooner or later, of that he had no doubt, and even her innocence would not bother his conscience.

She knew what she wanted and so did he. They were attracted to each other, but neither of them were interested in marriage. That was for naive fools who believed in hearth and home, or men who had run on hard times and needed to refill their coffers.

Rachael tugged on his sleeve. "Come on, luv, why don't we go upstairs? That's what you come for, isn't it?"

A corner of his mouth kicked up. "That's exactly why I've come, Rachael. And you're right, it's time we got to it. Get your pretty little bottom up to your room. I'll be right behind you." Adam followed her up, but even as he closed the door and turned in her direction, he realized he had made a mistake.

Only Rachael's skillful ministrations garnered his interest enough to make him hard. In the end, he, simply shoved her down on her knees and let her do the work, then buttoned up his breeches and came back downstairs.

It wasn't the night of debauchery he'd intended, and even at that, he felt oddly guilty, as if he had somehow been unfaithful.

Christ's blood, that was the trouble with women. Once a woman got her claws into a man, the poor fool just couldn't shake her. The thought made him even more angry, mostly at himself, and more determined than ever to bed Gwen Lockhart and get himself back in control. Once he'd had her, he was sure, she could no longer keep this stranglehold on him.

She was, after all, merely a woman, and he had certainly had more than his share of them.

The street noise barely penetrated his thoughts as Matthew proceeded to Brooks Club, St. James. He was looking for Adam Harcourt, hoping to gain his help. He had already been several other places. If he didn't find him soon, he would have to proceed alone.

Matt surveyed the smoky room, then he smiled. "St. Cere!" he called out, continuing toward a table in the rear, where Adam sat sipping a brandy. He reached him and extended a hand, which the viscount came to his feet and accepted. "I was hoping I might find you here."

Adam smiled warmly. "I thought you meant to rusticate at Belmore for the balance of the Season."

"Unfortunately, I had some unfinished business in the city. As soon as I find the man I'm after I'll be returning."

"Who are you looking for?"

"A bounder named Danny Fox. I've been prowling the city all day, asking questions. I've got a pretty good notion where he is."

"Perhaps I can help."

Matt clamped a hand on Adam's shoulder. "I was hoping you'd say that. Matter of fact, my next stop was the Cock and Hen. I thought if I couldn't find you anywhere else, you might be there."

Adam laughed. "I just came from there. I suppose I'll have to change my routine—I'm becoming far too predictable."

"Perhaps our age is starting to tell . . . beginning to settle us down."

"God, I hope not."

Matt just chuckled.

"Tell me how I can help," Adam said.

"I was hoping you might go with me. The kind of places this man frequents, it's good to have someone to watch your back."

"I think I can handle that."

"Hopefully that's all you'll have to do. Once I figure out where his is, I'll do the rest."

Adam studied Matt's taut expression. "From the look on your face, the fellow must have done something pretty bad."

He bunched a muscle in his jaw. "Bad enough. He's threatened my wife and family. The only mistake I made was in not doing something sooner."

Adam nodded. "Where do we start?"

"Sloane Street. The chap has a pocket full of money and a purse full of jewelry to sell. He'll be gaming away the coin and looking for a buyer for the jewels. Odds are that's where he'll go to do it." Matt smiled thinly. "He fancies himself a ladies' man. We'll begin by looking in the brothels. Chances are he won't be too hard to find."

Three hours later they were standing just inside the door of the Satin Garter, a sordid, low-roofed alehouse with rooms to let upstairs and a wench or two for comfort if a man had a shilling to spare. Across the rough-board floors at a scarred wooden table, his arm around the waist of a buxom tavern maid, Danny Fox sat cheating at cards.

It was the second time Matt and Adam had been there. This time, they weren't alone.

"Stay here," Matt said to St. Cere, "and keep the men out of sight outside. I'll bring Fox to you."

He crossed the room to where the yellow-eyed man sat playing whist, leaned down and spoke in his ear. "I want a word with you, Danny. You can come quietly or I can drag you out of here. Which is it going to be?"

Fox's face went pale, though his words held a touch of bravado. "Well, lookee 'ere, Connie," he said to the man beside him, "if it ain't 'is bleedin' lordship.'"

Matt's hard gaze swung to bone-thin Connie Dibble. He remembered him from his years in Buckler's Haven—and as one of the men who had attacked him at the fair. "You, too, Dibble. I want to see you both outside."

Fox sent Dibble a glance, one that said not to worry, that Matt was alone and together they could take him. But Dibble seemed uncertain.

"What do ye want wi' me?" he asked. "I ain't done nothin'.'"

"I'll be happy to explain . . . just as soon as we get out-side." Both men shoved back their chairs, which scraped against the roughhewn floor. The walls were bare and thin cracks of light seeped through them. Smoke hung in ropy spirals over the dimly lit tables.

Matt stepped out of Fox's way. "After you, gentlemen." He let them walk in front of him, then followed them out the door, Adam falling in beside him. The minute they stepped into the darkness, Fox and Dibble turned, their fists coming up, both of them swinging. Fox's blow landed harmlessly on Matt's shoulder. Dibble missed completely. Matt grabbed Fox's coat, slammed him up against the wall, and buried a fist in his stomach. A second blow slammed him back into the wall and elicited a low grunt of pain. Gripping Dibble by his lapels, Adam thrust the end of his silver-headed cane beneath the skinny man's chin and pressed the knob, releasing a small shiny blade.

"I'd advise you not to move," Adam warned.

"No . . . no, I ain't movin'."

Matt shook Fox like a rat. "I'm sure you've spent the money my wife gave you. What have you done with the jewels?"

Fox grunted. "So the lit'l tart told ya. I didn't think she'd 'ave the nerve."

Matt wrapped a hand around Fox's throat and gently began to squeeze. "Those jewels belong to my wife. Where are they?"

"Sold . . . sold 'em," Danny sputtered. "Spent the blunt . . . all but this." He fumbled for his coin purse, dragged it from his pocket, and pressed it into Matt's hand. "'Ere, take yer bleedin' money."

Matt smiled coldly. "I intend to—you'll hardly be need-ing it where you're going, Fox. And neither will your friend, Mr. Dibble." He motioned toward the shadows and six big burly bruisers stepped out of the alley into the street. Two of them carried stout oak clubs, the others had big beefy hands that were doubled into fists.

"Ye be goin' for an ocean voyage, Mr. Fox," the tallest of the men said, a red-haired sailor with a scar across his cheek. "Ye *and* Mr. Dibble."

"Jesus, Danny! It's a bloody press gang!"

"That's right, Connie," Matt said. "The captain of the *Harvest* is a friend of mine. He can always use a couple more good strong backs."

"I'll kill ya!" Fox threatened, his cheeks turning red with fury. "I swear it!"

"I don't think so, Danny. I think you'll be too busy swabbing decks and mending sail. Chances are, you'll never set foot on English shores again, but if you do, I'd suggest you stay as far away from me and my family as you can get. If you don't—if you ever come near them again—I'm the one who'll do the killing. I swear *that* to you."

Both men fell silent. The six big bruisers closed in on them, jerked their arms behind their backs and tied ropes around them. The last time Matt saw them, the press gang was prodding them off toward the docks, Fox and Dibble swearing all the way.

He turned his attention to St. Cere. "Thanks, Adam. You're a damned good friend."

"Anytime, Matthew." He grinned. "No matter what they say—one thing you aren't is dull."

Matt laughed and so did Adam.

"My town house isn't far. You can stay there for the night—what little is left of it."

"To tell you the truth, I think I'll head for home."

Adam glanced up. "You don't mean Belmore?"

Matt nodded.

"My friend, you've got it bad."

He smiled a bit stiffly. "I've grown used to the comforts of home and a warm, willing woman in my bed—that much I'll grant."

Adam just shook his head. Strickland might have gone half crazy over Jessie Fox, got himself leg-shackled—maybe even fallen in love—but Adam wasn't about to. Unlike Matt, he was ending his crazy obsession with Waring's beautiful stepdaughter before it went one bit further. As soon as he got the chance, he was taking Gwen Lockhart to bed.

*C*hapter *T*wenty

*T*he long warm summer slipped away, Jessie's days passed with an edge of fear, waiting for Matthew's orders to arrive, knowing the danger he would be facing in a battle against the French.

Knowing he might not return.

They took long walks in the garden, went for early morning rides, and worked together in the greenhouse, little Sarah often going with them. Today they were going on a picnic down by the lake. Carrying a basket heavy with cold meats, cheeses, gingerbread, and wine, Matthew led them out to the pony cart and lifted them in.

An hour later, Jessie was lying beside him on a blanket by the lake, pleasantly stuffed with food, Sarah wandering nearby, picking tiny yellow flowers, silent as always yet each day a little less afraid.

"What are you thinking?" Matt asked Jessie, watching her wipe the last of the cold roast partridge from her fingers.

"I was thinking about Papa Reggie. It isn't fair of us not to tell him you'll be leaving."

"I know. I've been thinking about it for days. I promise we'll tell him soon."

They talked about their childhood, Jessie telling Matt about the awful days after she had left the inn, Matt speaking briefly about his boyhood. "I was only six when my mother died. My father remarried, but we didn't see him much. He was busy with his properties, spending much of his time in London." He plucked a yellow clover daisy from amid the deep green grasses. "It was a difficult time for me. I was lonely, desperate for affection. I adored my stepmother but she didn't feel the least regard for me." A soft, bitter sound escaped him. "Ironically, she loved my father, but he cared nothing for her." He tossed the yellow flower away. "Love and pain. It's odd how closely they relate."

Jessie felt a pang of sadness at his words. And yet she couldn't deny the truth of them. Love often meant pain. Just the thought of Matt's leaving made a tight ache form in her chest. Reaching out to him, she cupped his face in her hand. "Your stepmother must have cared for you, Matthew. How could she not?"

A slow, uncertain smile spread across his lips. He lay down on the blanket, pulled her down on top of him, and kissed her deeply. They might have made love, there in the grass by the lake, if Sarah hadn't been with them.

If she hadn't tumbled just then with a thunderous splash into the lake. "Sarah!" Jessie leapt up and so did Matthew, both of them racing madly off toward the water. Sarah's head popped up just beyond a thin row of reeds, her eyes huge and her mouth gaping open for a scream. She flailed her arms and thrashed in the water, then her little pink ruffled dress dragged her down.

"My God!" Jessie cried. "Sarah's drowning and I can't swim!"

But Matthew had already pulled off his coat and jerked off his boots. Filling his lungs with air, he dived into the chilly pond.

"Oh, dear God . . ." Jessie stood ankle deep at the edge of the muddy lake, the hem of her gown clinging to her legs as she watched the line of bubbles that appeared where Matthew went down.

It seemed an eternity before he surfaced, another long instant before he jerked Sarah's tiny fair head above the water. She was crying, sputtering and gasping for breath, and

Jessie was crying, too. She ran to them while Matthew sloshed ashore, holding the child in his arms, a big hand cradling her head against his shoulder.

"She's all right," he said, but he was shaking, and not from his sodden clothes.

Jessie clutched the child's icy hand, the small blue veins standing out beneath the little girl's waxen skin. "We're taking you home, honey. You'll be warm and dry in no time."

Sarah turned her face into Matthew's shoulder and slid her small pale arms around his neck. "Papa," she whispered. "Papa . . ."

Matthew tightened his hold. "I'm right here, sweetheart. Papa's right here. Please don't cry. Everything's going to be fine."

Jessie stared at him and didn't say a word. Her throat had closed up and it ached too much for her to swallow. She had loved Matt Seaton since she was a little girl, but she had never loved him more than she did in that moment.

She walked beside him in silence as they made their way back to the blanket, which Jessie jerked up and wrapped around them against the chill. She grabbed the picnic basket and Matthew's abandoned clothes, hurried to the pony cart, and climbed in.

They left the horse and cart at the stable and made their way back to the house. Water dripped from the tail of Matt's coat but he didn't seem to notice, just climbed the stairs to the nursery and began to unbutton Sarah's soggy ruffled dress.

"Lord a mercy!" Viola bustled toward them, her round face dark with concern. "What's 'appened to me poor lit'l lamb?"

Through her huge, long-lashed blue eyes, Sarah looked up at Viola. "Papa saved me from the water," she said. And then she started to cry.

Vi's astonished gaze swung to Jessie, who turned to look at Matthew. Her husband merely smiled.

"Poor lit'l pet." Viola reached for the child, wrapping her

small shivering body in a blanket. Sarah snuffled a couple of times, then waved as Viola carried her off toward the fire.

Jessie dragged in a shaky breath. "Oh, God, Matthew, Sarah would have drowned if it hadn't been for you."

Matthew said nothing, but a muscle leapt in his cheek. It was obvious he had been thinking that same thing. And that the day would soon come when he would be gone.

Who would watch out for them then?

Matt strode the path leading down to the greenhouse. His father had told him Jessie was there, and now that his morning meeting with his tenants was ended, he was intent on seeking her out.

It didn't take long to reach his destination. He lifted the latch on the door and quietly slipped into the humid interior. The place was large, built of hundreds of panes of thick frosted glass and overflowing with big leafy plants. Flowers not usually found in the colder English climate grew in the earthen beds, along with exotic vegetables and fruits.

Jessie was busy working, digging in the rich black soil, her hands covered with dirt well past her wrists. She set a tiny orange tree into the soil, tamped the dirt around the roots, then bent over to pick up her watering can, giving him a tempting view of her firm little derriere.

He found himself grinning, walking as silently as he could, hoping to sneak up behind her. He had almost made it when his foot crunched on a pebble and she whirled to face him, watering can in hand, the holes in the long pointed nozzle spouting water all over his freshly polished boots.

A peal of laughter bubbled up from her throat. "You'll have to do better than that, my lord, if you plan to sneak up on me!" She laughed again at the stunned look on his face, at the water dripping off his shiny black Hessians.

A slow smile spread across his face, and he wickedly grinned. "Why, you little minx—you'll pay for that!"

Jessie shrieked as he made a grab for her, jumped out of his reach, and raced off through the rows of leafy plants, flowers, and more of the little orange trees, Matthew close behind her. Darting one way then another, dodging behind the heavy foliage, she finally reached the rear of the greenhouse, tore open the low wooden door to a small potting shed, and disappeared inside.

Matt just smiled. There was only one way out—sooner or later he would have her. Still, he moved forward, stepping into the dim interior. Waiting would work but the chase was much more fun.

As he moved toward the rear of the potting shed, jerking open each cupboard and peering menacingly inside, it occurred to him he had never behaved so playfully with a woman. Matt smiled to discover he was actually having fun.

He hauled away a mossy plank and searched beneath, but no one was there. "You might as well come out, Jess. You can't hide from me forever."

He searched the middle of the shed, then moved toward a corner where a paint-spattered canvas tarpaulin hung down from the rafters. She was back there—he could feel it. He grinned as he wrapped his fingers around the tarp. When he jerked back the heavy piece of canvas, he saw that she had climbed atop a rickety wooden ladder, but before he could haul her down, she tilted the rusty watering can, raining icy water over his head. Sputtering, grinning in spite of the chill, he charged the ladder, knocking Jessie off her perch, then catching her and tossing her over his shoulder.

"Now I've got you!" He laughed as he strode out of the shed, Jessie laughing and pounding helplessly on his back.

Chuckling all the way to an old wooden bench along the wall, he sat down and pulled her playfully across his lap.

Jessie didn't stop laughing, not even when he hauled up her skirts. "Matthew! What on earth are you doing?"

But his attention had already shifted, away from the teasing and mirth to the wriggling bundle of woman he held on his lap. "Perhaps you deserve another thrashing," he teased, but his voice came out husky and his hand merely smoothed over the curves hidden by her scanty chemise.

"When you were twelve years old," he said thickly, already hard and pulsing with desire for her, "it never occurred to me what a lovely little bottom you would have when you grew up." He lifted her chemise, baring her supple curves, then bent forward and pressed his lips to one of the rounded globes.

"Matthew!" Jessie sucked in a breath, conscious for the first time that now the game had shifted. He could feel the change in her heartbeat, and the rapid pulsing rhythm of his own.

He shifted her on his lap, his hand skimming down between the cheeks of her bottom, which felt warm and smooth, the muscles tightening wherever he touched. His other hand reached beneath her, cupping a breast, stroking it through her simple muslin day dress, then slipping inside her bodice to tease a nipple and make it crest. A shiver ran through her, then another and another, and the fire in his loins burned hotter.

It was strangely erotic, touching her this way, sensuous and wildly carnal. The greenhouse was humid, smelling of earth and flowers, but no one could see inside and no one ever bothered them when they were in there working. Jessie squirmed again, realizing as he had that they were alone and that he could do with her exactly as he wished.

His hand moved between her legs, parting them a little then stroking her there, feeling the slick hot wetness.

"Matthew . . . ?" His name came out on a hot breath of air.

"I told you you would pay," he said gruffly.

A tiny moan escaped. Her body trembled with shivers of pleasure, the same hot tingling that invaded his own. He delved deeper and began a gentle stroking. The muscles tightened across her stomach and the movement made the sinews in his thighs grow taut.

"Matthew . . ." she whimpered, but his sensuous stroking did not slow. If he meant to punish her, he was failing mightily. With every stroke of his hand, she gave up a throaty little purr, a sweetly feminine response to his playful domination.

His loins tightened, grew thick and heavy, desire pooling low in his belly. The breast he teased swelled into his palm, and tiny bumps rose over the soft white curves of her bottom. He teased the little bud at the core of her, and her body went taut. Little cries of passion slipped from her throat as she reached a shivery release, and Matt had to fight down a hot urge to take her.

Instead he continued his skillful caresses till the ripples of pleasure began to dim. She barely noticed when he lifted her onto her feet and bent her over, bracing her hands on the bench, keeping her skirts still bunched around her hips. He worked the buttons on his breeches and his shaft sprang free, pressing itself urgently against her. He had never felt so driven to possess a woman, never felt such a need to make a woman respond to him. He wanted her to need him, to crave him like a drug. He wanted her as ensnared by him as he was enthralled by her.

She squirmed against him and made a soft little whimpering moan as he eased himself inside her, burying himself to the hilt. Jessie cried out but still arched her back, driving him deeper still, sending thick waves of heat pulsing through him, nearly breaking his iron control.

"Easy, love," he soothed, tightening his hold around her waist, locking them more closely together. "You can't imagine how good you feel."

She moved a little and a shudder of pleasure rippled through him. "Yes, I can," she whispered.

His heart beat faster at her words. Withdrawing full length, he slid into her again, each long stroke sending waves of heat into his groin and a sliver of fire along his nerves. He massaged a breast, felt the tantalizing little tip go taut, and another surge of warmth shimmered through him. The tension returned to Jessie's body, straining the tightly leashed control he kept on his own.

Lowering his hands to her hips, he gripped them firmly, driving into her until she arched against him, moaning softly and begging him for more. He was pounding now, riding her fast and hard, giving her all he had and taking a good dose for himself.

Several long deep thrusts and her muscles clenched around him. She cried his name at the moment she reached her release, and with a groan, he followed, spilling his wet seed deeply inside her, holding her against him, savoring each sweet ripple of pleasure.

They stood like that for the longest time, Matt just holding her, still hard inside her, enjoying the closeness that veiled the trouble they faced ahead. He found himself praying that they had made a child, that before he went to war, she would be carrying his babe.

The thought crashed in that if he died, he wanted Jessie to have some part of him, something that would keep her from forgetting. The thought of never seeing her again made his throat close up, and when Jessie pulled away, he gathered her close in his arms.

He wished he could tell her something of how he felt, but it wasn't his way, and in truth he was still uncertain himself.

"Matthew? Is everything all right?"

He forced himself to smile. "Yes . . ." But inside he was thinking of the war and that he might not return. "Everything is fine."

Wordlessly, they helped each other straighten their clothes, then he turned her to face him. "There was a reason I came out here, Jess. I suppose I should have told you before, but I wasn't sure how you'd feel. I decided you had a right to know."

A worried frown creased her forehead. "What is it?"

"Last week when I went to London to see my solicitor, I also saw your brother."

The blood seemed to drain from her face. "How did you know where to find him?"

"I figured with the money and jewelry you gave him he'd head straight for the city. Once I got there, Adam Harcourt helped me."

"You didn't . . . you didn't kill him?"

"No." He smiled coldly, thinking of his encounter with Fox. "Your brother had a slight run-in with a London press gang—he and his chum, Connie Dibble." Matt explained about Long Dixon, the captain of the *Harvest,* and that Danny would be serving aboard Long's ship. "Odds are, my love, we'll never lay eyes on Danny Fox again."

Jessie glanced away, her long, dark gold lashes blinking furiously. "I wish I could say I am sorry, but in truth all I feel is relief."

"Fox made his own bed, Jess. Now he's suffering the consequences. All that matters is that you and Sarah are safe."

"And the Belmore name," Jessie said. "And your father's reputation."

"Yes, thank God." He smiled. "I do believe, Lady Strickland, your past is safely behind you."

Jessie just nodded. Matt had to admit it felt good to be free of the threat of scandal and able to look forward to the future. Jessie had come so far since those years of squalor above the Black Boar Inn. Perhaps now she would be able to forget them.

He hoped so. He wanted her protected, no matter what happened to him. Already he felt more for his wife than he had ever intended. He wasn't pleased about it, but he couldn't deny it was true.

Perhaps, once he was again at sea, he could come to grips with his newfound emotions, be able to bring them under control.

It was a goal that held more allure than he had ever expected.

Lady Caroline Winston walked across Bow Street to the three-story brick building near the corner and entered the office of one Willis G. McMullen, the investigator she had hired to look into the background of the newly titled Countess of Strickland.

"Come in, milady," the scruffy little man said. "I'll be right with you." His clothes, though clean, were wrinkled and unkempt, his face bore the signs of a two-day beard.

He pointed toward a rickety looking chair, but Caroline silently declined and stood carefully away from the stacks of yellowed newspapers that covered his desk and the floor.

"What have you found out, Mr. McMullen?" The office might be as shabby as he was, but according to her family's solicitor, McMullen was extremely good.

The little man scratched his head, making strands of his sandy brown hair stand on end. "That's the helluv it—beggin' yer pardon, miss. A little more than four years ago, yer Miss Fox, the woman in question, just sort of appears, practically like she come right outta thin air."

"What about her father, Simon Fox, the marquess's cousin from Devon? Surely you found some sign of him."

"Nary a trace, milady."

"Well, she can't just suddenly appear. She has to come from *somewhere*. You'll simply have to keep on looking."

"I realize that, milady, and that is exactly my intention. I've checked High Wycomb from top to bottom. She definitely ain't from anywhere near Belmore, but the marquess owns several other properties—one in Yorkshire and one in Wessex. Then there's Seaton Manor, near Buckler's Haven. That one belongs to his son, but I think I'll look into it, too."

"That's a good idea, Mr. McMullen." Caroline inwardly smiled. In this case, what hadn't been found was nearly as important as what had been. Jessica Fox wasn't from Devon, and there was no Simon Fox, which meant the marquess had lied. That being the case, odds were good there were a lot more lies to uncover.

Just thinking about it, Caroline had an insane urge to rub her hands together with glee. Or perhaps throw back her head and laugh aloud. Instead she arched a brow at the stocky little Bow Street runner.

"Let me know, Mr. McMullen, when you've found something of interest to report."

"Of course, milady."

Caroline left the office with the smile still clinging to her face.

*C*hapter *T*wenty-*O*ne

*I*n another part of London later that evening, Gwendolyn Lockhart stepped down from the Earl of Waring's fine black carriage, then crossed to where her mother and stepfather stood in front of the ornate doors leading into the Theatre Royal in Haymarket.

Since the night of his lascivious conduct at Vauxhall Gardens, the earl had been solicitous and perfectly behaved. He never mentioned his despicable behavior and neither did Gwen.

She had, however, been careful to stay out of his way.

Gwen sighed as she shoved back the hood of her mauve silk-lined cloak, a perfect match to her high-waisted brocade gown, and allowed a liveried footman just inside the doors to whisk it away. If only she could go to her mother, tell her about Waring's lewd advances and ask for the countess's protection. But her mother would never believe Gwen's story, or even if secretly she did, she would pretend that she did not.

She liked being the Countess of Waring. She liked the money, and the influence her husband wielded among members of the ton. If her daughter wound up paying the ultimate price, it would still be a small one . . . or at least so Lady Waring seemed to believe.

In truth, her mother was weak, especially when it came to the earl. Gwen knew when it came to Lord Waring, she was strictly on her own.

Except of course for St. Cere. He was the one man she had ever seen stand up to the earl. She admired him for it and of course she was grateful. She was also wildly enamored of the tall, gracefully handsome man, so much so that two days ago, she had sent him a note, telling him she would be riding in Hyde Park and asking him to join her.

He had, of course, but the encounter hadn't gone the way she had planned. Instead of the gallant lord who had rescued her at Vauxhall Gardens, St. Cere had played the rogue, urging her to meet him in private, asking her to steal away in the night to a place called Carlton House, as if she were one of his mistresses.

Not that secretly she wasn't tempted.

Just the sight of Adam Harcourt's dark good looks set her whole body to tingling. If he hadn't pressed her so hard, tried to force her to do his bidding with such typically domineering male tactics, she might have actually gone.

Instead she had simply said no.

She did, however, allude to the fact she would be attending the theater tonight, in company with her parents. She wasn't sure he would come, but she thought that he might. She'd neglected to mention, however, that Lord Bascomb, his friend, Lord Montague's oldest son, would be there as well, arriving even now to serve as her escort for the evening. She would let St. Cere discover that for himself.

"Lord and Lady Waring, Lady Gwendolyn, beg pardon for my tardiness." Bascomb swept off his cloak. "There was no way to postpone my meeting. I appreciate your indulgence in allowing me to join you here." Peter Montague, Lord Bascomb, was a slight man, average in height with thinning brown hair, perhaps ten years older than Gwen. In contrast to his plain features, he always dressed something of a peacock, which made his looks appear even more bland.

"It was a trifle," Waring said. "The play has not yet started, and we have only just arrived ourselves." Bascomb was a favorite of the earl's. At times she suspected he wanted

to see a marriage between them. Perhaps because her stepfather was involved in Lord Montague's business endeavors,
therefore exerting a great deal of control over him, and by
extension, his son.

Whatever the reason, Gwen was determined it wasn't
going to happen, not marriage to Peter or any other man.
She smiled at Lord Bascomb, made some sort of inane com-
ment about the play they were about to see, a controversial
satire called *The Tailors,* but all the while her eyes searched
the crowd for the dark good looks of St. Cere.

Halfway through the performance, Gwen was certain he
would not come. The theater was crowded, a three-story
building done lavishly in scarlet and gold with molded ceilings and heavy velvet curtains insuring the privacy of the
three tiers of private boxes where the wealthy patrons sat.
The rest of the audience watched from the pit.

Unfortunately for Gwen, St. Cere had not appeared in
either location.

Sitting glumly in her stepfather's velvet-draped box, she
ignored Peter's occasional toothy smile and stared down at
the stage. At least the performance had been interesting, not
so much the play itself but the catcalls coming from the pit. It
seemed half the tailors in London had come to see the show,
and they were not the least bit happy about the way they were
being portrayed.

Just before the candles were snuffed, signaling the end of
the second act, Gwen left the box on the pretense of a trip to
the ladies' retiring room, but instead simply made her way
down to the lobby for a moment away from the toadying
Lord Bascomb and the lewd glances coming from Lord
Waring.

"Good evening, my lady."

Gwen jerked her head toward the sound of the deep male
voice. "St. Cere . . . I-I didn't think to see you."

His sensuous lips went a little bit thin. "Apparently not,
since you are here with Bascomb." There was a slight edge
to his words, annoyance, or perhaps it was jealousy, though

she couldn't imagine the handsome viscount being jealous of another man and especially not Bascomb.

"I would rather it had been you."

A sleek black brow went up. Her frankness always unnerved him. Then a silvery glint appeared in those steel gray eyes and he pulled her around a corner into the shadows.

"If that is the truth, perhaps the situation can be remedied." He bent his head and took her mouth in a slow, sensuous kiss. He urged her to open for him, to allow him inside, his tongue like silk across her bottom lip.

"Get your parents to take you home early," he whispered, pressing soft warm kisses against her throat and shoulders, sending hot little shivers across her skin. "You can slip away and meet me at Carlton House, as I urged you to do before." He nibbled the lobe of an ear. "I'll have everything ready. You can come in through the back and no one will see you. We'll have the rest of the night to ourselves." Another soft kiss followed, making her knees feel weak, and God she was tempted.

Dear Lord, was she tempted! But something held her back, some feminine instinct that warned her to beware.

"I'm sorry, my lord, but I cannot meet you tonight. Lord Waring has had the evening planned for weeks. 'Twould be impossible for me to get away. Perhaps tomorrow we could meet . . . at the park, as we did before."

A muscle bunched in his cheek. "'Tis not in the park that I want you, Lady Gwendolyn, but in my bed. If I have spoken too plain, I am sorry, but 'tis a custom you yourself established. I want to make love to you. I want to kiss you and touch you and give you the greatest of pleasures. Come to me, Gwen. Meet me tonight."

It was one thing to be attracted to a man like St. Cere. It was another entirely to let him take advantage.

"I told you I cannot. If all you want is a woman to warm your bed, there are a dozen winsome tarts on the street outside the theater. I suggest you make use of one of them."

St. Cere cursed roundly as she turned and fled back upstairs.

He caught her at the top, at the end of the row of boxes. "I don't want another woman. Dammit, I want you. If you cannot come tonight, come tomorrow. Everything will be arranged, just the way I said."

Gwen jerked away, alarmed by the urgent, almost frantic note in his voice. "Do not bother, my lord. I will not be there." She heard another savage curse, but she didn't look back as she walked away, and this time St. Cere did not follow. Gwen's eyes filled with tears. She blinked and they clung to her dark lashes. Damn him! He was just like all the rest. She hated him for making her feel the things he did, and for making her cry—no man was ever worth that!

Before she reached her box, she fished through her reticule, pulled out a lace-trimmed handkerchief and wiped the moisture away.

That was when she heard it, the shouts from the pit that had risen from murmurs of discontent to a cacophony of threats and jeers and the crash of hurling objects. Elegantly dressed theater patrons had begun to stream from the boxes, forcing her backward, farther and farther from her mother and stepfather. She barely saw their heads as they appeared through the red velvet curtains and hurried toward another set of stairs at the opposite end of the row some distance away.

Even Bascomb didn't spare a glance, just hurried along beside Lord Waring till they disappeared into the crowd completely. The throng of people continued surging forward, forcing her down the stairs and into the melee streaming toward the double doors that weren't nearly wide enough to accommodate the hysterical mob trying to escape.

A worried glance toward the stage showed a half-dozen actors brawling with a throng of unhappy tailors, but it was the panic of the crowd fighting to reach the doors that gave Gwen her first real shot of fear.

Ahead of her a man went down and another man fell on top of him. People began to topple over themselves, stacking like cordwood beneath the weight of others trying to escape the fray.

"Get outta the way, lady!" Someone pushed her and she stumbled, caught herself just before she fell and righted herself, only to be shoved and stumble again. She would have gone down if a strong arm hadn't clamped around her waist and dragged her upright. She knew who it was even before she saw him and as angry with him as she was, relief surged through her.

"Come on!" he shouted above the din of shrieking, terrified people. "We have to get out of here."

Gwen simply nodded and gratefully clutched his arm. The theater had erupted into a full-fledged riot, people fighting in the aisles, shoving and pushing and cursing, tearing objects off the walls and hurling them at the stage.

Instead of moving forward toward the lobby and the doors leading out to the street, the viscount motioned her backward, leading her farther into the theater, then behind a row of boxes along one wall to a curtain hiding a set of stairs leading onto the stage. He turned away before they reached it, heading for a door that led out into an alley.

"How did you know that exit was there?" Gwen asked, leaning against the rough brick wall and inhaling a lungful of precious fresh air, along with a sweep of relief.

A corner of the viscount's sensuous mouth curved up. "There was a lady . . . an actress I once knew. Suffice it to say I've been backstage here a few times before."

More women, Gwen thought, suddenly disheartened. What was she doing with a man like St. Cere? Then she felt his hand at her waist, sure and determined, the only one who cared enough for her to see that she was safe.

They paused a moment more to catch their breath, then he urged her off to find his carriage. A few minutes later they were climbing inside and he was waving the driver away.

Gwen looked down at the deep vee of her neckline, saw the torn row of expensive mauve lace hanging down from the high-waisted bodice. "I must look a fright," she whispered. Her hair was mussed, her reticule missing, her slippers covered with mud.

The viscount turned her face with his hand. "You look lovely."

Her lashes swept down to hide a glow of pleasure she didn't want to feel. "Thank you for helping me. I'm not sure what would have happened if you hadn't come."

His face closed up. "People likely died in there tonight. You might have been among them." He looked at her hard. "They don't deserve you. None of them. They don't know what a treasure they have."

Gwen felt the burn of tears. No one ever stood up for her the way St. Cere did. No one. She reached up to touch him, rested her fingertips on his cheek. "Would you kiss me?"

He stared at her a moment more, then she thought he might have groaned. His head came down; their lips met and clung. His kissed her gently at first, slanting his lips over hers, teasing the corners. Then the kiss turned hot and fierce as he dragged her into his arms and his hands slid over her breasts.

By the time the carriage halted, she was breathless and dizzy, only vaguely aware of her surroundings, that the curtains were drawn and only a sliver of light from the brass coach lamps shone in. Her heart was pounding so hard she didn't hear the door being opened, but the viscount did, and he turned to hide her disarray behind his tall hard frame.

"We've arrived, my lord."

"Thank you, James."

With the draft of cold air that swept in as he climbed down, some of Gwen's senses returned. "Where . . . where are we?"

The viscount smiled. "Carlton House." He reached up for her, but she recoiled from his touch as if he were a snake—which in that moment, she was certain he was.

"Carlton House! I cannot believe you would bring me here!"

St. Cere frowned. "Don't tell me this isn't what you wanted,

Gwendolyn. No woman kisses a man the way you just did and doesn't want him to make love to her."

Embarrassment swept over her, mixed with a tide of anger. "Take me home," she said, her expression mutinous. "I appreciate your help at the theater—now I wish to go home." She sat back against the velvet squabs, refusing to budge from the carriage.

St. Cere clamped his jaw, bunching a muscle there. Then he swore a muttered curse. "I thought you were different, a woman who for once was honest about her feelings."

"And I thought *you* were different—a man I could finally trust."

A corner of his mouth twisted up. "You may trust me, Gwendolyn, to give you exactly what both of us want." But instead of hauling her out of the carriage, as she half-expected, half-hoped he would, he simply closed the door.

"Take the lady home, James," he called up to his driver. "Apparently that is her wish." At least for now, his thin smile said.

What would Jessie do in a case like this? Gwen suddenly wondered, and an image of her friend's slender frame draped over Matthew Seaton's broad shoulder popped into her mind. Jessie went after the things she wanted. If she had wanted Adam Harcourt, by now he might well belong to her.

Gwen was a woman of equal determination.

She wasn't sure if the shiver running through her was from fear of what she was thinking—or the promise she had seen in the viscount's silvery eyes.

Jessie spotted the uniformed rider and her heart slid into her stomach. Grabbing up her skirts, she raced out her bedchamber door in a highly unladylike manner and down the sweeping marble stairs.

Matthew arrived at the same moment and so did Papa Reggie, all of them gathered grimly in the entry, holding the very same thought.

The time had come at last for Matthew to leave.

The knock sounded again and tall, stately Osgood pulled open the door, his expression as carefully controlled as Matthew's suddenly appeared.

"A message for Captain Seaton," the uniformed young officer said.

"Come in, Lieutenant." Matt stepped forward to welcome the tired-looking navy man into the entry and accept the missive he carried. "It appears you've been on the road a while. Ozzie will see you to your refreshment, and you can rest before continuing your journey."

The lieutenant shook his head. "I'm sorry, sir. I'm afraid I'll have to decline. I've several more stops to make and not all that much time."

Matthew's smile looked brittle. "I understand." Still holding the wax-sealed message, he waited while Ozzie closed the door and turned away, then broke the seal and began to read, his stony expression confirming the content.

"It's from Admiral Dunhaven. Nelson is almost ready." He glanced up at Jessie. "It's time for me to leave."

"Oh, Matthew . . ." Jessie went into his arms and he held her tightly against him.

Papa Reggie cleared his throat, his face a little bit pale. "You're quite sure about this, son?"

"I'm certain I have to go. I am equally certain that I do not wish to leave. Belmore is my home now. I haven't yet left and already I miss it."

Jessie bit hard on her lip to keep it from trembling. "When must you go?" At least another week, she prayed, give us that long at least.

"The message is urgent," he said gently. "I must go as soon as I'm packed."

"But . . . But you can't possibly mean today!"

"I'm sorry, love, I must. It's a two-week sail from Portsmouth to Cádiz. That is where Nelson and his ships will be waiting. The French fleet is assembling. Time is of the essence now."

"But surely you can wait until tomorrow. Surely—"

"I'm ordered to leave today, Jess. That is what I must do." His hands came up to her shoulders. "Please don't make this any harder for me than it is already."

Papa Reggie reached for her hand and gave it a gentle squeeze. "Matthew is right, my dear. He must leave as he is commanded, and we must be strong."

Jessie simply nodded. Her throat had closed up and her chest ached as if a knife had pierced it. "I'm sorry," she said. "It's only that I had hoped for a little more time."

Matthew tipped her chin with his hand. "So had I." He smiled, but his face looked grim. "Come upstairs and help me pack?"

Jessie nodded, not quite trusting her voice. But once they reached his suite, instead of calling for his valet, he closed the door and dragged her into his arms.

His kiss was fierce, wildly possessive yet so achingly tender that tears sprang into her eyes. She kissed him back with equal desperation, her heart a knot of pain inside her chest. Matthew lifted her into his arms, carried her over to the bed, and began to strip off her clothes, kissing each part of her body, worshiping her even as he savagely claimed her.

They made love with wild abandon, then once more with gentle care. Still he did not linger.

"I'm sorry, my love," he said gently, unwinding his tall, powerful body from her embrace. "I'm afraid it's time. I can't put this off any longer."

Jessie swallowed past the ache in her throat. "I know." They dressed in silence, then she watched while Matthew and his valet packed the clothes he would need for his journey.

Two hours after the messenger from His Majesty's Navy had arrived, her husband stood at the bottom of the front steps leading into Belmore, dressed in his spotless blue uniform coat and tight white breeches, saying his final goodbyes.

He extended a hand to Papa Reggie, who accepted, looking

more fragile than he had in some time. "Take care of yourself, Father."

"Come back to us safely, my son." A sad smile touched his lips. "I'm too old to manage this place alone. Jessica and I need you."

Matthew just nodded. The marquess surprised him by leaning forward and enveloping him in a hug. Then both men stepped away, embarrassed by the brief show of affection.

At the top of the stairs, Viola set little Sarah on her feet. "Go on, now. Tell 'is lordship good-bye."

Yellow ruffles flounced on the hem of her dress as the child raced forward, stopping to stare up at Matthew, fascinated with the glittering gold buttons on his coat.

"Do you have to go?"

"Yes, sweetheart, I'm afraid I do."

Her big blue eyes filled with tears. "But I don't want you to go."

Matthew lifted the little girl into his arms. "I have to, sweetheart, but I'll be back just as soon as I can." He kissed her cheek and Sarah kissed him back. Then he set her back down on her feet.

"Bye . . . Papa." She waved to him as Viola led her away.

"Good-bye, Sarah," he called back to her.

Jessie watched as the others faded away, leaving them alone. Then she turned to her husband, who was standing perfectly erect, his shoulders squared, strong jaw thrust forward, proper as always for his last good-bye. She wanted to throw herself into his arms and beg him to stay, to whine and cry and beat her fists against his chest. Instead she lifted her chin, refusing to cry until he was gone.

"She's going to be all right," he said, his eyes still fixed on Sarah's small retreating figure.

"Yes, I think she is."

He focused the full measure of his formidable gaze on her. "And you, too, Jess, no matter what happens to me, you're going to be just fine."

Her heart clutched, squeezed inside her chest. She shook her head, fighting hard to hold back the wetness. "Please don't . . . please don't talk that way."

He lifted her chin with his fingers. "I'll miss you . . . more than I could ever say."

"I love you, Matthew." Jessie gazed into those fierce blue eyes, wishing with all her heart he would say he loved her, too, willing him to repeat the words, even if he really didn't mean them.

The muscles in his throat moved up and down. She thought he might speak, prayed that he would, but he only stared into her face as if he memorized her features. The beautiful words did not come. Matthew would never lie.

Long seconds passed. Finally, he bent forward and pressed a soft kiss on her lips. "Good-bye, Jess. Take care of yourself."

Sorrow smothered her. Tears burned the backs of her eyes. "Good-bye, Matthew."

He started to climb into the carriage, paused for a heartbeat, then turned back. Long strides returned him to her side and he swept her into his arms. His kiss was hot and deep, wildly possessive and so thorough her knees went weak, yet there was an aching tenderness to it and the tears she'd been holding rushed into her eyes.

Wordlessly he left her, striding back to the carriage, climbing inside and closing the door. A rap on the roof signaled the driver, and the vehicle lurched away.

Jessie watched until the shiny black conveyance rolled out of sight, then stood there for long minutes more. A brisk fall wind had come up, and a chill whipped through her clothes. Jessie didn't feel it. The only chill she felt was the icy fear that Matthew might never come home.

Reginald Seaton stood in the doorway to Jessica's make-shift schoolroom. The children were long gone, yet Jessica remained, staring morosely ahead, oblivious to her surroundings.

She had been that way for the past two weeks, ever since Matthew had gone. That she was in love with him was more than clear, as Reggie had suspected from the start. In time, he was sure, his son would come to love her.

If he survived his last, fearsome, blasted tour of duty.

She glanced up just then and he strode forward, enjoying the smile he had brought to her face. They didn't come often these days.

"A letter has arrived for you, my dear. From London. Your friend, Lady Gwendolyn, I believe. Apparently Lord Waring and his family are still in the city."

Jessica reached for the letter, studied the postmark and her friend's feminine scroll on the envelope. "I wrote to her last week. I told her Matthew had returned to the *Norwich*. I rather thought Lord Waring might have left for the country, since the Season had come to an end. But as you said, apparently he has not."

Reggie didn't leave then, as he normally would have, but waited instead for Jessica to scan the letter. "Nothing untoward has happened, I collect."

She smiled. "Just Gwen's usual mischief. She says she wishes that I were in London. I suppose she thinks, now that I'm a married woman, I could give her some worthwhile advice."

He chuckled softly. "I won't ask the nature of your friend's need, but I will say that in another way, her thoughts are running oddly parallel to mine."

"You think I can give Gwen advice?"

He smiled with amusement. "I can't speak to that. I was thinking that perhaps it would be easier for you to await word of Matthew if we were in the city."

Jessica glanced up. "You're thinking of going to London? But the Season is over."

"The time of year doesn't matter. There are always interesting diversions to be found in London. You hardly got a taste of it before you were married. Surely the theater and the opera, perhaps the occasional house party would make the time go faster."

She shook her head. "I could hardly enjoy myself knowing Matthew is in danger."

"The danger will not lessen simply because you wait here at Belmore—each day will only seem longer while you sit waiting for word. And Sarah would love it. Can you not imagine her excitement? That alone should make you say yes."

She didn't want to go. He could see it in her eyes and in a way he understood. She opened her mouth to argue, then paused, cocking a pretty blond eyebrow.

"Perhaps I am mistaken, but is it possible there is another reason for the trip? Perchance, while we are there, might you plan on spending a bit of time with Lady Bainbridge?"

He cleared his throat. Damnation, the girl was too quick by half. "Perhaps I would. Certainly, she could accompany us on occasion."

Jessie rounded the table and approached where he stood. "What about the scandal with the duke?"

"By now the gossip will have faded. And your appearance once more in Society will show them we have nothing to be ashamed of." He smiled. "Besides, most of the ton believe that Matthew was so mad for you he could not help himself. What he did was so completely romantic, they are willing to forgive him."

Jessie smiled. "I think the women would forgive your son almost anything and the men are half fearful of him. I only wish the story were true."

"Perhaps it is, my dear. Why else would my very proper son behave as he did?"

Jessie shook her head. "Because he wanted me. He never intended marriage—we both know that."

Reggie couldn't argue that one. "Give it time, my dear. Matthew isn't good at dealing with his emotions. He has bottled them up ever since his mother died. Captaining a ship only made things worse, and I suppose I am also to blame, since I have never been one for displays of affection. Still, there is always hope for change. Already, I believe he cares a great deal for you. In the years ahead, perhaps it will grow into love."

Jessica glanced away. "Perhaps," she said.

But both of them were thinking that the short time they'd had together might be all the time they would ever get.

Chapter Twenty-Two

Matt Seaton took his place near the end of the linen-draped dining table. He was sitting in Admiral Lord Nelson's luxurious cabin aboard the *Victory*, the admiral's flagship.

Nelson was commander-in-chief of the upcoming naval operation, in charge of four British frigates and twenty-seven ships of the line; Matt's ship, the *Norwich,* among them. Admiral Collingwood, also seated at the table, was second in command, and Captain Hardy captained the *Victory.*

Five other sea captains also attended the dinner, a lavish three-course meal of turtle soup, a turbot of halibut, freshly roasted goose, plover's eggs in aspic jelly, asparagus and fresh vegetables, and *meringues a la crème* for dessert. Three different wines had been served, and the men, at last replete, now sipped coffee and liquors.

Laughter drifted up from the far end of the table, but Matthew was distracted and missed the admiral's words. Setting his brandy glass back on the table, he glanced out the porthole to the gray, lightly rolling sea. He could hear the band up on deck playing "Rule Britannia," as they had done since he and the other ships' captains had first come aboard.

He took a sip of his brandy, surveying the group of officers in their spotless gold-trimmed uniforms, thinking the dinner had an almost surreal quality about it. Once they confronted the French and Spanish fleet, nearly fifty thousand men would be engaged in combat. The decks would run scarlet with blood; the damp sea air would be filled with the agonized shrieks of dying men.

Sitting as he was in a room of elegant moldings and fine silk draperies, surrounded by gleaming silver and crystal, if he had never been in battle, never seen the savagery of fighting, it would be impossible to believe.

And yet all of them were seasoned men, none of them novices to the carnage of war or oblivious to the threat of death that loomed so near at hand.

Perhaps this was simply their way of avoiding the brutal realities each man must face in the days ahead.

Nelson's voice drew his attention from the porthole. "Tell me, Captain Seaton, now that you've returned, does the *Norwich* and its crew still measure up to your stringent demands?" The admiral leaned back in his rosewood chair. He was a handsome man, just turned forty-seven, relatively young for the grave responsibilities he carried. His birthday had been celebrated aboard the *Victory* just a few days before Matt's arrival.

Matthew smiled. "Captain Munsen has done a commendable job in my absence. I've no doubt the *Norwich* will perform beyond your expectations under fire. The men are ready, even eager for battle. They will not disappoint you, Admiral Nelson."

"I'm glad to hear it, but not surprised. And I believe the ship will do even better with you at her helm. I thank you, Captain, for your swift return to duty. Experience is a key factor in any battle. I believe it could mean the difference between success or failure in the conflict that lies ahead."

Matthew swirled the burnished liquor in his glass. "How much longer, Admiral, before the French fleet begins to move?"

"They could sail from Cádiz any day. Once they do, we'll confront them. There are other factors, of course. The winds must hold, the seas must be manageable enough to maneuver." He leaned forward, beginning a discussion of his strategy for the coming confrontation. "My plan is a simple one. We'll attack in three lines—the *Victory* and fifteen other ships, including those of each man here, will go in at the front. Admiral Collingwood and his line will attack from the rear, and a third line, composed of our fastest vessels, will maneuver so that they can be used wherever they are needed."

Nelson went on with the details of his plan and each man listened with rapt attention. If anyone could win this battle, Nelson was that man. His men would follow him against the enemy into the depths of hell.

Matt was glad the *Norwich* had been chosen to come under Nelson's personal command, for his faith in the admiral was as great as the rest of his men. Still, he was worried about the outcome and dreading the losses that were certain to result from such a massive confrontation.

As the hours wore on, the admiral finished his briefing and the meal came to an end. With a final farewell and wishes for good fortune, the captains returned to their ships.

Feeling restless, thinking of Jessie and suddenly lonely, Matt crossed the deck of the *Norwich* and headed straight for his cabin, only to be interrupted by an insistent knock on the door. Discovering his friend Graham Paxton standing in the passageway, he stepped back and invited him in.

"Well, how did it go?" The brown-haired man ducked his head and stepped through the low wooden portal.

Matthew smiled. "You're not eager are you, Doctor?"

Graham chuckled, a quiet rumbling in his chest. "If you mean am I eager for battle the answer is no. If you mean am I eager to have this matter resolved, then yes, I suppose I am. It seems we've been waiting for this forever."

Matt walked over to the sideboard and poured his friend a brandy. "Here. You look like you could use it."

"Thank you." He accepted the snifter. "Perhaps it will help calm my nerves."

Matt motioned toward a chair in his small salon and both of them sat down. "The meeting went well, I suppose. There were the usual formalities, of course—a band on deck and a short speech of welcome. The meal was superb, though I find my age is showing. I grow impatient with the rigors of ceremony. Like you, I would simply like to see this business finished and be on my way home."

Graham leaned back in his chair. "Home . . . yes. You *are* beginning to sound like me. Those are definitely the words of a happily married man. I admit, I had wondered . . ."

Matt arched a brow. "You didn't think I would enjoy being married?"

"I didn't think you would let yourself fall in love."

Matthew said nothing for the longest time, just studied his friend and frowned. "What makes you think I'm in love?"

Graham simply smiled. "You forget, my friend, I have known you for a good many years. Since your return to the *Norwich,* you have spoken of your wife at least a dozen times and always with a tenderness I have never witnessed in you before. If you are not yet in love with her, there is no doubt you very soon will be."

Matt's scowl grew even darker. "I care for Jessica, yes. I am not afraid to admit it. But love?" He shook his head. "That I will never allow."

Graham finished his brandy and set the glass down on the table. "I have loved my wife since the moment I laid eyes on her more than ten years ago, and I haven't had a single regret. Loving someone doesn't make a man weaker, my friend. If the woman is the right one, the union makes him stronger. Together, each of them is more than either of them is apart."

Matthew shook his head. "Perhaps that is so, but there are other factors to consider. Loving someone doesn't guarantee you won't lose them. I lost my mother. I lost my brother. I've lost men I cared for in my crew. The pain was nearly unbearable. That kind of emotion can only bring pain. It isn't a risk I'm willing to take again."

The doctor regarded him closely. "What about children? Your wife is young and strong. There are bound to be offspring. Surely you plan to love them."

"Of course I will love them. I would be remiss in my duties as a father if I did not."

"But you will hold back from them. You won't let yourself love them too deeply."

Matthew said nothing. He had loved his mother and he had lost her. He had loved his stepmother and though she had never felt a deep affection for him, he had mourned her greatly when she died. He had lost dear friends in battle, and he had lost his brother.

"Granted there is a risk in loving someone," Graham said, "a wife perhaps most of all. But there is also the sweetest of rewards." The surgeon smiled. "Life is always a battle, my friend. Just as in war, you mustn't be afraid to face it, to claim whatever small victories you can. It is a difficult journey, even with someone to lean on. It is nearly unbearable with no one."

Matthew still did not answer. His friend's words rang with a truth he had never considered.

On top of that, he was trying to come to grips with the unsettling notion that Graham Paxton might be right—that perhaps it was already too late. Considering the painful longing he had felt for Jessie since his return to the *Norwich*, the loneliness, the aching he had suffered just thinking about her—maybe it was true.

Perhaps he had already fallen in love.

Gwen Lockhart glanced at the clock on the mantel above the marble-fronted hearth in her bedchamber. It was nine o'clock. Her mother and stepfather had gone out for the evening, but she had pled the headache. She would have to stay home, she'd said, take some powders and go straight to bed. In the morning, she would feel better.

But it wasn't her head that was pounding. It was her pulse, and it was racing with excitement.

Glancing again at the clock, Gwen dressed quickly in her cousin Henry's stylish clothes, the same ones she had worn to the Fallen Angel, never having returned them. With his

lavish wardrobe, Henry had never even noticed, and Gwen
figured she might have need of them again.

And of course, she did. Tonight she meant to use them by
attending, of all things, a boxing match. She had read all
about them, had heard Lord Waring discuss them, but actually attending such an event would, of course, be out of the
question.

Except Gwen was determined to go.

Wrapping her cousin's wide white stock around her neck,
she tied it into a stylish, oversized bow, then pulled on his
white pique waistcoat. It was too tight across the bosom,
which was probably just as well, since it flattened her breasts
and helped to disguise her female curves.

She glanced at herself in the mirror, surveying her handi-
work, eager to set off for the match. Tonight the champion,
Terrible Terrel, was scheduled to fight Rob Kilpatrick, the
Mclean, a big Scots bruiser the papers touted as the man
who would finally give Terrel his due.

Almost finished dressing—a task far easier for a man,
she'd discovered to her chagrin—Gwen adjusted the makeshift cuff links she had fashioned from two sewn-together
buttons. She straightened the waistcoat and her bottle green
tailcoat, then picked up her bowler and stuffed her hair up
under the brim.

She didn't bother with a false mustache. The fight was
being held at Honeywell's Bear Garden Boxing Ring, an
open-air arena in Haymarket, and the lighting wouldn't be
all that good. With any luck at all, she would pass among
the crowd unnoticed, just another young man engrossed in
the match.

It occurred to her that St. Cere might also attend, since
during their limited discussions he had mentioned his interest in sporting events, anything from horse racing to fox
hunting and everything in between.

Anything to help alleviate the boredom, he had said.

Gwen thought of him as she had every day since their last
ill-fated encounter, and a shiver of warmth raced through

her. If he did go, he might recognize her, since he had seen her dressed in these same clothes at the Fallen Angel. Yet the notion did not daunt her. In fact it made her pulse beat faster. Perhaps if she were lucky, she would see him but he wouldn't see her. It would give her the chance to study him, find out more about him.

And if he recognized her? Approached her? Gwen's stomach swirled, did a tiny little flip and neatly turned over. She wished she could convince herself he was merely a rake who wanted to bed her, that he cared nothing at all for her, that in thwarting him she had done the right thing. The problem was she wanted to be with him, to let him kiss her and perhaps in time, even make love to her.

Yes . . . perhaps Adam Harcourt would be there. If he was, who knew what the evening might bring? Gwen grinned as she headed for the door.

Adam Harcourt spotted Gwen Lockhart almost the moment she walked in. He blinked several times, trying to convince himself it couldn't be her, that after her nearly disastrous evening at the theater, the little hoyden wouldn't do such an idiotic thing.

And yet she was there, wearing the same, too-snug dandy's clothes she'd been garbed in at the Fallen Angel, the trousers and coat sleeves a bit too long, the bottle green jacket too snug across her breasts.

Good God, did she really think to fool them? Any man worth his salt would recognize the beautiful little bottom outlined in her nankeen breeches as belonging to a nicely curved female!

Adam cursed, long and fluently, wishing he hadn't seen her, that he didn't want to wring her pretty little neck—or drag her off somewhere and make slow, passionate love to her. Just when he had convinced himself to leave her alone, told himself Gwen Lockhart was a naive virgin who didn't deserve to be preyed upon by a seasoned rake like him, she appeared out of nowhere to tempt him.

Well, dammit, he was no saint. He had thought of her every day, imagined her sweet face and ripe little body a hundred times in his dreams. He had vowed to seduce her, to end his crazy obsession, and still he had left her alone. Dammit, enough was enough. He wanted her, and the way she constantly put herself in danger, if he didn't take her, sooner or later, some other man surely would.

He shoved his way through the throng of noisy spectators and came up beside where she stood in the middle of the crowd, but didn't make his presence known. He wondered how long it would take before she realized he stood there watching.

Gwen stared into the boxing ring, watching the two combatants slug it out. Sweat ran into their eyes and glistened over their half-naked bodies; their muscles bulged with the effort they were expending. It was exciting, she had to admit, in a primitive, animalistic sort of way, and watching them, the blood pumped faster through her veins. When the challenger landed a particularly wicked blow to Terrel's too-confident nose, she found herself cheering, raising a fist and shouting as loud as the rest of the people in the crowd.

There were women among them, she was surprised to see, some of them dressed quite fashionably. She wondered what kind of women they were and thought perhaps they were the mistresses of some of the men.

"Enjoying yourself, my lady?"

She jerked at the sound of the deep, familiar voice.

"Perhaps," the viscount said, "since you are so determined to pass yourself off as a man, you would care to step into the ring and go a few rounds with Terrel."

Gwen's spine went stiff. "Must you always be sneaking up on me?"

"Apparently I must. It seems I am doomed to come to your rescue time and again."

"In case you haven't noticed, my lord, the only one I need rescuing from is you."

His sleek black brows drew together over silvery eyes

that went hard. "In that, my lady, you are right. It is all I can do not to throttle you. You are a menace to yourself, Gwendolyn Lockhart. Surely there is someone, somewhere, who can keep you under control."

To her astonishment, instead of outrage, Gwen felt the sharp prickle of tears. "Why is it such a crime to want to learn about life? Why is it so different for you to be here than it is for me?" She looked up at him with the question burning in her eyes and the viscount's hard look softened, the sharp angles smoothing into a face more handsome than any she had ever seen.

"Perhaps you are right. Certainly to you it seems unfair. Unfortunately, life is rarely if ever fair."

"I only wish to understand, to experience life as you do. If I must take risks in order to do so, then that is what I will do."

His hand came up to her cheek. "You wish to learn of life, Gwen? I am more than willing to teach you."

She slowly shook her head, though she wasn't quite sure why. From the moment she had seen him, she had wanted the viscount to teach her everything he knew about life and loving, wanted it with a soft, sweet yearning unlike anything she had known.

He started to take her arm, then caught himself, realizing how unseemly it would look for two men to be walking together arm in arm. She thought she heard him curse as he urged her away from the ring, off toward the shadows at the rear of the garden.

"You can't stay here," he said, once they were alone. "Sooner or later, someone will realize you are a woman and that you are here by yourself. When they do you'll be fair game."

Gwen forced herself not to look away from those gray, determined eyes. "I came to watch the match, which is every bit as exciting as I suspected it would be. When it is over, that is when I shall leave."

St. Cere cursed blackly. "Little fool," he said, but there

was a note in his voice that sounded oddly like admiration. "If you are so determined, then I suppose I will have to stay with you. But I warn you, Gwendolyn Lockhart, there will be a stiff price to pay."

Perhaps there would. For now she didn't care. She was too caught up in his fierce silver gaze, too ensnared by the thrill she felt whenever he looked in her eyes. "We're missing the match," she said softly, and a corner of his mouth curved up.

"Well, we mustn't have that." He tipped his head toward the ring. "After you, my lady."

What fun they had! She never would have guessed. Once the viscount had accepted her presence, he relaxed and began to smile. It was a bright, white, devastating smile that made him look young and carefree. Standing in a place he commandeered near the front of the ring, they laughed and cheered the underdog, Rob Kilpatrick, on to a glorious victory. St. Cere even bought her a mug of ale, then grinned at the foamy mustache it left on her face.

"I believe I have seen you that way before," he teased. If she hadn't been dressed as a man, she was certain he would have kissed her.

They didn't wait for the last match to end, but still it was nearly midnight when they left Honeywell's boxing ring. Adam's carriage was waiting a few blocks from the entrance, but once he had settled her inside, his lighthearted manner seemed to change.

Very gently, he lifted the bowler from her head, then smoothed the thick dark curls away from her face. "You are so beautiful. You're so full of life . . . so incredibly alive— I've never met any woman like you."

She couldn't think of anything to say as he bent his head and took her mouth in a kiss so sweetly ravishing that every bone in her body seemed to melt away. His hands found their way inside her clothes, and he gently kneaded her breasts through her cousin's soft lawn shirt.

"It's time, Gwen," he whispered between sweetly coaxing kisses. "I told you there would be a price to pay. The time has come for you to pay it."

Her fuzzy brain could barely absorb the words. "Wh-What?"

"I said it's time. I'm taking you to Carlton House. I'm going to make love to you, Gwen. It's what both of us want and this time I'm not going to give you a choice."

The fog of passion began to clear. "Wh-What do you mean?"

"Just say yes, Gwen. Tell me you want me to make love to you."

She slowly shook her head. "We can't, Adam—not tonight. My parents will be home at midnight. It's nearly that late now. I have to be back before they get there."

Adam cursed roundly. "Tomorrow night, then. Come to me at Carlton House." His sensuous mouth curved up. "You're very good at getting away when you want to."

But sanity had begun to creep in. "Carlton House." Her voice went soft. "That is where gentlemen take their mistresses. Yesterday I heard my stepfather speak of it to his friends."

Adam looked at her and something shifted in his eyes. "My town house, then. I'll have my carriage waiting round the corner at nine o'clock to pick you up."

Wariness began to sift through her. "I-I'm not sure I can." She wanted Adam Harcourt, but there were consequences to pay from such a liaison. She might be headstrong but she wasn't a fool.

The viscount's face went dark. "I'm tired of waiting, Gwen. I'll expect you to come." He looked at her hard, his face as turbulent as a storm. "If you should fail to do so, I'll go to Lord Waring. I'll tell him about tonight—how you sneaked out of the house in men's clothes. I'll tell him about the night you went to the Fallen Angel."

She stared into those hard gray eyes and the color leached from her face. "You wouldn't . . . you wouldn't do such a thing."

"You were warned, Gwen. You knew the kind of man I was from the start. I'm used to getting what I want and I want you. If it takes a threat to convince you, then that is what I will do. Come to me tomorrow—or the earl will hear all about your little adventures."

Gwen's chest went tight. She desired Adam Harcourt, perhaps even loved him. Until this moment, in some strange way, she had trusted him as she never had another man. Dear God, how could she have been so wrong?

"You would do that?" she whispered. "You would actually go to the earl?"

A determined glint came into his eyes. "I'll do whatever it takes to have you."

Gwen bit down on her trembling lip, and Adam's hard look softened. "Come to me, love. It's what both of us want. I promise you won't be sorry."

Moonlight slanted into the carriage, shining on his blue-black hair, gleaming on his high, dark cheekbones. Gwen blinked to hide her tears and forced herself to smile. "Of course, I will come . . . exactly as you wish. As you said, my lord. I really have no other choice."

Adam frowned at her carefully chosen words and the odd expression on her face. Then the carriage stopped in the alley behind her town house, and the footman pulled open the door.

"Until tomorrow," Adam said, pressing a soft kiss on the back of her hand. The tender look in his eyes made her heart swell with longing for the man she had once thought he was.

"Good-bye, Adam." Dear God, if only he had been patient, if he had asked instead of commanded, respected her wishes as well as his own, she would have gone to him sooner or later. Instead he had threatened her, tried to force her to obey him.

Just like every other man she had ever known.

Gwen smiled bitterly as she made her way among the shadows and went in through the window she had left open at the rear of the town house. Like every other man, he believed she had no choice. But tomorrow night, just like the others, Adam Harcourt would discover the choice would still be hers.

Jessie rode through the streets of London as she had the first time she had arrived there, but the thrill of the city had dimmed beneath the film of loneliness that had enveloped her since Matthew had gone. She missed her husband unbearably and she feared for his safety. Any day word might come of the battle, of the casualties England had paid in men and ships, word that Matthew was among them.

Any day she might discover she had lost him.

Papa Reggie was worried about him, too. He seemed to have aged ten years since his son left home. It was the reason she had agreed to come to London. In the city, the marquess could be consoled by Lady Bainbridge, and he was right—the days would pass more swiftly where there were countless amusements to distract them from their fears.

Sarah helped, too, her eyes bright with the excitement of her first trip to the city.

And Gwen was here.

A message had been waiting at the town house. Gwendolyn begged the pleasure of her company at the earliest convenience. It was an oddly worded note that sent a thread of uneasiness through her. It was the reason Jessie had set off for Lord Waring's just hours after their arrival, as soon as they had unloaded their baggage and she'd had time to freshen and change.

Though dusk had begun to fall, she had left the residence alone, since Viola was busy with Sarah and Minnie was engrossed in ironing and freshening the clothes that had arrived in her trunks.

She wasn't even sure Gwen would be home, since she hadn't had time to confirm her arrival. It was hardly proper just to drop in, but propriety had rarely stopped Gwen, and the urgency of the missive had moved Jessie to bend the rules just a little.

When she reached Lord Waring's town house, she would think of something to explain her unexpected visit. Something besides Gwen's cryptic note.

It was nearly dark by the time the carriage rolled to a stop and the footman opened the door. "'Ere we are, milady."

"Thank you, Buckley." She smiled as he helped her descend the three iron steps to the paving stones. "I shan't be too long." Making her way to the wide, carved front door, she lifted the heavy brass knocker and rapped three times. The door came open an instant later and the butler peered down at her from the end of his long, hawklike nose.

She knew that look. Before she had come to Belmore, she had been on the receiving end more times than she cared to remember. It was just the impetus she needed.

"Good evening. The Countess of Strickland, here to see Lady Gwendolyn."

He stepped back hastily, taking in her elegant emerald silk gown and the fashionable upsweep of her hair that he had missed in the lamplight outside the doors.

"Beg pardon, my lady. Lady Gwendolyn forgot to mention you were coming."

Jessie gave him a haughty smile as she swept in. "That is hardly surprising, knowing our dear Gwen."

The butler simply nodded, as if there could be no truer words. He proceeded from the room and a few moments later, Gwendolyn burst down the stairs.

"Jessie! Thank God you're here!" The smaller girl's arms went around her and both women hugged. Gwen's hug lasted a few seconds longer.

Jessie gave her a worried glance as she followed her friend into a small salon off to one side of the town house and the uppity butler closed the door.

"All right, Gwen, tell me what's going on."

At first the petite dark-haired girl glanced away. "That's a fine greeting. You're supposed to tell me all about married life, how happy you are with Lord Strickland, then you can ask about me."

"Fine," Jessie said, taking a place on the brocade sofa. "I love being married to Matthew. He's a wonderful husband and I love him desperately—unfortunately, he is not in love with me. Even more unfortunately, he has gone off to fight in some terrible battle and I may never see him again." She swallowed back the ache that rose in her throat. "Now—tell me what's going on."

Gwen left her chair and sat down on the sofa next to Jessie. "Matthew will be all right, Jess. You have to believe that. And you have to believe he loves you. No man steals another man's bride who isn't at least a little bit in love with her."

Jessie just shook her head. She wanted to believe what Gwen said, but if Matthew loved her, surely he would have said so. "Tell me why your note was so urgent."

Gwen's pretty green eyes slid closed, her thick chestnut lashes forming crescents on her cheeks. "Adam Harcourt," was all she said.

"Oh, my God—not St. Cere."

"I almost fell in love with him, Jess. Perhaps I did, just a little."

"Tell me he didn't seduce you."

"If he had tried to seduce me, he might have succeeded." She brushed a tear from her cheek. "Instead he threatened me, tried to force me into his bed."

"I don't understand. What kind of threats could he make?"

Gwen glanced down at the hands she twisted in her lap. "He saw me the night we went to the Fallen Angel. Last night I dressed in those same clothes and went to a boxing match in Haymarket. Adam was there as well. Now he's demanding I come to him. I'm supposed to meet him tonight at his town house. If I don't, he'll tell Lord Waring what I've done."

"Dear heavens, I can't believe it."

"Unfortunately, it's the truth. He actually thinks his threats will work, that I'll trade my virtue for his silence."

She laughed bitterly. "The funny part is, I wanted Adam to make love to me. All I asked in return was that he feel some measure of affection for me. It wasn't that much to ask."

"Oh, Gwennie." Jessie put her arms around her friend's small shoulders and noticed how rigidly they were set.

"I won't let him blackmail me." She eased herself away, and dashed more tears from her cheeks. "I'm going to tell Waring myself."

"No! Dear God, Gwen, you can't possibly do that!" Jessie jumped up from the sofa and began to pace the room. "Let me speak to St. Cere. He doesn't even like Lord Waring. I don't believe he ever meant to tell him. He simply wanted you in his bed. Let me go to him, tell him his threats won't work." *Tell him what a rotten cad he is.* "I know I can convince—"

"No." Gwen stood up, too. "I know you want to help me. I wanted your advice, but mostly I just needed to tell someone. You came as I hoped you would, but my mind is made up. I won't beg St. Cere, and I won't have you do it in my stead—I would rather tell Waring the truth."

"Please don't do it, Gwen. You can't know what he might do."

"I know exactly what he will do—he will beat me. He hasn't for some time and lately he has been looking for an excuse. At any rate, I would rather face my stepfather than let St. Cere win."

Jessie put a hand on Gwen's shoulder. "This isn't about winning, Gwen. It's about love. Regretfully, that is the last thing most men are interested in, and the viscount least of all. I ask you again—please don't tell Lord Waring."

Gwen smiled faintly and Jessie noticed pale gray smudges beneath her friend's green eyes. "Thank you for coming, Jess. Perhaps I can stop by and see you . . . once this is finished. Or maybe you could come here."

"Oh, Gwen, of course I will come." She gripped her friend's hand as they walked back out to the entry. "When will you tell him?"

"Tonight. The earl is due home at eight. He is usually prompt and I would rather have this over and done."

"Dammit, Gwen—"

"Good night, Jess. Thank you for being my friend." Gwen leaned over and hugged her, then waited while she walked back out to her carriage, but all Jessie could think of was St. Cere—that it was a good thing she didn't have a pistol or she would probably shoot him!

Instead, she gave the driver directions to Hanover Square, where Matthew had mentioned Adam Harcourt lived, and prayed she'd be able to discover which of the expensive residences was his. She was trembling by the time she reached the square, praying that for once Lord Waring would be late. She had no idea what the viscount would say, or even what he might do when he discovered Gwen's intention. She only hoped he would be as appalled by the consequences of his actions as she was, and that he would find some way to help Gwen.

*C*hapter *T*wenty-*T*hree

*T*he minutes dragged past as the carriage rolled along, stretching Jessie's nerves to the breaking point. Finally the coachman called down from his seat atop the coach, "We're 'ere, milady," and she straightened on the seat.

"Thank you, Buckley," she called up to him. "Please pull over and let me out." She jumped from the carriage before it had quite stopped rolling, rushed up the closest set of stairs, and pounded on the door.

"Yes?" The stately butler peered through the small crack he had opened.

"I'm looking for Lord St. Cere—the Viscount St. Cere? His town house is somewhere on the square, but I seem to have forgotten exactly which one it is."

He eyed her up and down, taking in her expensive silk gown. "It's just there, milady." He pointed at a house across the way. "The middle house on St. George Street. The one with the pillars beside the door."

"Yes . . . I see it. Thank you. Thank you so much." In an instant, she was back in the carriage and they were rumbling toward the house down the block. A few minutes later, she was climbing the stairs, rapping fiercely on the viscount's gleaming front door.

It opened almost instantly, and St. Cere stepped back expecting Gwen to walk in, surprised a little that she had come so early. He was dressed elegantly, Jessie saw, in a perfectly fitted black tailcoat and dark gray breeches. His sleek dark brows arched up when he realized the woman who had entered was the Countess of Strickland instead of Gwen.

He recovered himself, of course, almost immediately. "Good evening, Countess. What a pleasant surprise."

"Hardly that," Jessie said, marching toward him, outrage glinting in her eyes. "Certainly not for you, since your little seduction will not be coming to fruition. And certainly not for my dear friend, Gwendolyn, who will suffer a brutal caning this night—thanks to you."

The color washed out from beneath his dark skin. "What are you talking about?"

"How could you do it?" Angry tears collected and spilled onto her cheeks. "She trusted you—maybe even loved you. How could you treat her that way?"

The viscount moved closer, took a firm grip on her shoulders. "I don't know what you're talking about. If you're speaking of Waring, I've said nothing to him about Gwen. He has no reason to harm her."

Jessie wiped the hot tears from her cheeks. "She told me what you planned, what you expected her to do. If you knew her a'tall, you'd know she would never submit to you by force. She won't take orders from Waring. She isn't about to take them from you."

"I tell you I said nothing. I never would have. I wanted her—yes. I thought if she had an excuse . . . if she could blame me for her seduction, she would come. Gwen is in no danger. I didn't tell Waring. I loathe the very sight of him. I—"

"Don't you understand?" Jessie glanced at the ornate grandfather clock in the entry. It was eight-thirty. "Waring was due home at eight. By now, *Gwen* has told him!"

The viscount swayed a little, reached toward the mahogany banister to steady himself. "She wouldn't . . . surely, she wouldn't do that."

Jessie looked into his eyes, as turbulent as a storm-tossed sea. "Do you actually believe there is anything Gwen Lockhart would not do, once her mind is made up?" His swarthy skin went even paler. "She said she would rather suffer a beating than allow you to coerce her."

St. Cere looked so distraught she almost relented, then she thought of Gwen with Waring. "She also said if you had asked her, if you had shown her the least amount of care, she would have come to you on her own."

St. Cere's knuckles went white around the banister. "God's blood," he whispered, sliding a shaky hand through his thick black hair. "It never occurred to me . . . I never imagined she would . . ." His head snapped up, his eyes suddenly dark with purpose. "Your carriage is still out front?"

"Yes."

"Stay here. I'll be back as quickly as I can."

Jessie caught him as he grabbed up his cloak and swung it around his broad shoulders. "You're going after her? You're going to stop him?"

"Of course, I am. Did you actually think I would stand here and let that filthy swine hurt her? If he's laid a hand on her, if he's harmed a single strand of her beautiful hair, he'll be lucky if I don't kill him."

Unconsciously, Jessie stepped back out of St. Cere's way. She had never seen such bloodlust in a man's eyes before, or a face so filled with self-loathing. If anyone could help Gwen now, it was Adam Harcourt.

She almost pitied Lord Waring.

In the drawing room of the Waring town house, Gwen stared into her stepfather's taut features, defiance clear on her face. On a tapestry sofa across the room, her mother pressed a lace handkerchief against her thin nose and sat there quietly weeping.

"You are a stubborn, willful young woman, Gwendolyn Lockhart—bent on self-destruction." Waring glared down from his lofty height more than a foot above her, his features swathed in self-righteousness. It was his cold dark eyes that held the glint of anticipation. "You realize you will have to be punished."

Her mother let out a wail and began to cry louder. "Must you, Edward?" she sobbed. "Gwendolyn came to us on her own. She didn't have to tell us. She could have kept silent but instead she told us the truth."

"Your daughter confessed her disobedience only because she knew that sooner or later we would have found out. She was simply trying to save herself. Unfortunately, I have no intention of ignoring her appalling behavior. Her punishment will be swift and severe."

Her mother wailed again, then fell silent, except for an occasional sniffle, and Waring turned his attention back to Gwen.

"Go to your room, Gwendolyn. Remove your outer garments and wait for me there. Perhaps a few stiff strokes of the birch will deter your nocturnal activities . . . at least for a time."

"Edward, I beg you," her mother pleaded.

"And you, Madame. You will retire to your chamber as well. I realize the task of disciplining one's children is an unpleasant one, therefore I shall spare you any part in it."

Keeping her eyes cast carefully down, her mother rose shakily to her feet. With a last sympathetic glance toward Gwen, she made her way out of the room. Gwen followed silently behind her, continuing past her mother's bedchamber door, far down the hall to her room at the opposite end.

Her little maid, Sadie, stood waiting. There was little the servants didn't know, not even a matter like the earl's penchant for discipline, or his stepdaughter's willful disobedience.

It didn't take long to disrobe. Dressed in her simple chemise, Gwen stood perfectly erect, stoically resigned to the ordeal ahead. Still, she started to tremble the moment Sadie left her alone. Moving woodenly to the bed, she picked up her wrapper and pulled it on, then stood in front of the fire, hoping to drive the chill from her bones.

Waring arrived a few minutes later, carrying a four-foot length of birch that had been smoothed, varnished, and polished to a sheen, one of his prize possessions.

"I am sorry, Gwendolyn, that we have come to this juncture yet again."

Gwen's mouth curved bitterly. "There is no need to lie, my lord. We both know you are not sorry at all."

Waring's square jaw tightened. "Remove your wrapper, Gwendolyn. And place your palms flat on the bench at the foot of your bed."

She was too old to be so thinly clothed in front of him, as he well knew. This whole charade was merely a pretense to disguise his lust and salve whatever scrap of conscience he retained. She removed her wrapper and turned away from him, hoping he wouldn't see the dark circles of her nipples through the sheer lawn fabric that covered her to just below the knees.

Her hands trembled as she bent and placed her palms on the padded velvet bench, her fingers digging into the plush pink fabric.

"Since my past lessons seem to have done so little good, I shall endeavor to make this one a bit more memorable."

Gwen closed her eyes as he lifted her gown, baring her as if she were a child. She had expected something like this, since each of his abuses had gradually grown worse, but still she didn't fight him. It was exactly what he wanted and in the end he was certain to win. It angered him more when she showed him only her disdain.

"Try to remember, my dear, I do this in your own best interest." The rod sang through the air and stung her flesh, sending a jolt of fire ripping through her. Gwen gripped the bench, hating Edward Waring, wishing him to the depths of hell.

Hating Adam Harcourt even more.

The birch whined again, landing with stinging heat across her bottom, raining down on her again, and again. The backs of her legs burned, blows fell onto her back and shoulders, then the flailing resumed on the soft flesh of her buttocks, his lordship's favorite target.

Gwen cursed him and fought to hold back tears. She wouldn't let him break her, not now, not ever.

Adam Harcourt rapped the knocker on Waring's front door so hard the whole house seemed to quake. When the butler pulled it open, he shoved past him into the entry.

"Where is Lady Gwen?"

The butler cleared his throat. "Her ladyship has retired to her chamber."

An instant of relief trickled through him. Perhaps she had said nothing after all. "And Lord Waring? Where is he?"

A faint flush crept into the old man's cheeks. "Attending to a family matter, I believe. At present, he cannot be disturbed."

Relief slid away, replaced by a gut-gnawing fear. "He's up there, isn't he? He's upstairs with Gwen."

The butler swallowed so hard the knot in his throat bobbed up and down. When he refused to answer, Adam grabbed his coat lapels and dragged him up on his toes. "Which room is she in? Which room!"

"The last door on the right . . . at the far end of the hall."

Adam started running before the old man had stopped speaking, taking the stairs two at a time, trying to ignore the fear pumping through his veins. He raced down the hall, gripped the silver doorknob, and jerked open the door, then stood frozen in the opening.

Two faces swung in his direction, one of them lovely and fair and glistening with tears. Waring's hand paused mid-stroke, the gleaming length of birch held threateningly above him. Gwen gasped when she realized he was there, her face heating up with embarrassment, glowing the same fiery shade as the welts that marked her legs and bottom. She straightened and the chemise fell back in place, covering her once more, but it couldn't erase the memory of the beating she had suffered.

Adam's stomach twisted with remorse. "I'm going to kill you, Waring. I'm going to wrap my hands around your throat and squeeze until the breath leaves your body." Untying his cloak and tossing it away, he moved forward, stone-cold menace in every step. "I'm going to end your miserable existence once and for all, but before I do, I'm going to punish you—ten times worse than you did this lovely girl."

Waring stepped backward. "Stay away from me, St. Cere. This is none of your concern."

His mouth twisted up. "I told you once before—I'm making it my concern." Adam's fist arched out the instant he reached the earl, slamming into his wide, square jaw and sending him careening backward, over a table in front of the hearth. Adam grabbed the fallen length of birch and slashed it down upon the earl's chest and shoulders, then whipped several blows across his face. Tossing the length of wood away, he bent and grabbed Waring by the front of his white lawn shirt, dragged him up on his feet and hit him again.

Several more blows rained down, bloodying Edward Waring's nose and cracking his lip. He dealt a couple of solid punches to the older man's middle, then, as the earl gasped for breath, leaned forward and wrapped both hands around the man's thick neck.

It felt so good to squeeze, to hear him wheezing for breath. Each second was for Gwen, each moment of pain he dealt lessened some of the guilt he suffered for what he had done.

"Adam!" It was Gwendolyn's voice, pleading for him to stop, and yet through the haze of his rage, he could barely decipher the words.

"Adam, please. He isn't worth it! Please—you mustn't kill him!" Vaguely, he felt her hands on his, trying to tug them loose from around her stepfather's neck. Waring's face was purple, his eyes bulging out, his fingers trying to loosen Adam's grip on his throat.

"Adam, please! Please don't do this!" It was the sound of her crying that finally reached him, cutting through his blinding rage and bringing the room back into focus. He released his hold and stepped away, working to suck in deep breaths of air. A few feet away, Gwen stood trembling, a wash of tears still gleaming on her cheeks.

Her face was as pale as Waring's, her breathing nearly as labored. Still, she looked beautiful, the thin chemise a useless attempt to hide her womanly curves. Adam cursed roundly, hating the earl, mostly hating himself. He grabbed his cloak and walked toward Gwen, settled the heavy silk-lined fabric around her shoulders, then lifted her gently into his arms, forcing himself to ignore her small hiss of pain.

"I'm taking you out of here," he said. "I won't let him hurt you again."

She didn't say a word, just turned her head into his shoulder and curled her trembling fingers into his shirt. She said nothing in the carriage, nothing when he lifted her up and carried her into his town house.

Then she saw Jessie and quietly began to weep.

Adam motioned for Lady Strickland to follow him upstairs into one of the bedchambers, then gently lowered Gwen onto the bed.

Adam pressed a kiss to the top of her head, then turned to Jessie. "Will you take care of her?"

"Of course," she said.

Adam simply nodded. His throat had closed up and his eyes burned. This was all his fault—every bit of it. He left the room and made his way downstairs.

An hour later, Jessie descended the stairs. Through the open drawing-room doors, she saw Adam Harcourt sitting alone in the semidarkness, only a single oil lamp and the embers of a dying fire seeping light into the room. His head hung forward; his shoulders slumped. His thick black hair was mussed where he had dragged his fingers through it.

He jerked upward at her approach and came swiftly to his feet. "How is she?"

"No one dies from a caning, my lord. It is Gwen's heart that is broken."

He swallowed and glanced away. "This is my fault—all

of it. I never meant to hurt her. I just . . . I just wanted her so badly . . ."

There was something in his eyes, something she had never thought to see in the eyes of a hard man like him . . . pain to be sure, and something else. "She's resting, now. She'll feel better in the morning, but I'm not sure . . ."

"You're not sure what?"

"Perhaps we shouldn't have interfered. We may have simply made things worse."

He moved closer. "What do you mean? Surely you can't believe she was better off staying there with Waring?"

"Perhaps she was. Sooner or later, she will have to go home. When she does, he's bound to extract some sort of revenge. Gwen will be completely at his mercy."

"She isn't going home," St. Cere said with finality. "She is staying here with me." Seeing the anguished look on the viscount's face, Jessie's anger began to slip away.

"Lord St. Cere . . . Adam, we both know Gwen can't stay here. Waring is her guardian and even if he weren't, the gossip would ruin her."

"The gossips would not dare. Not if we were married."

Her brow shot up. "Married!"

"That is what I said." His mouth twisted sardonically. "I know I'm not considered the best catch in London, but neither am I the worst."

Interest filtered through her. She had never expected an offer of marriage from St. Cere. Perhaps Matthew had been right about the viscount after all. "Gwen won't marry you, Adam. Not you or anyone else. She has vowed never to marry. And if you try to command her—"

"I won't command her. This time I'll ask her. Where Gwendolyn is concerned that is a lesson well learned. I won't try to force her. I'll get down on my knees and beg her, if that is what it takes."

A shuffling in the doorway drew their attention. Gwen stood stiffly in the opening, wrapped in the viscount's brown velvet dressing gown, several inches of fabric trailing across the polished inlaid floors.

"Jessica is right, my lord. I have no intention of marrying you." She drew herself up, but the effect was lost in the over-sized folds of St. Cere's robe. "I don't need your pity," she said. "I never did. Nor will I exchange one form of brutal domination for another." Her mouth curved, but it wasn't re-ally a smile. "I thank you, however, for tonight. It was quite gallant of you, considering that your threat, if executed, would have accomplished the very same thing."

The viscount strode forward, a dozen emotions flickering across the sharp planes of his face. When he reached Gwen's side, he took her hand and brought it slowly to his lips. "Gwendolyn, my love. I never meant to hurt you . . . never in a thousand years. I wanted you. It is as simple as that. I never would have gone to Waring, but I was willing to let you think I would. I would have done anything to have you."

Gwen tried to look away, but St. Cere gently caught her chin, forcing her to face him.

"I would have done anything, Gwen. Until tonight, it never occurred to me why. That the reason I wanted you so badly was that I was in love with you."

Gwen's eyes rose swiftly to his face, which shone with a mixture of regret, fear, and hope in the dim light of the fire.

"I swore I would never remarry," he said. "With Eliza-beth my life was hell. I scoffed at Matthew, swore I wasn't interested in a home . . . a family, but every time I saw you, the thought crept into my mind—what would life be like with a woman like Gwen?"

She only shook her head.

"I could make you happy, Gwen. I have something to offer you most men don't have."

She tipped her head back to look into his face. "What is that?" she asked softly.

"Your freedom. A chance to learn about the world. I can show you things you never imagined, take you places you

never dreamed of seeing. If there are times you're forced to
dress as a man to accomplish those ends, I don't care, as
long as I'm there to protect you. You can write your book,
Gwen. What husband would ever allow you that?"

She shook her head again, but with less force. "You would
grow tired of me, Adam. And I could never share you. That
is something I have learned."

A smile broke over his handsome face, lifting the darkness, easing some of the harshness away. He went down on
one knee in front of her. "I love you, Gwen Lockhart. I don't
want anyone else—not now, not ever. Say you'll marry
me . . . please?"

She glanced over Adam's head, searching for Jessie, finding her there, standing among the shadows. "What should I
do, Jess? I love Adam, but I don't want to be hurt anymore.
I'm frightened, Jess. I've never been so afraid."

Jessie's heart went out to her. She wanted to say that she
was frightened every day, that even if Matthew survived
the upcoming battle, there was still the chance she would
lose him. He didn't love her. He didn't even trust her. And
what if he discovered she had tricked him into marriage?

"Life is full of risks," she said. "If you love Adam, you
should marry him. That is what I would do."

Gwen stared down at the man who still knelt at her feet.
Her hand trembled as she slid it into his thick inky hair. "Are
you sure, Adam? You aren't doing this out of pity? Please,
for both of our sakes, you must tell me the truth."

He came to his feet and eased her into his arms, cradling
her gently, careful of her bruised and battered body. "I'm
crazy about you, Gwen. Madly, desperately in love with you.
I've tried every way in the world to deny it, but it hasn't done
an ounce of good. Tonight, when I walked into that room
and saw what Waring had done, I nearly went insane. I knew
then why I had threatened you the way I did. I was desperate . . . because I was in love. Please, my lovely Gwendolyn.
Say you'll be my wife."

She glanced once more at Jessie and then she smiled. "If

Jessica can put up with an ogre like Strickland, then I suppose I can put up with a rogue like you."

Adam threw back his head and laughed with sheer pleasure. It was a rich, deep, masculine sound that rang with such promise and joy it brought tears to Jessie's eyes.

She said nothing more to them, just slipped out of the drawing room, leaving them alone. Neither of them noticed she was gone. Gwen joined her the following morning, then spent the next three days at the Belmore town house. The day after that, she and Adam were married.

As happy as Jessie was for her friend, she couldn't help thinking of Matthew. She couldn't help missing him and wishing he were there, or stop the bittersweet ache of knowing he might never come home.

*C*hapter *T*wenty-*F*our

*T*he waiting was finally over. Matt lifted his heavy brass looking glass and focused on the line of French vessels on the horizon. The breeze was holding, allowing the ships on both sides to move into position. They were sailing off the beaches of Cádiz, not far from Cape Trafalgar.

Two days ago, the French and Spanish fleet had sailed from Cádiz harbor, their topsails hoisted and unfurled. At dawn this morning, the signal flags had spread the news: The enemy was coming in range—it was time to close British positions.

Matthew paced the quarterdeck, surveying the line of ships as they approached, praying Nelson's strategy of speed, audacity, and seamanship would win the upcoming battle.

As nearly as he could tell, Nelson's thirty-one ships would be facing a fleet of thirty-three. Odds were, Villeneuve and his forces would fight a defensive battle, using bar and chain shot to cut the rigging and halt pursuit.

Nelson's men would be aiming for the hull, their canons firing round shot to damage the ship so they could board her. Capturing a ship meant prize money: For every thousand pounds that went to the captain, two pounds—more than a seaman's monthly pay—went to each of the crew.

Matt folded up the glass and stood at the rail, staring out across the gently rolling sea. A steady breeze moved the air, leaving little need to trim the sails. The soft clatter and clank of rigging meshed with the whoosh of water against the hull. For weeks now they had been stalking the enemy, maneuvering the ships into position, Now with the time so near, he found his thoughts oddly drifting away.

He was thinking of Jessie, of the way they had parted, of what his friend Graham had said. Loving wasn't a thing a man did easily, especially not him. Caring that deeply often meant pain, he knew that firsthand.

And it also meant great risk. He recalled the way he had felt when he had thought that Jessie had betrayed him—a crushing, consuming agony that felt as if his heart had been torn out. Graham was right. He was afraid to love Jessie.

But the fact was, he did.

Matt shaded his face with his hand, lifted the glass and sighted through the lens, spotting the French ships *Redoubtable, Bucentaure,* and the Spanish ship, *San Justo.* A dozen others followed on one end of the line, an equal number rode the seas ahead. It was a formidable sight, indeed, as each man of the *Norwich* must have been thinking.

And wondering if at the end of the day he would be among those still alive.

It was an ugly thought Matt forced away. Turning from the line of ships, he strode off to the wheelhouse, where the rest of his officers stood tensely waiting. The decks of the ship were cleared for action, powder and shot ready at the guns, "Death or Victory!" chalked on the heavy iron barrels.

Though the sailors had stripped to the waist and wore kerchiefs around their heads to protect their ears from gun blasts, each officer wore his full-dress uniform, navy blue tailcoats perfectly tailored, gold epaulettes gleaming. It showed British superiority and gave the men confidence, or at least that's what they were taught.

It was a custom that had never set well with Matthew, since it also made officers easy targets for French sailors firing pistols from the rigging.

"We're closing, sir. It won't be much longer now." The words came with a grin from young Lieutenant Donnelly. Matt wondered how much longer the lieutenant would be grinning.

"Ease her a bit to port, then hold her steady."

"Aye, sir." The ship rose on a swell and in the distance he heard the band playing on the deck of the *Victory.*

Then the French ship *Fougueux* fired, a thunderous roar that overrode all other sound, and the battle at last was on.

"Fire a volley," Matt commanded. "We'll go in under a cover of smoke." A signal arrived to run up the British flag. It snapped in the freshening breeze as the *Norwich* plunged ahead, into the enemy's waiting canon. The first French broadside slammed into the sailors on the upper deck, slaughtering two men where they stood and leaving a dozen more wounded and bloody.

On the *Victory,* a blast of chain shot tore into the players in the band and for the next few minutes the ship fell silent. Several other bands played in the distance, the sound of "Britons Strike Home" echoing eerily across the water.

At a thousand yards, the *Norwich* began to fire its first round of broadsides, the concussion shaking the quarterdeck under Matt's booted feet. The *Bucentaure* returned fire, and the mizzen topmast of the *Norwich* blew away. A round shot split the hull of the *Bucentaure* above the waterline, then the whirring sound of grapeshot filled the air.

"Get down!" Matt commanded the young lieutenant who stood gaping in horror at the men sprawled on deck screaming in pain. Rivulets of blood darkened the holy-stoned planking beneath them, forming pools that dripped onto the deck below. A second later, a midshipman was blown to pieces not six feet from where Graham Paxton knelt beside one of the injured sailors.

Round after round thundered through the air. More of the sails were shot away, leaving the rigging in tatters and lengths of white canvas trailing in the water. A hole ripped through the main topgallant sail, and the sheer volume of shot blew the studding sails away.

At thirty yards, the *Norwich* fired the fifty guns on her port, then a minute later fired twenty-five more. A ball plowed across the deck, cutting tiller ropes and knocking a half-dozen men off their feet, breaking their legs and ankles. In the rolling sea beyond the ship, the fleet fought on, shrouding the ocean in smoke and littering the water with splintered wood and tattered sail. Matt's nostrils burned with the acrid smell of gunpowder. He was covered with sweat and black powder, the sky so thick with smoke there were times it blocked the sun.

The battle continued through most of the day, the badly damaged *Norwich* coming under fire from three different ships at once. A dozen sailors labored to clear the wreckage so they could continue firing. Matt's uniform was torn and streaked with powder, his white breeches spattered with blood.

"Brace yourselves!" he shouted as the yardarms of the *Norwich* locked with the Spanish ship, *San Justo*. Matt heard the sharp splintering of wood and the grinding of metal when the ships collided. At such close range the deafening roar and concussion of the guns pounded through his head, and a buzzing filled his ears. Canon thundered. Men staggered and screamed in pain. Sailors shoved dead men overboard to make room for the wounded.

"Lay on the grappling hooks!" Matt commanded, and a few seconds later, a wall of British seamen went over the side onto the ravaged *San Justo,* slashing their way across the decks, fighting hand to hand with the tough Spanish seamen, who in turn streamed aboard the *Norwich*.

Cutlass in hand, slashing and hacking beside his men, Matt fought his way up onto a deck box, his hands slick with blood, his jaw set with determination to defeat the Spanish vessel. Even more determined to survive the maiming grapeshot and musket fire, the cannon blasts and deadly cut of saber and cutlass.

Determined to return home to Jessie.

He blocked the thrusting blow of a blade and an image of her face rose in his mind. In the hours of bloody gore, and merciless destruction, the truth of his feelings had become crystal clear. He loved Jessie Fox—more than his own life. Losing her would be like severing one of his limbs.

A sailor shot up over the railing, his bloody sword raised above his head. He brought it arching downward, slicing through the air toward Matt's head. Whirling, he blocked the blow, felt the sword slash into his arm and the sharp sting of pain, saw the eruption of blood on his coat. His own blade sank in, burying itself deeply, and the sailor shrieked in pain. His weapon clattered to the deck and he slumped forward into a pool of blood.

A Spaniard swung down from the rigging. Matt fired his pistol and the sailor fell onto the deck, but two more men appeared. Matt's cutlass severed the hand that gripped a long-barreled cap-and-ball pistol. The gun exploded when it clattered to the deck. The second man stepped in, taking advantage of the precious instant it had taken to forestall the first. His pistol went off and Matt felt a searing jolt of pain.

He clutched the railing as he stumbled backward, fighting the dark swirling circles that pressed against his eyes, raising his saber to block the Spaniard's killing blow, fighting against death when the odds in that moment were a thousand to one he would live.

His saber flashed one final time, sank into flesh and bone. Matt sagged against the railing, thinking of Jessie, wishing he had told her that he loved her.

He prayed that Graham would live so that he might tell her, let her know that he had been thinking of her in the end, wishing he would have lived to give her children.

Wishing she knew that she had become his whole world.

Instead the darkness beckoned and he slumped toward

the deck, his vision no longer crowded with images of death and destruction. Memories of Jessie filled his mind: Jessie laughing at something he had said, of her riding hell-bent to birth a babe, of her risking her life in the fire to save him. He thought of her courage, her spirit, her loyalty to her friends. Of the way she had looked when she had said she loved him.

"Jessie . . ." he whispered, fighting the darkness, the sadness, and the unfamiliar sting of tears. *Jessie . . .* If he could only do things over. If only . . . His last thoughts were of Jessie before the thunder of cannonfire faded and Matthew drifted away.

Jessie sat next to Sarah in the breakfast room, across from Papa Reggie. A cold wind whipped the trees outside the window and flat gray clouds darkened the sky. The *London Times* sat open on the table in front of them. The headlines read, "Battle of Trafalgar, Capture of French and Spanish fleets, Death of Nelson." It was November 7. The first word of the battle had finally reached them.

"How long . . ." Jessie's voice sounded oddly high. She paused and started over. "How long do you think it will be before word comes of Matthew?"

Papa Reggie leaned forward in his chair. His snowy hair was neatly combed, but worry marred his features. "Not long, I should think. The first messenger has arrived. Others will follow close behind him." He gave her a weary smile. "We must remain optimistic. It says here that English losses were less than ten to one. Odds are good that Matthew is safe."

"Of course, he is safe," Jessie said. She swallowed and glanced away. "I would know—in here"—she rested a hand over her heart—"if he were not."

"No doubt about it," the marquess said firmly. But the worry didn't leave his face.

It was three more days before a message finally reached them. Jessie was reading to Sarah when Ozzie came to the door of the drawing room. "A courier, milady. From His Majesty's Navy."

The color drained from her face. "I-I'll be right there."

"Is it Papa?" Sarah asked. "Has Papa come home?"

"No, sweetheart, not yet." Jessie kissed the top of Sarah's head, turned and hurried from the room. A beefy red-haired sergeant stood in the entry, carrying a wax-sealed letter. The marquess walked up just as she took the paper from the sergeant's hand.

Jessie wet her lips, her mouth gone suddenly dry. Her hands were shaking so badly she couldn't get the parchment open. Papa Reggie's hand settled on her shoulder. Sliding the letter gently from her fingers, he carefully broke the seal and began to read.

"It's from Admiral Dunhaven."

"Oh, dear God . . ." Jessie's eyes suddenly burned.

Long seconds passed. Then Papa Reggie smiled. "He was injured—but he is mending—and the admiral says he is well on his way to recovery."

Jessie's legs nearly buckled beneath her. "He's alive. . . . Oh, thank God."

"It says he will be returning directly to London at the end of the month, in company with Admiral Dunhaven. There is to be a victory celebration and a number of the officers will be arriving to attend the affair, as well as Admiral Lord Nelson's funeral. Dunhaven believes Matthew will be fully recovered by then."

Jessie gave a very unladylike whoop of joy that brought Sarah to the door of the drawing room, an uncertain look on her face. Jessie smiled. "It's all right, honey. The letter just says your papa is coming home." The little girl's worried look turned into a grin. She called Jessie "Mama" now, and the marquess she called "Granpapa."

Jessie walked over and scooped her up, balancing the golden-haired child on one hip. "I was hoping we could go home, now that Matthew is safe, but if he is coming here—"

"Then we shall have to remain in the city," the marquess finished. He smiled and Jessie could have sworn he looked ten years younger. "It won't be much longer now. Perhaps for the next few weeks we shall actually be able to enjoy ourselves. And once Matthew arrives, we shall all go home together."

"Yes . . ." Jessie said, "together." And this time she would be the kind of wife he'd always wanted. *This time, I'll make him love me.* For the first time she felt as if they really had a chance, as if the past were truly over and they could make a new beginning. Jessie's smile went as wide as Papa Reggie's.

With a storm in the offing, the streets of London were less crowded. Fewer carriages rolled over the cobblestone streets, beggars ducked into vacant doorways; even pickpockets and thieves sought shelter from the cold and impending rain.

Braving the chill, Lady Caroline Winston stepped down from her shiny black phaeton, parked near the corner of Bow Street, gathered her fur-trimmed pelisse more closely around her, and went into the three-story brick building that housed the office of Willis G. McMullen.

"Good morning, milady."

"Good morning, Mr. McMullen." The office was a little less messy than it had been the time before. Caroline sat down in the hard wooden chair across from the little man's cluttered desk. "I received your note last week. I didn't expect to be returning to the city, but Father has friends in His Majesty's Navy. We've come for the victory celebration. And of course there is Lord Nelson's funeral."

"Of course." The small man sifted through the paperwork on his desk, then extracted a file with coffee stains along the edge. He opened it, briefly scanned the contents, then handed the file to Caroline. "I believe ye will find the information ye've been seeking."

For the longest time she simply read, her eyes growing

wider by the second, the sharp thrum of her heartbeat increasing with every word. "My heavens . . ."

"Exactly so, milady."

"Dear lord, this is an outrage—the woman is little better than a common trollop." Her head came up. "My poor dear Matthew. Somehow she must have fooled him."

"Folks down in Buckler's Haven . . . they said Jessie Fox was always a clever lass. Quick with a word, even quicker to steal a man's purse."

"Good Lord, the girl is a thief, too?"

"*Was,* milady. If you keep readin' ye'll see she went to that fancy Mrs. Seymour's Academy, just like she said. She was one of the school's finest pupils."

Caroline frowned. "A thief is a thief, Mr. McMullen. People rarely change."

"Some do," he said softly.

"Yes . . . well, it doesn't really matter. You have done your job. I have the information I need, and soon the Countess of Strickland will receive her just desserts."

McMullen said nothing, just sat there staring at the file she held so tightly to her bosom.

"Thank you, Mr. McMullen. I shall have a bank draft sent round first thing in the morning."

He simply nodded.

"And I shall be more than happy to recommend you to anyone who is in need of this sort of work."

But in that moment, thinking of the lovely young woman poor little Jessie Fox had become—and what Lady Caroline Winston would do to her with the facts he had unearthed, Willis McMullen wasn't sure he wanted to continue in his particular line of work.

Matthew paced the deck of the schooner, *Discovery,* that sailed toward the distant London docks. Instead of arriving yesterday morning as they had planned, they were arriving several hours past dusk. A rough sea and a driving head wind had delayed their journey two full days.

Now, as soon as they were docked, he and four other officers just returned from Trafalgar would head straight to the victory ball at the Pantheon in Oxford Street.

Wearing his full-dress uniform, gold epaulettes in place, brass buttons polished, black boots gleaming, Matt fought down his impatience and allowed himself a smile. If everything went as planned, in less than two hours, he would be with Jessie.

"Jessie," he repeated, just to hear the sound of her name. Then he said a small silent prayer that God had allowed him to live.

He hadn't thought he would, not in those final few moments when the ship had been overrun and he had taken a lead ball to the shoulder, leaving him at his enemies' mercy. But the men of the *Norwich* had rallied. They had come to his defense and beaten back the Spanish. They had captured the *San Justo,* and together with the rest of Nelson's fleet, had defeated the French in a stunning English victory.

In the end, many of the men survived the fighting only to drown in the terrible storm that swept in the following day. Through six grueling days of wind and rain, the *Norwich* remained seaworthy, even in her ravaged condition. She had carried the men who loved her to safety.

And now one of them was going home.

Ignoring the ache in his shoulder, Matt began pacing again, his impatience growing as it had every day since they had sailed from Gibraltar. He was desperate to see Jessie, to tell her the things he had learned. To tell her that he loved her.

In the days since the battle, he'd had plenty of time to think. The right woman, as Graham said, was an asset not a liability. She was a partner in life, someone to help share the burdens. Like the crew of a ship, they worked together as a team, supported each other in times of need. He imagined a life with Caroline and saw that such a woman was a burden not an asset. A dependent, rather than someone he could depend on.

Matt stared out at the approaching lights, thought of Jessie and found himself smiling. He couldn't wait to see her. He would make things up to her, make her happier than she had ever been before. As he had promised, this time he was home to stay.

*C*hapter *T*wenty-*F*ive

*J*essie leaned over the huge four-poster bed and carefully fluffed the pillows behind the marquess's white-haired head. "You're certain you'll be all right?"

"Blasted ague," he grumbled. "Bloody stuff always flares up at the damnedest times." He muttered something that might have been a curse, then looked up. "Of course I shall be all right. Go on to the victory celebration as the admiral's note requested. Hopefully your long-lost husband will arrive before the evening is ended. Matthew and I will have our reunion in the morning."

Her gaze traveled to Lemuel, Papa Reggie's ancient valet, who stood ramrod straight in the doorway. "I shall look after him for you, milady. I promise you he will be fine until your return."

She relaxed a little at that. "Thank you, Lemuel." The marquess was feeling under the weather, forced to miss his son's triumphant return, but his slight fever had already broken and his condition didn't appear serious.

Jessie smiled. "All right, then, I shall go. Adam and Gwen should be here any moment." She bent and kissed his cheek. "Oh, Papa Reggie, I can hardly wait to see him. Are you certain I look all right?" She glanced down at her high-waisted gown, a midnight blue velvet trimmed with satin and studded with rhinestones.

The old man chuckled softly. "My dear, you are a vision.

If Matthew is not yet fully recovered, he shall be the moment he sees you."

She smiled again then blew him a kiss as she sailed out the door, her heart beginning to thrum in anticipation. Gwen and Adam had already arrived and were waiting in the formal drawing room. They rose as she walked in.

"I hope the marquess is feeling better," Adam said.

"His fever has broken. I think he is much improved. Having Matthew home ought to make a great deal of difference."

"You must be so excited," Gwen said, smiling. "Now that I have Adam, I understand how worried you must have been." She tossed a warm glance at her husband, whose dark visage lit with a glow of pleasure. Jessie walked beside Gwen to the entry, and Adam set Jessie's cloak around her shoulders, a rich, midnight blue the same as the gown she was wearing.

They climbed inside the viscount's carriage and Gwen sat down beside her. "I've never really thanked you," Gwen said. "If you hadn't come that night . . . if you hadn't gone to Adam, the two of us might never have gotten together." The tall dark viscount sat across from them. Whenever his eyes touched on Gwen, a softness crept into his features. It took a special kind of woman for a man like St. Cere, but it was obvious they were happy, wildly so. They both looked very much in love.

"I'm just glad you're happy, Gwen. No one deserves it more." Jessie smiled, but seeing them together made her heart ache even more for Matthew.

They reached the ball at the Pantheon in Oxford Street, one of the most magnificent buildings in London. A long line of carriages waited to unload at the massive front doors, the viscount's elegant barouche falling in behind them. A few minutes later, they rolled up in front and a liveried footman helped them down from the carriage. A long red velvet runner led inside the structure, which was lavishly decorated in British red, blue, and white.

Admiral Dunhaven stood in the receiving line, along with Admiral Collingwood, Nelson's second in command,

and the Prime Minister, William Pitt, the Younger. Several British generals were in attendance, as well as the Lord Chamberlain and the Duke of York.

"Lady Strickland," Dunhaven said. "It's good to see you. I'm sorry your husband is not yet arrived, but the signals we've received from the *Discovery* tell us he and the others are on their way. I'm certain he'll be here very soon."

"I hope so, Admiral. I am more than eager to see him."

His rugged face curved into a smile. "And I am certain, my dear, that your husband is even more eager to see you."

She wandered on inside, hoping the admiral was right, praying that Matthew had missed her half as much as she had missed him. The Pantheon was filled to overflowing, its frescoed walls and Grecian columns obscured by the throng of elegantly dressed people crowding in. It was an odd sort of gathering, a celebration that the threat of French invasion had at last come to an end, yet most of those in attendance were dressed in somber colors in respect for their beloved fallen hero, Lord Nelson.

Jessie moved farther into the main salon, which was lit by huge chandeliers. The ceilings glowed with paintings of Grecian temples, the walls were lined with Corinthian columns and draped with heavy damask curtains. It was hard for a woman brought up in poverty not to be impressed.

Jessie smiled. Her life had certainly changed in the last few years. Who would have thought that a poor little pickpocket from Buckler's Haven would be a guest at a place like this? She surveyed the African marble floors and cut-glass chandeliers, then realized that in the pressing throng she had gotten separated from Adam and Gwen, and that standing as she was in the middle of the main salon, she was becoming the focus of attention.

She stepped backward, out of the way, but the eyes of the crowd seemed to follow her. At first she thought it was simply her imagination, but it soon became apparent the staring eyes were real. Perhaps it was the fact she appeared to be unescorted, or because her husband was something of a hero. But as the muttered words continued and the murmuring grew, it occurred to her it was something else entirely.

A flicker of unease filtered through her. Jessie glanced around for a familiar face, saw several women of Lady Bainbridge's acquaintance, but no one she really knew.

The woman next to her whispered to a friend, whose eyes went wide and she glanced away. Another woman stepped several paces backward, pulling her heavy silk skirts out of the way, as if something vile had just skittered across her path.

Jessie's heart started to thunder and her palms grew damp. Dear God, what was the matter? She glanced around in search of Gwen, but there was no sign of her or Adam. Someone snickered and pointed in her direction. An aging dandy rolled his eyes, said something to a pompous, gray-haired merchant, and the two of them laughed aloud. Around her, the crowd seemed to have moved even farther away, forming a half circle that left her once more the center of attention.

Panic set in. Jessie fought a wild urge to run. She forced herself to ignore it, to simply make her way to the door leading into another grand salon. She kept her head held high, but with every step she took, her legs trembled and people seemed to move out of her way.

Something was wrong. Very wrong. *Dear Lord, what could it be?*

"There she is," a graying matron whispered. "That's the one."

"Surely you can't mean Lady Strickland?"

The older woman merely grunted. "Hardly a lady. Why, the gel's a thief and cheat. Truth is, her mother was a doxy. Nothing but a dirty little whore."

Jessie swayed on her feet. *Oh, dear God.* She might have fallen if it hadn't been for the strong arm of the man who stepped out of the crowd to steady her and keep her from falling.

"Easy," he whispered. "Just hang on to me." Dressed in his

scarlet cavalry uniform, Adrian Kingsland, Lord Wolvermont, appeared like a knight in shining armor. He had never looked more handsome—or more welcome.

"Lady Strickland," he said smoothly. "Your friends have been looking for you . . . Lord and Lady St. Cere? Shall we join them?"

Jessie wet her lips, so dry she was afraid she could not answer. "Yes . . . ," she whispered. Beneath her skirt, her legs were shaking and her face felt bloodless and numb.

Wolvermont linked her arm with his and she took courage from his strength, letting him guide her out of the grand salon. Just as she passed through the doorway, from the corner of her eye she caught sight of Caroline Winston, gowned in white, standing in the glow of a chandelier.

A ruthless, triumphant smile lit Caroline's face and Jessie's stomach rolled with nausea. It was all she could do to keep walking.

"Steady," Wolvermont said, catching sight of the woman, too, knowing who she was and deducing just as Jessie had, exactly what must have occurred.

"I don't . . . I don't see my friends. You said they were looking for me."

He smiled darkly. "I'm certain they would be, if they realized you were in need of them. Unfortunately, in this crush, finding them might take a bit of time."

Her hand went tighter on his arm. "No . . . please, my lord. I-I should like to go home. Could I trouble you to take me?"

A brief nod of his head. "Of course, my lady. It will be no trouble at all. I'll just need a moment to have my carriage brought round." He started to leave her, saw the paleness of her face, felt the fine tremors racing through her. "On second thought, perhaps you had better come with me."

A few minutes later, Jessie was seated across from him inside the Wolvermont carriage, her face deathly pale, fighting to hold back tears. It was a losing battle. Salty droplets began to trickle down her cheeks.

"Lady Strickland," the baron's deep voice rose from the darkness across the carriage. "Your husband will be home soon. Matthew will straighten things out. Once he is here, everything will be all right."

Jessie's head snapped up. "Oh, dear God—Matthew." She clutched the baron's thick-muscled arm. "You've got to go back and warn him. You mustn't let him go in there. Please . . . promise me you'll wait for him, keep him from going inside."

"And what should I tell him, my lady?"

More tears washed down her cheeks. "Tell him they know the truth. Tell him they know about my mother . . . that I'm not the person they believed me to be." She gazed up at him through spiky, damp lashes. "Tell him how sorry I am."

"Lady Strickland . . . Jessica . . . please don't cry. People like that are not worth your tears."

But she couldn't stop them from falling. Everything she had worked for, all of her dreams had just burned to ashes and crumbled away. She said nothing as the carriage reached the Belmore town house. Nothing as the baron walked her to the door and waited while she stepped inside.

"Please . . . my lord. You mustn't let them hurt him."

"Your husband is a strong man, Lady Strickland. You can depend on him to stand by you in this."

Jessie said nothing. She could depend on Matthew. She never once doubted that. She was his wife. Honor demanded he stand with her. He would, no matter the cost. Matthew would suffer. Papa Reggie and the Belmore name would be ruined. All because she had tried to be something she was not.

Pain tore through her. And guilt. And regret. She had trapped Matthew into marriage, ended his plans for a life with Caroline Winston.

Well, she wasn't going to hurt him anymore.

Her legs still shaky, she silently climbed the stairs to her room and closed the door. A tapestry valise rested under the bed. She dragged it out and began to fill it with her most practical clothes.

Traveling clothes. She was taking little Sarah—another burden she had pressed on Matthew and Papa Reggie—and getting out of their lives for good. Matthew could tell them he hadn't known the truth about her or the child, that he and his father had been duped, the same as everyone else. Papa Reggie was clever at such things.

She thought of the dear old man, the only father she had ever known, and a hard lump formed in her throat. She would miss him so much. No one had ever been as kind to her as he was. The lump grew bigger. At least he wouldn't be ruined. Once she was gone, Matthew could have their marriage annulled, and in time, the ton would forgive him, allow them both back into the fold.

Jessie's heart constricted with a pain that tore into her chest. Ignoring the trembling in her hands and the heavy ache inside her, she packed a bag for Sarah, praying she wouldn't wake Vi. But just as she reached Sarah's bedside and bent down to retrieve the sleeping child, the older woman stirred.

Viola blinked and slowly awakened, glancing around as if she weren't quite sure where she was. For a moment she said nothing, just sat staring into the darkness. Then she spied the satchel beside the bed where Sarah still lay sleeping.

"So . . . the time 'as come, 'as it? I was afraid they'd find out, sooner or later."

Jessie's throat ached. Tearfully she nodded. "I guess I should have known it, too. I suppose in my heart I did. I just didn't want to believe it."

Viola sighed. "Poor lit'l lamb. I wish thin's was different, but for our kind it 'ardly ever is."

"I have to go, Vi. I can't hurt them any more than I have already."

Vi heaved her oversized body out of bed. "Did ye think to leave me be'ind? Go off on yer own wit' the wee un'?" She harrumphed and started to pull on her clothes.

"You don't have to leave, Vi. The marquess will take care of you. You'll always have a place at Belmore."

"Me place is wit' ye. I love ye like the daughter I ne'er 'ad. And lit'l Sarah needs me."

"Oh, Vi . . ." Jessie went into the stout woman's arms. "I love you. If you want to come, there is no one I would rather have with me."

"Where do ye figure to go?"

Jessie reached for Sarah. "Wherever the next ship out of London is headed, I suppose. I've saved a little money, enough to buy passage. We'll go down to the docks and see." She lifted Sarah onto her shoulder, heard her fussing as she slowly awakened.

"I'll get the child ready," Vi said. "Ye go do whate'er ye 'ave to."

Jessie nodded. With a last glance at Vi, she headed out the door. At the entrance to her husband's room, she paused. Tonight they would have slept there together. They would have made beautiful love and fallen asleep in each other's arms. She had loved Matt Seaton for as long as she could remember. For years she had dreamed of being his wife.

Always she'd had her dreams. Always. They had seen her through times she was hungry, times she was cold, times she was desperately lonely.

But she didn't have dreams anymore. She'd discovered they had just been pretty illusions.

She opened the door with a trembling hand and walked in, then paused at his dresser, her hand coming up to touch a few of his things: a silver-backed comb, a small leather-bound volume of poetry, an ivory-framed porcelain miniature of his mother. She took a steadying breath and caught a lingering trace of his cologne and the masculine scent of leather.

Her throat closed up. She tried to conjure his face, then thought how empty her life would be without him. Inside she felt crushed and broken, like a small bird who had fallen from its nest.

Forcing her feet to move toward the gilded writing desk in the corner, she drew a sheet of foolscap out of the drawer with a hand that trembled, picked up a quill pen, and dipped it into the inkwell.

My Darling, Matthew, she began, ignoring, with each word, the silent tears slipping down her cheeks.

Matthew stepped out of the hackney coach he and Eustace Bradford, another Trafalgar captain, had hailed down at the dock the moment the *Discovery* had arrived in the harbor. Three other ships' captains followed in another rented hack, all of them eager to reach the victory celebration.

Matthew even more so. At last he would see his beloved Jessie, and his pulse hammered mightily at the thought. He smiled to think that a woman could affect him so, particularly the feisty slip of a girl who'd done her best to thwart him since she was a child.

But the fact was she had stolen his heart and now that he had accepted the fact, he thought he was just about the luckiest man in the world.

He had almost reached the door to the Pantheon when a tall man stepped out of the shadows.

"Matthew?" It was Adrian Kingsland. "I'm afraid I need a word with you."

He glanced wistfully at the door. "Go on in, Captain Bradford," he said to his companion. "I'll be there in just a moment." He turned away from the craggy-faced officer and swung his gaze to Wolvermont instead. What he saw in the handsome man's features made his stomach tighten with worry. "What is it, Adrian? What's happened?"

A muscle clenched in Wolvermont's cheek. "A problem's come up, I'm afraid."

Dread swept through him. "It isn't Lady Strickland? Nothing's happened to Jessie?"

"She's all right, Matthew. She hasn't been injured or anything . . . it's nothing like that, but . . ."

"Where is she?" He glanced toward the building, turned and started walking, but Wolvermont blocked his way.

"Your wife has gone home. I took her there myself. She

asked me to come back and wait for you. She wanted me to warn you . . . to tell you they've discovered the truth about her."

"The truth? What truth?" Nothing made sense, he couldn't seem to think for the worry that was gnawing at his guts.

"I did some digging when I got back. Apparently they've found out about her mother . . . that Jessie isn't really your father's distant cousin. It's only a guess but I believe your jilted fiancée may have been behind it. Whoever it was, they did a very thorough job of ravaging your wife's reputation."

Matthew closed his eyes, gathering his composure, but inside he was aching for Jessie, for the terrible pain she must have suffered at the hands of his so-called friends.

"It was her greatest fear," he said softly. He turned back toward the street. "I have to go to her. Get her away from London. For now protecting her is all that matters."

He started to call for a hack, but Wolvermont stepped up beside him. "My carriage is waiting. I'll take you home."

Matthew just nodded. All he could think of was Jessie. The terrible pain she must be feeling—that he wished he could have been there when she had needed him most.

Matthew pounded up the wide porch steps of the Belmore town house, his heart thumping louder than his boots. Only a single lamp burned in the drawing room. He didn't look for Jessie there, just took the stairs two at a time up to her room and strode in. She wasn't there and the bed hadn't been slept in. The door was open between their two rooms. He strode in quickly, but it was empty, too. The knot in his stomach went tighter.

A small lamp burned on his writing desk, the wick turned low, a yellow glow lighting the single sheet of foolscap on the green leather surface.

Matthew reached for the page with a hand that shook, his insides feeling leaden. He forced himself to scan the words.

My Darling Matthew,

By the time you read this, I shall be gone. You will never know how sorry I am for the damage I have done. Please believe I never meant to hurt you, or your father, who has always been so very good to me. I regret that I repay his kindness with scandal. At least with my leaving, perhaps the damage can be repaired.

My dearest love, I pray you obtain an annulment of our marriage at your earliest convenience. Tell them I tricked you into speaking the vows, that I deceived you just as I did them.

Do not worry about little Sarah. I am taking her with me so there will be no chance that in the future her background will embarrass you. Again, I say that I am sorry. Know that I will always love you from the very depths of my heart.

Jessie

The words began to blur through a film of tears, until he couldn't read them at all. He crushed the note in his hand, his chest so tight he couldn't breathe. Whirling toward the door, he walked back into the hall and down the stairs, stopping at the sight of Ozzie's ravaged visage in the entry.

"Where is my father?"

"In the drawing room, milord."

He turned in that direction, saw the room still bathed in shadows and realized his father had been sitting in the darkness all along. Long strides carried him toward the man who sat rocking before the nearly dead embers of the fire.

"She's gone," Matthew said without preamble.

The old man merely nodded. The dark glow of the fire outlined his grief-stricken face and the tracks of dried tears on his cheeks. "What will you do?"

Pain squeezed into Matt's chest, a tight knot of overwhelming grief. "What will I do?" A bitter laugh tore from

his throat. "My wife and a frightened little girl are somewhere out in the darkened streets. They have stolen off into
the night in some misguided effort to protect me, and you
ask what I will do?" He stared at his father but there was no
hint of retreat. "Was I really so bad?" he said brokenly. "Did
you actually believe I would sacrifice Jessie and Sarah to
protect the Belmore name?"

His father stirred. "I believed that you cared for them. I
wasn't certain how much."

"Then for once I shall be clear. I'm going after them. Jessie is my wife. Sarah is my daughter. They are my family
just as much as you are. I love them more than life itself, and
I don't give a damn what anyone thinks."

The marquess sat up straighter in his chair. For the first
time since he had read the note on his son's desk, Reginald
Seaton felt a ray of hope steal into his heart. "The coachy took
her to the docks. He was worried that something was amiss so
upon his return he spoke to Ozzie. Ozzie came to me and I
found the note she left you. I thought it best to await your return."

"How long ago did they leave?"

"More than several hours. Do you think you will be able
to find them?"

Matt crumpled the note even tighter in his fist. "I'll find
them." Without a backward glance, ignoring the pain that
throbbed in his shoulder, he started for the door.

His father's deep voice stopped him. "Matthew?"

He turned. "Yes, Father?"

A gentle smile touched the old man's lips. "Welcome home,
son."

Chapter Twenty-Six

*T*hey called her Lady Blue. Jessie bent over the scarred wooden table at the Red Horse Inn, scrubbing away a sticky puddle of ale that spread across the surface. Lady Blue. A sad name for a woman whose face betrayed the ravages of the grief she carried inside.

She wiped her work-roughened hands on the apron tied over her plain brown skirt and returned to the bar for a round of grog for the sailors who had just wandered in. The tavern sat on the quay overlooking the harbor in Charleston, a small seaport city on the South Carolina coast.

Over a month ago, she, Sarah, and Viola had made the rough sea journey to America, sailing aboard one of the three ships they had found that were leaving the London docks with the morning tide. Another had been bound for the West Indies, one sailed for the far-off shores of India. America had seemed the most logical choice.

And the captain had agreed to keep their passage secret, just in case Papa Reggie might have discovered them gone and tried to stop them. Jessie thought of him and a lump rose in her throat. She missed him so much. She hoped he was well and that the scandal hadn't overset him too badly.

She tried not to think of Matthew. Whenever she did, she would cry, and crying was something she had done more than enough of since she had fled the shores of England. Still, the grief must have shown in her face, for the men in the tavern spent hours trying to cheer her. They told her stories of their journeys around the world, brought her small gifts, and sang her songs. They treated her with a kindness she hadn't expected, protecting her when a stranger got rough, or a sailor's bawdy jokes became a bit too crude.

They called her Lady Blue—because, they said, even when she smiled she looked sad.

She smiled sadly now, thinking of little Sarah, asleep on a pallet on the floor of the room the three of them shared above the stable, wishing the child wouldn't have to face the same sort of life Jessie had suffered.

Perhaps she wouldn't. Perhaps she would escape. Perhaps . . .

Jessie sighed as she set the mugs of grog down on the table in front of the men.

Sarah wouldn't escape. None of them would.

That was a dream and Jessie had long ago stopped dreaming.

"Over 'ere, lassie!" a sailor called out. "I be sorely in need o' a tankard. Get a move on, gel."

"Keep yer breeches on, man," one of the regulars, Jake Barley, called out. "Can't ya see the girl's movin' as fast as she can?"

Jessie smiled her gratitude and turned to do the sailor's bidding.

"She can hustle her pretty little arse over here as soon as she's finished," another gruff voice called out, and across from him, a brawny Irishman shoved back his chair.

"Keep yer foul mouth closed," Sean Nolan warned. "Can't ya see ye're talkin' to a lady?"

The man eyed her sharply, but he only grunted.

A lady. She was hardly that and it was clear she never would be. It surprised her that the thought could still make her sad.

Matthew stood at the rail of the brigantine *Windmere*. They were one day out of Charleston, one day from his destination. It was the longest day he could remember.

Shading his eyes from the sun, he squinted toward the Carolina coast, praying once he arrived he would find the woman he searched for. It had taken him three weeks to discover which ship she had sailed on. He'd had to be certain. The wrong choice could have cost him months of sailing in the wrong direction. If that had happened, he might have lost her trail for good.

In the end, the offer of a substantial reward had done the trick. One of the dockhands had remembered seeing three women boarding the *Gallant* for America. The man was able to describe them, and another man eventually came forward to substantiate the story of the first.

Matt had set sail two days later, on a grueling voyage that seemed to take forever, each day spent agonizing over the myriad dangers two women and a child might encounter in the world alone. Now as he stared out at the water, his fingers curled tightly around the rail, he thought of Jessie and prayed that she was safe.

He wondered where she was and if she missed him half as much as he missed her.

He prayed God would answer his prayers and help him find her, and vowed he wouldn't give up until he did.

Inside her tiny clapboard room above the stable, Jessie leaned over the golden-haired child asleep on a pallet stuffed with straw. Tenderly, she smoothed the silky hair away from the little girl's face. Sarah had been fussy tonight, asking after Matthew, wanting to know again why her papa hadn't come with them. Jessie told her he had wanted to come, but he had to stay and take care of the people at Belmore.

Sarah wanted to know who was going to take care of them?

Jessie swallowed past the lump in her throat, a pang of regret lancing through her. She had wanted more for Sarah. A home and family, a mother and father who would love her. She had tried to make her own life better, but she'd still wound up slopping ale in a smoky taproom. It didn't seem fair. But then, as Wolvermont said—life was rarely if ever fair.

At least she wasn't a whore. She knew she never would be. In her heart she was still Matthew's wife and nothing would ever change that.

Whatever happened, whatever life held in store, she would never do anything that would make him ashamed of what she had become.

Matthew strode along the street that fronted the Charleston quay, his booted strides ringing on the rough hewn boards laid over the muddy street. He had arrived in the seaport city yesterday aboard the *Windmere.* It had taken him a day and a half to find her—the woman they called Lady Blue.

Strange, how the name had affected him. A mixture of guilt at the pain he had caused her and joy that the love she felt for him appeared to run as deeply as the love he felt for her.

Now he was here and all he could do was worry that she was all right and think what he might possibly say. A thousand phrases sailed through his head but none seemed to convey the loss he had felt since his beloved wife had left him.

The words would come, Matt told himself. This time he would say them.

He stopped outside the doors of the Red Horse Inn, his heart like a trip-hammer inside his chest, his mouth as dry as cotton. Praying the women were all right, he wiped his hands on his breeches and shoved open the doors leading into the smoky taproom.

Jessie wrung the harsh lye soap from the rag she was using to scrub the heavy wooden tables in the taproom, then winced at the sting to her rough, reddened hands. It was early in the day. Only one table held patrons, a group of sailors off the *Windmere,* just in from England. They laughed as they leaned back in their chairs, gaming away the afternoon playing cards.

Jessie forced herself not to look at them, not to cross the

room and hound each man for news of her homeland. She wanted to. Dear God, she would be happy just to hear the crisp, clipped tones that marked an Englishman's words.

Instead she bent over the table, scrubbing even harder, trying to banish her painful memories and ignore the group of sailors. Still, thoughts of England and Matthew crept in, and her heart started hurting.

Jessie wet the rag and wrung it out, began to scour a table in the corner. Strands of her light blond hair had come lose from the kerchief she wore and whispered against her cheek. She tucked the unruly curl away and kept on scrubbing. She barely noticed when footfalls echoed behind her, didn't pause when she felt someone's presence, not until dark-tanned fingers reached out to gently still the hand that scoured away.

"Fairly menial labor, isn't it, my love? For a countess . . . ?"

The hand trembled slightly over hers. Jessie turned to face him, unable to believe the deep voice was really his. "Matthew . . ." She drank in the beauty of his strong chiseled features even as her mind screamed that she must send him away. "You shouldn't have come."

Deep blue eyes moved over her face. Tenderly, he lifted her work-roughened hand and pressed it against his lips. "You're my wife, Jess. Did you really believe I would not come?"

She blinked hard, fought to hold back tears. Dear God how she loved him. "I-I left you a note."

"Yes . . . I suppose you thought that was enough."

Her chest squeezed painfully. "All you have to do is—"

"All I have to do is have our marriage annulled. Is that right, love?"

A wave of misery moved through her. "That's right." She glanced away, unable to face him, the pain in her chest nearly unbearable. "You don't have to feel guilty. None of this was your fault. I tricked you into marrying me. That night . . . at the inn . . . all you did was kiss me. That was all that happened. I-I lied about everything else."

She thought he would be angry, but the line around his mouth appeared to soften instead. "Why?" he asked gently.

She stared into those blue, blue eyes. "Because I was in love with you."

"And are you still?"

She swallowed past the tight lump aching in her throat. "Yes . . ."

Matthew said nothing, just blinked and glanced away.

"You deserve a lady, Matthew. A real lady, not an impostor like me."

He turned back to her and a muscle jumped in his cheek. "A lady? Is that what you said? For godsakes, Jess, you're more of a lady than any woman I've ever met. You're generous and caring, you're intelligent and determined, you're loyal to a fault." His eyes bored into her. "All I have to do is have our marriage annulled—give up the best thing that's ever happened to me. All I have to do is walk away from the only woman I'll ever love, spend the rest of my life grieving for you and Sarah. Leave you behind—and never know a moment's peace."

In an instant she was wrapped in his arms, clinging to him, repeating his name over and over. "Matthew . . . Matthew, I love you so much."

"Ah, God, Jess." He slid the kerchief from her hair, ran his fingers through it, then buried his face in the strands curling softly beside her cheek. "I've missed you so. I love you, Jess. I love you more than life. Don't ever leave me again."

Jessie closed her eyes, felt tears seeping out from beneath her lashes. "No . . . I'll never leave you again." She couldn't, she knew. She wouldn't survive it. The pain was simply too great.

She pulled away to look at him. "How can we go back there, Matthew? What will we do?"

"We don't have to return to England." He eased her back into his arms. "At least not for a while. Wolvermont owns a plantation in Barbados. We can stay as long as we want. If we like it, perhaps we'll buy one ourselves. If not, we can always come back here." He smiled. "It doesn't really matter, Jess. Not as long as all of us are together."

"Matthew . . ." Jessie slid her arms around his neck and

pressed herself against his solid length. She felt fine tremors running through it. Eventually the rustling of chairs and the sound of men's voices broke through the haze of their awareness.

When Jessie glanced up, she saw Jake Barley standing next to Sean Nolan and a half-dozen other familiar faces. And all of them were grinning.

"Ya come to fetch yer lady home?" Sean asked.

Matthew just grinned. "The lady is my wife and yes I have."

"We figured sooner or later her man'd be a comin'," Jake said. "He didn't, he'd sure be some kinda fool."

Matthew looked down into her face. "That he would, my friend. That he would." He bent his head and kissed her full on the lips, a fiery, thorough, passionate kiss that said the Earl of Strickland was a lot of things, but he was not a fool.

*E*pilogue

*R*eginald Seaton sat beneath the last warming rays of a late afternoon sun that spilled in through the windows in the drawing room. Little Sarah Seaton, now his son's adopted daughter, sat on the tapestry sofa beside him, On his knee, he playfully bounced year-old, towheaded little Reginald Matthew III.

"Tell us another story, Granpapa," Sarah said. "Please?"

The marquess chuckled softly. "I don't think so, sweetheart. Granpapa's getting too old to do so much talking." He gazed across the room to where Cornelia Seaton, the newly titled Marchioness of Belmore, sat laughing at something Jessica had said. His wife's eye caught his and her warm look said he wasn't so very old at all. She must have said something of the sort to Jessie, for it was she who laughed this time.

Reggie smiled, pleased at the sound that had been missing from the halls of Belmore for the past two years. It had taken him that long to smooth the way for his family's return. Two years of machinations, of money changing hands here and there, a suggestion to Landsdowne, along with the return of his unpaid overdue note, that his daughter's information might have been mistaken, that somehow things had gotten confused.

His daughter had objected, of course, but once the earl had seen her married to the stern, straightlaced Lord Burbage, a friend of Matthew's from Oxford, her husband had insisted the lady make amends for the error she had made and the trouble she had caused.

The Bow Street runner had been easy to convince. It merely took an offer of a high-paying position in a London security firm.

There were markers to call in, of course, debts long due the Seatons that would now be finally paid. It took every trick he knew, including falsified documents to prove Jessica's legitimate birth, but he had finally succeeded. The Belmore name had been restored, the Earl and Countess of Strickland once more accepted among the ton.

Not that it mattered so much anymore.

What really mattered was that they were a family again.

And that they were once more together.

Reggie's bones cracked as he rose from sitting so long on the sofa with the baby in his lap. He smiled as he carried the sleeping child over to its mother.

"So when, my dear girl, may we expect another little Seaton to make his presence among us? I told you I expect to see a house full of grandchildren before I meet my maker."

Jessie laughed. "Papa Reggie, you've been preparing to meet your maker since the day I met you. In truth, you'll probably outlive us all."

"Yes, you old schemer," Matthew chimed in. "When I look back on it, there are times I think you faked your entire bout of illness just to get Jessie and me together."

The marquess's thick white brows shot up. "How can you say such a thing?" But the twinkle in his eye and the wink he gave Cornelia was enough to make both of them wonder.

"Even if you planned the whole thing," Matthew said, "I would thank you for it, Father. Marrying Jessie was the best thing that's ever happened to me, and if you are to blame, then I shall be forever grateful."

Jessie smiled at her husband's words, leaned forward and kissed his cheek. A wicked glint came into his dark blue eyes. Matthew whispered something in her ear and her smile grew broader.

"The children are sleepy," Matt said. "And Jessie and I could use a rest as well." His gaze held tenderness along with a trace of heat. "I believe we shall retire to our bedchamber for a nap before supper."

"Good idea," said Reggie with a glance at his lusty son. "As I said—"

"I know," Matt put in. "You want a whole house full of grandchildren before you meet your maker."

The marquess, wily as always, simply looked over at him and grinned.